Praise for *Imaginary Things* by

"Rarely does a book surprise me. But completely off-guard! Andrea Lochen writes with vivid scenes, unforgettable characters, and oodles of heart. With a page-turning plot and an utterly unique concept, *Imaginary Things* entertains, inspires, and provokes thought—a perfect book club pick."

—*Lori Nelson Spielman, bestselling author of* The Life List

"*Imaginary Things* takes place in a Midwest made so vivid and alive, so much its own character, that it becomes thrillingly believable that as Grandma styles the local brides' hair into ringlets and the next door neighbor may be fighting a pain-killer addiction, a T-rex is running through the back yard. This isn't just a psychological thriller, but a love story, and Andrea Lochen has put words to a reality that is as imaginary as it is rock solid."

—*Laura Kasischke, bestselling author of* In a Perfect World

"Cleverly written with the perfect touch of magic, *Imaginary Things* will take you on a journey of the unexpected, and leave you contemplating the power of your own mind."

—*Liz Fenton & Lisa Steinke, authors of* Your Perfect Life

"If it's possible to write a witty modern fairy tale about a down-on-her-luck young mother, her erratic ex, and her charming four-year-old boy, Andrea Lochen has done it. Anna is not your typical overwhelmed mom, but her story feels like a friend's. *Imaginary Things* reminded me again and again that the act of raising a child is a love story, a test of strength, and a thrill ride."

—*Susanna Daniel, author of* Stiltsville

"Have you ever thought about seeing into someone else's imagination? Neither had I. Then I read *Imaginary Things*. This is an honest, charming novel that blends reality and magical possibilities, hard struggles and small victories, starting over and daring to dare."

—*Cathy Lamb, author of* What I Remember Most

Praise for *The Repeat Year* by Andrea Lochen

"An intriguing premise and some surprising twists make this an engaging, satisfying read that explores friendship, love, and who we really are when it truly matters. A debut novel that offers a fascinating glimpse into one woman's opportunity to rewrite her past and change her future."

—*Kirkus Reviews*

"For anyone who has ever needed a 'do over,' this novel gives hope for change and redemption."

—*RT Reviews*

"Lochen's twist on the theme, with relationships taking center stage, makes this a perfect light summer read…"

—*Library Journal*

"A clever novel about the myriad ways we second guess and sabotage ourselves in the name of finding happiness."

—*Margaret Dilloway, author of* How to be an American Housewife

"Warm, touching, and thoroughly enjoyable… Anyone who has dreamed of getting a second chance at love will not be able to resist this book."

—*Janis Thomas, author of* Something New *and* Sweet Nothings

"A magical realist rom-com of great charm, *The Repeat Year* reflects with lively wit (and a surprising undertow of poignancy) on questions of fate and karma, chance and choice."

—*Peter Ho Davies, author of* The Welsh Girl

"*The Repeat Year* is a magical, fairy tale-like debut, and I will certainly be on the lookout for Andrea Lochen's future releases. This book is for anyone who believes in second chances, fate, and the power of true love."

—*Luxury Reading*

imaginary things

andrea lochen

ASTOR
+BLUE
EDITIONS

IMAGINARY THINGS
Astor + Blue Editions
Copyright © 2015 by Andrea Lochen

Astor + Blue Editions
New York, NY 10036
www.astorandblue.com

Publisher's Cataloging-In-Publication Data

LOCHEN, ANDREA. IMAGINARY THINGS.—1ˢᵗ ed.

ISBN: 978-1-941286-11-1 (paperback)
ISBN: 978-1-941286-13-5 (epdf)
ISBN: 978-1-941286-12-8 (epub)

1. Contemporary Women—Magical Realism—Fiction. 2. Young mother begins to see son's imaginary friends—Fiction 3. Women's fiction—Fiction 4. Fantastical elements—Fiction 5. Coming of age—Fiction 6. Women & Family—Fiction 7. Wisconsin I. Title

Jacket Cover Design: Julie Metz

For my sister, Steph, the best childhood playmate and co-adventurer in pursuits of make-believe a girl could ask for, and for my parents, Mike and Linda, with my deep love, admiration, and gratitude.

CHAPTER ONE

There was something about driving an ancient Dodge Caravan packed with all of my worldly possessions, including my four year-old son and my cat, that reeked of failure and desperation. The back of the minivan was crammed with duffel bags of clothing and cardboard boxes filled with pirate action figures, perfume bottles, matchbox cars and race track pieces, sketchbooks, a remote-controlled dinosaur, mascara wands and eyeliner pencils, markers and stubby crayons, and black garbage bags stuffed with everything else: David's rocket ship comforter, my flat iron, winter coats, story books, sandwich baggies full of earrings, and half-eaten boxes of Little Debbies that were probably smushed by now. I'd sold my bed, couch, and kitchen table for a fraction of their worth and had given my TV to Stacy for all the times she'd watched David for free. I'd also asked her to hold on to my rocking chair, the one piece of furniture I couldn't bear to part with, until I could come back for it. I'd taken bags of clothes and toys that David had outgrown plus my old dresses, purses, and shoes to Goodwill, and still the minivan was bursting with the painfully mundane trappings of my life.

If I'd sped past myself on the highway five years ago (and undoubtedly I would have, because this Caravan wasn't exactly capable of high speeds), I would have looked at the maroon minivan missing its hubcaps, the back windows blocked by lumpy garbage bags and last-minute additions to the trunk like Candy Land, a bag of kitty litter, a dustbuster, and then at the driver—a pretty, twenty-two-year-old girl with dirty blond hair and a perfect nose, sporting glamorous sunglasses, a bleach-stained T-shirt, and frown lines, and thought—*where the hell did she go wrong?* And then I would've zipped past, changed lanes, secure in my own bright future, and forgotten her.

Ha. What a sucker I'd been. What a sucker I still was.

I raised my eyes to the rearview mirror and caught a glimpse of David rocking back and forth in his booster seat, singing quietly to himself, "*The tie-ran-a-suss rex had big big teeth, big big teeth, big big teeth. The tie-ran-a-suss rex had big big teeth when dino-suss roamed the earth.*" In her pink crate on the seat next to him, Vivien Leigh was mewling her dissatisfaction, as she had been since we'd left Milwaukee an hour ago.

"How you doing back there, buckaroo?" I called over my shoulder.

He lifted his blond head and squinted thoughtfully. "Me and kitty are singing," he said.

"I can hear that. Do you need to go potty?"

He squinted again and cocked his head. "No."

Which meant yes. I popped a stick of watermelon gum into my mouth. "We'll stop at a gas station in a few minutes and you can go."

The AC had been wheezing and puffing out only a tepid breeze, so as soon as I pulled off at the next exit, I cracked the windows and the pungent, familiar smell of manure blew in. Yep, definitely not far from our new home now. Strands of my hair whipped across my face, and I wished I could remember where I had packed my brush—probably in one of the duffel bags at the very bottom of the pile. Oh well. Who was there to impress at this Podunk gas station anyway? There were only four pumps, and a homemade sign advertising BAIT! BRATS! HOTDOGS! God, I hoped there were indoor bathrooms.

"Can kitty come out, Mommy?" David asked as I unstrapped him from his booster seat. Sensing freedom was near, Vivien Leigh was yowling for all she was worth.

"No, she's fine," I said and held out my arms for him to jump down. "We won't be long."

David curled his pointer finger around one of the metal bars of her crate sympathetically. "Do you want food, kitty? Do you want to play? Do you need to go potty?"

I glanced inside her crate. She shot me a haughty look and then, seeming to think better of it, let out a pitiful meow. "Oh, don't be such a diva." I manually propped the side windows open an inch.

David looked unconvinced, but he slid into my arms anyway.

Inside, a country music radio station played over the speakers, and the tiled floors looked like they hadn't been mopped or swept in twenty years. Crystals of salt leftover from winters long ago stuck in the soles of my sandals. David galloped straight for the candy aisle.

"No candy," I said in my best *I'm-not-in-the-mood-so-you-better-not-start* voice. The man at the register craned his neck to get a good look at us, but I ducked behind a rack of trucker hats as I steered David's little body to the restroom. Suspicious of what state the bathroom would be in, I flung the door open and flicked the light on with my elbow. It was pretty much in keeping with the rest of the gas station: sad gray tiles, scrunched-up paper towels on the floor, drippy faucet, toilet seat flipped up to reveal what I hoped was a ring of mildew.

"Don't touch anything," I instructed David and guided him inside.

He stood in front of the toilet for a second and then faced me. "Go outside, Mommy."

"Just go potty, David."

He frowned. "Go outside. I'm a big boy." It was his rebuttal to everything lately.

I glanced at my phone—it was three o'clock already, and I'd told Duffy we'd be there around one—and blew out a sigh of resignation. "Fine. But don't touch *anything*, and wash your hands when you're done. I'll be right outside if you need anything."

When the door closed with another click, the cashier's head darted up again. Unluckily, we had a direct view of each other as I waited outside the bathroom. He was middle-aged with a thick brown beard and a green plaid shirt. I supposed he was a nice enough guy—somebody's uncle who sent birthday cards with a twenty inside, the best bowler on his team, maybe—but all I felt right then were his eyes crawling all over me, undoubtedly trying to determine the color of my bra and the cut of my underwear. Yuck.

I narrowed my eyes at him and then feigned interest in the odd assortment of items shelved nearby—windshield wiper fluid and ice scrapers right alongside boxes of tampons and bags of Funyuns. My gum was starting to lose its flavor, and I hadn't heard the toilet flush or the water run yet. I pressed my ear against the door.

"Everything okay in there, buckaroo? Need any help?"

David didn't respond, but I thought I could hear him singing softly: *"When dino-suss roamed the earth…"*

I pressed on the door handle, but it wouldn't budge. "David!" I called. Was the door stuck or had he locked it? "Let Mommy in, okay?" I was acutely aware that the bearded cashier was watching the whole scene with interest.

"It's time to go, David. Let me in so we can wash up and then go to Grandma and Grandpa's house." I jiggled the handle again, but no luck. I squatted down to be at his level and spoke into the crack. "Did you lock yourself in? You need to turn the knob or the little dial thingy, okay?"

"I know how to lock and unlock the door," David said. It sounded like he was crouching, his mouth hovering near the door jamb.

"Great. Then unlock it so I can come in." I stood up and swung my purse back over my arm.

"Need any help there, honey?" the cashier called.

I didn't even bother to look up. "No, thanks. We're fine."

"Alrighty then," he said, heavy on the skepticism. "Let me know if you change your mind." Like he was worried my son was going to wreak havoc in his precious, pristine gas station bathroom. Right.

"David, unlock the door right now," I hissed.

"If I unlock the door, can I have candy?"

"No deal. Unlock the door this instant, David." My tone was stern, but I wasn't fooling anyone. My four-year-old clearly had the upper hand here. The cashier knew it, I knew it; even David knew it.

There was a long pause, then the sound of water rushing. I could only imagine what he was doing inside. Unscrewing pipes? Playing in the toilet? Licking the floor?

"It's time to go, David. Please unlock the door for Mommy." I was so tired. I'd been up until three the night before, packing the minivan and attempting to cover up the holes in the walls and scrub out the carpet stains for our apartment inspection. Not that I'd gotten my deposit back anyway.

The water stopped. "If I unlock the door, can I have animal crackers?"

Fine. Given the circumstances, it seemed a small concession to make. I was starting to worry Vivien Leigh was dehydrating into cat jerky in the minivan. "Yes, if you unlock the door you can have a snack."

"Animal crackers?"

"Sure. Whatever. Just open the door."

A few seconds passed and then the door clicked, and I scrambled to open it. David looked up at me with his wide brown eyes.

I gripped his shoulder a little too tightly and peered in the toilet. The water was grungy, but not yellowish at all. "Did you go potty?"

"No, Mommy. I told you I don't need to go potty."

"David," I said, and then stopped, too angry to continue. *Count to ten, twenty, a hundred, whatever it takes,* Stacy was fond of saying. *You can't take back your words.* I bit my lip. "Don't ever do that again. Now let's get your snack and get back on the road before Grandma Duffy starts to think we changed our minds."

Of course there were no animal crackers, so we settled on a dusty package of mini chocolate muffins, which I was pretty sure had been sitting on the shelf a few years past their absent sell-by date, but David wouldn't be dissuaded. The cashier enjoyed a good close-up of my cleavage in my V-neck as we checked out but then sent me a disapproving look as I handed the muffins over to David. Great, even he thought I was a totally incompetent mother.

I buckled David into his booster seat somewhat gruffly, but enamored with his mini muffins, he didn't seem to notice. The standoff in the gas station was just another one of the footholds I lost with him every day. Sleeping in his T-ball jersey and socks? Sure, why not? As long as the cleats came off. Eating a Swiss Cake Roll for breakfast? Fine. How different was it *really* in nutritional value from a Pop-Tart or doughnut? Burying and then digging up his action figures in various holes in the backyard like a dog? Whatever. As long as it kept him occupied. I was a disaster at discipline because David knew my Achilles heel—I didn't have any energy left in me to fight.

As I pulled out of the gas station, I did a double take. Leaning against one of the pumps was a blond man wearing a leather jacket, despite the heat. He was much too tall and heavyset to be Patrick, but my pulse accelerated anyway. No matter how much time passed, Patrick would always be my own personal boogeyman, lurking behind every corner.

"Tell me a story," David said around a peaty mouthful of chocolate muffin.

My head felt like a wasp's nest—brittle and buzzing. "Not now, buckaroo. Maybe later if you're good. I need to focus on the road now."

It would've been easier to think of our stay with my grandparents as a fresh start if their home in Salsburg hadn't been the place I'd been shipped to whenever I needed to recover from my other failures in life. My mom had first sent me to stay with them the summers I was seven and eight, after serious "behavior problems," as she called them. Then after some spectacular mischief my sophomore year of high school, I was exiled to Salsburg again for the entire duration of the school year. Most recently, when I was eighteen, they took me in for part of my pregnancy.

So the symbolic significance of the fact that I was going there now, after I'd lost my job as a receptionist at Lakeview Dermatology, was not lost on me. Or them, I was sure. But they had always been good about taking me in, dusting me off, and attempting to set me back to rights again. Winston and Duffy Jennings were not stern, preachy types, nor were they permissive, indulgent pushovers. Since my mom had made them grandparents before they were even forty, much too young to be dubbed Granny and Pops, Duffy had insisted I call them by their first names instead. She owned a small beauty salon and over the years had learned to talk auctioneer-fast, pausing rarely to catch her breath, lest someone interrupt her. She called it like she saw it; sometimes she called me a dumb-ass and sometimes she called me a snickerdoodle, and whichever it was, usually rightfully so. Winston was a semi-retired farm equipment mechanic who had adapted to his wife's loquaciousness by speaking up only when necessary; his silence was occasionally restful but most of the time kind of unnerving.

My grandparents rarely left their one square mile of southeastern Wisconsin, their beloved population-of-one-thousand town, and they acted as if driving all the way to the "big city" of Milwaukee was as treacherous and cumbersome as hitching up a team of horses to a covered wagon and setting out for the great unknown. Driving alone both ways with a baby was unappealing to me, and I was an appallingly lazy correspondent; I patted myself on the back if I remembered to send them a Christmas card with a recent photo of David in it. So the pathetic fact was that the last time we'd come to Salsburg for a visit was for David's second birthday, and if I was nakedly honest with myself about it, I'd admit it was because I had been flat broke (though nowhere near as destitute as I was now), and I had known I could count on them to buy cake and presents.

Still, when I had called Duffy two weeks ago to explain my financial woes and plead my case, I had barely squeaked out that I'd lost my job, when she'd interjected, "Why don't you two come and stay with us for a spell? You know, Anna, that we've got those two spare bedrooms just collecting dust and storing Winston's old Revolutionary War junk, and it would be so nice to spend some time with you and Davey. Why, I haven't seen the little guy since he was still in diapers! It would be good for him to get out of that big city and get some fresh air and experience a taste of small town living."

And that had been that. What I'd hoped for, of course, as I had dialed their number, and though the length of a "spell" had not been agreed upon, something about this stay seemed much more permanent and serious than all the others before it. I had no home to return to this time. I was leaving no one behind who really gave a damn. This was not merely a respite from my life. This *was* my life.

"We're almost there," I sang out to David, as we passed the ostentatious wooden sign welcoming us to THE VILLAGE OF SALSBURG; POPULATION: 1,140; THIRD LARGEST GROWER OF SNAP BEANS IN WISCONSIN; HOME OF THE FAMOUS SALSBURG FIREMEN'S PICNIC; PROUD SISTER VILLAGE OF BORKENDORF, GERMANY. It was the kind of town you could completely miss if you were focused on changing the radio station or lighting a cigarette. One church, one cemetery, one volunteer fire department, one restaurant, one gas station, one bank, one drugstore, one post office, one beauty parlor, and five bars. No stoplights. No sidewalks.

Of course by this time, David was dozing in his booster seat. I rattled down Main Street and hung a right on Steepleview—so named for its vantage of St. Monica's white steeple reaching heavenward. Duffy and Winston's house was a large brown and white split-level adrift on a sea of rolling green lawn. Not that you could see much from the street except for a long blacktop driveway and a wishing well; towering Douglas-firs hid the rest. A shiny blue SUV was parked at the top of the driveway, and I was careful not to block it with the Caravan.

I rolled the minivan door back as slowly and gently as possible, which was about as quiet as a freight train squealing its rusty brakes. David blinked up at me with stormy eyes and a furrowed brow—a sure indication of an impending cranky mood. That made two of us.

"Guess what, buckaroo? We're finally here! Grandma and Grandpa's house!"

He looked unimpressed. I unbuckled and lifted him into my arms. When I tried to set him down, he clung to me and pressed his hot little cheek against my neck.

The screen door slapped shut, and Duffy's voice rang out. "Glad to see you finally made it!" She was wearing a metallic purple apron and one latex glove; the other dangled inside out from between her pinched fingertips. Her platinum hair was teased into a cloud twice the size of her head. "I wish I could roll out the welcome wagon for you right now, but I'm in the midst of coloring Edna Franklin's hair, and it's very touchy business. Just one minute on too long, and it could turn out more Paradise Peach than Autumn Auburn."

"You're doing her hair *here*?" I asked and adjusted David on my hip.

"That's right. With the economy being what it's been, I decided to downsize and bring my business home." She took a step forward, squinting into the sun. "But my goodness, that can't be my great-grandson! He's as leggy as a grasshopper, and still towheaded just like his mommy. What a handsome little devil. Hello, David. Do you remember your great-grandma Duffy?"

She reached her ungloved hand out to stroke David's hair, and the chemical smell of the hair dye wafted toward us. He jerked away, banging his head against my chin, and then started to cry loud, gasping sobs. Vivien Leigh chose this moment to join in—gazing up at me with her green, expressive eyes, scratching desperately at the bars of her crate, and crooning her most plaintive meow yet. I had named her because of those eyes, as well as her noble bearing, and not to mention that *Gone With the Wind* had been my favorite movie as a teenager. With the luxurious brown and black fur bordering her eyes on her otherwise snowy white face, my cat looked like she was perpetually wearing a feather-tufted masquerade mask.

"He's a little overtired," I said apologetically. His warm, clinging body was starting to make me feel like I was wearing a heavy fur coat. My arms were aching and my chin was smarting.

"Oh my, oh my, oh my," Duffy said soothingly. "There's no need for tears, sugar cookie. I'm sure it's been a long ride from the big city." She peered past us into the minivan. "Is that a cat? Anna Grace

Jennings, you never mentioned anything about a cat!" She frowned and almost put her gloved hand on her hip, but thought better of it. "But I've been out here much too long already—Edna's hair will be turning pink! Come inside now for a cool drink and then you can get Davey all settled in for a nap before dinner. I sent Winston out for some groceries, but he'll be back soon, and then he can help you get all this unloaded."

She was back inside the house before I could reply. I rubbed David's bumped head. "Be a big boy now. I need you to walk on your own so that I can carry kitty's crate."

He grudgingly slid down. We made our way up the front steps together and pushed open the screen door. Late afternoon sunlight spilled through the windows, liberally coating the living room and dining room in a buttery glow. Very few alterations had been made to their house since I was seven years old. Same beige shag carpeting, same mauve-colored walls, same floral couch and matching curtains, same hutch displaying dusty wedding china and family photographs. The only concessions made to time passing were a new flat screen TV and entertainment center, which looked sorely out of place amidst all the other 90's country-chic decor. The house was so quiet I could hear the ticking of the grandfather clock and Duffy's constant chatter floating up from the basement. Suddenly, I felt very, very tired. Almost too tired to remain standing.

David tugged on my hand, and I switched on my auto pilot. Two glasses of water? Check. Another trip to the potty? Check. Tucking David into the twin-sized bed in one of the spare rooms despite his protest that he wasn't sleepy and that the sheets smelled funny? Check. Sitting by his bedside and humming "On Top of Spaghetti" until he fell asleep? Check. Returning to the minivan for the litter box? Check. Closing the other bedroom door before springing Vivien Leigh from her crate? Okay, I forgot that one. She ran from the room, a blur of black, brown, and white fur, and disappeared before I could catch her.

I sat on the bed, feeling numb, feeling a little like a child who's being punished. An old-fashioned black-and-white illustration hung across the room from the bed. It depicted a crush of bodies, rifles, bayonets, horses, drums, contorted faces, and blood. Some battle from the Revolutionary War, I inferred. Not exactly what I wanted to look at every night before I went to sleep and every morning when I woke up.

I tried to remember what it had replaced, and the image instantly clicked into focus: a high school portrait of my mom, Kimberly. A long mass of honey curls framed her face; a poof of bangs at least two inches high crowned her head. Her face was narrower than mine, and her eyes were a hazel to my brown, but the flawlessly straight nose, high cheekbones, and Cupid's bow lips were an exact match. She had worn a high-necked royal blue sweater and a string of fake pearls.

It was a photograph that had initially served as a warning—*don't become like me, Anna*—and later as a taunt as I had lain in her childhood bed, eighteen years old, six months pregnant, and unmarried. *How could you have been so stupid, little girl? Didn't you learn anything from my mistakes?*

So maybe the gruesome Revolutionary War print was an improvement. And hopefully, I wouldn't be looking at it for that long anyway.

CHAPTER TWO

"Let's see here." Duffy flicked the spatula back and forth as if it were a wand. "We've got scrambled eggs, sausage links, cottage fries, toast with blackberry jam or peach preserves…"

Perched on a kitchen chair, David swung his short legs back and forth as he burned a hole with his gaze through the screen door that led to the backyard. I wasn't looking forward to explaining to Duffy that David refused to eat eggs in their many incarnations, had to practically be force-fed any type of meat, and was distrustful of basically all food that didn't come individually packaged in cellophane. Last night for dinner we'd been spared a scene because Duffy had fortuitously served David's all-time favorite meal, spaghetti.

Duffy raised her eyebrows questioningly at me as she continued, "We have yogurt and strawberries and granola. A few types of cold cereal, or I could even make some oatmeal. To drink, there's orange juice, apple juice, milk, and coffee."

"Do you want a piece of toast with jelly?" I nudged David. "And Grandma Duffy's cottage fries are really yummy. Almost like McDonald's."

"Better than McDonald's," Winston said gravely. With his thick black hair, steady brown eyes, and flyaway gray eyebrows, he had always reminded me of a great horned owl. I couldn't really fault David for feeling a little intimidated by him. Giant birds of prey were designed to be intimidating.

David violently flopped his head to one side, as though he wished he could hide his face entirely in his armpit. "I'm not hungry," he whined. "I want to play outside."

"You can play outside as soon as you eat something," I said with as much authority as I could muster. "Duffy, would you make me up a plate with a little of everything? David and I can share. He'll take orange juice and I'd like coffee."

We had survived our first night with relatively little incident. Winston had helped me lug the haphazardly packed contents of the minivan inside with no comment. (They were currently piled in the corner of my bedroom.) David had woken up from his nap eager to explore the house, and he had become downright giddy over the spaghetti dinner, even going so far as to perform the chorus of "When Dinosaurs Roamed the Earth" for Duffy and Winston before he remembered he was supposed to be bashful around them. He'd slept peacefully through the night, unlike me, who had bolted upright, heart pounding, at two in the morning when Vivien Leigh had launched herself at my chest. She'd then wrapped herself around my head, purring as loud as a lawnmower, preventing me from falling back asleep for over an hour. Of course, I hadn't gotten up to close my bedroom door, and when I'd woken up this morning, she had disappeared again.

Duffy set a steaming plate in front of me, and the complicated dance of wheedling, bribing, and begging my son to take a bite, just one small taste, one little nibble, began. David glowered murderously at the sausage and spit out a clump of scrambled eggs, but managed to down a few forkfuls of cottage fries, a tiny square of buttered toast, and a glass of juice.

I didn't fare much better. As far as breakfast went, I was more of a coffee and doughnut kind of person. Big farm breakfasts with all the food groups represented (at least the Wisconsin food groups—eggs, cheese, sausage, potatoes, and grease) were not my forte. Duffy knew this, but perhaps she was optimistic that I'd changed. I ate a bite of everything and then nursed my cup of coffee.

When David's anxiously swinging legs started to get closer and closer to assaulting the table leg, I said, "All right. You did a pretty good job, so you can go outside now."

He rocketed off his chair and out the screen door, and I drifted behind, halfway hoping that either Duffy or Winston would offer, *I'll keep an eye on him, Anna. Why don't you go back to bed?* Neither did.

I stood on the wooden deck, squinting at the sun and the vibrant greenness of the backyard. Compared to the tiny, malnourished lawn we'd had on 57th Street, the huge swaths of grass were almost obscene. There were few interruptions to break it up: one tree encircled by bricks, a flower bed (presided over by the ceramic cast of Snow White and the Seven Dwarfs), and an immaculate shed. A row of pines loomed at the back of the huge lot, but nothing visually demarcated where my grandparents' lawn ended and their next-door neighbors' began.

Plates and skillets clattered in the kitchen. "I don't know why I even bother…" Duffy's voice rang out and was then muffled by the sound of running water.

"*I* enjoyed it," Winston returned.

"Well, *you're* supposed to be watching your cholesterol!" More clanking and running water.

I walked to the railing of the deck, trying to summon a shred of guilt, but *I* hadn't been the one to suggest she cook a breakfast fit for a caravan of famished truckers. *I* would've been happy with black coffee and a Nutty Bar. Or better yet: forgone breakfast entirely for an extra hour of sleep.

David was pinballing across the lawn, surveying his new kingdom. I leaned forward, resting my elbows on the railing with my head in my hands. The sun felt warm and comforting on my scalp and forearms. I longed for a fashion or gossip magazine, like the good old days when Duffy would bring them home from the salon for me, and I would spread out an old comforter on the grass and lazily page through them in my little red bikini, drinking raspberry lemonade from a thermos.

I glanced backwards at the pair of chaise longues on the deck, which were looking increasingly more inviting, and took a step toward them, nearly stumbling over a bushel basket filled with toys. Winston must have put it there for David. I recognized some of the toys from my childhood—the Skip-It, hot pink soccer ball, water guns, hula hoop, and multicolored frisbee—but others looked like they'd been newly purchased. My grandparents were way too generous with us. I nudged the bushel basket out of the way with my foot and moved it closer to the steps.

"Toys up here," I announced to David, who was squatting in the shade cast by the shed.

He didn't dash toward the deck or even acknowledge I'd said anything. Balanced on the balls of his feet with his hand extended, he was staring intently at something I couldn't see.

The sun must have been blocked by a cloud because the backyard was momentarily—eerily—ten degrees cooler.

"David," I yelled. "Grandpa Winston left some toys up here for you."

His head shot up this time, and he raced toward me from his crouched position, like a track runner erupting from the starting blocks. As I watched him pump his skinny arms, I thought I saw something move behind him, from out of the shadows. Had Vivien Leigh managed to sneak out of the house? But, no. It was bigger than a cat. More the size of a dog. For a split second, the sun glinted off its fur. I expected to see it streak across the lawn back into whichever neighbor's yard it belonged, but suddenly it was just gone.

David was pulling each toy from the basket and inspecting it.

"Was there a dog back there?" I asked, cupping my hand over my eyes, studying the patch of grass that had just swallowed up the animal.

"No." His expression told me my question was on the same scale of stupidity as, "Do chickens moo", or, "Would you like a pork chop with sauerkraut for lunch?"

"You're sure you didn't see an animal up there by the shed?"

"No animals." Grinning hugely, he held up a styrofoam glider over half his height. "Is this for me?"

"Go ahead," I said. "But if you see any pets wandering around, don't touch them. You come tell me, okay?" But he was already running down the stairs holding the glider aloft. I called after him, "And try not to get the plane stuck on the roof!"

I stretched out on one of the chaise longues, thinking about the elusive dog I could have sworn I had just seen. Okay, so I was a little fatigued. And I'd misplaced my knock-off designer sunglasses when I'd arrived yesterday, so all this squinting into the sun was probably screwing with my retinas. I closed my eyes. That felt better. Yes, that felt really nice. The sun caressed my face and licked my bare legs. I rolled up the sleeves of my T-shirt and raised my arms over my head.

The deafening drone of a lawnmower broke through my bliss. I sat up, the heaviness of my limbs and grogginess in my head quickly cluing me in to the fact that I hadn't been catnapping for just a few minutes. I scanned the lawn for David. Not over by the shed. Not by the pine trees. Not by the dwarfs and their garden. Maybe he'd gone inside and was with Duffy or Winston? Heart hammering in my dry mouth, I sprang from the chaise longue and noticed David sitting cross-legged on the chair beside mine.

I sank back down and tried to breathe. "Are you done playing?"

His nose and cheeks were pink. Sunburned. What kind of inept mother let her fair-skinned child play for hours in the late June sun with no sunscreen? Me, of course.

"The man told me to play on the deck."

"What man? Grandpa Winston?"

"That man." He pointed.

I followed his finger to the source of the teeth-gritting whine that had awakened me: a man pushing a lawnmower. Cutting my grandparents' grass. Not Winston, whose love for cutting grass was only surpassed by his love for Massey-Harris antique tractors and carnival food. My grandparents' orderly, predictable lives had changed; Duffy had lost her salon and Winston was no longer cutting his own grass. With these changes, I caught an unpleasant whiff of the hardship aging would bring them.

I stood at the top of the stairs and stared down at the man. He was wearing headphones—not cute little ear buds, but honking recording-studio size padded, noise-canceling ear muffs—over his shaggy, shoulder-length black hair. His beard was unkempt, and he was clothed head to toe in shades of black or dark gray, despite the heat. My grandparents had hired a badass wannabe rocker to do their yard work.

As he rounded the tree in the middle of the yard, his gaze met mine, and I became fiercely aware that I hadn't showered in over twenty-four hours and I was wearing tiny sleep shorts and a T-shirt with no bra. I longed for my sunglasses, which helped so much in the aloof sneer department, but I settled for a tight frown.

"Let's go inside, David," I said. "Did you put the plane away?"

He slid from the chaise longue and studied his feet. "The plane flew on the roof."

"You're telling me that was Jamie Presswood mowing your lawn?" I balked.

Duffy handed me a crusty, fishy-smelling skillet. She'd half-suggested, half-informed me after dinner that I'd be helping her wash the dishes. "The one and only."

Jamie Presswood was Winston and Duffy's next-door neighbor's son and my one-time childhood friend. He was a year younger than me, and during the summers I'd spent in Salsburg when I was seven and eight, he became the closest friend I'd ever had—the sibling I'd always yearned for. When I'd returned as a sixteen-year-old and we'd gone to the same high school for a year, I'd been embarrassed by his freshman status and quickly ditched him for the company of the cool kids. I hadn't heard or seen much of him since I'd met Patrick and moved out on my own.

"He *still* lives at home?" I asked, before realizing what a total hypocrite I sounded like.

Duffy stooped to put a mixing bowl in the cupboard. "He's been back for a few months now," she said. "After he graduated, he went away for a couple of years. Somewhere out west, I think. Kansas or Nebraska. But it must not have worked out. Personally, I don't know why anyone would ever want to leave, but of course that's just my opinion." She playfully wiggled her eyebrows and smiled at me.

I groaned and continued to scrub the bottom of the pan. "And you're paying him to mow your lawn, why?"

"Winston set it all up. I think he's trying to do him a good turn and help him get the word out about the landscaping business he's trying to start. But you know Salsburg—it's going to be a tough market to crack. And I don't know what he expects to do the other six months of the year, but he'll figure it out, I guess."

In Salsburg, everybody took meticulous care of their own yards and gardens, if they had them, that is, and the rest was farmland. Coupled with the fact that most residents' idea of landscaping was a discarded tractor tire planted with petunias or a smattering of gazing balls on pedestals, I agreed with Duffy that Jamie's plan did not seem like a very bright business venture.

"Jamie Presswood," I repeated, rinsing the skillet. His name conjured up simpler times: ferris wheels and sparklers, picnics by the river, Neapolitan ice cream.

"Now, Anna. He's not the same boy you were best buddies with. You know I'm not one to gossip, but he's been through some struggles in his life since you knew him. Some of them inflicted by the world, but others inflicted by himself. Winston wouldn't take no for an answer, but I'm not entirely happy having him around, especially now that you and David are here. If you cross paths with him again, and you're bound to, living right next door, you don't have to be rude to him or anything, but I'd encourage you to keep your distance."

From Jamie? The boy who had cried when he realized he'd killed his fireflies by neglecting to punch holes in the jar's lid? The teenager who'd single-handedly organized a Thanksgiving food drive at the high school?

"Really? I find that hard to believe," I said. "No offense, Duffy, but I'm perfectly capable of forming my own judgments about people."

She swiped the washcloth from me and began scrubbing down the kitchen table, sweeping crumbs into the palm of her hand. I could hear the solemn tones of news anchors coming from the living room where Winston was watching TV and David was settled in with his remote-controlled dinosaur and a bowl of mint chocolate-chip ice cream.

She flicked the crumbs into the garbage can and rinsed and wrung out the washcloth. "Like you did with Patrick?"

Her words landed like a swift punch to my kidneys. I inhaled sharply. "That was really low. Kimberly-low. What, are you stealing pages from her playbook now?"

"Anna! You know I don't like you talking about your mom that way." She sat down heavily on one of the kitchen chairs, her expression pained. "I'm sorry. I didn't mean to throw that in your face. I know you didn't know—that nobody, not even his own parents, knew at the time. It's just a fitting example, is all. Sometimes we think we know a person, but we don't really. People change, and sometimes it's for the better, and sometimes it's for the worse."

I leaned against the sink, reluctant to sit down at the table with her. "Why are you talking in clichés all of a sudden? If there's something you want me to know about Jamie, you should just tell me."

Duffy stared straight ahead at the napkin holder and salt and pepper shakers, a Dutch boy and girl kissing. "You know I can't abide gossip, especially spreading unverified rumors."

She had once explained her process of "verifying" a rumor to me. As a hairdresser and the owner of the only beauty shop in town, all rumors went through her, and she viewed it as her duty to sift and winnow out the truth while squelching falsehoods in their tracks. Therefore, a rumor only became verified if at least three reliable sources, one of which needed to be an involved party with firsthand knowledge, corroborated it.

"So you say," I muttered. Duffy delighted in her role as the hub in the rumor mill almost as much as she delighted in rereading and thus "solving" her Agatha Christie mysteries. "Unverified or not, you must believe it, if you're warning me away from him."

Duffy patted the chair next to her. "Mind you, I didn't want to believe it. Jamie was such a lamb chop as a boy, taking you under his wing like that when you arrived here for the first time, alone and friendless, mad at your mom, mad at the world. He lifted your spirits and overlooked your...eccentricities. He really was a special kid, and I let Wendy know it. I permed her hair and trimmed his for free all that year."

That wasn't quite my remembering of the events, but I didn't want to interrupt. I sat down.

"Vickie Eberhardt told me first, and you know she's about as reliable as the Channel 8 weatherman, so I dismissed the rumor right off the bat. But then only a few days later, Joanne Gehring came in for an updo—it was her goddaughter's wedding, and you should've seen how her hair turned out, it was just breathtaking; I did it all up in ringlets—and she said the exact same thing. And you know her son Marshall used to be good friends with Jamie in high school, and she said they'd been hanging out some since he's been back. But the nail in the coffin was Laura Schiff."

I furrowed my brow. "The waitress at Ruby's Diner?"

"No, that's her mother-in-law, Lorraine Schiff. Laura's maiden name was Armentrout. I think she's a couple years older than you. You might've crossed paths with her at the high school?"

I was starting to feel overwhelmed by the Old Testament style genealogy of all the relationships in Salsburg. "I really don't remember. So, anyway, what did Laura tell you?"

"Well, Laura is the pharmacy tech at the drugstore, so strictly speaking, this is very confidential. Poor Wendy Presswood came down with MS a few years ago—that part's not confidential; we had a church fundraiser for her to help pay her medical bills, poor thing—but since Jamie's been back, he's been picking up all her medications for her, and Laura said they're refilling the painkillers twice as often. He even had them call and ask the doctor to write a new script for something stronger." She raised her eyebrows in expectation, but when I didn't say anything, she rushed on, "Now Vickie thinks he's selling the drugs to other people, but Joanne was certain he's taking them himself and is an addict. Can you imagine taking away medicine from your own sick mother?"

I put my elbows on the table and leaned in. "Maybe the drugs *are* for his mom. Maybe her MS is getting worse. Maybe she's in terrible pain. Did you ever consider that?" My cheeks felt hot. I hadn't known Wendy Presswood had been diagnosed with multiple sclerosis. It seemed monumentally unfair. She was an incredibly kind woman, always plying me with Danish butter cookies whenever I came to her house, which admittedly, hadn't been in several years.

"Oh, Anna, I wish that were the truth. But Marshall Gehring told his mother that when Jamie was out west, he had—"

"Just stop. Stop. I don't want to hear any more, Duffy." I stood up quickly, nearly knocking an amateurish acrylic painting of Lake Michigan off the wall. I tried to straighten it, but it kept slouching to the right. "You've warned me. I got it. You did your duty, and now I really don't want to talk about this anymore."

I wondered what Edna Franklin and Vickie Eberhardt and Joanne Gehring and all the others said about me behind Duffy's back. That I was a little slut who'd gotten knocked up and hadn't even been able to trap the father into marrying me? That I was an unfit mother who fed her son crap for three meals a day? That I was a loser who couldn't even hold down a stupid secretarial job? An ungrateful mooch who exploited the generosity of her grandparents who were much too nice for their own good? According to my grandmother's standards, these rumors were probably all triple-verified and gold-stamped.

"You're the one who brought him up and seemed so interested," Duffy said mildly. She stood up too and wrapped her warm, steady hands around mine as we readjusted the painting together. "I painted this two years ago from a photograph of the lighthouse in Port Ambrose. I've been dying to get an artist's perspective."

"I'm not an artist."

"Well, I think you are. You used to take all those classes and you're certainly very talented. So what do you think?" Duffy fingered the grainy wooden frame.

The lake was both lumpy (in an effort to depict waves, I assumed) and dimensionless. The water was a monochromatic deep navy, and the sky looked like a solid wall of gray. You could see the pencil lines under the watery white paint where she'd first sketched the light-house. *"A basement masterpiece,"* Mr. Schneider, my high school art teacher, would've designated it.

"I knew it was a painting of Lake Michigan immediately," I said. She nodded eagerly, so I continued, "And the proportions of the lighthouse seem very accurate." I racked my brain for something else innocuous to say. "Maybe it would help to actually go to Port Ambrose and get a feel for the place and then try to paint it from memory, instead of a picture in a book?"

She sighed and sat back down. "That's not practical. It's much too far away."

"Duffy, it's half an hour away." Standing behind her, I bent down and rested my chin on her rounded shoulder. She smelled like hair spray and oatmeal raisin cookies. "We could go together if you like, make a day trip of it with David. I could drive."

Duffy patted my cheek twice, leaving it feeling slightly itchy. "That's thoughtful of you, Anna, but you know I don't like to leave our little paradise here. Salsburg has everything I need and plenty of scenic places to paint if I want to do it your way."

No lakes or lighthouses though, I thought, but didn't say. I straightened up and stretched my arms over my head. "Well, let me know if you change your mind. I'd better go get David ready for bed now. He probably needs a bath. Whenever he eats ice cream, he manages to get it in the weirdest places—in his ears, up his nose."

Duffy smiled fondly, but she wasn't the one who had to scrub the gunk off a bawling, squirming, complaining child.

I had one foot in the dining room before I remembered the other question on my mind. "Oh! I meant to ask you earlier. Are there any dogs in your neighborhood? Big ones? I thought I saw one in your backyard this morning."

Duffy squinted in thought. "Let's see. The Presswoods never had any pets, and Duane and Rose Dawes next door just have cats.

Melody Yarbrough across the way has a yappy little dog, but I'm pretty sure it's never without a leash. Off the top of my head, I can't think of anyone who has a big dog, and I don't think anyone in the neighborhood would let their pet roam free with the highway only a couple of miles away." She looked up at me in concern. "Was it bothering you and Davey? Did it seem like a stray?"

"I don't really know," I said, remembering the way the animal had been illuminated in the sun and then seemingly sucked into the shadows. Almost like an image from a movie projector. Except that it had seemed solid. I bit the inside of my cheek. "I think David was trying to play with it, but he didn't want me to know."

"Hmm. Well, let me know if you see it around here again, and we'll try to get to the bottom of it. In the meantime, make sure Davey knows not to get too close to stray dogs—"

"He knows," I interrupted.

"Alright, alright. Just a suggestion. I suppose it's something you need to teach your little ones right off the bat when you're raising them in the big city."

I drifted into the living room, where the TV was still on and a lithe couple in matching red-sequined costumes was tangoing. Vivien Leigh, crouching under the coffee table, flicked her tail back and forth, as if she were hunting some invisible prey. Winston was asleep on the couch, his head back and mouth open; David was curled up on the opposite end, in deep conversation with his plastic dinosaur. "I want to play with *him* now…" he murmured to his toy, his little voice drifting out of earshot. "But I still like you…"

I pressed my pointer finger to my lips when David spotted me. "Bedtime," I whispered.

He stood up on the couch, holding the remote control that activated the dinosaur's roaring only inches away from his grandpa's face, threatening to click it. "Will you tell me a story?" he countered. Four-year-old bargaining tactics were ruthless.

"Okay. But we need to get you cleaned up first. You're like one big ice cream cone." I pretended I was going to lick his face, and he giggled.

Storytelling was the one area of parenting I felt like I was doing right. In David's infancy, I had babbled repurposed fairy tales to him whenever I cuddled or rocked him. Those early stories were thinly veiled accounts of my own life as I saw it: a princess who escaped the evil queen's snare in order to be with her true love, a prince who had been transformed into a beast and hopefully one day would magically change back into a prince. I could've been reading my baby the phonebook for all he knew; the stories' true purpose was to help me keep my sanity.

But as he grew up, he took an active interest in my stories and even started requesting characters and settings. His tastes skewed toward woodland creatures, space explorers, and pirates. My shining storytelling moment happened when David's preschool asked me to visit for storytime, and instead of reading Dr. Seuss in a singsong voice like all of the other parents, I had invented a story on the spot about a muskrat named Glenn. The children had been rapt the entire fifteen minutes, and afterwards, the teacher had told me without a hint of sarcasm that I should write children's books.

Though it was an almost nightly ritual David and I both cherished, it could be exhausting sometimes, especially when I was feeling un-inspired like I had been for the past several months. David was also becoming a more critical listener, demanding reasonable explanations and tidy endings. "What about Wolfy?" he would ask, and I would try to devise something that would appeal to a four-year-old's sense of logic. "Wolfy was taking a nap," I'd reply. "Mona will come back for him when he wakes up and he's nice and rested." But sometimes all I wanted to say was, *Because I am tired. Because it is time to go to sleep. Because I am a lazy mom. Because I am just a husk of my former self.*

David tried to wriggle out of my grasp as I scrubbed the stickiness off his face, neck, and hands with a washcloth. A full-fledged bath was definitely in order, but we were both too irritable and impatient to wait while the tub filled and then dig for his bath toys in our mess of still unpacked bags.

The evening installment of Mona, the space explorer, and her dog, Wolfy, was my least imaginative story yet. Usually Mona traveled to planets made entirely of food—peanut butter, for example—and after a few minutes of eating and enjoying the food, some sort of conflict arose—Wolfy's mouth got stuck together, so he couldn't warn Mona about a peanut butter bog up ahead. Luckily, a swim in the milk river saved the day. But tonight, I was having a hard time finding a conflict on Planet String Cheese. Even David looked bored.

My mind kept drifting to what Duffy had said about Jamie Presswood. As kids, we both never would have imagined that we'd return to Salsburg one day as hapless, stunted adults. I felt a certain kinship with the neighbor boy I hadn't spared a second thought on in years. A kinship born out of pity, curiosity, and my own sense of humiliation. But maybe it was just because, for once, it was refreshing to be appalled by someone else's life other than my own.

CHAPTER THREE

When I was seventeen years old, Patrick Gill entered my life like a missile fired from a rocket launcher. Whoosh! And suddenly my hair was on fire, my breast impaled, and my clothes flaking off my body into ashes.

It probably had something to do with the fact that I had just returned to Milwaukee after a ho-hum, "safe" year in Salsburg, and my mom had preemptively enrolled me in an all-girls Catholic school, even though we weren't practicing Catholics. It probably also had something to do with the fact that Patrick was the most captivating creature I had ever seen. He had the dark, mournful features of an archangel, but bleached blond hair with one black stripe defiantly streaking across the back of his head at a diagonal. His lean ropy muscles were covered in elaborate black tattoos—a wild mustang, a hawk, a Chinese dragon, a panther, a Celtic cross.

We met in a church, of all places: the Basilica of St. Josaphat. My class was taking a field trip, and we were shuffling along the marble floors in our hideous uniforms (olive green polo shirts and unflattering gray skirts) like we were walking the green mile. Some of us clutched clipboards to our waists with worksheets attached that demanded the answers to such mind-numbing questions as: *What church was the Basilica commissioned to resemble? What events led to the martyrdom of St. Josaphat?* I had ditched mine almost immediately.

My friend, Pippa, had just stepped outside for a cigarette, and I was contemplating joining her even though cigarette smoke made my eyes itchy and watery. It was oppressively quiet inside the church; I felt like the eyes of Jesus and all the saints were watching me from every which angle, and they didn't like what they saw.

Ahead of me, Marguerite Clemens and Billie Van der Wal, the two most popular—and therefore, most hated—girls in the junior class, were whispering and laughing behind their cupped hands. I followed their gaze, and there he was: lying on a pew, stretched out on his back, his leather jacket balled up beneath his head like a pillow. He was gazing up at the dome, furiously scribbling in a sketchbook.

"Yum," Billie Van der Wal breathed.

"Sex on a stick," Marguerite murmured.

He was oblivious to our class, oblivious to everything really, except the kaleidoscope of saints rendered in the dome and the pad of paper in front of him, so I was able to memorize his every detail. I savored him in little pieces, sneaking sideways glances of him with my eyelashes lowered.

"Earth to Anna," Pippa sang in a cloud of minty breath. She had managed to wiggle back into her place beside me in line. "Do you want to check out the gift shop with me? I promised my mom I'd pick up a rosary for my little sister's first communion."

The crowded gift shop gradually emptied out as Pippa dawdled over which rosary to buy and our classmates rushed to board the waiting bus. I studied the rack of postcards, thinking it might be fun to send some to my Salsburg and Lawrenceville friends. I imagined scrawling, *Aren't you glad you're NOT here? This is what passes as a field trip at my new school!*

The postcard rack started swiveling, seemingly of its own accord. I reached out, stopped it, and turned it back to the column of Basilica exterior photos I'd been considering.

"Oh, sorry." The bad-boy-artist's head appeared from the other side of the rack. "I didn't know someone else was looking. Are you an art aficionado, too?"

I couldn't breathe. I'd been an expert at talking to boys since I'd budded breasts, but Patrick wasn't your typical boy by any stretch of imagination. In my frumpy school uniform, I'd never felt more branded as a high schooler, when normally most of my friends said I could pass for twenty or twenty-one. Also, I wasn't positive what "aficionado" meant, but I thought I got the gist of it.

"I love art," I said, looking at him flirtatiously from behind a clump of hair that I'd let fall in front of my face. "Just not *this* kind of art. I'm not really into angels and cherubs and gold-plated halos."

"Oh?" Patrick stepped around the postcard rack, and I could see that his tight jeans were covered in zippers and artfully placed rips. "What kind of art *do* you like?"

I thought back to the art class I'd taken last year with Mr. Schneider and tried to remember the artists he was always going on and on about. "Mark Rothko?" I wagered. "Kandinsky?" I put my hands on my hips and tossed my hair out of my eyes.

"Ah, so you prefer abstract art. Then I can see why this isn't your taste." He nodded and plucked a postcard from the rack and offered it to me. "But take a look at this and tell me that it's not the purest, most humbling Madonna you've ever seen."

She wasn't holding baby Jesus, as I'd seen her portrayed in most paintings, but being bathed in light by an angel and a dove. Mary looked young, younger than me, and pale, almost afraid. Her arms were folded across her chest, and her head was bowed, light brown ropes of her hair falling behind her shoulder.

"It's lovely," I said, though I wasn't sure I meant it. Something about the painting was vaguely troubling, but I couldn't put my finger on it.

"Let me buy it for you. It's a whopping fifty cents. My treat."

Before I could protest, he'd taken it to the cash register and paid for it. Then he handed me the postcard with a wink and hurried off, and it wasn't until I was seated on the bus that I thought to flip it over. On the back he'd scribbled: *I'm having a party tomorrow night. 719 N. 22ⁿᵈ St. Apt. 4. Ten o'clock. Please come?* I'd never seen anything so suave; of course Pippa and I had to go. I told my mom, who had made the effort to send me to an all-girls school and had therefore absolved herself of any other attempts at parenting for the year, that we were going to see a late night movie.

It was the first college party I'd ever attended. I don't know what I'd been expecting—frat guys in togas hitting a beer bong, maybe—but it certainly wasn't that. Instead, about a dozen people milled around the tiny, nearly furniture-less apartment drinking from real glasses, not disposable plastic cups. An old record player set up on the floor emitted a staticky never-ending guitar solo. Patrick and I sat cross-legged, face to face, knees touching knees, on the worn carpet and talked about art, for real this time. I didn't try to impress him by dropping the names of artists and movements I knew little about. Instead, I described the way I felt when I brushed paint onto a canvas, almost like I was revealing its true image by stripping away the white, and he listened carefully to me, watching me, studying me, nodding, and murmuring his understanding.

He was an art major. He showed me one of his sketchbooks, and though most of the drawings were of religious artwork he'd copied from churches and museums, there were a few striking originals. A man with a violin for a face. "My father," he said simply. Two disembodied torsos tangled in the branches of a tree. The last page in the book was a hastily outlined face. It took me a moment to recognize it was mine. He had captured me, apparently from memory, in a way no camera ever had. My graphite-rendered eyes seemed to sparkle from the page, my upturned nose reflected a kind of haughtiness, but the set of my lips divulged my true insecurity. I asked if I could have it, and he laughed and said no. We talked and drank vodka with pineapple juice and ate peapods and dried apricots until Pippa demanded we go home; she was bored to death, and she thought she'd been a good friend and toughed it out long enough.

I started sneaking over to campus to meet him weekly. And then daily. I spent whole weekends at his apartment, telling my mom I was going with Pippa's family to their lake house in Muskego. Now when I looked back at those early months, everything seemed like a clue, a gigantic neon-lit arrow, and I couldn't help wondering why I hadn't suspected anything at the time. Patrick's impulsiveness: buying me a kitten when I'd never mentioned wanting one, skipping classes and encouraging me to do the same so we could take the train to Chicago to visit the Art Institute. His overly grand gestures: sending a thousand dollars' worth of orchids and lilies to my house, much to my mom's rage (since she hadn't known I was dating anyone), after our first argument. His firm belief that he was the next Raphael and I was his Muse, and the way he'd keep me up until five in the morning, alternating between making love to me and drawing me in various poses. Exhausted, I'd finally beg him to let me sleep, and he'd oblige and set about doing something else—banging out a history paper or walking to the nearby coffee shop—but never seemed to need his own rest.

Perhaps it was just the way I'd always wanted to be loved by someone. Wholly, single-mindedly, almost to the point of obsession.

Of course I got pregnant. I'd been so furious with my mom when she'd marched me into Planned Parenthood my freshman year of high school to get me on the pill, that I'd refused to take it and relied on Patrick for condoms instead. *I wasn't like her*, I'd fumed. I was smarter. I was immune to the same weaknesses and mistakes that she'd made. When my period failed to come two months in a row, and the smell of bacon started to make me throw up, my illusion shattered and I hated myself, even more than I hated my mom, for once. Patrick didn't believe in abortion, and he seemed so genuinely excited about our having a baby together, that I knew it was my way out, my way of being different from my mom. I would prove her wrong. I would have the baby *and* stay with its father *and* give it a loving and happy home.

I spent my senior year at an abysmal Milwaukee public school, where at least I was in good company with ten other pregnant girls. I lived between my mom's house and Patrick's apartment. When my mom's incessant litany of my failings got to be too much, I went to Patrick's. When there was nothing left in his fridge or I couldn't get any sleep or do my homework because he was constantly talking or wanting me to pose for him, I went to my mom's.

I had almost entered my third trimester when I returned to Patrick's apartment one day to find his normally bare living room crowded with baby stuff. Bags of onesies, sleepers, bottles, pacifiers, plastic keys, and fuzzy caterpillars. An enormous mahogany crib still in its box. A stroller, a car seat, a bouncer, and a plastic bathtub shaped like a whale. A stuffed giraffe nearly as tall as me.

"What is all this stuff?" I asked, struggling to make my way through the clutter to the bathroom.

Patrick looked up from the pair of yellow baby booties he was holding in his palm. He rose from the futon and gestured to the crib box, where it was leaning against the wall, as if it might speak for itself. "I wanted to prepare for our child, Anna."

"That's thoughtful, babe, but it must have cost a fortune! Your mom said she still has your old crib and some of your baby stuff and we're welcome to it. The rest we can buy at rummage sales or Goodwill. This is too much, Patrick. Way too much."

He frowned. "Don't worry about the cost. I'm going to support you and our baby. I know we don't have a lot right now, but I'm really close to having my first exhibit, and once that happens, we'll be set."

I headed toward the bathroom, rolling my eyes. He'd been saying the same thing since I had first met him. He was always on the verge of "scoring" an exhibit. "I'm about to wet my pants. I'll be right back."

When I came out, Patrick gently tugged me onto the futon, lifted up my maternity shirt, and rested his cheek gently against the taut skin of my belly. "Hello, Baby Panna," he said, a combination of our names that he'd taken to calling our unborn child, and then whispered something I couldn't hear. He kissed my stomach and raised his face to mine, studying me with his somber, archangel eyes.

"What do you think about turning our bedroom into a nursery? You and I can move the bed out here. I could paint the walls in the nursery to look like a farm—rolling hills and a sunflower patch, a little red barn, some sheep and cows."

I closed my eyes as he talked and let his words wash over me. I imagined the small, dingy bedroom transformed into a little piece of the idyllic countryside for my baby.

The next morning I woke up to find the crib box unpacked and hundreds of tiny pieces and tools scattered about the living room, but no Patrick. It was a Saturday, and I imagined he'd gone to the coffee shop or grocery store to get us some breakfast. By noon, he still hadn't returned, and I'd abandoned that hypothesis, replacing it with the more likely explanation that he was off drawing somewhere and had lost track of the time, which was oh-so-typical. When he didn't show up by ten o'clock that night, I started to worry. He wouldn't answer his cell phone, and none of his friends knew where he was either. I was close to calling the cops and reporting him as a missing person when he finally strolled in on Monday morning. He had buzzed most of his hair off.

."Where were you?" I hissed through my teeth, too livid and relieved all at once to even look at him.

According to Patrick, he had gone to the Basilica to look at "our dome" (as he called it) for inspiration and strength, when he'd stumbled upon a friendly tour group who'd invited him to join them. He'd tagged along with them to the Harley Davidson Museum and then the Miller Brewing Company, where he sampled a little too much beer. The tour ended at this point, but some of his newfound friends invited him to go downtown and get some more drinks. He didn't remember much after that. He didn't know where he had slept. He thought he'd gone down to the lake at some point because he had sand in his pockets, and he vaguely remembered looking in a mirror and realizing his blond hair with the black stripe was holding him back from reaching his true potential and therefore needed to go. That was all.

"Patrick, you can't do this! *I* can't do this," I shouted. "We've got a baby on the way. You didn't even leave a note. Did you not think about me even once to wonder if I was worried sick about you? You can't go wandering off on me like this and then drinking so much that you black out. You don't even remember where you stayed? How do you know that you didn't pick up some girl and cheat on me?"

I left for my mom's house and stayed there for an entire week before her diatribes got the best of me. *I could tell he was trouble just by looking at him. I knew you were going to end up raising this baby all by yourself, just like I did. And if you think for one second that I'm going to be the one raising it for you, while you go about your glamorous life, you've got another thing coming…*

Patrick was sweeter and more devoted than ever when I returned—rubbing my swollen feet with lavender-scented oil and making sure the freezer and cupboards were stocked with my pregnancy cravings: waffle fries and powdered sugar doughnuts. He kept apologizing for his behavior and telling me that if he ever lost me, he didn't know what he'd do. He started curling up in bed beside me and sleeping at night for the first time since I'd known him and even slept later than me most days. Then he stopped drawing, and I knew something was wrong.

I got home one afternoon from the part-time waitressing job I'd picked up to find him in the nursery, still in the sweat pants and T-shirt he slept in, surrounded by the paint cans we'd bought for his farm mural, and crying.

I wrapped my arms around him as best I could with my huge stomach between us. "What's wrong, babe? Tell me what's wrong."

"I've lost it," he said. "I can't see it anymore. It's just gone. Even when I close my eyes, there's nothing there."

"What's gone? What did you lose?"

But he couldn't tell me. I ended up painting the nursery myself—a solid light blue since that was the color we had the most of—with a handkerchief tied around my face like a bandit to keep out the paint fumes.

Patrick stopped leaving the apartment, even to go to his classes, and was suspicious of me and irritable whenever I went to work or any of my doctor's appointments. When I got home one night, cranky and tired from being on my feet for ten hours straight, and he had the nerve to ask me if I'd been out with someone, I erupted.

"God, Patrick! I'm not cheating on you! I'm hideously fat and seven months pregnant and busting my butt so we can have some sort of income while you stay home and do God knows what with God knows who."

Patrick tried to put his hand on my shoulder, but I shrugged it off.

"I'm sorry," he said. "It's just that I don't know what I'd do if I ever lost you, Anna. I'd kill myself if you ever left me. You're the only good thing in my life. Everything else is turning to shit. School. My art. My future."

It wasn't the first time he'd threatened to commit suicide. His first few threats had flattered my ego and made me feel even more wretchedly in love, as if our fates were as tortuously entwined as Romeo and Juliet's. But the next several threats had dragged me into my own black hole of depression. By now, I'd become practically numb to them.

"Maybe you should talk to someone about it," I said as gently as I could. As a college student, Patrick was entitled to at least five free sessions with a mental health counselor. I knew this because I'd looked into it after his period of going missing, but since then I hadn't found the courage to broach the subject with him.

"I am," he said. "I'm talking to you."

I took a deep breath. "Someone more qualified than me. Someone at University Health."

"God damn it, Anna. They can't help me. They don't know the first thing about me. The only person who can help me is you. Just promise me that you'll never leave me for someone else. That you'll always be my muse."

Even unshaved and disheveled, with the recent weight loss that made his arms nearly as thin as mine, he was still the most achingly beautiful creature I had ever seen. My heart was overwhelmed for him with love, pity, and guilt.

"I love you so much, babe," I said. "You know I don't ever want to leave you, but you worry me, and I only want for you to get better. If you really loved me, you'd at least try for me and see a doctor."

"There's nothing they can tell me that I don't already know. I had a light inside me—I was tuned in to everything. I was so close to God, and every time I put my pencil on a page, this amazing energy flowed through me, and I saw the world as it really was. As it should be. But now that light is gone, and I don't know how to get it back. But I know you're part of it, and if I lose you too, I'll have lost everything."

"You won't lose me, babe," I said and swallowed hard. "We'll go to the doctor's office together tomorrow. You can explain to them exactly what you just explained to me, and they'll know what to do."

"You're not listening to me!" He picked up a ceramic piggy bank that was sitting on the counter, a graduation/baby shower gift I'd gotten from Valentina, one of the other pregnant teens at the high school. I think I knew, even before he did, that he was going to fling it at me. I clutched my belly and felt the air next to my cheek stir. The piggy bank exploded into little shards against the wall behind my head. We both stared at each other in stunned silence.

Patrick raised his hands over his head, as if showing me he had no other weapons. "I'm so sorry. I didn't mean to—I promise you I would never hurt you."

I backed away from him, but there was nowhere for me to go; he was blocking my exit. Even in his penitent state, he looked wild and capable of a violent, smothering kind of love. He crumpled to the worn carpet, dragging me down with him, and stroked my hair. He bathed my belly with his tears and whispered promises I knew he wouldn't be able to keep.

Small ceramic chips dusted the shoulder of my maternity shirt, and I tried to brush them off. There was a dent in the plaster mere inches from where I had been standing, a tangible mark of the intangible thing that had broken between us.

That night when he was sleeping, I called Duffy and broke down weeping on the phone. I told her I didn't know what to do and that I had no one to turn to. She said I was always welcome in her home, but I tearfully reminded her that I had no way of getting there. I think it was the first time in over ten years that Duffy left Salsburg. She drove the two hours to Milwaukee in the middle of the night to pick me up. I was so consumed by my own drama that we were almost to her house by the time I noticed her hands were trembling on the steering wheel.

She agreed with me that Patrick had a mental health problem and needed to seek help, and that it wouldn't be a good idea for me to live with him until he had done so. She encouraged me to call his parents, whom I'd met only once when we'd broken the news about my pregnancy, and clue them in to what was going on to see if they could persuade him to get treatment. I stayed with Duffy and

Winston for two months, almost up until the time of my delivery. During that time, Abigail Gill, Patrick's mom, called me routinely, filling me in that Patrick had been diagnosed with type I bipolar disorder. They'd withdrawn him from his classes, and he'd moved back home with them. His doctor had put him on a regimen of mood-stabilizing drugs that Abigail claimed were helping. She suggested I come live with them; they were quite wealthy and had a "guest suite" above their garage.

I wanted to stay safe—wrapped up in my cocoon somewhere between conception and birth, between childhood and motherhood, in the care of my grandparents, but I missed Patrick. I was hopeful that the medication had restored him to the man I'd fallen in love with. I was hopeful that I could still prove my mom wrong and claim the life I'd always known I'd deserved. So I went back to Milwaukee.

Patrick wasn't the bad-boy-artist I'd fallen in love with. Neither was he the insecure, temperamental man that I'd left. He was somewhere in between—a colorless, hollowed-out version of himself. But when I gave birth to David Patrick Jennings Gill on September 14, our son seemed to reach inside his shell with his little fists and bring him back to life for a few precious months. He started painting again and even got a job working at a hardware store. We were able to save up enough to rent the upper-half of a house on 57th Street, where I met Stacy, a married mother of two in her thirties, who would become a great friend to me and a convenient babysitter for David.

When David was five months old, I found out that Patrick had stopped taking his medication. I came home from the grocery store to find David sitting in his whale-shaped bathtub in chilly water with Patrick nowhere to be seen. I picked up the wailing baby, wrapped him in a towel, and clutched him to my chest, murmuring in his ear over and over again, "It's okay, it's okay. Everything's all right now. You're okay," while in my brain, I screamed, "He could've drowned! He could've drowned! Just one little slip and he could've drowned."

Patrick was in a corner of the basement that we shared with Stacy, rifling through some plastic bins and boxes. He later explained that he was looking for a green frog towel that we had wrapped David in when he was a newborn, but then gotten sidetracked by all his art supplies and old paintings.

"Oh, you're home," he said cheerily, as if he hadn't just almost killed our infant.

We fought into the middle of the night. We fought until I went through an entire tissue box and my throat was raw and hoarse from screaming. Patrick said he had stopped taking his mood stabilizers because it made his head feel all cloudy and he'd gained some weight as a side effect. I replied that I was sorry, but I'd rather have him feel a little cloudy than accidentally drown our son with his negligence. Why hadn't he talked to his doctor and tried a different dosage or new medication instead of just stopping without telling anyone? I told him that I no longer trusted him with David, and that if he didn't start getting treatment again, we were through.

He promised he would see his doctor and start taking his medication again. "I just wanted you to love me like you used to," he admitted. "But you don't love this doped-up me. You love the manic me. You fell in love with my creativity and energy, and there's no way I can get that back if I'm in the cloud all the time." His calm, hopeless assessment nearly broke my heart.

"I don't want you to be in the cloud either," I said. "But these manic episodes aren't good for you. They're killing us. We need to get you on more solid ground."

He disappeared again a month later. He was gone for nine days before the cops picked him up for breaking into a mansion in Fox Point. He'd insisted he lived there and even brandished a crowbar at the real homeowner. While in police custody, he tried to hang himself and was put on emergency detention. His parents persuaded the homeowner not to press charges and had Patrick admitted to the best psychiatric hospital in the state. Meanwhile, I moved all of his stuff back to their guest suite, had my landlord change the locks on our apartment, and started the arduous process of petitioning for sole legal and physical custody of David. After Patrick was released from the hospital, his parents pushed for him to have supervised visitation with David. This lasted for only a few months before Patrick's behavior became so frightening—screaming and cursing at me as though I were a stranger, squeezing David until he was red-faced and howling, and finally threatening to kill us and himself so that "we could all be together as a family"—that I filed for an injunction against him, and the court granted it, stating that he couldn't make contact with me or David for the maximum sentence of four years, except through his parents to determine any necessary financial matters.

You didn't know, Duffy had said. *Not even his own parents knew.* That was true, and yet sometimes, I felt like I was drawn to mania. That Patrick was right, and I had loved him only during his manic episodes. That mania *was* true love. And it could consume you like it had consumed Patrick, or it could leave you feeling tired and used up, like it had left me. Nothing seemed to exist in between.

CHAPTER FOUR

David wiggled his arm between one of the big gaps in the fence. "I want to pet the cows!"

The cows were all thankfully out of his reach, grazing several feet away from us in the pasture. "The cows are eating their breakfast, so they don't want to be petted right now. We'll just have to look at them from a distance, okay?"

"Moo," he called to them and wiggled his other arm through the fence. "Moo moo mooooo."

I tugged him back before he could land face first on the other side in a pile of manure. "What are you saying to them?"

He grinned. "Hurry up and eat breakfast and come play with me."

We walked around the fenced-in pasture, David unsuccessfully trying to call the cows over every so often. I couldn't blame him for being disappointed. That morning when Winston had asked us if we wanted to tag along with him to the Englebrooks' farm while he repaired a manure spreader, David had been so keen on going that I'd managed to get him to eat an entire wedge of cantaloupe. I supposed he'd envisioned Old McDonald's farm or the petting zoo his preschool had visited. My motive had simply been getting out of the house. I'd been in Salsburg for an entire week and hadn't left my grandparents' neighborhood once. Even a stinky old farm seemed like it would be a breath of fresh air.

But it wasn't, of course. We'd been there for nearly an hour already, and no sign of Winston yet. I wondered how much longer it could possibly take to fix a manure spreader.

"Which cow has the most black on it? Which cow has the most white?" I asked David, and he studied the herd thoughtfully before pointing them out. "If you could name one of these cows, what would you name it?"

"King Rex," he said, and I didn't bother to correct him and tell him that cows were females.

Droopy from the heat and our long walk around the fence, we collapsed in the shade of a tree near the cornfield. I hadn't thought to pack any water bottles or juice boxes because I hadn't known the trip would last so long. David seemed content examining the leafy stalks of corn, which were only about a foot high. Still I prayed that he wouldn't start whining he was thirsty.

"That will grow into corn in another month," I said. "Yummy corn on the cob like we sometimes eat in the summer. But right now it's really young and needs a lot of sunlight and water to grow big and tall—even taller than you or me!"

David's eyes widened. He stepped into the row of corn and stroked one of the glossy leaves with his thumb.

"Don't go too far. Stay where I can see you."

A light breeze ruffled the corn plants, and I followed David's sky-blue shirt with my eyes as he skipped through the neat rows. From my shady seat, the farm looked more picturesque. I tried not to let the red barn and tall silo remind me of the nursery mural that Patrick had finally painted in our apartment on 57th Street, the same walls that I had forced myself to paint over when David had turned three.

I returned my gaze to my son, and something caught my eye. I immediately scrambled to my feet. Darting through the corn behind him was a coppery-colored animal. It was taller than David, almost as tall as me. And it seemed to be running on two legs.

"David!" I shouted. I searched for a stick, for anything, to ward off the threatening-looking animal, but there was nothing, so I simply launched myself into the cornfield. I would put my body between them.

I was thirty feet away. Twenty. David was leisurely jogging toward me, with flushed cheeks and a goofy smile, apparently unaware of the creature in hot pursuit. It looked like something out of a horror movie. Leathery skin covered its lean body, and its lizard-like tail stood out behind it like the rudder of a boat. Its face…its face was terrible. Yellow eyes with black slits and a mouth full of knife-like teeth. It seemed to be emitting a black mist that drifted over the corn stalks like a low-lying, poisonous fog.

I shivered. I was only ten feet away now, and I'd opened up my stride so I could swoop in, collect him in my arms, and keep running. "It's okay, David. Everything's going to be okay. It's not going to hurt you! Just come here."

He reacted to the panic in my voice, tears immediately wetting his eyes. Instead of tumbling into my arms, he stopped in his tracks. The black mist crept up his bare ankle. "Mommy?"

The fearsome creature stopped too, just inches behind him, and seemed to taunt me from over David's shoulder. Its coppery scales flashed in the sun; its yellow eyes penetrated mine.

I charged forward and scooped David into my arms, carrying him to the edge of the field. When I looked back, there was nothing there except for our shadows; even the dark smoke had dissipated like a bad dream. I turned in a slow, searching circle, but there was nowhere for a creature as tall as me to hide in the glaring late morning sunlight.

My grandfather, however, was just then ambling down a hill to reach us. His plaid shirt was darkened by sweat, and grease smudged his forearms, but he wore the expression of a man in charge. I had never been happier to see another human being before in my life. I wanted him to lift both David and me in his sturdy arms and hold us tightly against his barrel chest.

"Sorry that took so long," he called. "The bed chain was giving me—"

"Did you see it?" My words came out in all one breathy gasp. "Did you see that…that *thing*?" I set David down and pointed one shaky arm at the cornfield.

Winston squinted at the now empty rows of cornstalks. He pulled a handkerchief out of his back pocket, squinted at me, and then squinted at David. Genuine concern was etched on his face. He arched one shaggy eyebrow upward. "I'm sorry. I didn't see anything."

"It was chasing David."

Winston's eyebrow climbed higher. "Was it a wild turkey? They can be aggressive if you startle them. Or a raccoon? It's unusual for raccoons to be out at this time of day, but if it was sick…" He dabbed at his forehead with the handkerchief. "There haven't been coyotes around in these parts for years, and they're mostly nocturnal, too. What did it look like, Anna?"

A predatory, oversized reptile running on two legs. But this description sounded insane, even in the privacy of my head; I could only imagine how nuts it would sound if I spoke it aloud. I looked down at David, whose tears had evaporated. He looked calm and no longer frightened, and I tried to channel his easy resilience.

"I didn't get a good look," I lied, wishing it were the truth. "But whatever it was, it gave us quite a scare."

I had just settled David in for his afternoon nap and decided that a nap of my own might not be a bad idea. I flopped backwards onto the bed and squeezed my eyes shut. When that didn't work, I got up and yanked the curtains closed and returned to bed. I pressed my palm over my eyes and massaged my eyeballs through their lids. But that didn't work either, because it wasn't the sunlight that was keeping me awake: it was the images flickering behind my eyelids.

There were no two ways about it: I was seeing things. Things that weren't there, that other people couldn't see. In particular, a scaly monster that was stalking my son, who was completely oblivious to its existence. The first time, I could write it off as the sun in my eyes combined with a lack of sleep. But the second time, I had stared into the creature's eyes. I had been so close to it that I could almost smell its foul breath, could imagine what the texture of its skin would feel like beneath my fingertips. I could feel the temperature change. It was certainly no raccoon or golden retriever.

There were two possibilities I could think of to explain these bizarre events. Either a) there was a giant lizard on the loose in Salsburg, or b) I was going crazy. The former didn't seem very likely.

I rolled onto my stomach and buried my face in the pillow. When Patrick had finally been diagnosed with bipolar disorder, I'd tried to learn as much as possible about the disease. The more I'd learned, the more convinced I'd been that it was a cruel, cruel illness, lulling you into thinking you would live a normal, happy life, until it suddenly pulled the rug out from under you in your late teens or early twenties. But I wasn't suffering from mood swings. I was suffering from hallucinations. What could that mean? Schizophrenia? What chance in life would my poor son have with a bipolar father and a schizophrenic mother?

I lifted my face from the damp pillow, sat up, and wiped my eyes. There had to be some other explanation. I didn't *feel* schizophrenic, although I didn't suppose anyone ever did. I wasn't having several delusions—only one. And it had only happened here in Salsburg. Maybe we needed to go back to Milwaukee. Maybe I was getting too much fresh air and relaxation, and my brain was restless and had started inventing boogeymen. Or maybe my grandparents' yard and the Englebrooks' farm was haunted...by humongous reptiles. Right.

I commandeered the old desktop computer situated in the hallway nook outside my bedroom. Duffy and Winston rarely used it, as evidenced by the sheen of dust on the boxy monitor and the flurry of sticky note instructions attached to the desk. *Make sure the green light is on and there is paper loaded in the tray before trying to print,* one note instructed.

A cursory search of the internet turned up several stories of people who'd had hallucinations of large reptiles and lizards (whew!), but this was only after ingesting LSD or shrooms (damn!). Certain types of brain tumors could create disturbing visions, but that was a possibility too dreadful for me to ponder long, so I quickly changed tacks. Apparently the state of Wisconsin was brimming with weird creatures—everything from werewolves and lake monsters to Bigfoot and even something called a Hodag. Rhinelander's legend of the Hodag initially seemed promising, because the horned animal was described as part frog, part dinosaur, and part elephant, but with a little more digging, I found out it had been confirmed as a hoax a long time ago and was now just a cartoonish tourist attraction and festival mascot, not the very realistic creature I had witnessed.

In frustration, I pushed my chair away from the computer desk. So what *was* I seeing? And what did it have to do with David?

Outside, the familiar growl of a lawnmower roared to life. I strode through my bedroom, drew the curtains back, and peeked out the window, which overlooked the backyard. Sure enough, Jamie Presswood, dressed all in black, was mowing our lawn. I guessed it was a weekly thing. I glanced at the reflection of myself in the glass of the Revolutionary War picture, making sure my eyes weren't still puffy from my earlier cry. Then I shut down the computer, grateful to close the images of the horned beast (imaginary or not, he was still ugly as sin), and ran downstairs.

He didn't notice me at first, waving at him from the deck, so I walked barefoot toward him.

"Hey!" I called out. "Jamie Presswood! Fancy meeting you here!"

Jamie squinted at me and motioned to his huge headphones. "Sorry! I can't hear you!" he shouted over the roar. "Hold on a sec." He slipped the headphones around his neck and released the handle of the lawnmower, and the yard fell silent. Up close, I could see that this was Jamie Presswood, my childhood friend, not just some strange man with a beard and gothic wardrobe. He was staring at me expectantly, waiting for me to say something.

"Do you remember me?" I found myself asking.

He brushed dismissively at some drops of sweat on his forehead. "For the love of God, Anna, of course I remember you. But I'm surprised you remember me."

"I hardly recognized you at first," I admitted, curling my toes into the soft grass. "What's with this whole scraggly bearded look? Are you trying to replace the lead singer of the Foo Fighters?"

Jamie scowled, but then a shadow of his former boyish grin flickered across his face. "Why? You think I could pull it off?"

I laughed. "I think you should shave your face."

"Well, if that's all you wanted to say..." He replaced his headphones and reached for the bar of the mower.

"No, that's not all I wanted to say." I wanted to express my sympathy for his mother's illness. I wanted to remind him about the time we took Duffy's penny jar to the bank, converted it into $22 in paper money, and spent it all on gas station candy that we'd consumed that very same day. I wanted to ask him if he was a drug addict. "What are you doing back here?" I asked instead.

Jamie gestured to the mower, deliberately misunderstanding me. "Just cutting the grass."

"I know *that*. What are you doing back *here*? In Salsburg. My grandma told me you went out west."

"Did she? Then why don't you ask your grandma?" He narrowed his brown eyes, and the tough guy facade slipped back into place. "It doesn't really matter though, does it? I'm here now, and I've got a lot to do today, so I'd better get back to work."

"Fine." I put my hand on my hip, leaned forward, and quipped, "I was just trying to be neighborly."

Jamie mumbled something under his breath that didn't sound very neighborly. He jerked the cord on the lawnmower, and the prohibitive noise bubbled up between us. "I could ask you the same question, you know," he yelled over the noise. "Why *you're* back here."

"You could!" I yelled back. "So why don't you?"

His words were almost swallowed up. "Because I'd honestly rather not go down that road again, Anna." Then he stared straight ahead at the swath of grass he was cutting.

A rush of hot blood flooded my face and neck. I turned on my heel and stalked inside, suddenly wondering if Duffy had been watching our interaction. But I could hear her voice from the basement downstairs, where she was working on a client's hair, and Winston was nowhere to be found. Despite the noise, David was still fast asleep.

I sat down at the kitchen table, propped my head in my hands, and watched Jamie's steady progress through the back windows until he disappeared to do the front yard.

The kinship I'd imagined between us was clearly that—imagined. It seemed that Jamie was one of those immature people who kept old high school grudges, and it simply couldn't be helped. But pleasant or not, talking with him had been a welcome distraction. At least while I focused on my indignation, the fear I was losing my mind couldn't rise up and overwhelm me.

Duffy let the refrigerator door swing closed. "I just don't feel like cooking tonight. Let's go to Ruby's instead. Winston, sweet potato, would you be up for it? What about you, Anna?"

"*I* could cook," I offered, even though my cooking expertise didn't extend much further than boiling noodles or punching buttons on a microwave. Staying with my grandparents and eating their food had made me feel like a total freeloader, and letting them take David and me out to a restaurant somehow seemed even worse. Public freeloading.

"That's sweet of you, but not necessary. I think we could all do with a night out," Duffy said without a hint of irony.

"Ruby's has some great specials on Saturday nights," Winston added.

"If you guys really don't mind, okay," I said. "Let me just go get changed first."

"You do realize this is Ruby's we're talking about, right?" Duffy hollered after me, as I dashed up the stairs. "Ruby's Diner? The only restaurant in town? No fancy attire required!"

It was only my second foray out of the house, but a busy diner was certainly a different story than a dairy farm. The chances were incredibly good that I would bump into someone I knew, or someone who knew someone I knew, and I wanted them to give a glowing, somewhat envious report of me, not a pitying or disapproving one.

I brushed out my hair until it fell down my back in a smooth, gleaming sheet. I slipped out of my jean shorts, T-shirt, and rubber flip-flops in favor of a white-and-pink belted sundress and high-heeled sandals. I looked like my old self, my best self, the one who only got to make an appearance once or twice a year these days. I only wished I'd had time to give David a bath or at least a quick face-scrubbing, but it couldn't be helped.

The diner was crowded by Salsburg standards; we had to wait ten minutes for a table, and I endured a lot of curious stares from the other patrons, who were mostly middle-aged and wore their patriotic or Harley-Davidson T-shirts tucked into faded jeans.

David was very impressed by the swiveling stools lined up at the counter and therefore upset that we would be sitting at a booth instead. He showed his displeasure by folding his skinny arms across his chest and making half-whining, half-growling sounds under his breath.

"You need to behave," I warned him. "Grandma Duffy and Grandpa Winston are being very nice by taking us out to eat, so be a good boy."

He scrunched up his face and climbed into the booth next to me, stepping on the flared skirt of my dress with his dirty sneakers in the process. Winston set about the very serious business of deciding what to order, and Duffy made a not-too-subtle survey of all the other diners in the room, turning her head to and fro, and smiling and waving at a few she recognized. I tucked my skirt under my legs to prevent further damage and tried to discreetly pull up the bodice of my dress so that my hot pink bra wasn't peeking out.

"Why look who it is! You brought the whole family in!" Lorraine Schiff, our waitress, crowed. She tucked her order pad into her apron to free up her hands to better pinch David's cheeks. "My, my. What an adorable great-grandson! What's your name, honey?"

David scowled at her and threw himself into my arms.

"I'm sorry," I said. "He can be a little shy. His name is David."

Lorraine smiled indulgently; she was the type of overly friendly, insincere waitress who you just knew would turn on her heel and badmouth her customers in the kitchen. "Well, he's a positive cherub. I'm envious. I keep asking my son and daughter-in-law when they're going to make me a grandma, but they keep telling me not to rush them, that they want to get their careers established, and save up to buy a house first. Imagine that! Why, Anna, I think you went to school with my daughter-in-law, Laura. Laura Armentrout? Do you remember her? She was the secretary of the student government and graduated salutatorian, and now she's a pharmacy tech and even wants to go back to school to become a pharmacist. Too busy for babies, I guess." She pursed her red lips in an exaggerated pout.

I hugged David, who seemed to be trying to put his head down my dress, closer to me. If I had to hear about this Laura Armentrout-Schiff one more time… "Good for them. I wish them the best," I managed to say.

Duffy leaned forward. "Yes, certainly. You have a lot to be proud of, Lorraine. Tim's a real success at the bank, and Laura always was a bright girl. It takes a lot of skill, I always say, counting all those little pills and making sure you put them in the right bottles, and working the cash register to boot. Just make sure she doesn't wait too long to start a family. You know what they say about a woman's eggs: they've got an expiration date." She cocked her head toward me and gave me a sly wink. "Well, anyway, we're all ravenous. Would it be okay with you if we ordered now?"

Lorraine's gloating smile faded, and it was clear she was trying to figure out if she and her daughter-in-law had just been insulted. She fumbled for her order pad.

There wasn't a children's menu, so we ended up ordering what turned out to be a mountainous plate of spaghetti for David. I shuddered to think what he would look like when we left the restaurant, but there was nothing else he'd eat, and the spaghetti seemed to take the edge off his crabbiness. I tucked one napkin into his collar and spread another across his lap. But after only a few bites, he claimed he was full and wanted to play in the "PlayPlace." I told him this wasn't McDonalds, and there was no PlayPlace, but if he ate a few more bites, he could have dessert. He wailed that he didn't want dessert and became increasingly antsy, until Winston had the brilliant idea of asking Lorraine for some paper and crayons. David pushed his plate away and set about coloring immediately.

"We'll get a doggy bag and take it home," I said apologetically. "He and I can eat the leftovers."

"If he doesn't like it now, I'm sure he won't want it reheated," Duffy said. "Oh, honestly, Anna. No need to look so stricken. Sometimes you act like we've never dealt with a cranky four-year-old before. It'll be fine. Although we do need to do something about this picky eating, I'm afraid, or he won't get all the nutrients he needs to grow into a big, strong boy." Here, David looked up, and Duffy grinned at him. "Instead he'll turn into a pile of spaghetti! Or a meatball! A big, Davey-sized meatball! And then how are we going to keep Grandpa Winston from eating you?"

David giggled and reached for another crayon.

"Why—it *is* you!" a familiar female voice exclaimed. "Lorraine said you were here with your grandparents, but I didn't believe her!"

I turned around to see a petite young woman with unruly brown curls grinning at me. Carly Cardwell, a friend from high school and one of the few I'd bothered to send a birth announcement to when David was born. She'd been famous in our class for throwing the wildest parties at her parents' house on Long Lake whenever they went out of town. Drunk boating, drunk skinny dipping, drunk jumping on a trampoline. The stupid, death-defying stuff of teenagers' dreams.

Duffy helped me scoot David aside and then swapped places with me, so that I could slide out of the booth and hug Carly. She came up to only my chin and was a genuine hugger—the kind who gave you a good tight squeeze and held on just a few seconds longer than the norm.

"It's wonderful to see you!" I said into her nest of chestnut ringlets.

"Same to you! What an absolute trip to run into you here at Ruby's again like the good old days! You look just the same, but you've got your little boy with you now." Carly studied him with a look akin to wonder. "He's got your hair, of course, and your chin and oval face, I think. He's beautiful."

"Thanks." A lot of people instantly professed that he looked just like me, because of our blond hair, but in truth, he looked much more like Patrick with his dark, serious eyes and expressions of intense concentration. Carly had managed to pinpoint the few small similarities that I myself had sought out many times in my son's face. "So what's new with you? It's been ages."

Carly rocked backwards on her heels, and for the first time, I noticed she was wearing an apron. Was she waitressing at Ruby's? She made a face. "It's just my gig for right now to get some experience," she explained. "I started doing the desserts and pastries here. I'm working toward having my own bakery one day. If I ever do, Sam always jokes that I have to name it the One Day Bakery. That's another new thing, I guess—I'm engaged, and oh, you should totally come to our party! One week from tonight. At our condo in Lawrenceville. Please tell me you'll come! We have some serious catching up to do."

"I'd love to!" I said, perhaps a little too enthusiastically, but the thought of socializing with someone other than my grandparents was incredibly appealing at the moment.

Carly wrote her address and phone number down on an order pad and then insisted my grandparents and I order dessert on the house. She recommended the cheesecake, which we all enjoyed except for David who was suspicious of its name and consistency.

"What you drawing there, kiddo?" Winston asked David, after he'd flipped over his fifth or sixth sheet of paper.

"My friend," David said, without looking up. He'd worn the tip of his crayon flat. He reached for another.

Winston sipped his coffee. "Does your friend have a name?"

"King Rex."

The name caught my attention. I set down my fork and glanced across the table, expecting to see a black-and-white cow, but instead, the drawing was an odd reddish-brown shape.

"Can I see that?" I asked.

David obligingly handed me the paper. As with most of his artwork, a thin strip of green grass lined the bottom and an egg yolk sun smiled down benevolently from one corner. Centered in the page, floating a centimeter off the grass, stood the reddish-brown blob. Its little head with black eyes balanced atop a cylindrical body. Two claws sprouted from its chest, two webbed feet grounded its body, and a long triangular tail sailed behind it. Most startling, however, was the mouth. Nearly taking up the whole head, the mouth was a wide circle filled on all sides with a jumble of pointy, yellow teeth, like a sea lamprey.

My sweaty fingers dampened the paper's edges as I clutched it and stared disbelievingly. It looked like a fairy tale creature, a monster, a dragon—something that existed solely to steal children away from their mothers in the dead of night.

It looked like the creature I had seen chasing David earlier in the day.

"What is King Rex?" I asked, raising my eyes to my son's face. I could no longer bear to look at the waxy image before me. The talons. The mouth of razor-sharp teeth. The way it conjured up the terrifying likeness I had seen with my own eyes.

"My friend," David repeated. He rifled through the stack of drawings before him and held up another one, similar to the one I clutched in my hands. It depicted the same brown creature, but standing next to it was a boy with yellow hair, long orangutan arms, and a big smile. David, himself.

Fear and slow comprehension squeezed my heart. "You said that," I said. "But what *is* he?"

David smiled, his own blunt baby teeth as perfect as pearls. "A tie-ran-a-suss rex, Mommy."

CHAPTER FIVE

It was an overcast morning, threatening rain. The sky was grayish-white, bleaching the landscape. David stood on the top step of the deck facing the yard, hesitant as though he were on a diving board, about to leap into a swimming pool. He turned to me with wide, questioning eyes.

"It's okay, buckaroo. Show me how you play."

He descended the stairs. I stood at the railing, my cup of hot coffee the only thing anchoring me to reality. When I'd tucked David in last night and asked him if he was afraid of King Rex and if King Rex had ever hurt him, he'd replied adamantly, "No! He's my friend," as though it had never occurred to him that friends, especially of the dinosaur variety, could harm him. I had eked out only two hours of sleep the whole night, and even those hours were filled with terrifying, *Jurassic Park*-like nightmares. And yet I'd woken up this morning with the cold certainty that I needed to face this thing head on. I needed to see the creature again to help me understand, so I could figure out how best to protect my child.

David seemed self-conscious at first, jogging around the yard in circles, looking at me over his shoulder occasionally. But in five minutes he had forgotten me and lost himself in the world of play. He raised his arms, curled his fingers, and stomped across the grass in a stiff Frankenstein walk that I now recognized as his impression of a dinosaur. He was being a T-rex. His loop-de-loops around the yard seemed random at first, but I soon noticed a pattern. It seemed like he was following someone, or someone was following him. But still the creature didn't appear.

I sipped my coffee and set the mug down on the railing. It had been such a relief—in a very perverse way—to think that my delusion was not just mine. It was shared with my son, and so therefore, maybe I wasn't losing my mind. But as I tracked David's progress across the yard, I wondered if I was only grasping at straws, trying to explain my hallucination in any way possible. Maybe his artwork was only a coincidence.

The clouds were turning a smoky gray, and I knew we'd have to go inside soon before the sky broke open. David careened past Snow White and her ceramic dwarfs, and suddenly, something caught my attention. Level with David's head was an odd patch in the air—an oval of dull muddy-brown. The patch expanded and swelled, taking shape like it was being painted by some invisible hand. The head appeared, the body filled in, the tail elongated. And then the details slowly came into focus, like I was examining it through binoculars now. Reptilian scales. Sinewy muscles. Golden eyes.

Hugging my ribs, I fought the urge to cry out or run to David. But he didn't seem the least bit startled that his dinosaur pal had decided to show up. In fact, he continued to play in the same manner as if the creature had been there with him all along. Maybe he had. Maybe I was just starting to perceive him.

Seeing the creature materialize was like watching your child trapped in a hungry lion's enclosure at the zoo. Or waking up from a nightmare to find your dream stalker standing over your bed. It was terrifying, it was illogical, it was certifiably batshit-funny-farm-one-sandwich-short-of-a-picnic-basket crazy. But there it was, in the flesh, following my son around the yard. A miniature freaking T-rex.

The dinosaur lurched past the shed, its tail whacking against the door, but the contact made no hollow drumming noise as I'd expected. Its nostrils flared, and its short arms flailed ineffectually, as if reaching for something it knew it could never quite grasp. Both David and the dinosaur disappeared from view for a moment, as the shed hid them from me. I lunged forward, prepared to throw myself off the deck and between them.

"Anna?" The exasperation in Duffy's voice suggested she'd been calling my name for a long time. "You're both going to get soaked. It's time to come in now. Davey, darling! Come now, hurry inside!"

Steady rain clipped my face, a prelude to a fierce downpour. I wiped the moisture from my blurry eyes to discover David scurrying toward us, unaccompanied, his blond hair slicked to his skull and his gray T-shirt speckled by raindrops. How long had it been raining?

"What happened here?" Duffy asked.

It took me one heart-stopping minute to realize she wasn't referring to the surreal scene that had just unfolded in her backyard; she was pointing at my feet where the white coffee mug had shattered, and the liquid had dripped through the cracks. I hadn't even noticed when it fell.

"I'm sorry," I murmured, as a cold raindrop slid down the back of my shirt and trailed down my spine.

David bounded up the stairs, eyes bright. His fingers were still curled into claws, and he ducked away from the lavender bath towel Duffy tried to wrap him in.

"Rawr!" he snarled as he stormed across the wet deck. "Rawrrrrrrrr!"

I stooped to sweep a pile of jet-black curls and silky, coppery clumps into the dust pan. The mass of hair looked like an animal of some sort—a newborn puppy maybe, but somehow sinister.

"Thanks for helping out," Duffy said and set down a laundry basket heaped with dirty towels. "Hot water cycle, please. This is my busiest season, you know. Weddings and weddings and more weddings. And with just one of me..."

She drifted off, examining our surroundings. I followed her disparaging gaze. It was a typical unfinished basement—a gray cement floor with a drain in the center of the room, white-painted brick walls, exposed pipes in the ceiling, two small glass-block windows, a washer, dryer, and utility sink. Winston had dragged her black leather stylist chair from the salon, and they'd repurposed an old mirrored bureau from one of the guest rooms. Duffy had re-used a lot of the old decorations from her French-themed salon, but in this stark space, they didn't have quite the same effect. A framed photograph of the Eiffel Tower, a stack of fancy hatboxes, a wrought iron fleur-de-lis, an assortment of porcelain poodles, and a wooden plaque with curly, pink letters proclaiming, "Ooh La La!"

It was a far cry from the cute little salon space she'd rented on Division Street. *Savon Vivement* was the whimsical name she'd given it, after only a cursory look at a French dictionary. (We'd later discovered upon closer investigation that it meant something along the lines of "soap smartly" and gotten a good laugh.) The salon had three stylist chairs—one for Duffy, and two others she rented out—a store-front window, vintage black-and-white tile floors, and pink toile wallpaper. It smelled like rose-water and French-milled soap instead of mildew and dryer sheets.

"I'm happy to help," I said, returning the broom to its cobwebby corner. "I think it's a true testament to your talent that your customers will follow you anywhere. The space doesn't matter. It's you they want."

Duffy harrumphed. "I don't know about that. I lost a lot of my regulars when a Super Shears opened up in Lawrenceville a year ago. How could I compete with ten dollar haircuts?"

"Well, you get what you pay for. I bet they *look* like ten dollar haircuts," I said and was rewarded with her pleased little smile. "Besides, you offer a lot more services." I set the laundry basket on the edge of the washing machine and started dropping in the wrinkled towels one by one. I hadn't been lying when I'd said I enjoyed helping. Cleaning up after her appointments kept my hands busy and my mind off the worrisome problem of what to do about the lethal dinosaur in our backyard.

It had been raining heavily for the past three days, and the dreary weather and muddy yard had forced us all inside. David had been insufferably crabby, whining for toys he hadn't played with in months, toys that I had donated to Goodwill prior to our move. When I explained to him that his once beloved corn popper toy was probably being played with by another child right now, he stared at me with an expression of utter betrayal before bursting into loud sobs. I was willing to put up with the irritable mood though, if it meant staying indoors and away from the realm of the T-rex, which it appeared was primarily an outdoor creature. At the moment, Winston was keeping David occupied with a bucket of Lincoln Logs he'd found in the attic. Winston was working on a careful model of a Revolutionary War fort, and David was stacking blocks as high as possible and then gleefully kicking them down.

"I've got an hour until Martina Napier comes in for her practice updo," Duffy said, returning a color mixing bowl to one of the bureau drawers. "Would you like me to give your hair a trim?" She swiveled the chair around to face me.

In twenty-two years, I'd gotten pretty good at dodging Duffy's attempts to cut or style my hair. At the age of eight, I'd made the mistake of letting her curl my hair, and the Shirley Temple effect had lasted for days. It wasn't something easily forgotten, especially when Duffy's own white-blond hair was currently shellacked into a feathery wave not unlike an umbrella cockatoo's head.

I lifted a few strands of my hair and examined the ends. "Thanks, but I don't think it's necessary."

Duffy squinted hard at me, as though she could detect the split ends from where she was standing. "Just half an inch," she promised. "Not even half an inch. A quarter of an inch. A light dusting. Your hair will feel and look so much healthier. It'll look nice and fresh for Carly's party."

She was playing to my vanity over my hair and my desire to make a good impression on my old friends. I didn't stand a chance against these appeals. "Alright." I sighed and sank down into the chair. "A quarter of an inch, and that's it."

Duffy fanned the black cape out, and its butterfly-wing weight draped over me. She tied it in the back and gently gathered my hair in her hand and smoothed it over the cape. "Such beautiful, thick hair," she said, as she spritzed it with a water bottle and ran her comb through it. "You're lucky you got your mother's hair."

I gritted my teeth and refused to acknowledge her comment. I stared straight ahead at my reflection in the bureau's mirror. With my damp hair parted down the middle, I looked like a little girl. Duffy pressed her palms on my cheekbones and lightly adjusted my head.

"Are you sitting straight? Chin up."

For the next few minutes, the only sounds were the churning of the washing machine and the snipping of the scissors. I closed my eyes and let Duffy's magic descend over me. Because there was something magical about it—sitting in a special chair with your feet off the ground, trusting someone else to transform you into something you hoped to be. But in that quiet, peaceful place, a pair of golden eyes with black reptilian slits rose up and glared at me. I jerked slightly, snapping my eyelids open.

"No moving," Duffy commanded, gripping my shoulder.

"Do you think it's weird for a four-year-old to be obsessed with dinosaurs?" I asked.

Duffy's scissors paused briefly. "No. No, I do not. I think it's very normal for little boys and girls to fixate on things that interest them. Trains, trucks, construction equipment, outer space, you name it. When your uncle Luke was a boy, he had this thing with earthworms. Collecting them in jars, naming them, trying to get them to race. He got over that phase pretty quick once Winston taught him how to fish. And Edna Franklin was just telling me the other day that her grandson is obsessed with watching a documentary about the Titanic, over and over, up to four times a day! At first, Edna's daughter was a little worried about autism, but their doctor said not to worry, and that it's perfectly healthy and he'll grow out of it."

I tried to stifle a relieved sigh. At least an obsession with dinosaurs was slightly less ghoulish than an obsession with a sinking ship that had caused the death of a thousand people. But I doubted Edna's grandson had the Titanic as a playmate either. "But dinosaurs?" I persisted, trying to keep my head still.

"Oh, sure. What fun! I mean, big old scary reptiles that are now extinct and therefore harmless—what's not to like? It's a little boy's dream."

"I guess I just don't even know where he picked up his whole fascination," I said. His remote-controlled dinosaur was made of acid-green plastic and had googly eyes and an inane smile. Part of its repertoire was jerking along to a recording of "The Ants Go Marching." The T-rex in the yard looked like it had escaped from the Milwaukee Public Museum. Or even worse, the Jurassic period.

"Well, you said he learned that song he sang for us from his pre-school. He probably picked it up there." Duffy pulled strands of my hair forward on either side of my face and matched the ends. Apparently dissatisfied, she snipped a few more pieces off.

She was referring to "When Dinosaurs Roamed the Earth." Of course! Why hadn't I thought of that? His pre-school had probably done a unit on dinosaurs or read a book about them for storytime. Surely that's what had led to the appearance of the very realistic King Rex.

"Is it weird for him then to… want a dinosaur for a playmate?" I asked.

Duffy set down the scissors on top of the bureau and stood in front of me. "Do you mean—like an imaginary friend?"

Beneath the lightweight cape, I was sweating. King Rex was David's imaginary friend? My son had a ruthless dinosaur for a not-so-pretend companion? I could feel the bare backs of my thighs sticking to the leather chair. I couldn't bring myself to reply, to repeat her casually flippant phrase—*an imaginary friend*—so I nodded.

"My goodness!" She laughed. "A dinosaur for an imaginary friend. Well, I suppose stranger things have happened. Would you like me to blow dry your hair? We still have about fifteen more minutes until I'm expecting Martina." When I didn't respond, she picked up a bottle and began spraying my hair and running her fingers through it. "A lot of kids his age have imaginary friends, you know. I think it's a sign of intelligence and creativity." She peered down at me. "You remember, of course, that you had an imaginary friend when you were a girl, right?"

"No," I murmured, taken aback. I slid my finger under the collar of the cape, which was feeling rather constrictive. I had imperfect memories of my childhood, pieced together by what others had told me and colored by disappointment and frustration. "I don't remember that."

"You most certainly did! Up until the point you were getting a little old for that kind of thing, to be quite honest." Duffy turned on the hairdryer, and as the hot air blasted my head, I tried to bat away all the gnawing gnats of associations that were starting to dive-bomb me. If King Rex was David's imaginary friend, and I could see King Rex, that meant I could see David's *imagination*. I could see as clear as day the things he was inventing in his mind. And apparently he had inherited his over-active imagination from me.

The hairdryer clicked off. "Gorgeous. Just gorgeous," Duffy said, fluffing out my hair around my face.

I looked in the mirror just long enough to see that she had taken off much more than a quarter of an inch, at least two inches, but it was still quite long, and the bottom looked fuller and healthier overall.

"Looks good," I said. "Thank you." I turned to face her and tried to sound offhand. "Now about my imaginary friend. Do you know what it was?"

"Not a dinosaur, that's for sure!" Duffy brushed off my cape and then untied it. "It was just a girl, I think. A little girl about your age. You had a name for her, I can't remember what. Maybe Winston will remember."

"Winston?"

Duffy smiled. "You brought her with you that first summer you stayed with us. Winston got a kick out of playing along. Setting out a plate and cup for her at dinner, that kind of thing."

"Oh," I said, remembering the comment she'd made earlier about my childhood eccentricities. I stood up from the beauty chair, glad to be free of its hot sweaty union with my legs. "How did I play with her?"

Duffy grabbed the broom and started sweeping up the slivers of blond hair, which looked like chaffs of wheat on the floor. "You know, I'm really not sure. But if you have questions about that time in your life, you know who you should ask?" She paused significantly. "Your mother."

"Thanks, but no thanks."

"I'm serious. Winston and I were just talking about Kimberly the other night. She usually visits us twice a year, but we haven't seen her yet. I know she'd love to see David, and he deserves to see his grandma—his *real* grandma. We could set something up, just a short visit, you wouldn't have to even be there the whole time if you didn't want to, and if you did, you could maybe ask her some of your questions."

"No," I said forcefully. "And if you bring her here, we're leaving."

"Anna, it's just an idea. No need to get upset. I would never do it without your permission, you know. Just something to think about."

"My mind was made up a long time ago," I said and started to climb the stairs. "Thanks for the haircut."

When the next day dawned lemony bright and cloudless, David rejoiced, and I trembled. Would his imaginary friend re-appear, and would I behold it? Was this bizarre blip becoming a part of our reality, a permanent break from normalcy, and if so, what would happen to us? I envisioned troubling phone calls from teachers, unsuccessful play dates, whispered criticism, and a long line of therapists—some for me, some for David.

The rain had turned Duffy and Winston's backyard into a giant mud puddle, so we walked to St. Monica's parking lot, where a hopscotch grid and a four-square court were painted. I tried to teach David both games, but he lost interest quickly, and soon enough, was galloping around the parking lot in his T-rex stance.

King Rex appeared almost immediately this time, my eyes detecting him all at once. He popped out of thin air like a magic trick. I hovered nearby, pacing slightly, too anxious to stand still or sit down. Across the street from the parking lot was an old cemetery, and it was unsettling watching the dinosaur dart to and fro in front of a backdrop of crumbling tombstones and monuments.

My eyes shifted to David, who was wearing his favorite red T-shirt with a pirate ship screen-printed on the front. He looked so small and fragile next to the towering dinosaur, but his face was contorted into an expression of total absorption and joy. His brown eyes glittered as he whirled around the blacktop, chased by a prehistoric being of his own making.

It was awful in both senses of the word: awe-inspiring *and* terrible. To be given a glimpse into my son's vivid imagination! I knew that most parents, especially the ones at David's preschool—the ones who packed oat bran pretzels and gluten-free applesauce for their kids' snacks and condescendingly tried to give me advice about "establishing a routine" and time-outs and following through on a punishment—*those* parents would have given their front teeth to be able to see what I could see. Because it was a gift, even I realized that. But it was a fairytale gift, a be-careful-what-you-wish-for gift, the kind you wanted to return almost immediately after it happened.

Even if David's imaginary friend hadn't been a fearsome, carnivorous king of the dinosaurs, but something more innocuous, like a talking giraffe, it still would've been scary. Because peering into someone else's mind and imaginary life *was* downright scary. It wasn't the type of thing you could ever be prepared for.

I sat down on the warm asphalt cross-legged and rested my elbows on my knees. David ran parallel to the steepled, cream-brick church, King Rex staggering behind him, as though they were playing a bizarre game of Follow the Leader. Despite the heat of the day, I shivered and hugged my knees to my chest.

When had my son become a conjurer of dinosaurs? When had he become his own little person, separate but still so much a part of me?

CHAPTER SIX

I sprayed my hair lightly with a can of Duffy's extra hold, extra shine hairspray. I set the bottle down amongst the clutter on the small pink-marbled vanity, and a tube of mascara and a bottle of perfume fell into the sink. Gritting my teeth, I retrieved the mascara and perfume and set them on the toilet tank instead. It was my old routine from high school—getting ready in the teeny-tiny guest bathroom that I could hardly turn around in without knocking my elbow on a towel bar or banging my hip on a corner of the vanity. Only this time, I had a whiny four-year-old darting in and out at intervals to boot.

I held up a small mirror, carefully turned around, and examined the back of my head. I'd coiled my hair at the nape of my neck, like a twist of fresh, golden bread. It looked super sophisticated. With my low-backed, sleeveless turquoise top, having my hair up revealed the smooth, tan, uninterrupted expanse of my narrow back since I wasn't wearing a bra. I hoped Carly had some cute, single friends.

David raced a matchbox car along the edge of the bathtub, and it promptly fell in, just like the other five or six that were now hidden behind the ruffled, coral-colored shower curtain. "Don't go, Mommy." It had been his refrain since seven o'clock, when I'd first started getting ready, but it was starting to sound more panicked and tearful.

I sat down on the toilet-seat lid and slid my feet into black pumps. Since I'd been trying to reassure him for the past hour, my patience was wearing thin. "You'll hardly know I'm gone, buckaroo. Grandpa and Grandma will tuck you in, and I'll be back before you wake up. I promise." I patted his thin shoulder as I stood up.

Examining my reflection in the mirror one more time, I couldn't help noticing a few of the decorative beads on my top had fallen off. It wasn't too conspicuous, and there wasn't time to change anyway, but I felt somehow less pretty, like there was a chip in my otherwise polished veneer.

On instinct, I opened the mirrored cabinet, the one that Duffy never thought to clean out. The top two shelves still housed some essentials from my high school stays: bubble-gum scented lip gloss, a rainbow of nail polish colors, and a half-empty bottle of antacids for my terrible heartburn during pregnancy. The bottom shelf, which was starting to rust, held items that had been there for many more years, and I'd conjectured had once belonged to my mom when she was a teenager. A purple comb and wide-toothed hair pick, a tube of bright red lipstick, and a cough drop tin that housed a folded poem, written in sloppy, boyish handwriting: *Kim, I see stars in your eyes, I hear angels when you speak, I taste honey on your lips, I smell strawberries in your hair, I touch heaven when you're in my arms.* I'd thought about throwing her junk away several times, but something always stopped me. Was the poem from the boy who'd knocked her up, my nameless, faceless father? I shut the medicine cabinet with a soft click.

"Mommy, don't leave me," David howled and threw himself at my legs.

I disentangled him momentarily, and we half-walked, half-wrestled down the hallway. "I won't be gone for long. Just a couple of hours and I'll be right back." He'd never had this kind of separation anxiety when I'd left him with my neighbor, Stacy.

"Take me with you."

"I can't, David. This is a grown-up party. You want Mommy to have fun with her grown-up friends, right?"

"No." His face turned tomato-red, and he threw himself on the living room carpet. "No no no no no!"

Duffy poked her head out from the kitchen. "All set to go, Anna? Davey, darling, I have a very important job for you in the kitchen.

See, I just made some chocolate pudding, and I really need someone to lick off the beaters and let me know if it's any good."

David stopped squirming on the floor and looked suspiciously from me to Duffy. It was clear he knew it was a trap but didn't have the willpower to resist.

"Enjoy your pudding! And be good!" I called after him as he followed Duffy into the kitchen. "Thanks, Duffy! I won't be out too late."

I scowled at the rusty minivan parked in the driveway; it didn't fit my image, but it was all I had. I figured I could park a block away so no one would know I drove a clunker.

The drive to Lawrenceville took less than ten minutes, and once again, it saddened and amazed me to think that this was a trip Duffy refused to make, which was the reason why Winston had done the grocery shopping for the past ten years. I forced this thought from my mind, switched off the radio, and listened to the rhythmic thumping of the tires against the road instead. Twilight pearlized the sky. Every mile I put between myself and my grandparents' house allowed me to breathe a little easier. I felt like I was traveling into the past, when everything had seemed so shining and full of potential.

Lawrenceville boasted four times the population of Salsburg and therefore warranted a supermarket, a multiplex movie theater, a smattering of fast food restaurants, a couple of apartment complexes, and William Payne High School, the modest school I had attended my sophomore year. The slightly larger town had been and continued to be the hang-out place for bored teens who had cars, since Salsburg had so little to offer.

I didn't have any trouble finding Carly's condo. It was on the edge of town, which was quickly getting built-up. The condo was clearly new construction—a long building that alternated exteriors between red brick and gray siding to give the impression of separate townhouses—with brand new shoots of grass, baby shrubs, and freshly paved gleaming white sidewalks. It was the type of place Patrick would've written off as "soulless." Parking a block away became a true necessity because there were so many cars crowded together on the street.

Their front door was ajar, so I let myself in. The interior smelled like new carpet and fresh paint and looked like one of those model apartments featured in upscale rental magazines. Gas fireplace. Faux granite countertops and matching tile floors. An oval coffee table with candles and various knickknacks artfully arranged on top of it. Even more disconcerting were the people. Young twenty-somethings like myself, yet dressed like forty-somethings at a family backyard barbecue. To say I was overdressed would be putting it mildly. But the worst thing of all was the stack of cards and presents on the wrought iron and glass table against one wall. Was this some kind of engagement or housewarming party?

Carly spotted me before I could slowly back out the front door.

"Anna! I'm so glad you could make it!" At least *she* was wearing a brown slip-dress and a chunky amber necklace, and had her wild hair tied back in a cute ponytail. She linked her arm through mine and walked me toward the kitchen. "Can I get you something to drink? Where's your little guy? I thought you might bring him."

"I'm sorry," I said. "I didn't know kids were invited. And I didn't realize that this was a special party to celebrate…?"

"Our engagement. Oh, please don't worry about it. We had the 'official' dinner with our relatives to tell them the news last month, and we just thought we'd have some friends over so they could see our new place and kill two birds with one stone. It was *supposed* to be very low key." She frowned at the cheese platter and shrimp ring on the buffet-style counter and spun to open the fridge. "I said no gifts necessary on the invite, but you can see a lot of them didn't listen. So what can I get you? Beer, wine cooler, soda, lemonade?" She handed me a berry-flavored wine cooler before I could respond. "Try this one. You'll love it. It reminds me of those fruity schnapps drinks we used to mix in Libby O'Mallon's basement."

"Yum, thanks." I used a cutesy dishtowel hanging on the oven to twist my wine cooler top off with. "So when do I get to meet the sainted Sam?"

Carly grinned the self-satisfied grin of a woman head over heels in love. "I think he's out back playing ladder ball, but I'll bet they'll be in soon. Let me introduce you to some other people first." ✴

Ladder ball? I felt like I'd wandered into my grandparents' neighborhood block party by mistake. This was definitely not the boisterous, broken-up-by-cops-at-two-a.m. type of party that Carly had hosted in high school. But what had I expected? We were adults now, and apparently adults stood around talking about adjustable rate mortgages and nibbling on toothpick-skewered cheese cubes. Or perhaps they were just playacting at being grown-ups, self-consciously slipping into the role because it seemed like the thing to do now, much like I had after David's birth. But I couldn't imagine why anyone would deliberately choose to sacrifice their freedom and their coolness at the altar of adulthood so early. Damn, what I would have given right then for a naked swim in Long Lake—the water a chilly, black void below me, the stars above me so bright they stung my eyes. To feel sixteen again with my whole life spread before me.

Carly guided me through the crowd, introducing me to several people, some of whom I vaguely remembered from high school, but most of whom were new and equally uninteresting to me: Sam's club baseball teammates and Carly's friends from culinary school. Dull as they were, it seemed like every single one of them belonged to a couple. Grant and Heather. Amy and Tim. Drew and Chelsea. Carly left me with one such couple, so she could see to her other hostessing duties. They were deep in discussion, speculating if a guy named A.J. hadn't made it to the party because of his bossy, controlling girlfriend.

I excused myself to go to the bathroom, and there confirmed that my hair and makeup were still ridiculously perfect. What a waste all my primping had been! I would have fit in better if I'd simply stayed in my grape juice-spattered tank top and wrinkled shorts; the last thing I wanted was to come across like I was trying too hard. I loosened a tendril from my chignon and let it fall in front of one eye. I practiced a nonchalant face in the mirror and resolved to seek out Sam to make his acquaintance before taking off.

The yard was a square slab of concrete with a grill and lawn chairs and a narrow channel of young grass that was blessedly dinosaur-free. Tiki torches to keep away mosquitos bordered the patio. It looked like the ladder ball game had ended, and now five guys were standing around drinking beer in the waning light.

"Sam?" I called out, and one of the guys, medium height and build, wearing a Brewers baseball cap, turned to face me. Actually, all the guys turned to face me, but he was the first one. "Hey, I'm Anna, Carly's friend from high school. I need to take off soon, but I wanted to meet the guy that managed to tame her wild ways first."

"Anna," Sam said, and stepped forward to shake my hand. "Carly's told me so much about you."

"Uh-oh," I said, playing with one of my dangly earrings. "Only half of it's true, I promise."

"Do you really have to leave already?" Sam asked. "The party's just getting started."

I could have pulled out the mommy card, but something stopped me. Probably the fact that with the exception of maybe Sam, no one else out here knew I was a mommy. And Sam's friends were staring at me with the kind of male appreciation I'd been hoping to inspire when I'd chosen my outfit earlier that night. Not to mention the fact that one of them, a tall guy with chiseled features and tousled blond hair, was sending me a come-hither signal with his gray, brooding eyes.

"I guess I can stay a little longer," I said.

"Great. What are you drinking? Colin was just heading inside for some more beer." He pointed to the tall blond, who shot me a devilish smile. I held up my berry wine cooler, and he nodded and disappeared inside. Sam pulled up a canvas chair for me.

"So how did you guys meet?" I asked. "I didn't get to hear the story."

Sam folded his hands across his slight paunch, clearly pleased to be asked that particular question. "Carly didn't tell you? It was a little over a year ago. I was driving along 33 when I saw this little black poodle wandering around looking lost on the side of the road. I was worried he was going to try to cross and get hit, so I pulled over and tried to corral him. He had a collar on, so I knew he belonged to somebody, but he wouldn't let me get close enough to see if there was an address or phone number on his tags. Another car pulled up, and it was this gorgeous girl, wanting to help. She was able to lure the poodle with some beef jerky she had in her car, and then we were able to call his owners and return him. Afterwards, we went to Ruby's to celebrate. Even though I was incredibly late for work, I didn't even bother calling in. She was that amazing."

"Carly keeps beef jerky in her car?" I quipped, but my throat felt tight with emotion. Sam's smile radiated some serious wattage when he talked about Carly, and I was happy for her—I truly was— but beneath that joy was a riptide of self-pity. Would I ever meet someone who grinned irrepressibly whenever he talked about me? Someone sweet and safe and uncomplicated? I wondered if it would be enough for me.

"I guess for just those kinds of occasions," Sam said. "You never know when you might need some jerky."

A cold drip of water landed on my bare leg, and I looked up to see Colin holding the wine cooler above me. The drip slid along my inner thigh toward my kneecap, and every inch of my skin tingled.

"Thanks," I said, accepting the bottle.

Sam handed me a bottle opener. "Anna, this is Colin. We work together at the marina in Port Ambrose."

"Oh?" I had no idea what a "marina worker" did, but I imagined Sam and Colin dressed in matching striped sailor shirts and high-waisted white pants, tying up expensive yachts in their slips, and then mopping the docks or something.

"Yeah." Colin pulled up a chair next to me and sank into it. "Last week we had our annual sailboat race from Muskegon, Michigan, and now we're organizing a fishing derby for next month." He leaned forward. "What do you do, Anna?"

"I used to work for a group of dermatologists in Milwaukee," I said. "Lakeview Dermatology. But I'm in between jobs right now."

Colin's storm-cloud-gray eyes gazed into mine as though saying, *I knew you weren't from around here. I knew you were far too special.*

A few more people trickled out into the backyard, some of the Heathers and Chelseas and Tims I'd met earlier, but I hardly noticed them because Colin and I were now thoroughly immersed in a conversation about downtown Milwaukee's restaurants and bars and lakefront. The tiki torches cast an exotic, sexy glow over the small backyard, and we could've been on a tropical island, instead of Lawrenceville, Wisconsin. Every time I finished my wine cooler, a new one magically appeared in such delicious flavors I felt like I was drinking Kool-Aid: strawberry, raspberry pomegranate, blueberry, peachy orange.

Colin was wearing a blue chambray shirt with the top three buttons undone, revealing tan, marina-worker-worthy pecs, and I couldn't help wondering what he looked like without his shirt. Also maybe his pants. Despite the cool night breeze, I was really, really warm, so I pressed my wine cooler against my neck and cleavage.

"Gehring, man! So nice of you to finally show up!" a voice, maybe Sam's, shouted. "I hope you didn't bring any of that Pabst Blue Ribbon shit."

Gehring? The name sounded familiar, but I didn't know why. Probably because when it boiled right down to it, there were only about twenty different last names in the Salsburg area. When you walked through the cemetery, the tombstones were easily grouped into families. Gehring, Jennings, Eberhardt, Presswood...

"Now don't you go hating on PBR," a man, presumably Gehring, called back. "It'll put hair on your wife-to-be's chest."

A round of loud guffaws. I turned in my chair to catch a glimpse of Gehring, but I didn't recognize him at all. He was a short, slim guy with reddish spiked-up hair. But standing next to him, half-concealed in the shadows, was someone I *did* recognize. Black wavy hair, black scruffy beard, black T-shirt, black leather wrist cuff. Jamie Presswood. My ego was still slightly bruised from the way he'd given me the cold shoulder last week. Well, two could play at that game.

I set my bottle down in the mesh cup holder built into the arm of my chair and crossed my legs, returning my attention to Colin.

"...take you sailing sometime," he was saying.

"I would love that," I said loudly, toying with the tendril I'd freed earlier from my twisted bun. My back felt especially naked knowing that Jamie Presswood was right behind me, perhaps watching me. My shoulder blades burned. I reached across the short distance between Colin and me and touched his right hand, where he wore a silver and turquoise ring on his ring finger. "Does this mean something special?"

Colin held onto my hand and laughed. His fingers were long and elegant, and his touch was soft. "I could make something up, but really, I just thought it looked cool."

"It does." I giggled. "Look cool."

"Glad you like it." He gave my arm a gentle tug. "Hey. I'm headed inside for a bit. Want to come with me?"

I let him pull me into a standing position, rising to my full height in heels. I cast a backward glance at the yard to see if Jamie had noticed. He had. He, Sam, Gehring, and another guy were standing in a half-circle holding cans of beer. The other three guys were talking intently, but Jamie was squinting straight at me, as though my mere presence miffed him. Our eyes met, and something that felt too raw, too bitter, and much too intimate passed between us. I looked away carelessly, as though I didn't even recognize him.

"Easy, Anna," Colin said, and he put his palm on my lower back to guide me toward the house.

The condo was quieter and nearly empty. It seemed that most of the fuddy-duddies had left, and now the real party was taking place outside. Colin led me down a hallway, applying gentle pressure to my back, and into what I guessed was the second bedroom. He shut the door and swept me into his arms.

"God, you're sexy," he whispered and leaned in to kiss me.

I kissed him back, gripping his muscular shoulders, pulling him closer to me. His desire intoxicated me. It felt so good to be held, kissed, *wanted*. He slipped his hands under the back of my shirt, caressed my sides, and slid them around to the front to cup my bare breasts. He groaned and pushed me a few feet backwards, then stopped. I opened my eyes to see what had given him pause.

There was no bed. Moonlight spilled into the little bedroom, revealing that the walls were painted a pale yellow. Carly and Sam weren't using their spare bedroom as a guest bedroom or an office. The only furniture in the room was a small dresser and bookcase. A child-sized dresser and bookcase.

Colin drenched my neck in kisses as he pressed me up against the wall. "Let's go to my place."

My eyes were still open. I looked at the empty wall where I knew they would put a crib and changing table one day, and overwhelming sadness washed over me. This was how it was supposed to be. The wedding, the home, the baby. The stability. God, how I envied Carly and her boring, ordinary life at that moment.

"No," I said, stepping away from him and smoothing my shirt back into place. "I'm sorry. I need to go home."

Colin studied me with a confused expression. "Okay. I'll drive you."

"No." I stumbled toward the door and opened it. Suddenly all I wanted to do was get the hell out of their condo. I thought I heard him swear under his breath, but I was already fleeing the room. I didn't know what had happened to my purse. Had I left it somewhere outside or had Carly taken it from me when I arrived? I didn't remember.

I poked my head in their bedroom and discovered a small pile of sweatshirts, jackets, and purses heaped on their bed. I found mine in the jumble.

Carly and a couple of her girlfriends were still in the living room, sipping glasses of wine. When I hurried by, Carly called something after me, but I didn't slow down. "Thanks for inviting me," I said in passing. "We should get together again soon."

Without the light of the tiki torches, it was incredibly dark outside. Apparently the neighborhood was so new that the streetlights weren't even functioning yet. I wrapped my arms around myself and took a deep breath. Soft footsteps rustled the grass and bushes only a few feet away from me, and I nearly jumped out of my skin.

"Anna." I thought maybe it was Colin with one more attempt at seducing me, but the voice was lower. Kinder somehow. Jamie appeared in front of me. "Please tell me that you're not about to drive drunk."

I bristled. "I'm not drunk." Wine coolers were notoriously low in alcohol content, and I'd had only three. Four? Maybe five? I tucked my purse under my arm and tried to step past him, but he blocked my path.

"You're not? Well, what else would explain you hanging all over a douchebag like Colin Bentley?" He grabbed my upper arm, and unlike Colin's soft touch, Jamie's hand was rough and calloused.

I shook loose of him. "What I do is not your concern, which you made abundantly clear to me last week, in case you've forgotten already. So leave me alone."

Jamie followed me. "Please let me drive you home."

"I'm fine." I whirled around and faced him. "Besides, why would I trust you? How do I know that *you're* safe to drive and that you don't want to take advantage of me?"

"Right." Jamie laughed. "The world according to Anna. Every guy that lays eyes on her must want to sleep with her."

I scowled and pushed past him. The hulking shape of the minivan was only twenty feet away now, and my footsteps were the only ones clicking on the sidewalk. Jamie had stopped in his tracks. Good.

But then he spoke quietly, and the hard, joking edge had vanished from his voice. "Please," he said. "I want to drive you home. Just as an old friend, okay?"

Standing still, the ground felt slightly shaky under my feet. Maybe he *was* looking out for me. Maybe a part of him did still care. I dropped my keys into my purse. "Fine. Where are you parked?"

Jamie was driving a red pick-up truck with white lettering on the door: DEMETER LANDSCAPING SERVICES, LLC. When he turned the key in the ignition, music blared out from the speakers but not the heavy metal kind I'd expected. Instead, he'd been listening to country music. He quickly turned the dial down until it was just a low hum. I laughed to myself imagining him mowing my grandparents' lawn in his all black get-up listening to country and western on his headphones.

We didn't talk. I stared out the window, watching the gravel shoulder of the road and tall grasses beyond fly by in a blur. It was soothing—the quiet drone of the radio, the higher-up view of the road from a truck as if I'd been granted an alternative vantage of my life, and next to me, my wannabe-rescuer's sturdy presence. I pressed my forehead against the cool glass of the window and nearly drifted off. But something stopped me. A slight tickle in my memory.

"Jamie," I murmured. "When we were kids, do you remember me having an imaginary friend?"

He was quiet for what seemed like a long time. Finally, he replied. "Yes."

"You do?" I turned my head slowly to face him. "Do you remember what her name was?"

"Yeah." His eyes were focused intently on the road ahead. His left hand balanced on top of the steering wheel; his right rested on the console between us. "Her name was Leah Nola."

Leah Nola. The name was instantly familiar to my ears and lips. It had an almost magical quality to it. But it didn't conjure up her face or the time I'd spent with her, the games we'd played, as I'd thought it might.

"Did you ever see her?" I whispered into the shadowy cab of the truck.

"Did I see her?" Jamie's lips quirked into a smile. "No, Anna, I can't say that I ever saw your imaginary friend. Man, I'm glad I drove you."

The truck decelerated as we entered the town limits. There was no decorative welcome sign on the eastern approach to the city. Just a green reflective road sign with the name and population.

"I suppose you'll need help tomorrow getting your minivan back," Jamie said with a sigh.

I didn't appreciate his snippy tone. "Don't worry about it. I can get Winston to help me."

He turned onto Steepleview, and my grandparents' house appeared with its outdoor lights on, blazing like a lighthouse. But instead of feeling relief at being back, I felt only intense loneliness.

Jamie pulled into the driveway and turned off his headlights.

"Thank you for the ride," I said stiffly and started to open the door.

"Anna—" he said, and then stopped abruptly.

"What?" I clutched my purse to my chest, ready to climb down from the truck. Had he remembered something else about Leah Nola? Or was he going to apologize for the way he'd treated me the week before? Maybe we could be friends again after all.

He gave his head a slight shake, as though he had changed his mind about whatever he'd been about to say. "You're welcome."

I closed the passenger side door quietly and hurried up the front steps. Jamie didn't drive away until he'd seen I was safely inside the house.

CHAPTER SEVEN

Someone or something was stroking my back and hip in a repetitive motion. Down my shoulder, over my ribs, and onward to the curve of my butt. Again and again with a feather-light touch. What the heck? I hadn't gone home with Colin, I was positive because I remembered with painful clarity going to bed all by my lonesome the night before. I cracked open one eye to see that my son was using me as a makeshift racetrack for his matchbox cars.

"Mommy's sleeping," I grumbled into my pillow.

"Grandma said to wake Mommy up." A miniature red hotrod careened off my shoulder and landed by my chin.

"What time is it?" I flicked the toy car away and rolled over for a glimpse of the digital clock on my nightstand. 11:49.

"Lunchtime," David sang.

I lifted the sheet up like a wing. "Come here, sweet child of mine." David clamored under the covers with me, and I hugged his small body to my chest. He smelled singularly like my son—a mixture of baby shampoo, cinnamon and bread dough, dirt, grass, and worms. He snuggled against me, digging into me with his bony elbows. In this dim bedroom, it was just me and him again, like it had always been. No dinosaur, thank God.

"Did you have fun with Grandpa and Grandma last night?" I murmured into his hair.

He nodded against my chest. "We ate pudding and read stories."

"That sounds nice. What stories?"

"Not Mona and Wolfy. Stories from picture books. We read a story about a naughty monkey and a story about a teddy bear."

I pulled the sheet over our heads, and David giggled. We stared at each other, nose to nose.

"Did you play with King Rex last night?" I asked.

David shook his head. "King Rex doesn't like pudding," he said gravely.

"What does King Rex eat?" I prayed that his response wouldn't be "people" or "little boys" in particular.

He thought about this for a moment. "Pickles and bologna," he said at last. Two of his own least favorite foods. How interesting.

"Really?" I walked my fingers toward the nape of his neck, his most ticklish spot, and David squirmed in delighted anticipation. "And where does he live?"

"At the Piggly Wiggly," he replied immediately.

"That's convenient," I said, fluttering my fingers against his neck. "Do you think he could pick us up some groceries for dinner?"

"No!" He laughed and wiggled under my touch. "Dino-suss can't shop for groceries."

"They can't?" I withdrew my hand and flipped down the sheet, so we could breathe fresh air again. "What *can* dinosaurs do?"

"Dino-suss can run and jump and play and ROAR." He opened his mouth wide with a menacing growl. "Dino-suss are never scared."

I could feel his finch-like pulse beating against my skin. My heart gave an uneasy lurch. He was so delicate. So small and breakable. I knew that as a figment of his imagination, King Rex was more or less under David's control. It was the "more or less" part that concerned me. Was it possible that David's imagination would ever turn on him? Was it possible for his dinosaur to physically hurt him?

"Tell me a story about dino-suss," David begged.

My head still felt dull and heavy from last night's wine coolers. I folded my pillow in half and wedged it under my neck. "We don't have time for a long story right now because I need to get ready. But why don't *you* tell *me* a quick story about dinosaurs?"

He screwed up his face in concentration. "Once there was a tie-ran-a-suss rex named King Rex," he started, endearingly following the format I used to open all of my stories. I couldn't help smiling.

Duffy's exasperated voice carried from downstairs. "Anna Grace Jennings! This is not a hotel!" It was like being in high school all over again.

"He ran and ran and chased the bad cat away," David continued.

I tousled his hair and forced myself out of bed. "Good story, buckaroo." Although I hoped it wasn't based on fact and that the "bad cat" wasn't Vivien Leigh or one of the poor neighborhood cats. "Why don't you go downstairs now? Tell Grandma Duffy not to hold lunch for me and that I'll be down as soon as I've showered."

When I entered the kitchen, still detangling my wet hair with a comb, the atmosphere smacked of Duffy's disapproval. The room was brimming over with it, much like the bubbling pot of macaroni noodles on the burner. Unfazed, I sat down in my usual spot at the kitchen table. I'd endured my fair share of Duffy's lectures in my day, and I'd learned they usually didn't last longer than ten minutes if you didn't try to contradict her too much.

I confirmed that David was out of earshot, playing with Vivien Leigh and her jingly balls in the living room, and then said to Duffy's turned back, "Okay, let me have it."

She rounded on me with pursed lips and her hands on her hips, but her tough demeanor quickly melted away when she saw my jokingly contrite expression. "Why, you little brat." She chuckled and swatted at me with a dishtowel. "Don't think I don't realize that you're only twenty-two and that most people your age are doing much worse than staying out late and drinking. Lord knows it must be hard on you, seeing your old friends still footloose and fancy-free, while you're already tied down with a little one. I don't blame you for wanting to pretend for a little while, but you better not make a habit of it, you hear?"

The timer beeped, and she turned off the burner and strained the noodles in a colander. That was it? It had to be her shortest lecture yet, and I was certainly feeling like I'd gotten away with something when she slammed the jug of milk on the table in front of me.

"Please pour some for everyone except me. I'll have water." Her pursed lips had returned.

I stood up to get glasses from the cupboard.

"Jamie Presswood stopped by this morning," she said.

"Oh? Time to mow the lawn again?"

"No." Her voice was dangerous. "He offered to help Winston get your minivan back from Lawrenceville. It seems he drove you home last night."

I focused on pouring even amounts of milk into the glasses. I'd told him no, that I didn't need his help. Why had he insisted on showing up anyway and causing trouble? If he was trying to win over my grandmother, it certainly wasn't working.

"He did," I said. "I swear I didn't have that much to drink and I was fine to drive, but Jamie wanted to make sure I got home safely. It was actually very chivalrous of him. And believe me, nothing happened."

Duffy banged bowls of steaming macaroni and cheese one by one onto the table. "How could you do that? How could you accept a ride from him, of all people? Didn't I warn you to stay away from him? How did you know he was safe to drive, that he wasn't mixing alcohol with prescription drugs? You could've been in an accident!"

"Duffy," I said levelly, hoping she would follow my lead and calm down. "I don't know where you got this idea that Jamie is some kind of druggie, but I can assure you he's not. I've known him since I was seven years old, and I know it's been awhile, but I can tell he's still a good guy. A decent guy. And apparently Winston thinks so too. Did they get the minivan?"

"Yes." She scowled. "Well, he may have managed to pull the wool over Winston's eyes, but not mine. Poor Winston's so naïve, always wanting to think the best of everybody."

"What's so wrong with that?" I asked, remembering the way Jamie's voice had softened last night when I'd walked away from him. *Please. I want to drive you home. Just as an old friend.* If ever I could use an old friend, it was now.

"We both know what the problem with that is." Duffy popped a grape in her mouth before arranging the bunch in a plastic bowl. "How disappointing it is when it turns out you're wrong." She called Winston and David to the table.

My grandfather sat down in the chair across from me, and when Duffy got up to get some napkins, he winked at me. Unsure if I'd really seen what I thought I'd just seen, I smiled at him with a question on my face. He winked again, slow and exaggerated, as if he were blinking a gravely important message in Morse code. It was a wink of solidarity.

So we were in this together, he and I. Whether it was out of wisdom or just plain wishfulness, we both wanted to believe in Jamie Presswood.

It was hot. Too hot to move, too hot to think. Lying face down in a sun-induced coma, I could hear David talking to himself. Or rather, talking to King Rex and the newest addition to their twosome, Weeple, who was, according to my internet research, a Brontosaurus (or, as the paleontologists were calling them these days, an Apatosaurus). A long-necked, green, Volkswagen beetle-sized Brontosaurus who had showed up in our backyard yesterday afternoon. Though I approved of his gentler features (no scary talons, and more rounded herbivore-type teeth), his weight alone I feared could easily crush David with just one wrong step. But my four-year-old prince of the dinosaurs hardly seemed daunted.

"No no no," he criticized, as though directing some kind of invisible stage play. Invisible, that is, to everyone but us. "Weeple needs a bath first. King Rex, you need to wait."

I sat up, adjusted my bikini top, and reached for my thermos of raspberry lemonade. David had somehow sneaked Duffy's pink-handled loofah brush outside and was using it to scrub what he could reach of his dinosaurs' backs and legs. Oh well. What she didn't know wouldn't hurt her. Today she was booked with updo appointments for a wedding and probably wouldn't emerge from the basement until the early evening.

"Hey, buckaroo. How are the baths coming?" Sweat dripped down my inner arm, and I rubbed it off with my beach towel.

David looked up at me like a harried father with newborn twins.

"Would it help if you had some water?"

I found the sprinkler where Winston kept it in the shed and unspooled the hose from the side of the house. David had grown out of last summer's swim trunks, so I simply stripped him down to his Spiderman briefs and coated his pale chest, back, and shoulders with waterproof sunscreen. It was an oscillating sprinkler, the kind that lazily arced back and forth in a predictable pattern, but David shrieked in surprise every time the stream of water rained down on him. He and the two dinosaurs darted in and out of the sprinkler's spray. It was quite the spectacle.

"Mommy, Mommy! Ah!" David squealed as the sprinkler showered down on his head. "Come in, come in!"

"I'm okay up here." I leaned against the wooden railing of the deck, which scorched my elbows. Running through the sprinkler, or even just lying beneath its spray in the damp, cool grass, did look delicious. And if it had been just David, I probably would have. But with those two prehistoric creatures slinking around, I wasn't so sure I was brave enough.

Maybe David sensed this. King Rex and Weeple detached themselves from his side and slunk to the far reaches of the sprinkler, so that only a few drops of water hit them. Their wet scales gleamed like rainbow oil slicks, and their eyes solemnly watched David as he ran circles around the sprinkler and leaped over it.

I tentatively walked down the steps and joined him. The water was colder than I expected, and I let out a sharp hiss as ice cold droplets slithered down my shoulders and stomach. David screamed in laughter and dragged me closer into the sprinkler's direct spray. We danced around together in a ring, slipping in the wet grass;

all the while, the two dinosaurs looked on from the periphery like beefy bodyguards.

There was someone else on the periphery, too. For one heart-stopping second, I thought it was Patrick, but then I realized the man was too tall and his hair was too long for it to be David's father. It was Jamie, and he'd shaved his beard. In the moment it took my brain to process this, David's dinosaurs were making snap judgments of their own.

King Rex was the first to move, creeping stealthily toward Jamie, lowering and rearing its head like it was trying to decide where to take a chunk out of Jamie first. Weeple was not far behind, stomping closer and closer to the perceived intruder, menacingly swinging its thick tail. The air around us crackled with energy, like before a lightning strike, and a plume of black smoke erupted from the wet grass. Jamie, oblivious to the danger he was in, stood right in the dinosaurs' path.

My son was frozen, white-faced, on the other side of the sprinkler. He looked just as terrified as I felt. I wanted to shout at him to call off his dinosaurs, tell him that Jamie was my friend, but the frantic words were lodged in my throat. If I spoke up now, not only would it sound kooky to Jamie, but it would also broadcast loud and clear to David that I could see what he was imagining, and I was even more terrified to breach our fragile grasp of what was reality and what was fantasy. *They're imaginary, they're imaginary, they're imaginary*, I repeated to myself. But the dinosaurs looked so realistic and ruthless that it was hard to have faith that their teeth and talons would pass through Jamie ineffectually instead of ripping into his flesh.

With its deadly snout only an arm's length away from Jamie's exposed bicep, the T-rex faked right and chased the smoke plume instead. It leaned forward, opening up its stride, and raced across the yard into the pine trees and disappeared. The black smoke evaporated. Weeple turned around and shuffled to David's side like a guard dog.

"Jamie! You almost gave me a heart attack. We were just playing, and David, my son, was…What are you doing back here? Are we in your way? Do you need to mow the lawn?" I knew I was babbling, but I couldn't seem to stop. My knees felt wobbly, and I was worried they were going to buckle beneath me.

Jamie wore a puzzled expression. I could only imagine how ridiculous I sounded to him. "Sorry to startle you," he said. "It's been such a hot, dry week that Winston asked me to skip it this time."

It took me a few beats too long to process what he'd said. My eyes were still darting toward the tree line, watching for King Rex to return. "Then why are you here?"

He motioned to something tucked under his arm I couldn't see. "I brought you something. But if this is a bad time…"

I was suddenly very aware that I was wearing only a bikini. I folded my arms over my lower stomach, where white hair-line stretch marks scarred my skin. "What is it?" I asked suspiciously.

He frowned and held it up, and I could see that it was a thin, spiral-bound sketchbook. It looked just like any of the cheap sketchbooks you could buy in a drugstore, except the cover of this one was decorated with Sailor Moon stickers. "When you asked me last week if I'd ever seen your imaginary friend, Leah Nola … well, I guess I lied."

My heart accelerated. I nervously wrung out my wet hair and glanced over his shoulder to see Weeple lie down, folding his enormous legs as if he were a camel. The T-rex was still nowhere to be seen. "What do you mean?"

"In here," he said. "You drew pictures of her. Of us. It's from the second summer you stayed here, and you gave it to me before you left because you said your mom would be mad if she saw it."

"Really?" I reached for the sketchbook, which felt warm from Jamie's hands and the sun. I ran my fingertips over the faded stickers. His offering was so kind and unexpected, the perfect olive branch. I didn't have many artifacts from my childhood. My mom hadn't been sentimental enough to keep much, and the handful of items she had kept—boxes filled with my baby book, a few dolls and stuffed animals, and some elementary school projects—had supposedly been ruined in a basement flood after I moved out. The only pictures I had of my childhood were in photo albums Duffy had compiled. "Thank you," I said, hugging the sketchbook to my waist. The words felt inadequate, so I repeated them with more emphasis. "Thank you so much."

"No problem." He shoved his hands into his pockets. Without his beard, Jamie looked much younger and more like the boy I had once known. Shaving had revealed his full, well-formed lips, lips I had always thought were such a waste on a guy. They were the lips I'd practiced kissing as a little girl.

"Well, we'd better go inside," I said, bending down to retrieve my lemonade thermos. Out of the corner of my eye, I noticed Jamie studiously not noticing my breasts as they swelled over the tight triangles of my bikini top. "David and I," I clarified quickly. "He's overdue for his nap. But thanks again for this. And for"—I dug deep—"your help last week. I know I made it pretty clear to you that I didn't want it at the time, but it was really nice of you."

"No problem," he repeated, struggling to withdraw his hand from his pocket to gesture dismissively. Was it just me, or did he look both disappointed *and* relieved? He took a few steps backward, his eyes never straying from my face.

"David," I called. "Time to come inside and get dried off."

My son galloped toward me without Weeple, wielding the loofah in front of him like a sword. Its spongy surface glistened with something speckled and shiny. He shot Jamie a curious glance as he approached. I knew I was being rude by not introducing him to Jamie, but the dinosaurs' reaction to my childhood friend still had me wound-up. Was it possible that David had sensed something about Jamie that I could not? Something threatening that had raised his dinosaurs' figurative hackles?

We climbed up the stairs to the deck together. I draped a faded beach towel around David's shoulders and pried the long-handled sponge away from him. Up close, I could see its head was coated in something gelatinous and gleaming, like a thousand tiny frog eggs. Ew. He must have left it lying in something gross in the yard, because imaginary dinosaurs certainly weren't capable of sloughing off their imaginary skin, were they? Of course not! Dang it, now I couldn't return the loofah to Duffy without her noticing. I'd have to throw it out and buy her a new one.

I looked up to see Jamie crossing the yard back to his house. I lifted my hand in a wave, but he must not have seen me.

Inside, the only sound was the humming air conditioner on full arctic blast. Duffy was still ensconced in her basement salon, and Winston was volunteering at the pioneer village. David's bare skin contracted into tiny goosebumps, and I tightened the towel around him.

"Let's hurry upstairs and get you in some dry clothes," I said, vigorously rubbing his arms with my palms. "Then it's time for a nap."

I wanted to talk to him about his dinosaurs' aggressive behavior but didn't know how to broach the subject without revealing that I could see them. Surely it wasn't a good idea to divulge to my son that I had a less-than-normal relationship with his imagination unless I wanted to condemn him to a life of therapy. My greatest fear was that by acknowledging my ability aloud, it would make David believe in them even more, and they would somehow become even more real. With more weight, more substance, more of their own agency, more potential for violence. I had no idea how this phenomenon worked, but I really didn't want to be responsible for unleashing that.

Drowsy from the sprinkler and the sun, David climbed into bed without his usual pre-nap protest.

"That man we saw lives next door," I told him. "I think you've seen him mowing our lawn? His name is Jamie, and I was friends with him when I was a little girl. Just a little older than you."

He stared up at me, clearly shocked by the notion of my being a child once. I pulled the sheet up to his chin.

"You seemed upset when you first saw him," I said. "Any reason why?" I suspected there had been something primal and protective in his response. Maybe it wasn't that he'd sensed anything threatening about Jamie in particular, but that he was simply a stranger, and a male one at that, when David hardly had any interaction with men.

His first instinct had been to defend us. But it scared me that he'd sicced his dinosaurs on someone in order to do that.

David leaned his cheek against my hand and closed his eyes. He mumbled something that sounded like, *I thought it was him.* When I asked him to repeat himself, he said, "I don't like the bad cat. King Rex and Weeple chase him away."

"What bad cat?" I asked, but he didn't respond. "If you want to keep playing with your dinosaurs, they need to be nice. No chasing cats or people, okay? I don't want them to hurt you or someone else. They can eat all the pickles and bologna they want, but they need to be good." I stroked his cheek and quietly left the room.

I changed out of my bikini and sat cross-legged on my bed with the sketchbook Jamie had brought me. Vivien Leigh jumped up beside me and butted her head against my thigh. Scratching her white chin with one hand, I inspected the front and back covers for any writing, my name or otherwise, but found nothing. After engaging with David's monstrous imaginary friends, I was a little hesitant to uncover more about my own. But mostly, I wanted to extend the pleasure of anticipating what would be inside—a message from my eight-year-old self. Maybe learning about my own childhood would shed some light on my son's creations.

I slid my pointer finger under the lip of the front cover. The first drawing, disappointingly, was not of my imaginary friend. Instead, it was a colored-pencil sketch of the river and the grassy banks around it. It was actually pretty good for an eight-year-old, I had to admit. I flipped to the next one, which showed a barn, and the next one, a Ferris wheel. My landscape phase, apparently.

A third of the way through the sketchbook, I came across a portrait of a little girl. Black pageboy haircut, large lavender-gray eyes, a hint of a smile playing on her lips. Charcoal gray jumper with a white blouse underneath. LEAH NOLA was written in my girlish, bubbly handwriting. She looked pretty and self-contained somehow, like an orphaned yet tenacious heroine in a children's book. I studied each line of the drawing, trying to remember her, willing myself to hear her voice. Had she sounded sweet and ghostly? Or loud and bossy? But the drawing stared silently back at me.

I paged through the rest of the sketchbook. There were drawings of Leah Nola and a blonde girl of the same height—me—and there were drawings of us with a slightly smaller, wide-eyed, brown-haired boy. Jamie. I closed the book, and Vivien Leigh immediately settled herself on top of it. She yawned, revealing the tiny pink cave of her mouth, and I stroked the delicate arch of her back.

Jamie had said I'd given my drawings to him for safekeeping because my mom would've been mad if she had seen them. But why? They were lovely, precise sketches, full of promise, and even though my mom had never really encouraged my interest in art, she certainly hadn't prohibited it either. So clearly, it had something to do with their content—my imaginary friend. The imaginary friend who, until a few weeks ago, I'd had no memory of. And if I'd been hiding the drawings from my mom, that meant that she had known about Leah Nola and disapproved.

A disquieting idea crossed my mind: *had she been able to see my imagination as I was able to see David's?* But it seemed unlikely because in order to see my imagination, she would've needed to have paid attention to me. And if there was one consistent theme of my childhood, it was that her time was too precious to spare much of it on me. Kimberly Jennings was a vanishing act. Now you see her, now you don't.

Even if she hadn't been able to see Leah Nola, she certainly could've been aware I had an imaginary friend. Probably I had talked about her in front of my mom, asked her to set out an extra place setting like Winston had done, that sort of thing. Had my mom been disturbed by my overactive imagination? Had she worried I was a troubled or abnormal child? It seemed too big a coincidence that the first two summers I'd been sent to stay with my grandparents—tumultuous years with my mom, years she claimed I exhibited "behavior problems"—paralleled my friendship with Leah Nola.

And why could I remember so little about her? Why, until both Duffy and Jamie had mentioned her, had I totally forgotten about the gray-eyed girl in the jumper? I didn't have a steel trap memory like Jamie, yet I could remember a lot of other details from my summers here. But not Leah Nola. It was almost like I'd repressed the memory of her. The only interaction with my mom I was able to pluck from my memory that related to Leah Nola was my thirteenth birthday party. She had muttered my imaginary friend's name hatefully under her breath.

When I turned thirteen, all I wanted for my birthday was a sleepover party. I'd been to plenty of them before but had never hosted one at my own house mostly because my mom was too flaky and unpredictable. But I'd finally worn down her resistance by playing up how all of my friends thought she was the youngest and prettiest mom, and therefore The Coolest Mom in Our Grade, and how they just knew we'd throw the best sleepover ever. My mom took unprecedented pride in her new title and, in an effort to live up to it, granted me one of the best weeks of my life leading up to my birthday. We planned the party together, harmoniously side by side, acting like a mother and daughter who actually liked each other. We sent out glittery invitations, ordered a real bakery cake with pink icing roses, rented R-rated chick-flicks, and made up little party favor bags with lip gloss, ring pops, and glow stick bracelets.

By the time my first guest arrived, my skin was nearly shooting off little sparks of happiness. As planned, I showed my room to the eight specially-chosen girls, and then we set about playing a dating board game until the pizzas were delivered. But my mom didn't call us down and some of the girls were starting to complain they were hungry, so I went downstairs to investigate. My mom was sitting at the kitchen table, frowning at the mound of beautifully wrapped gifts. When I asked her about dinner, she snapped, "Mark went to go get them, so we didn't have to pay some idiot driver a tip."

Mark was her current boyfriend, a bald-headed cook at the restaurant where she worked, who almost exclusively referred to her as "mama." She'd had a lot of boyfriends over the years, but Mark definitely ranked in my Top Ten List of Losers.

When Mark finally showed up with the pizza, my mom berated him for forgetting to pick up the cake as well. They argued right in front of us, and Mark shouted at one point, "It's not like she's my fucking kid, Kim!" My mom said nothing in reply, but her hazel eyes told a different story. They flashed indignantly: *I wish she wasn't my fucking kid either.*

My friends politely pretended to be busy choosing their pizza slices. I was disappointed to see that my mom hadn't thought to order my favorite pizza toppings—ham and pineapple—or if she had, Mark hadn't remembered. The birthday cake never did get picked up because by the time my mom had won the fight, the bakery had already closed for the evening, and Mark returned empty-handed and fuming.

The party limped along. Half of the girls were resigned to treating me with patronizing kindness; the other half had given in to malicious whispering about my screwed-up home life. When the credits on the last movie rolled and the majority of my "friends" were drifting off to sleep, I felt only immense relief. That is, until Katie Birch nudged me awake. Her pretty face was pale and drawn in the moonlit living room. "I don't feel good," she whispered and immediately burst into hot, gulping tears. I hurried her into the bathroom before she could wake the other girls and held her shiny black hair back as she hurled the contents of her stomach into the toilet bowl.

"I want my mom," Katie whimpered, before retching again.

"Wait here." I gave her a wet washcloth to wipe her face.

I tiptoed past the living room to my mom's bedroom. In the pitch dark, I knelt by her bed to gently prod her awake. But she wasn't in the bed. Neither was Mark. I did a quick search of the rest of the house and found they were both gone. Both their cars were missing too. No note, no nothing.

Since I was eight, my mom had been leaving me home alone with only our downstairs neighbor, an elderly man named Vern, as a vague kind of "in case of emergencies" babysitter. She'd leave for hours at a time, but she had never left me alone overnight. At least not that I knew of. I wondered if maybe Mark had murdered her. In my righteous adolescent anger, I almost hoped that was the case, instead of her intentionally leaving me all by myself to fend with a situation I didn't know how to handle.

"What did your mom say? Did she call my mom?" Katie asked. Her face looked even whiter than when I'd left her, and her slight shoulders were shaking.

"Do you really think we need to call your mom? I mean, you threw up, so hopefully you'll feel better now, right? Why scare her and make her come out here in the middle of the night?" I chattered nervously. I was scared to death that Mrs. Birch would find out how negligent my mom was and that we'd somehow get in trouble.

Fat tears rolled down Katie's cheeks, and she rubbed at a smear of vomit on the corner of her lips. "Anna, please. My mom won't mind, I promise. I just want to go home."

"Okay," I whispered. "I'll call."

True to Katie's word, her mom wasn't angry or annoyed to have to come get her at 3:30 in the morning. She was still wearing her pajamas—a matronly pink-plaid short set that revealed the varicose veins in her legs, unlike the lace and silk nighties my own mom wore—and her eyes were bleary, but when she saw Katie, she heroically scooped her into her arms and let out a string of comforting phrases, "Sweetie, it's okay. I'm here. There now. Everything is fine, Katie girl."

When I told Mrs. Birch my mom was a heavy sleeper, she didn't seem the least bit suspicious. Instead, she stroked my hair and said, "Poor Anna. I'm sorry this had to happen at your birthday party. Thank you for helping Katie and calling me. You did the right thing." I watched them walk to their station wagon, Katie's skinny form leaning against her mother's sturdy one, and I wanted to go with them. I wanted Mrs. Birch to be my mother and to never again have to wonder where my mom was or if she would be there for me when I needed her.

My mom had miraculously reappeared by the time everyone woke up the next morning, with a box of frosted long john doughnuts with sprinkles, as though that could somehow make up for everything else. I gave her the cold shoulder the more she tried to cajole me and win over my friends with her knowledge of current trends and celebrities. Finally, all the girls had been collected. I stood up to go to my room.

"What's *your* problem?" my mom asked, struggling to squeeze the empty bakery box into the garbage, which was already jammed with foul-smelling pizza boxes. "I throw this extravagant party for you—which was not cheap, let me tell you—and I don't even get the slightest thanks?"

My face burned. I tried to keep my mouth shut, but my anger was flooding my throat like a tidal wave of verbal vomit, and I couldn't hold it back any longer. "What do you want me to thank you for?" I shouted. "Embarrassing me in front of everyone? Not standing up for me to stupid Mark? Forgetting my cake? Leaving me all alone in the middle of the night to fend for myself with Katie puking…and her mom…" I was sobbing at that point, and my words were thick and wet and probably hard to understand. I cried until my sinuses ached from the pressure.

"Are you done?" my mom asked. She was sitting at the kitchen table with her hands folded primly and her face bland and expressionless. I had never hated her more than I did at that moment.

"I know this is hard for you to understand, but please try," she started. Without her makeup on, she looked older than her thirty years. "Sometimes life can be disappointing. It can turn out in ways that you didn't expect. You're thirteen now, a teenager. You need to know that not everything is always going to be perfect, least of all me, and you need to learn to deal with that."

"Really, Mom? Life can be disappointing, and you're not perfect?" My voice dripped with sarcasm. "You think I'm just figuring that out now?"

"With that bad attitude, you've got a lot more disappointment coming to you, Little Miss Anna. Life is not gentle with girls like us."

"Don't say that. I'm nothing like you!" I spat. "I hate you!"

I'd finally pierced her composure. She leapt from the table with her palm raised as though she were going to strike me. She pounded the tabletop instead. "It's a terrible thing to hate your mother. But I've known it for a while now. I've seen it in your eyes. Ever since Leah Nola."

We stood glaring at each other, raw wounds exposed, unrelenting. I couldn't bring myself to contradict her. Why couldn't she have just hugged me and told me she was sorry? Why couldn't she just say, "I love you Anna"? Why was she always trying to preach to me about life's harsh lessons, when she was dishing out enough of them as it was?

"Take out the trash and then go to your room," she said at last, and I couldn't tell who had won the argument. Like most relationship-defining fights, we had both lost something important.

CHAPTER EIGHT

Carly Cardwell was a hard woman to turn down. When she'd called to invite me to spend the day at her parents' lake house, I'd had a hundred reasons to say no, not the least of which was that I'd finally started my job hunt in earnest. (Which was code for "browsing through the classified ads" instead of simply freaking out about my finances: no money to chip in for my grandparents' bills; no money for a security deposit on a place of our own, much less steady rent; no money for school supplies or new clothes for David.) But as I sat in front of my grandparents' ancient computer, scrolling through postings seeking receptionists, customer service reps, sales associates, office managers, wait staff, and daycare teachers, all with unbelievably high expectations and even more unbelievably *low* pay, I started to feel more and more discouraged.

"Who else is going to be there?" I asked her, remembering the Tims and Heathers at her engagement party. I held my cell phone between my ear and shoulder as I clicked on an ad for an elementary school art teacher. Unfortunately, a Bachelor's degree and a state teaching license were required. Boo.

"Just you, lovely," Carly said. "I thought we could catch up. Maybe take the pontoon boat out for a spin."

"Your dad still lets you drive that thing after you crashed it into your neighbor's dock?" I teased.

"Of course," she scoffed. "It doesn't hurt that my parents are divorced now, and my mom got to keep the house *and* the boats. She spends most of her time with her boyfriend in Port Ambrose anyway, so Sam and I come out here a ton in the summer. What do you say?"

My desire to escape—from the stifling house, from the demands of my tedious life, from David's sullen mood, and from his dinosaurs who weren't really there but somehow were and oh, God, what was that about, anyway?—was physically overwhelming. I could almost feel the cool lake water lapping against my skin as I floated in an inner tube. I knew Duffy would probably be willing to watch David for the rest of the day and wouldn't begrudge me a little "girl time" as long as I didn't come home too late or show up in Jamie Presswood's truck.

When I parked in the small parking area above the Cardwells' house, I was already perspiring through the halter top and jean shorts I'd layered over my bikini. The Dodge Caravan's AC was now officially out of commission. I passed the familiar, ugly big-mouthed bass mailbox before descending the steep stone steps that led to the house. Peeking in the screened-in side porch, I couldn't see or hear Carly, so I climbed down another flight of narrower stone steps that led to the lake. The pleasantly musty smell of lake water rose up to greet me. Each step I took felt like I was traveling back in time to my high school days. There was the trampoline where Carly, Libby O'Mallon, and I had sprawled out on our backs and exchanged secrets about boys. The bonfire pit. The dove-gray, sparkling water where I had first gone skinny-dipping. And Carly herself, looking sixteen again in a sexy black bikini, her skin as smooth and brown as a chestnut.

She gave me an energetic wave from the dock. "Hey! I packed a cooler full of bottled water and wine coolers, and I have the perfect place in mind for us to drop anchor and swim. Ready to cruise?" She jammed a baseball cap over her springy hair and swung open the boat's gate for me.

Carly was a more competent captain than I remembered, and I didn't fear for anyone's dock this time. She piloted the pontoon boat slowly and precisely around the perimeter of the lake, pointing out Sam's and her dream house, asking all about David (I left out the part about the dinosaurs), and filling me in on their plans for their May wedding. We found an eighties music station on the radio and sang along to Bananarama, the Go-Go's, and the Bangles. I drank one wine cooler, promising myself I would switch to water next.

"Where's Libby these days?" I asked, relaxing against the bank of sun-warmed vinyl seats.

"San Francisco." Carly cut the engine as we entered a small cove. The pontoon boat glided into a private area where there were no houses and marsh grass grew in tall bunches. "She's with a ballet company there."

"Really?" Out of the three of us, Libby had always seemed the least ambitious. And yet there she was, and here we were.

Carly raised her eyebrow as if she was totally on the same page as me. "I *know*. I'm super happy for her, though. If I ever get out to California, I'm supposed to call her, and she'll get me free tickets to a performance." She walked to the back of the boat to throw out the anchor. "Let's see. Who else that you know is still in the area? Oh. Well, you probably already know this because he lives next door to you, but Jamie Presswood is back."

I nodded quickly. "Yeah, I know. I saw him at your party." Something stopped me from telling her about Colin, the wine coolers, and Jamie driving me home. Maybe Sam had already told her, or she'd seen Jamie come to pick up my minivan the next morning. Carly was many things, but judgmental was not one of them. "He mows my grandparents' lawn, so he's out there weekly. And he actually gave me something the other day from when we were kids."

"Oh yeah?" She twisted off her water bottle cap and took a swig. "I'm surprised he'll talk to you. It took him a while to warm up to me, and only then because Sam and Marshall persuaded him. We were such bitches to him in high school, weren't we?"

I bit my lip as I remembered how dismissive I'd been of Jamie my sophomore year. The weekend before I started at William Payne, Duffy and Winston had invited him over to join us for dinner. We'd spent the whole night reminiscing about our childhood summers together, sitting so close our bare legs touched. It had been Jamie's first year at William Payne, too, as a freshman, but school had already been in session for a month, so he had tried to prepare me and give me lots of practical advice. He'd eased my anxiety, and since we had the same lunch period, he even promised to sit with me at lunch, so I wouldn't run the risk of eating alone. But on the big day, I immediately met Carly and Libby in my first period class, who tucked me under their wings like a baby bird. Not only did I not sit with Jamie for lunch that day, I also went so far as to pretend I didn't even know him, and we'd coldly avoided each other the rest of the year, both at home and at school. The awful memory made my cheeks burn.

"Me more so than you," I said. "Jamie and I had been best friends, and then I just dropped him."

"We were all pretty horrible. Evil teenage brain syndrome, I call it, because what else would explain being so vicious to such a nice kid? Remember how you dared me to ask him to homecoming? We had this whole elaborate idea for how to dump him the day before the dance. But he wouldn't even say yes because you and Libby were laughing so hard that he knew all along it was a prank." Carly lowered herself to the aluminum edge of the boat and dangled her legs into the water. She took off her cap and shook out her hair. "But the joke was on us because he really grew into one fine specimen of a man, didn't he?"

"I guess so. He's not really my type." I slipped off my halter top and shorts and joined Carly on the back deck. The water felt warm and soothing on my toes and calves.

"That's right. You always had a thing for the bad boys, didn't you?" She dipped her fingers in the water and sent a playful splash my way. "Speaking of which, I wonder where Zack Winslow is these days. Prison, perhaps?"

"Probably." I splashed her back. "By my grandmother's standards, Jamie *is* a bad boy."

"By Salsburg standards, sure." Carly stretched her arms out in front of her, pressed her palms together, leaned forward, and dove into the water. I followed suit.

Beneath the top foot of clear water where the sunlight had warmed it, the lake was crisply cold and otherworldly. Darting fish, weeds undulating like mermaid hair, alternating patches of sunlight and shadow. I would take a lake over a chlorinated pool any day. There was no pressure to swim laps in a lake; just floating or treading water was perfectly acceptable. Even the flecks of silt and sand that I would find in my swimsuit afterward made me feel truly organic, a part of the ecosystem.

When I emerged, I slicked my hair back out of my eyes. Carly was breast-stroking toward a clump of fragile-looking lily pads.

"Do you think the drug rumors about him are true?" I asked. Since her fiancé was friends with Marshall and Jamie, she probably had inside information about him.

"Beats me. Probably not, but at the heart of every rumor is always a kernel of truth. Why don't you ask him?" She paddled around to face me. "You seem awfully interested in Jamie all of a sudden. Have you dated anyone since Patrick?"

"It's not like that. I'm just curious. I've known the guy since he was six! And no, I haven't dated anyone—at least seriously—since Patrick. In case you've forgotten, I'm a single mother of a four-year-old."

We swam lazily around the cove, and I brought her up to speed about my injunction against Patrick, which would be expiring in October, and how I was deeply disturbed by what that would mean for me and David. I knew that it was one of my major motives in escaping to Salsburg and cloistering myself for a time.

Climbing back into the boat, we let the sun dry us off. We talked about her job at Ruby's Diner and how soul-crushing she found it to bake walnut brownies every day and instead wished she could experiment with rainbow-colored macarons and crème brûlée. She asked me about my art, and I admitted I hadn't done a single oil pastel since David was six months old and that I, too, would be reentering the world of dream-crushing jobs soon. Then she pulled up the anchor and started motoring back to shore.

When she guided the boat back into its slip, we noticed a small fire smoking in the pit up the hill. "Sam must be here," she said, securing the pontoon boat to the dock with a nylon rope. "Do you want to join us for dinner? In the summer, my mom's house is always stocked with brats, hotdogs, and s'mores fixings."

Suddenly I wanted nothing more than to have David with me. The boat ride, the bonfire, roasting marshmallows, he would have loved it all. It was something I wrestled with daily: craving time to myself, time with other adults, and then when I finally stole a few hours away from him, I desperately missed his wide, excited eyes and warm, heavy body, perpetually in some kind of contact with mine. I worried I was missing something important and fleeting that couldn't be reclaimed.

I was also torn between feeling prudent and reckless about leaving David with someone who couldn't see his dinosaurs. This was the way the world worked for 99.99% of parents, I reasoned. Imagination was a private, mental creation by definition, and it was merely a fluke that I could see the images David was projecting. If anything, my perceiving and reacting to his dinosaurs was maybe making him more susceptible. Still I couldn't help feeling like I was leaving my child alone with a particularly dangerous breed of dog. A breed that seemed loyal and safe one minute but might rip someone's face off the next.

I stepped into my jean shorts and buttoned them up. "Thanks," I said. "I'd like to, but I probably should be getting home soon." I'd told Duffy I didn't know if I'd be home for dinner but that I'd definitely be back in time to tuck David in and tell him a story. The sun was still gleaming on the lake's surface, misleadingly making it look like only three or four o'clock, when I knew it was probably closer to six or seven.

Boyish whoops carried down the hillside to us, and three male figures appeared on the stone steps, too far away to identify.

"Oh, I guess he brought friends, too," Carly said, craning her neck to make them out. One of them let out a low wolf whistle when he spotted us. "What a bunch of goons."

The first guy was scrawny and red-haired—Marshall Gehring, I remembered. Jamie's friend. Next came Sam, lugging a case of beer. And behind him—no, it couldn't be. Messy blond hair and broad shoulders under a sky-blue soccer jersey. I wanted to positively die. Colin Bentley, my misguided conquest.

I yanked my halter top over my head and retied it. My bikini wasn't totally dry yet, and I hoped I wouldn't have wet booby circles through my shirt. "Thanks for having me over. This was just what I needed, but it's almost David's bedtime. And probably mine too, after all the sun we got today." I yawned as if to prove my point.

Carly looped her arm around my waist as we walked toward the guys. "Well, let's do it again sometime then. I'm so glad you're back in the area. I know it's selfish of me to say, but I really hope you'll stick around."

"Hey!" Sam bent down to Carly's tiny height and kissed her. "I tried calling to warn you, but you know how terrible cell phone reception is out here. We were in the mood for a bonfire and some night fishing." He set the case of beer down and straightened up. "Anna! So good to see you again! I don't know if you remember my friends from the party, Marshall and Colin."

I smiled noncommittally. Colin was sizing me up as if he couldn't decide whether to write me off as a lost cause or give it another crack. I hadn't just been wearing my drunk goggles; he really was gorgeous in a Burberry model kind of way. Maybe a bit too pretty for my liking. Carly was right about my preference in men; bad boys were my downfall.

"You're both staying, right?" Sam asked. Marshall added another log to the fire, and Colin righted a fallen lawn chair.

"I'll help you with the brats, babe, and then leave you to your guy time. Anna was actually just taking off," Carly rescued me, God love her. "I held her captive on the pontoon boat all afternoon, and we're both pretty beat."

"Bummer," Colin said, his pearly gray eyes sparkling like the sunlit lake.

"Yeah," Sam agreed. "Well, next time then."

Carly and I parted ways with a hug at the top of the first flight of steps, the lower entrance to the house. She went inside to beer boil some brats, and I continued to climb the steps that would take me back up to the road where I'd parked my minivan. I passed the screened-in porch, turned the corner, and almost planted my face directly in Jamie Presswood's chest. He smelled like cedar shavings and dried sweat.

"Ah!" I backed up quickly. "What are you doing here?"

"Sam invited me." He gestured to the fishing pole he was carrying at his side. "What are *you* doing here?"

"Carly invited me." I glanced back at the screened-in porch, almost expecting her curly head to pop up at any minute. She'd seemed so mindful of my questions about Jamie earlier. Was this some kind of a set-up? If it was, both Carly and Sam were playing it awfully cool. "I was just leaving though."

Jamie made as if to shoulder past me without another word. I remembered what Carly had said. *I'm surprised he'll talk to you. We were such bitches to him in high school.* I wished I could go back in time, erase my bad behavior, and we could be the friends who had once caught fireflies for their wish-granting abilities and picnicked by the river together, again.

"I looked through the sketchbook," I said. "It brought back some good memories. Thanks again."

He raised one shoulder and let it drop. "It was yours. I was just returning it."

"I still can't believe you had it after all these years. I mean, that it wasn't thrown away." I hooked my car keys around my pointer finger and jingled them.

Was I imagining it, or did Jamie's cheeks pinken? "My mom's a packrat," he said. "She kept everything I so much as wiped my nose on as a kid. It's all sorted in boxes and labeled by year in the attic. When you mentioned that summer, I knew where to look."

I leaned against the stone stairwell. "I still don't remember much about her—my imaginary friend. It's like I completely blotted out her memory. But I've been thinking about the 'picnics' you and I used to have by the river. Do you remember? You would steal a tin of butter cookies from your mom, and I would pack a cooler full of Cokes and fruit roll-ups and freezy pops. Of course, the freezy pops would always melt by the time we got there."

Jamie's posture noticeably relaxed. "I'd forgotten about that. You know what I remember? The carnival at the Firemen's Picnic. Remember how my mom or Duffy would take us for a few hours during the day and buy us a couple of hot dogs and some tickets for the rides? Then later that night—it was probably only 9:00, but it felt like it was midnight—Winston would take us again, so he could buy himself a funnel cake without your grandmother knowing. He'd give us ten bucks each to spend however we wanted. He just let us run off. We just had to meet him by the gate at a certain time, and that was it. I always wanted to play the ring toss game and win one of those gigantic stuffed animals, and you always wanted to—"

"Ride the Ferris wheel," I finished eagerly. It was thrilling hearing him speak more than one sentence at a time. His tumble of words reminded me of how open and earnest he'd been when he was fifteen. Before he'd stopped speaking to me, that is.

I'd only vaguely recalled those late-night, unsupervised visits to the carnival, but as soon as Jamie described it, I could almost smell the fried dough and powdered sugar of Winston's forbidden funnel cake. I could feel the night breeze on my feverish cheeks as we rode the Ferris wheel to the top for the hundredth time. I could see Jamie's shoulders hunched in disappointment as he missed the three required bottles and the grand prize again. And there was something else. A girl with a black pageboy brushing against my arm: "Let's go on the Ferris wheel again, Anna. It's so magical! You can see the whole town from up there! The whole world, practically."

Leah Nola. I sat down on one of the steps. So she had been there. She was *still* there, pressed in between the cracks of my memories.

"It's probably the smallest, lowest-budget fair in the country, but, man, I thought it was cool back then." Jamie propped his fishing pole against the stairwell. He looked like he wanted to sit down but was conflicted since I was already occupying the stairs.

I wanted to keep the easy, comfortable feeling growing between us. I wanted to hear more about Leah Nola. "Tell me the truth. Was I a weird kid?"

"Come on. Would *I* have been friends with a weird kid?" He laughed. "Okay, don't answer that."

I fought back a smile. "Didn't you think it was strange that I had an imaginary friend?" I pressed. "I mean, I was in first and second grade at the time. That's a little old to be playing with pretend little girls."

Jamie shrugged. "I was only six when we met. What did I know?"

I tried to fathom the strange dynamic that must have existed between the three of us. Had Jamie tried to share Leah Nola with me? I could imagine him making incorrect assertions about her whereabouts and behaviors: "Leah Nola wants to go to the river," or "Leah Nola fell asleep on the deck," and my bossy, seven-year-old self setting the record straight. I wondered if he'd given up trying.

"You know, that's wrong," Jamie said softly. He gazed off in the direction of the leafy trees separating the Cardwells' property from their neighbors. "I *do* remember. It didn't seem weird to me, it seemed amazing. I mean, there I was, an only child in this boring neighborhood with absolutely no children, and all of a sudden, this girl shows up next door who's super imaginative and always assigning me roles in her elaborate games, and on top of it, she tells me that she has a secret friend who no one else knows about or can see but she's going to play with us too? It was awesome." His eyes flicked back briefly to meet mine. In the fading daylight, his irises looked like melted chocolate.

I let his compliment sink in. I'd been labeled a "problem child" so frequently by my mom that it was nice to have someone else remember me as a kind of gift. "Thanks, Jamie." I patted the space on the step next to me, and to my surprise, he actually sat down. It was a tight squeeze. His hip was only inches away from mine.

We were hidden together in the stairwell, frozen halfway between coming and going. Carly probably assumed I was long gone; Sam had maybe given up hope of Jamie showing up to the bonfire. It was rapidly approaching nightfall, and the cicadas had already started their frantic buzzing. I needed to get home to tell David a story, but I didn't want to leave just yet. And something told me Jamie didn't want to either. I thought about saying something apologetic about high school—my coldness toward him my first day of school and thereafter, that horrible homecoming prank—but he spoke up before I had the chance to.

"Look, I know you've probably heard some rumors, and I'd prefer you hear the truth from me." Jamie leaned forward, clasping his hands tightly between his knees. His leg brushed mine.

I considered playing dumb. I considered being a good friend and saying, *You don't need to tell me anything. I knew they were all lies right from the start.* But my curiosity got the better of me. "Okay. But it's really not necessary. I mean, who am *I* to judge? You know I haven't led a life of sainthood—the whole town knows it."

"What you think matters more to me than what the town thinks." He stood up and started pacing on the small landing. My perch on the steps felt suddenly lonely and much too spacious.

His pronouncement was flattering, but I tried to focus on the issue at hand. I contrasted Duffy's "verified" gossip that Jamie was filling his mom's pain meds for his own purposes with Winston's unwavering faith in him. My own instincts were more muddled. I wanted to believe in Jamie because he was Jamie, the gentle-natured boy I'd known since I was seven. Unfortunately, I also knew from too much experience that good people sometimes did bad things.

"Then tell me." My hair had dried in tangled waves, and I gathered it together and pulled it over one shoulder.

He spun on his heel and continued his pacing. "My big plan was to drive out West, hiking and camping in all the National Parks—Yellowstone, Mesa Verde, the Arches, the Grand Canyon, all the way to Yosemite and the Redwoods. I'd saved up some money, and I figured every so often I'd settle down for a month or so, get a job, earn some cash for food and gas, and then just pick up and go. But I didn't get very far.

"I made it to Sioux Falls. South Dakota. The Badlands was going to be my first stop. But I never got there because I got into a car accident. A sleep-deprived trucker drifted into my lane and ran me off the road. I dislocated my shoulder, cracked some ribs, and strained my back pretty good. I was laid up in the hospital for a week, and that drained my savings."

"That's horrible," I said, imagining him lying in a hospital bed in an unfamiliar state, all alone. "Did you call your mom?"

He paused mid-stride and pressed his lips together. "What could she have done? She'd been diagnosed with multiple sclerosis at that point and had to give up her driver's license. Knowing would have just made her feel helpless."

I hadn't seen Wendy Presswood since I was sixteen, and it was hard to picture her as anything other than her strong, independent self. Jamie's dad had left when he was four, and Wendy had filled the "father" void— playing catch with Jamie, mowing the lawn, cleaning out the gutters, changing the oil on her car. Occasionally Duffy would send Winston over for a particularly challenging, two-person task, but otherwise Wendy took care of things herself. Until Jamie had gotten old enough to help around the house. Once she'd been diagnosed with MS, how had she been able to spare him? How had she managed to let him go?

"They prescribed oxycodone for my pain," he continued. "It was amazing. It did more than just take away the pain. It made life more bearable. It made the prospect of my road trip ending—before I'd even seen anything—and returning to Wisconsin, to my mom's illness, more bearable. But then the prescription ran out, and they wouldn't refill it." Jamie ran his hand through his shaggy black hair. "Around that time, the insurance settlement from the trucking company came in. I moved into a motel room I could pay for by the week, and I found someone who could sell me oxycodone under the table."

So, he had been a drug addict. Not just taking the pills for his pain, but addicted to the high they had given him. Maybe he still was. He was watching me, trying to gauge my reaction. I stared back at him with a mild expression (I'd gotten quite good at my poker face living with Patrick), waiting to see if the story had a happy ending.

"That went on for longer than I care to admit," he said. "But then I met a guy, Mike Mueller, and he gave me a job at his nursery shoveling mulch, watering flowers, that kind of thing. I really needed the money at that point. I worked hard for him because he was a good guy, but also I was working to pay for more OC. Then one day, he called me into the back room to tell me he knew about my addiction. He didn't want to fire me, he said, but he cared about me and wanted me to get my life back together. He'd researched some rehab facilities, and he wanted me to sign myself into one. He said my job would still be waiting for me when I got out."

"So you went?" I asked.

"I went. And it was the hardest thing I've ever done in my life." Jamie slouched against the wall as if just the memory of it was exhausting. "The program encouraged me to get in touch with my mom, so I called her and told her where I was and how I was doing. She was pretty bad off at that point and had a nurse coming for a couple of hours every day, but it didn't sound like enough. Still, I just couldn't bring myself to go back yet. I stayed on with Mike a few more months, and then finally, I decided it was time to come home. So here I am."

His tone of finality told me the story was over, but was it really? I wanted to ask him if he was really clean, but I remembered how important my opinion seemed to him, and I didn't want him to think I didn't trust him.

"I'm glad," I said, and I really, really meant it. When I'd packed up and left Milwaukee, Jamie Presswood had been the furthest thing from my mind. But seeing him in my grandparents' backyard had been bizarrely comforting and reassuring, a steady link to my past, like Duffy and Winston. Talking to him like this made me feel trustworthy and on less shaky ground.

"I wasn't at first," he said. "My mom's condition had worsened so much, it was shocking, and I felt so guilty for leaving her like that. I felt like such a failure coming back here in so many ways."

That made two of us.

"But then you came back," he said and turned to face me. His tone sounded almost accusatory. His face was half hidden in shadow and somehow at the same height as mine. Everything was suddenly too quiet—even the cicadas in their desperation to mate had paused in their relentless humming—and all I could hear was the steadily increasing tempo of my heart. His eyelids were lowering, his full lips were softening, and I started to think that he might kiss me. And that I might kiss him back.

"Whoa! Didn't know anyone was up here!" A loud voice broke our silence. Colin. He held up his hands in mock surrender as he surveyed the scene. "Sorry if I interrupted anything! Forgot my tackle box in my trunk. Pretend I'm not here." He met my gaze as he climbed past me on the stairs. His eyes said, *I knew you were a slut.*

I hugged my arms across my chest and waited for him to leave so we could continue our talk, but Jamie was already stooping to retrieve his fishing pole. He stood up, his back ramrod straight. "I'd better go," he said in a hollow voice. "They're waiting for me."

I searched his face for a clue to his sudden change in demeanor. It was Colin, of course—the reminder of Carly and Sam's party—*What else would explain you hanging all over a douchebag like Colin Bentley?* Jamie had asked. But it seemed like there was more to it. I tried to analyze the tense moment between us before Colin had bounded up the stairs. Jamie had nakedly confided in me because my knowing the truth mattered to him. How could that feeling of intimacy dissolve so quickly?

"Excuse me again. Carry on!" Colin ran past us, this time carrying a battered green tackle box. We could hear him shout down the hill to Sam and Marshall, "Guess who's finally here, guys! Presswood!"

Now there was no turning back for Jamie, but it was time for me to go anyway. I hoped that David was still awake so I could give him another installment of Mona and Wolfy's latest adventures. This time, I decided, they would fly to Planet Hot/Cold, where freezing ice cream mountains mingled with boiling hot fudge springs and they never knew where they stood or what kind of trouble they were going to get themselves into.

CHAPTER NINE

Duffy pulled a retractable clothesline from the shed and clipped it to a metal hook screwed into the tree trunk. "That's what Winston said too, more or less," she said. "Now be a biscuit and help me hang these sheets."

I hadn't wanted to betray Jamie's confidence, but trying to straighten out my grandmother's vendetta against him seemed even more important, so I'd told her a (somewhat edited) version of the truth, emphasizing the horrific car crash and intolerable pain, his kindly paternal boss, the successful rehab, and his heroic return to take care of his ailing mother.

I lifted the first wet sheet from the laundry basket. It was the top sheet from my own bed, pale yellow with tiny pink rosebuds. With two clothespins and two efficient movements, Duffy had it hung up. I bent to retrieve the matching fitted sheet.

"Then why did you warn me to stay away from him? He's changed, Duffy. Just because he's had troubles in the past doesn't mean that you should totally write him off as a bad guy."

"No, of course not," Duffy mumbled around a wooden clothespin in her mouth, "and I'm sorry if it seems that way to you." She lined up the sheet to allow it to share a clothespin with the previous one. "I just don't want to see you get involved with another troubled young man. Especially for David's sake."

"Get involved? We're just friends." I handed her the navy blue sheets from David's bed and tried not to think about the scene Colin had stumbled upon last night. The interrupted kiss—which had seemed so inevitable at the time, so large and magnetic that it filled up the stairwell and squeezed my drumming heart—seemed like a distant dream now. Something silly and probably misremembered. "I always have David's best interests in mind. Don't confuse me with my mother." I glanced quickly to the deck where David was playing a complicated game involving his pirate action figures, the Lincoln logs, the hula hoop, and one of Vivien Leigh's cat toys. It was such a relief to see him playing with something other than his dinosaurs for once.

"Listen to me, cupcake. You may look like Kimberly, and sometimes you're both a little too stubborn for your own good, but there the similarities end. Believe me, I know." She laughed and scooped the laundry basket up from the grass, balancing it on her hip. "You're a loving, doting mother, and you deserve to be loved and doted on too. Those things don't have to be mutually exclusive. One day you'll meet someone, and it will be a clean slate for you. No more tears, no more drama. I just don't think that someone is Jamie."

"Will you stop bringing him up? I already told you we're just friends." I looked over my shoulder at the Presswoods' empty backyard.

"Are you sure he feels the same way?" She squinted at me skeptically. With her white blond bouffant and pink-and-green paisley print apron, she looked like a seventies housewife.

I remembered the way he had hustled off, desperate to get away from me, after Colin had discovered us. "Yeah, I'm pretty sure."

David clambered down the steps, delighted by the sight of the sheets billowing in the breeze. "Let's play hide-and-seek, Mommy!"

"What fun!" Duffy said, bending down to ruffle his hair. "I wonder where a little grasshopper like you will hide." She gave me an exaggerated wink over his head. "That reminds me. Edna Franklin and I were talking the other night about setting up a play date with her grandson, Gunner. Isn't that a nice idea? Poor Davey's been cooped up with only us old folks for company this summer. Wouldn't you like to play with someone your own age for once?"

David shrugged before disappearing behind the fluttering partition of bed sheets.

"Sure," I said. "It will be good for him." Even if Gunner sounded like an oddball to me with his morbid Titanic obsession, I still thought it would be wise to get David interacting with other children again. Perhaps his fascination with his dinosaur playmates would wane. Maybe by the time kindergarten started, the phase would have run its course. (Unless he turned out to be a late bloomer like me—four more years of this was inconceivable!)

"Excellent! Edna will be so pleased," Duffy trilled. "Oh, and Anna bean, I've been meaning to ask you to warn Davey from playing too close to my flower bed. Some of my petunias got positively trampled the other day. I'm sure it was an accident, but if you wouldn't mind reminding him to be careful."

"Of course," I said. "I'm sorry about that. It won't happen again." Their backyard was a veritable Garden of Eden of uninterrupted grass for him to play on, and of course, my son had chosen the one forbidden flower bed to clomp through. I raised my voice. "David. You heard Grandma Duffy. You need to be extra careful around her plants, okay? No setting foot in the flower bed."

"Okay," he sang out from behind the clothesline, and my grandmother seemed satisfied.

I turned around, covered my eyes with my palms, and started counting to ten out loud. I could hear Duffy creaking up the patio steps and closing the door behind her, the soft *thwack* of the damp sheets as the wind kicked them up, and David's giggle not far away. "Nine. Ten. Ready or not, here I come!" I called.

At the end of the clothesline, on the far right, I could see David's silhouette through my grandparents' ivory, queen-size sheets. His dingy sneakers poked out beneath the hem.

"Where could he be?" I asked myself aloud theatrically. "Is he inside the shed?" I poked my head through the shed's open door, which housed the lawnmower, some extra lawn chairs, gardening equipment, and miscellaneous tractor parts. "Nope. Not in here! Well, I'm stumped. Where else could he be?"

I marched back to the row of sheets, swelling like sails. "Could he be hiding behind here?" I raised the edge of my rosebud top sheet, peeked behind, and let it drop. "No. I guess not. Oh, no. Is he lost? What if I never find him?" I pretended to cry. More giggles came from behind the ivory sheet at the end of the clothesline.

I lowered my voice an octave, doing a version of my Wolfy voice, which was just about the only male voice I could impersonate. "Where are you, David?" I growled. "I'm going to *find* you…I'm going to *get* you…"

I dramatically flapped David's navy blue sheet and found myself face to face with yellow eyes so close to mine I could see a sliver of myself in their narrow black pupils. My nose was inches away from a ridged snout. He huffed through his nostrils, and a warm, foul-smelling current wafted toward me. King Rex.

I almost screamed my lungs out but was able to repress the sound into more of a panicked yelp. I stumbled backward, landing pain-fully on my tailbone in the grass. The sheet came unpinned, hanging crookedly like a door off its hinge. The Tyrannosaurus rex stepped through this new gaping space, looming over me. I scuttled on my hands and backside until my head collided with the deck railing. My heart was jittering in my chest like a wind-up toy, and useless tears were leaking down the side of my nose. I had felt its *breath*.

"Mommy?" David called tentatively, still in his hiding place. I tried to reply, but the fright and my fall had knocked the wind out of me. I hastily wiped at the moisture on my cheeks. David's disembodied head appeared between the sheets. His lips were trembling as if he were about to sob. But there was something else wrong. As he stepped between the sheets, his body seemed to have a shadowy aura around it.

I shook my head, refocusing my eyes, but it was still there. A black corona radiating from my son, head to toe. Like Peter Pan's legendary shadow. But then, just as suddenly, the dark wreath slipped away and sank to the ground. King Rex let out a shrill, reverberating scream, as hair-raising as a lion's roar with the otherworldliness of a peacock's cry. My toes curled involuntarily into the grass. I was sure the whole neighborhood had heard the dinosaur's roar and would descend on our backyard any minute now to see what all the ruckus was about.

But instead of turning on me or David as I feared, the T-rex pivoted on his taloned feet and pursued the shadowy substance with lightning speed. Weeple lumbered from behind the bed sheets and set off after the mysterious aura as well. They chased it to the tree line and then continued to stand there, bodies heaving with exertion and their backs and tails turned to us. Guarding the boundary. Guarding it from *what* I did not know.

I dragged myself into a sitting position. My lower back was sore, bruised probably, and I was certain I'd have a nice bump on the back of my head too. I inhaled, counted silently to ten, and then exhaled. I still felt hysterical, so I counted to one hundred. David crumpled wordlessly beside me, and I pulled his head to my chest. I knew I should try to compose myself for his sake and say something to dispel the terror we had both just witnessed, but my hands and knees were trembling and my mouth felt parched. I swallowed hard.

I had just learned three things. One: the dinosaurs and the black smoke were separate beings. I had assumed from the start that the two were entwined, that the shadowy plume heralded the dinosaurs' arrival in a way. But now, I realized that I had been mistaken and they were two very separate creations.

Two: some sort of psychological drama I didn't understand was playing out in David's imagination. He seemed almost haunted by the black shadow, but what did the shadow represent? The dinosaurs appeared intent on keeping it away from him, as though they were in fact his bodyguards.

And three: I couldn't do this anymore. Couldn't live with the frequent shots of adrenaline. Couldn't live with the fear of a dinosaur behind every door or, in this case, bed sheet. Couldn't deal with ominous shadows threatening my son. It wasn't normal. It wasn't right.

Something needed to be done. We needed to meet with a professional, although I wasn't sure into which category this would fit. I doubted I would find a listing in the phonebook. A child psychiatrist slash paleontologist?

Dr. Nicole Rosen was not what I had expected at all. She didn't look old enough to have graduated from high school, let alone medical school. In her oversized white coat and black wedge sandals, she looked like a little girl playing dress-up. But she was sharp. Sharper than David's regular pediatrician in Milwaukee, Dr. Bob Komanski, who had been practicing medicine for over forty years and was stone deaf.

"At David's age, imaginary playmates are incredibly common," Dr. Rosen said, crossing her legs at the ankle, revealing a coral-colored pedicure and a toe ring. A slender, silver toe ring. Did people really still wear those? "In the past, the literature used to treat them as some kind of warning sign of a child in crisis, but recent studies show that about two-thirds of children have an imaginary friend by the age of seven, and those children even turn out to be better communicators and more creative in general."

I'd found a clinic in Glacial Hills affiliated with the medical complex in Milwaukee we normally visited, so I knew they'd have all David's medical records in their computer system. Unlike her other, probably older and more experienced colleagues, Dr. Rosen was able to squeeze us in within the week, and I was too antsy to wait. Apparently I couldn't make an appointment directly with a child psychiatrist; I needed a referral from a family medicine doctor or pediatrician so they could rule out any other health problems first. I figured it couldn't hurt for David to have a check-up anyway because he'd be starting kindergarten in a month and would need to be current on all his immunizations.

David had been measured (43 inches) and weighed (40.7 pounds). Dr. Rosen had physically examined him from head to foot, and when she'd gotten to his toes, she had pointed out a bruised toenail I hadn't seen before.

"What happened here?" she asked David, lightly pressing the blackened nail of his big toe, which caused him to squirm and let out a small yelp. "Did something fall on your foot?"

He shook his head and looked up at me helplessly, but I couldn't explain it to her either. With all of David's running around barefoot, I wasn't too surprised that he had a black-and-blue toenail. What surprised me was that he hadn't complained about the pain or cried when it first happened. He was a tough kid. Maybe too tough.

"Well, the good news is I don't think it will fall off," Dr. Rosen said briskly. *Whew.* I hadn't known that was a possibility. "But I think it will take a few more weeks for the discoloration to totally go away." Then she had typed a few additional notes on the computer in the examining room and stood up, clearly on her way out the door.

"Any other questions or concerns I can help you with today?" she had asked, hand on doorknob.

"Yes," I'd said. "Actually, there is one." She had reluctantly sat back down, and I had explained to her about the recent appearance of the dinosaur duo and the shadow they chased. Not their literal appearance to me, of course—I didn't want her to call a psych consult on her patient's wacko mother—but their appearance in David's life.

After rattling off her statistics, Dr. Rosen assured me that childhood imaginary friends weren't an indication of mental illness. I found myself letting out a breath I hadn't realized I'd been holding. The fear that had been with me since Patrick's diagnosis—the hereditary threat of bipolar disorder—was always present in the back of my mind, and though the fear would persist until my son was much older, at least these imaginary friends were not warning signs of it. There was still hope.

"Do you know why kids create imaginary friends?" I asked. It had been the question preoccupying my thoughts lately.

Dr. Rosen jiggled her foot, the one wearing the toe ring. "There are a lot of possible reasons, actually. Usually it's linked to some kind of transition in the child's life: the birth of a sibling, the first day of school, a household move. But it could just be that the child is bored and wants a new way to be entertained."

It certainly was a time of transition for both of us right now. The move from Milwaukee to a new home, new environment, new routine, and new group of people. I wondered if he missed Stacy and her kids, who were much older than David but really sweet with him, and the handful of friends he'd made in preschool and on the T-ball team. I wondered if he missed our tiny apartment which smelled like cat pee whenever it rained and was so close to the railroad tracks you could practically set your watch by the Amtrak timetable.

"We just moved to Salsburg, which is when the dinosaurs first showed up, but otherwise he seems to be adjusting well," I said. "So it's probably not a warning sign of a child in crisis, like you said," I added hopefully.

She cocked her head with a slight frown. "Is there any reason to suspect David is in crisis right now?"

"I don't think so. It's just, well, dinosaurs and shadows seem kind of scary, don't you think?" I knitted my fingers together on my lap and glanced at David, who was busy sliding the colored beads of an abacus across each row. Only the most educational toys at the doctor's office, of course.

She studied him, too. "That depends. Does David seem afraid of them?"

"Not the dinosaurs, but the shadow…" It was hard to describe the complicated relationship both the dinosaurs and David seemed to have with the black smoke without revealing I could see their actions. "From what he says about them," I started carefully, "I think part of the dinosaurs' job is to keep the shadow away."

"Hmm." I didn't like the sound of that *hmm*. Dr. Rosen spun in her chair and typed something in David's chart. "You mentioned moving recently. Do you and David live alone? With his father? Other family members?"

"With my grandparents," I said. "Temporarily. I'm a single mom. David's father isn't in the picture. Hasn't been since he was a baby."

She dragged her eyes from the computer screen to level them at me. They were a pretty dark blue with curly lashes. They were the kind of eyes that inspired immediate trust. "And you feel safe there?"

I laughed, taken aback. "Yes, totally."

"And David feels safe there too?"

"Yes," I said. I knew she was probably required by law to ask these questions, but I was starting to feel unsettled.

"And before your move, where did you live?"

"In an apartment in Milwaukee, just the two of us."

She scrolled rapidly through David's chart and fired off a list of questions at me. "Any changes in appetite? Increased irritability? Mood swings? Trouble sleeping? Any injuries?" She double-clicked the mouse with every "no" I gave her.

"All right then. I'd like to talk to David now, one-on-one, so if you wouldn't mind stepping outside for just a bit…"

"Step outside? Why?" I exclaimed. "He's only four years old! He needs his mother with him."

David looked up from his abacus, apparently reacting to the panicked tone of my voice.

"It will just be for a few minutes, Ms. Jennings," Dr. Rosen said in an infuriatingly calm tone. She rolled her stool toward David with a big smile plastered on her face. "David, your mom is going to be right outside this door, so that we can get to know each other a little better. I just have a few questions for you about your dinosaurs. I'd love for you to tell me about them." She turned back to me with a look meant to drive me from the room.

When I opened the exam room door and stepped into the hallway, the nurse who had ushered us into the room and taken David's vitals gave me a wide grin. But when David didn't come out as well, and I shut the door behind me, her expression changed to a hard, wary one. My face flushed, and my stomach felt queasy. In her mind, and apparently Dr. Rosen's too, I was not to be trusted. A suspected child abuser maybe. I turned away from her and pretended to study a poster on the wall about the benefits of breastfeeding. The door was either soundproof or Dr. Rosen was talking very quietly.

With each minute that passed, it seemed more and more likely that I would throw up. The rational part of my brain knew I hadn't done anything wrong and they were just taking precautions like they would with any child. But the insecure part of my brain worried that David would blurt out some of my less proud parenting moments, and this, combined with the troubling imaginary friends, would be enough for them to take him away from me.

I was seriously regretting bringing him for a check-up today when Dr. Rosen cracked open the door. "All done in here," she said cheerfully. "Why don't you come back in so we can wrap things up? Please, have a seat."

David looked totally calm sitting near the basket of books and toys on the floor.

Dr. Rosen crossed her arms, which looked like they were drowning in the sleeves of her white coat. "Overall, I'm not too concerned about David's overactive imagination. I think it's a perfectly normal, healthy phase for him to be going through right now with all the changes in his life."

It was the exact thing I'd been praying to hear, but it brought only a hollow kind of relief. Because Dr. Rosen knew only half of the story. She could make this pronouncement in the clinic's sterile, climate-controlled exam room, but if she stepped outdoors into the merciless heat, into the cloaking shadows and glaring sunlight, and could lay eyes on the terrors of David's imagination like I could? Would she consider my ability a "perfectly normal, healthy phase" for me as well? Or would she write a psychiatric referral for me so fast that it would make my head would spin?

She'd also lost some of my confidence by suspecting me of harming David or allowing him to live in a dangerous home, which was so contrary to the way I had struggled to remove him from Patrick's poisonous moods that it made my eye sockets pulse with a dull anger.

"Now if there are any concerning changes in his mood or behavior, you might consider meeting with a child psychiatrist. I can definitely refer you to one if you'd like to explore that option. I also have a book I can lend you that I think you will find very informative and reassuring. If you can wait here for a minute, I'll get it for you."

The book was a thin, glossy publication called *Imaginary Friends, Your Child, and You.* The cover featured an outrageously happy-looking mom with her outrageously happy-looking daughter hugging a teddy bear with a huge red bow tie, sitting together on a bed.

It looked about as helpful for my situation as a child's water pistol would be in the face of a wildfire, but I thanked Dr. Rosen anyway and slipped the book into my purse.

"More coffee?" Lorraine Schiff asked. She'd been hovering around my table for the past hour, and I knew it was because she was curious about what I was doing there with a battered leather portfolio rather than because she needed to clear my table for other customers. It was mid-afternoon on a Tuesday, and there were only three other customers in Ruby's Diner.

"Sure," I said, mostly because I'd turned down her other five offers of refills and I wanted her to stop asking. "You don't have any almond macarons, do you? Or crème brûlée?" Maybe if enough customers started asking, Carly would be given a little more creative license in the kitchen.

She looked baffled. "No, we don't. But if you're interested in dessert, we have fresh cheesecake, walnut brownies, and ice cream sundaes. The special of the day is berry cobbler."

The berry cobbler actually did sound delicious, but I couldn't justify spending money on a high-calorie treat for myself when I couldn't even afford new swim trunks or shoes for David.

"No, thanks. I think I'll just stick with coffee." At least that was only one dollar and bottomless. Lorraine snuck one more peek at my leather portfolio before drifting away to pester more customers.

After weeks of indiscriminately sending out my resume, I'd finally gotten an interview at a chiropractic office in Port Ambrose. I'd cast a wide net—some businesses in the Milwaukee area, some in the Salsburg/Lawrenceville area. It somehow seemed easier than making a conscious decision about where to live, like I was leaving it to chance. If the job was in a fifteen-mile radius of Salsburg, I used my grandparents' address on my resume; if the job was closer to Milwaukee, I used my old address. I figured if any job-related correspondence ended up there, Stacy would let me know.

But the interview had been atrocious, and I had no hope of getting a good news call from Dr. Lippmann or his bookkeeping, jealous wife Mindy. As soon as I'd walked through the door and Mindy had eyed my cleavage and measured how many inches my skirt fell above my knee, I knew there was no way I would get hired if she had any say in the matter. Poor Dr. Lippmann had tried to interject easy questions into the interview as Mindy had assaulted me with a relentless stream of incredibly technical questions about chiropracting or chiropractory, or whatever the heck the verb or noun would be, and a medical records computer system I had no experience with before.

"We have several more interviews this week, but we'll be sure to call you if we're interested," Mindy had said in a smug way that let me know they were very much not.

Winston and Duffy would be disappointed on my behalf, so I was prolonging the inevitable. But the longer I waited, the more optimistic they'd probably become, thinking maybe the office had hired me on the spot and was having me fill out paperwork or something. Just one more cup of coffee, and I would leave to shatter their hopes.

I unzipped the leather portfolio that enclosed my résumé, list of references, a pen and notepad, and *Imaginary Friends, Your Child, and You*. I had thought I would maybe have a few minutes to peruse the book before my interview, but they'd been ready for me immediately. Now I opened the book to its first chapter.

Self-Expression. *You can tell a lot about your child by the form his or her imaginary companion takes. For example, superheroes often reveal the desire to have special powers or more control over his or her life. If your child's imaginary friend is attached to a stuffed animal, such as a teddy bear, it might indicate a need for security and comfort. Whether your child's imaginary friend is a talking dog or a "shadow man" (refer to Chapter Nine), however, what is most important is how your child relates to his or her playmate. Listen carefully to the way your child describes his or her friend.*

Does your child claim, like Mariah D., age five, that her imaginary friend, Muffin, is an only child with no brothers or sisters? This might indicate that your child is trying out the idea of what it would be like not to have siblings. Imaginary companions allow children to try on alternate identities and explore other realities. It can be a great learning experience in empathy. Though Mariah D. initially stated, "Muffin is the happiest girl in the world" because she had no siblings, only a few weeks later, she showed a more mature perspective by saying, "Muffin says she's sad because she doesn't have a little brother like me. I told her we could share." Therefore, an imaginary friend can be a mouthpiece for the child's own concerns, desires, or developing opinions and beliefs about the world.

I marked my place in the book with my finger and looked up. This, of course, was the most frustrating part of being able to see David's imaginary friends—it was like watching a silent film. Maybe he was using them as his "mouthpiece," but I still had no idea what he was trying to say through them. I took a tiny sip of my coffee and twirled the pen between my fingers. Without intentionally setting out to do so, I pressed the pen's tip to the notepad's blank page and started to sketch.

King Rex's curved spine and musculature took shape under my pen. I scribbled in a few scales and charted out the spiky lines of his teeth with a few flicks of my wrist. It was hard to effectively capture his eyes in black and white, and even harder, with just a ballpoint pen, to shade in the area where the black shadow had lurked. I longed for the full range of colors, textures, and effects my oil pastels could produce, but this would have to do for now.

I tilted the drawing up, scrutinizing it to see if I'd accurately depicted the moment emblazoned in my mind—the terrifying seconds just after King Rex and I had come face to face and he had roared and sprung after the shadowy figure. I followed the impression of the pen lines with my fingertips, looking for a clue. What was it that David's dinosaurs were protecting him from, and was it a common childhood fear or something more concerning?

"More coffee?" Lorraine asked. I looked up to see her peering over my shoulder at my sketch. Her penciled-on eyebrows were so high they almost disappeared into her ash-blond hair. I flipped the portfolio closed, but it was clearly too late.

Great. Just what I needed, another rumor about me: the crazy girl who sat alone drinking coffee and drawing dinosaurs.

CHAPTER TEN

I didn't get a call from Lippmann Chiropractic, but I did get a call from my old neighbor, Stacy. Not about any mailed responses to my resume, but about my rocking chair. Her husband, Brett, had gotten a job up in Rhinelander, and she wanted to know if I wanted to come and get the chair before they moved so far away. She called on a Friday, and they were packing up and heading out that Sunday. Meteorologists were predicting record high temperatures that weekend, and driving all the way to Milwaukee by myself in the stifling hot minivan sounded about as pleasant as a root canal. Winston's car was too small for hauling a rocking chair, and besides, he and Duffy both had plans for that Saturday. Duffy had her "blue rinse brigade" ladies booked all day, and Winston had hired himself out to fix some farm machinery on the Larsons' farm. As far as I could see, that left only one other person who I could ask to help me. Someone I knew who had a truck.

Jamie Presswood.

It was after dinner, seven o'clock, and the day's heat didn't show any sign of relenting. Throughout the neighborhood, sprinklers gracefully bowed in timed precision on front lawns. Practicing what I would say in my head, I hastened past the wishing well and across the green no-man's land that connected my grandparents' yard to the Presswoods'. I had prepared myself to knock on their door and catch up a little with Wendy before casually asking to speak with her son. I had not prepared myself for the contingency that Jamie would already be outside. Shirtless.

On the driveway sat a pile of mulch about the size of a small elephant. Jamie stood in front of it, dressed only in khaki cargo shorts and flip-flops, shoveling mulch into a wheelbarrow. He didn't have the scrawny physique of a fifteen-year-old that I remembered; instead, his shoulders were wide and sturdy, his biceps were thick and shapely, and his chest and stomach muscles were well-defined. As he dug into the pile with his shovel and scooped more mulch into the wheelbarrow, his back muscles rippled and glistened with sweat. I bit my lower lip. He didn't notice me until the wheelbarrow was full and he lifted the wooden handles to swivel it in my direction.

"Anna!" He was startled, to say the least; he made my name sound like a curse. He ran his fingers through his damp, wavy hair and frowned at me like I was the last person on earth he'd expected to see instead of his next-door neighbor. "What do you need?"

I prickled at his automatic assumption that my visit meant I needed something from him, but of course it did. "What are you doing?" I asked stupidly. This wasn't going how I'd envisioned it at all.

Jamie glanced down at the wheelbarrow, the shovel, and the mulch pile, and then back up at me. It was the kind of look David often gave me when I asked him something exceedingly obvious. "I'm putting down a new layer of mulch on our flower beds."

"It smells good." *Ah!* I needed to stop with the kindergartener observations! But to my surprise, the corners of Jamie's mouth curved upward into a tiny grin.

"It's my favorite too. White cedar. It's got the added benefit of keeping the mosquitoes away." He started pushing the wheelbarrow down the driveway. When he turned and saw that I was still standing in place, he waved impatiently at me to follow him. We stopped at the front of the yard where a flowerbed shaped like a half moon was bordered by blue and gray river rocks. It contained all kinds of flowers and plants I didn't know the names of.

He punched the sharp edge of his shovel into the mulch pile, lifted it from the wheelbarrow, and then gently sprinkled the contents over the earth, avoiding the plants. The braided muscles in his arms leaped and danced with the movement. He repeated this process several more times. I tried not to look as utterly hypnotized as I felt.

"You want it at least two inches thick," he said. "That way it keeps in the moisture and keeps out the weeds." The wheelbarrow was nearly empty now, and Jamie squatted down to smooth out the clumps of mulch that were spread too thickly. "Can you thin out that patch over there?" he asked.

I stared down at him. "With my bare hands?"

Expression sober, Jamie said, "Well, it is highly unorthodox, but you could use your butt if you wanted."

Well, then. So even if he didn't look like my dopey childhood friend, he still had the same maturity level. I punched him in his very muscular arm.

Jamie pretended not to notice. He reached into his cargo shorts pocket, produced a pair of leather work gloves, and handed them to me. "Here. So you don't dirty your pretty little hands."

"Thank you." The gloves were stiff from sweat and dirt and about three times too big for my hands, but I slipped them on anyway. I crouched down at the opposite end from where Jamie was working and started sifting through the mulch. Up close, it smelled even more fragrant. It reminded me of the cedar hangers Duffy kept in the coat closet, so that when you opened the door and pulled out your winter jacket, it smelled like a forest.

"So, what's going on?" Jamie asked. His naked torso was only a foot away. At this distance, I could see that an angry red scar, about the width and length of an earthworm, curved around his right shoulder socket. I had the sudden impulse to take off my glove and trace my fingers over it.

Instead, I gently patted the mulch around the base of a bush with flowers that looked like a hundred bluish-purple butterflies all resting together. Had Jamie and his friends talked about me after I'd left the lake house? I wished that *he* had sought *me* out after his big confession instead of the other way around. Or did he think it was my turn now to extend an olive branch? I felt presumptuous and bumbling, which were new and not very welcome emotions for me. "I was wondering if you'd do me a favor."

Jamie dusted his hands off on his shorts and stood up. "Oh, yeah? What kind of favor?"

"I left some furniture in Milwaukee. Only one piece of furniture, actually—a chair. My minivan's not up to the task, and Winston's car isn't big enough, so I was wondering if you'd let me use your truck." I bit my lip. The request had sounded so much more reasonable in my head.

Jamie raised his thick eyebrows. "You want to drive my truck?"

"No," I said. "I want *you* to drive your truck."

Jamie laid the shovel in the empty wheelbarrow and started pushing it back up the driveway. He didn't look back or invite me to follow this time. "When?" he called.

"Ideally, tomorrow," I called back, realizing then what unbelievably short notice I was giving him. He was probably scheduled to do landscaping stuff for his business, or maybe since it was supposed to be one of the hottest Saturdays of the summer, he had plans to go to Long Lake or the beach at Port Ambrose.

He didn't say anything for what felt like a long time, just continued to shovel mulch, and I was about to tell him to forget it when he finally responded. "Fine. I'll pick you up at seven o'clock tomorrow morning."

"Eight thirty," I countered. "I've got to drop David off at a play date at eight."

Jamie glanced at me over his shoulder, with an expression somewhere between exasperation and amusement. "Whatever you say, Anna."

I dropped my chin so he wouldn't see my triumphant smile. "Great," I said casually and stepped toward my grandparents' house. "Thanks. See you then."

Edna had been delighted when I'd called her yesterday to ask if it was her Saturday with her grandson and if we could set up that play date she'd suggested. But all the bribery and persuasion in the world couldn't convince David that his dinosaurs need not come along on said play date. King Rex and Weeple watched us, hunkered down in the front yard like the two largest, ugliest garden statues ever made, as David and I went down the same conversational path we'd already been down many times before.

"You'll have a friend to play with at the Franklins' house. A boy your own age. You won't need to have other friends along."

"But I want to play with my dino-suss."

"You can play with your dinosaurs whenever, but you don't always get a chance to play with another kid. You'll have a lot of fun with Gunner. He's going into kindergarten just like you in the fall. Besides, King Rex and Weeple won't fit in the minivan."

David eyed the Dodge Caravan parked in the driveway. "They can run."

"It's too far away for them to run."

His lower lip pooched out as he considered the minivan again. "King Rex can fit."

Fantastic. Of the dinosaur duo, the carnivore with the murderous eyes and teeth was the one I least wanted to send along to an unsuspecting household. But I knew it was a battle I couldn't exactly win. Even if I forbid King Rex from getting into the minivan, how could I stop him from materializing at the Franklins' house whenever David wished it? Transport was kind of a moot point with imaginary friends.

"I expect you to be on your best behavior," I said when we pulled up to their house. I turned to face the backseat, where David was buckled up and King Rex was ridiculously crammed into the trunk space like a hairless, leathery Doberman. "David, are you listening? King Rex, I'm talking to you, too. Be nice, share toys, say please and thank you, and absolutely no chasing, roaring, or biting. You're here as guests, so be good." Oh my god—was this really my life? I rested my forehead against the steering wheel for a second.

David took my hand as we walked up the brick pathway to Edna and Chuck's house, King Rex staggering a few paces behind us. David wasn't usually the hand-holding type unless he wanted to pull me along more quickly, so I suspected he was nervous. A boy with orange hair and dark freckles flung open the door before we could even ring the doorbell.

"Hi. I'm Gunner Nathaniel Rasmussen." He articulated loudly and carefully as though he feared we might both be dim-witted.

"Hi, Gunner. I'm Anna, and this is David. Is your grandma home?"

Edna's head poked around the door, as though she, too, had been waiting eagerly for our arrival. "So glad you could both come. When Duffy mentioned that David's birthday was the day after Gunner's, I just knew they were destined to be friends." She beamed down at the two boys and then up at me, corralling us into her house with her bony arms. "And can you believe that they'll both be starting kindergarten next month? Lord have mercy, where has the time gone? It seems like just yesterday that I was sending my little Joy off to kindergarten, and now she's a mom herself and enrolling my precious grandson at Port Ambrose Elementary. Have you decided if you'll be sending David there as well? Gunner has Mrs. Banaszynski—all the kids call her Mrs. B—and I hear she's fabulous."

It was hard to imagine Duffy and Edna as good friends. How two such rapid-fire, tangential talkers could hold a conversation without tripping all over each other was beyond me. Perhaps one monopolized the discussion for an hour and then they switched. Or maybe they simply talked over each other, totally oblivious and content.

"I haven't decided yet," I admitted, adding it to my ever-growing list of worries. Hopefully, kindergarten enrollment would be open for at least a few more weeks until I could secure a job. I hated the thought of having to uproot David from a school once he had already settled in somewhere.

"Well, I'm sure there's still plenty of time," Edna said, but her pinched face betrayed her true opinion. "I just made a pitcher of iced tea. Would you like a glass?"

"Oh, I'm so sorry. I wish I could stay." I looked down at my watch. Eight twenty-two already. "I have an errand in Milwaukee today, but I should be back by lunchtime."

Edna looked incredibly put out, like she'd been expecting us to drink iced tea and gossip the whole time Gunner and David played. I could only imagine what kind of dirt she'd been hoping to get from me. "Oh. I didn't realize. Gunner, I bet David would like to see Grandpa's collection of ships-in-bottles."

At the mention of the collection, David's face brightened and his grasp on my hand relaxed. "That sounds really cool," I said. "Why don't you go check it out?" I squeezed him against my hip and then released him. He followed Gunner down the hallway, with King Rex creeping along behind them as though trying to be as small and inconspicuous as possible, which, as could be imagined, was *not very*. My hopes rose like little effervescent bubbles; maybe this play date would be even better for David than I had imagined. Maybe it was what he'd needed all summer. I chose to ignore the galling voice in my head pointing out that even with six-year-old Jamie as my next-door neighbor, I had continued to play with Leah Nola.

"Remember, boys, look with your eyes, not your fingers!" Edna called after them.

"I really appreciate your watching him," I said and gave her David's backpack and my cell phone number on a slip of paper. "I'd be happy to return the favor sometime."

Edna smoothed her auburn hair. "Of course. Well, enjoy your trip to the city."

Jamie's red pickup was idling in my grandparents' driveway when I returned. Inside the air-conditioned cab, he was fidgeting with his cell phone. His face was clean-shaven, but he was wearing his all-black ensemble again. Black jeans, black T-shirt, black leather wrist cuff with silver studs.

I buckled my seat belt and glanced up at the house as we backed out of the driveway. Duffy was standing at the front door in her purple metallic apron. I gave her a little wave, but if she could see me, she didn't wave back. Jamie asked for my old address, and when I told him, he seemed to know exactly where we were headed. The radio was turned off, and a cool, awkward silence settled between us.

"Why Demeter Landscaping Services?" I burst out. "Why not Presswood?"

Jamie shrugged as though it hadn't occurred to him, as though naming his business after the Greek goddess of agriculture had been a thoughtless accident. "It's kind of embarrassing, actually. Ever since middle school I've been a Greek mythology freak." He turned onto the county highway that would lead us out of Salsburg. "I think I liked the idea of this wise council of beings sitting up on a cloud planning out your fate for you, and if you didn't like it or something went wrong, you could just pray to a specific god or goddess, make a sacrifice, and everything would magically work out."

"That does sound kind of nice," I agreed. "Except for the sacrifice part." I slipped off my sandals and arranged myself cross-legged in the seat. I recognized the back of the wooden welcome sign as we flew by it, and then the Milwaukee River raced alongside us for a while. "So how is your business going?"

Jamie glanced over at me, taking in my cozy position and lack of shoes. "My outlook changes hourly. Do you want my cautiously optimistic answer or my dark, despairing answer?"

"Let's go with dark and despairing."

"I'm worried," he said and blew out a sigh. "Right now, I'm just mowing, planting, and weeding, which doesn't really pay the bills; it just takes the cash out of neighbor kids' pockets. But I know if I can just get a few bigger projects and prove myself, I'll get some referrals, and business will pick up. I put a bid in on a brick patio in Lawrenceville that I'm hoping to get to build because I'm guessing I'm the lowest estimate by a long shot." He clenched and unclenched his hands on the steering wheel. "I figure I'll give the company at least a year before calling it quits. This fall, Marshall's going to try to get me in at the printing factory, and I'll stay there indefinitely if I have to. I'll do whatever it takes to keep the house and take care of my mom."

I examined the peeling red nail polish on my toenails. My own financial woes seemed insignificant next to Jamie's. I didn't have a family home to lose. I didn't have the crushing weight of medical bills for an ailing mother. I had grandparents who were willing to take in my son and me when I had nowhere else to turn. Who did Jamie have to turn to?

Without meaning to, I found myself mentally cataloging the ways he and I would never work as more than friends. We were two people with major responsibilities that demanded all of our time and energy, responsibilities that limited our choices and defined our day-to-day lives. Though not necessarily in a bad way, I reminded myself, thinking of David's flushed, earnest face as he listened to my bedtime stories. But how would Jamie ever have time for a serious relationship with his landscaping business and Wendy's care? And how would I ever find someone to whom I could entrust my heart, and more importantly, my most precious possession—David? It seemed unthinkable.

"I hope you get to build that patio," I said. "And I hope business picks up. If I hear anyone talking about needing help with their yard, I'll be sure to give them your name."

Jamie gave me a wry smile. "Thanks."

"How's your mom?" I asked.

"She's fine." He leaned forward and turned the air conditioning down a notch. "A little depressed because she can't do all the things she used to do. But her doctor says she's in remission right now."

"That's great," I said. "Does that mean she's getting better?"

"MS isn't like cancer. It doesn't go away. But there are periods of remission, and then there are relapses." He turned his head to examine a dilapidated barn. "We're not going to talk about my pathetic life all the way to Milwaukee, are we? Tell me about you."

"Oh, so you'd rather hear about *my* pathetic life?"

"Yes, please. Maybe it will make me feel better about myself." We both laughed a little.

Despite my best intentions to present myself as a competent, successful woman who'd had only a minor setback in life, I found myself revealing way too much information to Jamie. His gentle brown eyes encouraged me somehow. I told him about Lakeview Dermatology's downsizing, closing the clinic location I worked at, and my losing my job. I told him about selling my bed and sleeping on the couch so

I could pay our electric bill. I told him about selling my couch and sleeping on the floor to pay for groceries. I told him about my fear of overstaying my welcome in my grandparents' house, my haphazard job search, and my inability to make up my mind about what to do or where to go next. I told him that I was worried I'd never amount to anything.

"*Amounting* to something," Jamie said. "I've always thought that was a weird expression."

My incessant talking had gotten us all the way to Milwaukee. We were on the zoo interchange, only a few short miles away from the exit we would take to get to my old apartment.

"It makes it sound like life is an equation," he continued. "If you do a, b, and c, you will be happy and successful. You will *amount* to something." He turned to look at me, his voice suddenly low and as soft as a caress. "But you already *are* something, Anna. You always have been."

I tried not to show how much his words affected me. I took a deep breath and focused on the billboards on the side of the road. I hadn't been gone for even two months, and already many of them had been changed. Some of them advertised the upcoming Wisconsin State Fair in August. When we pulled onto South Avenue, I was surprised to see all the medians planted with red and purple flowers. Summer was still marching on in Milwaukee even if David and I weren't there.

"Which house is it?" Jamie asked, as we crawled down 57th Street.

"The green and white bungalow on the left," I said.

"Right. The one with the moving truck parked in front. That would make sense." He grinned sheepishly.

Stacy and Brett were arguing in the detached garage when we strolled up the sidewalk.

"It's ugly, and it hasn't worked in years! We're either going to junk it here, or we're going to junk it once we get to Rhinelander, so I say we junk it here and save ourselves the trouble of hauling it," Stacy said. She was a tall blonde with a trim figure; she'd always liked to joke that she could've been mistaken for my older sister.

"I've had it since high school," Brett said and held up the item presumably in question. It was a neon-lit sign for a beer company, the kind that hung in bar windows. "I think one of the tubes needs to be replaced, and if that's the case, I think it would look really cool in our new rec room."

Stacy huffed out a heavy sigh. "You said that five years ago when we moved here, and you've still never fixed it. Don't you think it's time to just let it go?"

Jamie shot me an amused look. I had a feeling that the argument would go on for a lot longer if we didn't interrupt.

"Hey, guys!" I called out, and Stacy literally sprinted from the garage to crush me in a hug.

"You have no idea how happy I am to see you, Anna! I've missed you and David so much!" She pulled back to squeeze my upper arms and spotted Jamie over my shoulder. "Well, well. Who's this?"

"An old friend," I answered hurriedly, lest she get ideas. "Jamie."

"He's *hot*," she whispered in my ear before pulling away to shake his offered hand. Brett, who'd been a burly, muscular football player in high school and was now a burly, muscular construction worker, came out of the garage to say hello as well. After the introductions were through, I noticed him slink away with the neon sign tucked under his arm, to put in the moving truck, I suspected.

"Where are the kids?" I asked.

Stacy squinted toward the house as though she had X-ray vision that allowed her to see through the siding. "Breanne is at her friend's house, saying her goodbyes, and lamenting what horribly unfair parents she has. And Nick is still cleaning out his closet, I think." She gave an exaggerated shudder. "You don't want to see some of the things that kid's unearthed in there. Where's your kiddo?"

"He's playing at a friend's house," I said.

"Wow, making friends already? Way to go, David." Stacy wiped a smudge of dust off her shorts and eyed Jamie appreciatively again.

Calling Gunner a "friend" was a bit of a stretch. Probably he was subjecting David and King Rex to a viewing of his Titanic documentary at that very moment.

"Yeah, we're adjusting alright to life in Salsburg," I said, testing the statement out to see if it was true.

"I'm psyched to get out of this city too," Stacy said. "The house we bought in Rhinelander comes with three acres of land, and I think it's going to be so good for the kids. I'll write down our new address, but my cell phone number will be the same, so there's no excuse not to keep in touch. You hear me, Anna?"

"Loud and clear."

Brett reappeared empty-handed and sidled up to Jamie. "Want to give me a hand with the chair? It's not heavy, but you can drop the tailgate for me, and I can help you tie it down." They walked inside the house together.

"He's really cute," Stacy gushed once they were out of earshot. "Are you two seeing each other?"

"No," I protested. "We're just friends. He's my grandparents' next-door neighbor, and we've known each other since we were little kids. He's practically my brother."

"I think the lady doth protest too much." Stacy batted her eyelashes.

"Stacy—"

"Alright, I'll shut up. Anyway, I have something important to tell you." She motioned for me to follow her to the tiny backyard. The yellowish grass was still pitted with little craters from David's digging phase. "I didn't say anything on the phone because I didn't want to alarm you—"

"What? What's wrong?" A swift range of horrible scenarios flashed before my eyes. Stacy had cancer. Brett was cheating on her. She was cheating on Brett. My last rent check had bounced, and a collection agency was going to come after me.

"I'm sorry. I know how upsetting this will be," Stacy said. "Patrick stopped by a week ago."

CHAPTER ELEVEN

"Patrick? Patrick stopped by here?" I sat down on the grimy, bird poop-stained picnic table. I tried to take a deep breath, but it felt like something was caught in my throat.

"Yeah. He knocked on the front door and asked if I knew where you guys were."

"He did? What did you say?"

"I told him it was none of his damn business and that he had no right to try to contact you with your restraining order still in effect."

God bless Stacy and her absolute fearlessness. "How did he seem?" I asked.

"I don't know," she said thoughtfully. "He was dressed nice and trying to act friendly to me, but underneath it, he seemed agitated. I just wanted to give you the heads up in case you want to report it to the police."

My heart was sinking slowly like a weighted corpse in a lake. I gripped the picnic table's wooden edge. The last time Patrick had broken the injunction was an absolute nightmare. Two years ago, I had come home from grocery shopping one evening to find him waiting for me, concealed in the shadows of the outdoor staircase, barefoot and wearing only a pair of jeans despite the 40 degree weather. Startled, I had dropped the bag of groceries I was carrying and grabbed for David's arm to pull him behind me. With the tattoos on his naked chest and arms gleaming in the moonlight, Patrick had ranted about Caravaggio, Saint Paul, and the road to Damascus in a voice not his own. I kept trying to back away from him and escape to the front of the house and Stacy's doorstep, but Patrick kept obstructing my path. Thankfully, Stacy had heard the commotion and called the police. I was also grateful for the small favor of David being too young to remember the frightening ordeal.

"He doesn't have your grandparents' address, does he?" Stacy asked, voicing my own concern.

"No, and neither do his parents. He knows they live in Salsburg though, and it's a pretty small place."

She toed a divot in the grass with her sandal. "It's probably nothing. Just one bad day off his meds. I just thought you'd want to know."

"Yeah," I said, hardly knowing what I was agreeing to. "Thank you for telling me." The feeling of vertigo I got around Patrick, or even at the mention of him, was back. His boldness in coming to the front door this time instead of waiting for me in the shadows was almost scarier in a way. It showed his brazen disregard for the injunction.

"Got the chair in the truck bed," Brett hollered triumphantly. He and Jamie joined us in the backyard. When Jamie caught sight of my face, he raised his eyebrows questioningly. I stared straight ahead at the outdoor stairs that led to the upper flat, my old apartment. *Our* old apartment. I remembered how Patrick had threatened to jump from the top landing on a few occasions. *Please, Anna. Don't make me do this.*

"Do you all want to stay for some lunch?" Brett asked. "The grill's probably around here somewhere. We could put some burgers on."

"No, no," I said. "Please don't go to any trouble for us. We actually need to get going. I've got to pick up David soon. Stacy, thanks so much for calling about the chair. We'll have to talk soon once you're all settled."

"Yes, of course." She squeezed my hand. "I'm so glad you were able to come on such short notice. And it was so nice meeting you, Jamie." She gave him a not very sly wink.

Back in the cool cabin of the truck, I wanted to be alone with my thoughts, but Jamie sensed my distress. "Is something wrong? You seem upset."

"It's nothing."

His hand drifted across the center console, like he might take mine, but it stayed there and didn't come any closer. We were quiet for a long time until we were well out of the city limits.

"So, what's the story behind the chair?" Jamie asked.

"It's the chair I rocked David in when he was a baby." I peered through the back window for the first time at the cherry wood rocking chair strapped down in the bed of the truck. It had a blue padded back and seat tied to it. "Rocking David was the only thing that soothed him for the first six months of his life."

I could tell Jamie wanted to ask more questions, but he politely held his tongue. Asking a woman about her unplanned teen pregnancy could be a touchy subject. *So when did you get knocked up? And why didn't you stay with the father? If you could go back and do things differently, would you?*

"It was Patrick's chair. His mom rocked him in it when he was a baby too. She said she wanted me to have it. For her grandson to have it. I asked a few years ago if she wanted it back, and she said no. To keep it."

"That was nice of her. Patrick is your ex-husband?"

"No. I wasn't stupid enough to get married. Just stupid enough to get pregnant."

He was silent for a long time, clearly unsure how to respond. Finally, he said, "You know I saw you once. When you were pregnant."

"Really?"

"Yeah, my junior year. I was outside, putting away some tools in our shed at night, and I saw you in your backyard. You were standing on the deck, and you were really pregnant. You had one hand on the railing and the other on your belly, and you looked so sad, like you were on the verge of tears. I thought about coming over to talk to you."

I turned to study him in profile. "Why didn't you?"

"Pride, I guess. I was still mad at you."

"I'm so sorry about that," I said, feeling the shame anew. "I wish I'd had half a brain and been a loyal friend to you."

He held up his hand between us like a peace offering. "I'm sorry, too. Obviously you were going through a lot and could've used a friend that night."

I closed my eyes briefly, remembering the night Jamie had witnessed. "I was crying because I'd found out Patrick was bipolar. He kept disappearing and he became really unreliable. Threatening. He refused to take his meds consistently." It was such a short summation of Patrick and all that he was. All that he had been to me. Bipolar. Unreliable. Threatening. But Jamie seemed to accept it for what it was.

I thought about confiding in him what Stacy had just told me, that Patrick was looking for David and me. I considered telling him about the four-year injunction against Patrick, which would be expiring this fall. But I didn't want him to view me as even more of a victim than he probably already did. And I didn't want to think about the restraining order lifting in only a few short months...unless I could somehow be granted a renewal in light of recent events. I wondered if the court would grant me an extension based on Patrick's two incidents of harassment. Maybe even a permanent restraining order? But instead of calming me, this possibility made me feel worse, like a jagged rock had lodged itself in my stomach. To be the one who settled things irrevocably, the one who determined there was no hope for Patrick to change, no chance for him to ever be in his son's life? I didn't know if I could bear the weight of that responsibility.

Jamie was slowing down in the right lane, like he was going to get off at an exit, but we were still half an hour away from Salsburg.

"What are you doing?" I asked. I could see from his fuel gauge that he still had half a tank.

"I thought maybe we could stop for a bite to eat," he said. "There's this amazing sandwich shop out here. Best hand-scooped malts in the state."

"That's a nice idea," I said, "but we really can't afford to stop. I told Edna I'd be back to pick David up by lunchtime, and it's already twelve o'clock."

"Oh, okay." Jamie flicked off his directional and slammed his foot on the accelerator. A car behind us honked and sped around us. The driver flipped us the bird as he passed.

"Maybe some other time," I said, but even as I said these words, I realized that there might not *be* another time with all of the turmoil in my life. The sharp stone in my belly felt even heavier.

"Okay."

I could tell he was disappointed, but I was suddenly desperate to lay eyes on David. Hearing about Patrick's audacity had given me the same foreboding feeling I got after watching a horror movie—that something bad was waiting for me just out of sight. As soon as I got home, I would call Abigail Gill and find out if she knew what her son was up to; from there, I would determine if the police needed to get involved again. I doubted they would find his chat with my former neighbor as concerning as I did, but at least they would document it and maybe give him a fine or something. And then if I decided to petition for a renewal, all the evidence would be on file. I slipped my feet nervously in and out of my sandals and watched the blue numbers on the dashboard clock creep higher.

"Do you mind if I make a quick call?" I asked Jamie. "Just to let the babysitter know I'm running a bit late."

He shook his head. "Of course not."

I pulled my cell phone from my purse and dialed Edna's number. "Hi, it's Anna. I just wanted to let you know I'll be there in about twenty minutes. The errand took a little longer than I expected. How did things go?"

"Terrible," Edna replied tartly. A little boy was wailing in the background; I couldn't tell if it was David or Gunner.

I flattened my ear against the phone. "What happened?"

"Your son," she hissed, "attacked my grandson."

"Attacked?" I repeated. It seemed like such a melodramatic word for the slap or push that forty-one-pound David had maybe inflicted—and even that seemed out of character. When playing with other children, David was usually generous and eager to please. The pushover type, not the aggressor. "Is Gunner okay? Did you see what happened?"

"No, I didn't," she huffed. "But it looks really bad. He's bleeding. I might have to take him to the doctor." The wailing got louder, and I could differentiate now that this was not my son's sobs but the frantic cries of an injured Gunner.

"I'm so sorry. I'll be there as soon as I can."

Bleeding? A visit to the doctor? Pictures flashed through my mind of the freckled boy, puncture wounds and cuts all over his body. It wasn't possible. There was no way. David was as gentle as a lamb, and King Rex was imaginary and therefore incapable of physically affecting anything or anyone. Right? Unless I didn't know my own son. Or unless…I dried my sweaty palms on my thigh and dredged up my hide-and-seek encounter with the T-rex and how I'd thought for just a split second that I could feel and smell his awful prehistoric breath. But that clearly had just been the result of my shock because it was one thing to see my child's imaginary friends; it was quite another to believe they might be becoming tangible… and dangerous.

When we got back to town, I hardly waited for Jamie to unload the rocking chair and carry it into the house. I thanked him profusely and then apologized just as profusely for having to take off for the Franklins' house to collect my son. Jamie just nodded. "It's fine. I get it," he said. "I hope everything is okay."

Edna opened the door with David's backpack slung over her wrist, as though she couldn't get rid of it and him fast enough. "David! Your mom's here!" she called sharply and thrust the backpack at me. He raced toward me and clung to my knees. His eyes were pink from crying, and his nose was runny. King Rex's absence felt somehow ominous.

"How is Gunner?" I asked, looking past Edna to the living room, since she clearly wasn't going to invite me in for a glass of iced tea this time. I could see Gunner sprawled out on the couch with a handheld videogame. He didn't look bloody or mangled, thank goodness.

"I think he'll be okay," Edna said grudgingly. "He's more shook up than anything else."

"Well, that's a relief." I stroked David's hair, brushing the tear-dampened strands from his eyes. He was huddled against my legs. "I'm so sorry about all of this. It's just so unlike David. I wish I knew what caused it."

She scowled at me, as though I'd just suggested Gunner had had it coming to him. "All I know is the boys were getting along just fine, making a fort in the den, when one of them started screaming. Before I could get to them, Gunner came running out with this huge mark down his neck and chest, dripping blood. He said that, out of nowhere, David jumped on him and started scratching him." She narrowed her eyes at the back of my son's head.

I doubted that version of events, especially the part about its being unprovoked, but I wasn't feeling up to going head to head with Edna. "Well, I will definitely talk to him about fighting," I said, "and he'll be punished when we get home. Has he apologized to Gunner yet?"

Edna shook her head vehemently. "Gunner, sweetheart, please come here by Gram-Gram a minute."

Gunner ambled toward the door, still playing his videogame. I could see the bright red line against his pale skin as he came closer. It wasn't a fatal dinosaur bite but it wasn't a kitty-cat scratch either. About half a centimeter wide, the scrape ran from the top of Gunner's neck to somewhere beneath the stretched-out collar of his white T-shirt. Bright pink, inflamed skin was revealed, and in one place, a few speckles of wet blood shone. The scratch ran along his jugular vein. If what Gunner said was true, David had literally gone for his throat.

I peeled David off my legs and turned him around. "Tell Gunner you're sorry for scratching him," I instructed.

"But it wasn't me," he wailed through a fresh batch of tears, trying to bury his face in the fabric of my shorts.

My stomach clenched like a fist, but I ignored it. "David," I warned, and he whimpered out an apology. Gunner cast him a glance and then walked back to the couch, his videogame revving like a racecar engine the whole way.

David's damp hair smelled like baby shampoo. He had eagerly climbed into my lap the instant he'd gotten out of his bath and spotted the rocking chair Jamie had set in my room. I pressed my nose to his scalp, and together we rocked.

"Tell me what happened today," I murmured into his ear.

He'd already had his lecture on the drive home about never scratching or hitting someone and using his words instead. He'd been so tearful I hadn't been able to get a straight answer out of him about what had actually transpired. No dessert after dinner and an early bedtime was the extent of his punishment until I could figure out what exactly I was punishing him for. I figured the warm bath and the rocking would coax him into opening up to me now.

David pressed his nose against my collarbone, and I stroked his soft, brushed-cotton pajama top.

"It's okay, buckaroo. You can tell me what happened. Why did you scratch Gunner?"

Nose still pressed into my clavicle, David finally spoke up. "I didn't scratch him. King Rex did."

I drew in a sharp breath. I had been prepared for opening up this can of worms, but he had still put my deepest, darkest fear into words. I knew it was irrational and the least likely explanation, the one that most children with an imaginary friend would probably offer up in the face of punishment. I'd consulted the book Dr. Rosen had given me as soon as we'd gotten home.

Negotiating Blame and Responsibility. *A vase breaks. Cookies are missing from the cookie jar. Chances are, if your child has an imaginary companion, he or she will not confess to the deed and will instead insist that* *his or her imaginary friend is the one at fault. Do children really believe their imaginary friends are responsible or are they simply using them as scapegoats? As a parent, how should you navigate this difficult situation? Insisting that your child is a liar is unproductive but so is allowing him or her to keep passing the buck to his or her imaginary companion.*

A child's sense of power and control is developing at this stage. With this newfound realization of their ability to make things happen, children also experience the aftermath of their agency—praise or punishment—and while eager to garner the former, they are much more reluctant to accept the latter. Is a child testing you when he or she blames the misbehavior on his or her friend? Yes and no. While your child might be testing the waters to see what he or she can get away with, he or she might also be feeling that the imaginary friend is the one with the power and that he or she is less in control. For children who feel themselves to be impotent in their home life or at school, having an authoritative imaginary friend can be a great reassurance, but this kind of imbalance should be discouraged over time so the child can learn how to properly stand up or act for him or herself.

If your child blames his or her mischief on the imaginary companion, patiently and thoroughly ask him or her questions and then listen. *When Taylor B.'s mom found a chunk of cake missing from her husband's just frosted birthday cake, Taylor B., age six, blamed her imaginary cat, Caramel. But after she had been asked several questions, Taylor B. admitted that while she hadn't been the one to "cut the cake," she had in fact eaten "some" of the cake. Her mom could then appropriately discipline her (by not allowing her another slice of the cake at the party that night) and explain why Taylor B. and Caramel's behavior was wrong for ruining the cake before its rightful owner could have a slice of it first.*

But stolen cake and an imaginary cat didn't seem to fit into the same constellation of problems as the possible physical evidence of a Tyrannosaurus rex attack. I also couldn't help wondering if Taylor B.'s mom had had the same ability as I had and had peeked in the kitchen at the right moment, would she have witnessed Caramel up on the counter, slicing the forbidden cake for her master? Of course the developmental psychologist author of *Imaginary Friends, Your*

Child, and You hadn't thought to speculate on that possibility because it was sheer lunacy. But I wanted to know just how submerged children were in the world of their imagination. Did they actually visualize their imaginary friends doing these physical actions they claimed they did or did they just invent their actions later in story form? I wished for the hundredth time that I could remember my own experiences with Leah Nola.

I gently lifted David's head, so we could see eye to eye. "I need you to tell me the truth."

"He hurt Gunner," he maintained. His little chin quivered.

"Why did he hurt Gunner?" I asked, trying a different tact. "Did you tell him to?" David's orchestrating King Rex's aggressive behavior was a disturbing thought, but even more disturbing was the thought that David was losing his control of the dinosaur. Did he feel powerless in his home life as the book speculated? Was he making up for it by having a fierce defender?

"No," he whispered and played at stretching out the cuff of his pajama top. "Gunner didn't want to play dino-suss. He said dino-suss are for babies."

"That wasn't very nice," I said. "But that's not a reason to hurt someone."

David's words came out in a breathless rush. "He wanted to watch his movie, and I didn't like it. I shut my eyes and hid in the fort. He knocked down the fort and made me watch. He called me a baby and sat on my tummy. I couldn't get up. Then King Rex pushed him off and Gunner cried."

I pictured the red-haired boy pinning David to the ground and taunting him. In a four-year-old's mind, being called a baby was the ultimate insult. So David, or King Rex, had shoved Gunner away, a bit too forcefully. I envisioned the long scratch on Gunner's neck, trying to determine if David's ragged fingernails or King Rex's talons were a better match. Gunner had claimed that David had jumped on him and scratched him, but of course, he wouldn't have been able to see the dinosaur. He would've felt himself get pushed off, seen David lying there, and assumed it was him. It would be crazy to believe anything else. Absolutely crazy to believe King Rex had done this, I scolded myself.

"Oh, David." I tightened my arms around him. "What Gunner said and did was wrong. But you have to promise me you won't hurt anyone or let King Rex hurt anyone either. If someone says something mean to you, tell an adult or just walk away, okay?"

He grunted his consent.

I rocked a little faster. The chair had a slight squeak in it that I'd always found comforting. He wasn't the chubby, fussy infant that I'd rocked to sleep. He wasn't my troublemaking, into-everything toddler anymore either. He was becoming a full-fledged boy with his own personality and an interior life that was growing more knotty and complex with each passing day.

"Just love 'em," Winston had told me once, late in my pregnancy when we'd made a midnight run to buy two pints of chocolate chip cookie dough ice cream. In between spoonfuls, I'd been venting my increasing anxiety about becoming a parent, single or otherwise, and Winston had listened stoically, not contradicting me or assuring me that everything would be all right as Duffy would have done. "Love 'em because they're yours," he said, the grocery store parking lot lights illuminating his craggy profile. "Love 'em because of their sweet selves, but most importantly, love 'em in spite of themselves."

Though I had recognized the truth in his words, love had still seemed like such a paltry thing in the face of all my doubts then, much the way it felt now. David had worries my love couldn't touch, fears my love couldn't easily dispel. I didn't know where he'd be going to kindergarten yet, but he'd be going, and I didn't know how to protect him. I didn't know how to protect him from the other kids, and I didn't know how to protect him from himself. My love seemed like a well-worn blanket instead of the titanium shield I needed.

I bent down to sweep his hair off his forehead and saw that he had fallen fast asleep.

With all the excitement in the hours following David's catastrophic play date, I hadn't had time to call Patrick's parents yet. Duffy and Winston were curled up on the couch—my disloyal cat snuggled between them—watching a Miss Marple rerun on PBS, so I stepped outside with my cell phone. I didn't want to alarm them until I knew for sure if I had something to be alarmed about. Duffy was already all keyed up about Edna's handling of the boys' fight, and I was starting to think that maybe David and I and all our baggage were getting to be too much for even my sainted grandparents. It was exhausting to me, and I was only twenty-two. They deserved to be easing into retirement and enjoying each other's companionship, not slaving away on side jobs and dealing with our drama. But I knew Duffy wouldn't agree. "Family," she was fond of saying, "are the people who put up with you even when you're being a tremendous pain in the heinie."

The evening air was shimmering with heat, and the old air conditioner was working double time, cranking out a warm, musty breeze as a result. I walked as far away from its blowing heat and rattling noise as I could without leaving the deck. I scrolled through my contacts on my cell phone and speed-dialed the Gills' home number.

On the fourth ring, a man answered. Patrick's father, Quentin, the Milwaukee symphony violinist.

"Hi, this is Anna," I said. "I was hoping to talk to Abigail."

There was some muffled discussion before Quentin spoke again. "Anna, it's nice to hear from you! Abigail will be right with you. How are you and David doing?"

"We're good," I said, trying not to sound as guarded as I felt. "How is everybody there?" Which of course meant, how is Patrick?

"We're hanging in there," Quentin said, and then something loud crashed and clunked. What had I caught him in the middle of doing? Demolishing a building? "Patrick has been working on his art a lot, which makes us all very happy."

Quentin had never been as open about his son's illness as his wife. There was no asking him straightforward questions about Patrick's drug regimen or mental health because Quentin preferred to pretend those problems didn't exist. And reading between the lines with him was a skill I hadn't quite mastered. If Patrick was painting again, did that mean he was totally off his meds and unblocked? Or had they finally found a dosage that allowed him to still feel productive and creative?

"That's good. So he's still living with you?"

"Of course," Quentin retorted, as though Patrick hadn't been disappearing on and off for the past five years. More loud banging. This time it sounded like metal against metal. A wrench whacking a pipe? "Anyway, it was nice chatting with you, Anna. Here's Abigail."

"Anna," Abigail breathed into the phone, and she sounded genuinely happy to hear from me. "How are you? How's our favorite little guy? We miss you both so much."

"We're good," I repeated, trying to speed the conversation along. "How is Patrick doing?"

Abigail was silent for a beat. I could still hear the banging sounds in the distance, but they were quieter, as if she'd moved to another room. "It's been an uphill battle, but I think maybe this is finally it." Abigail had believed "this was it" several times before and had been wrong every time. She loved her son so much and was unwilling to give up on him, and for that, I was glad; Patrick deserved someone who could give him that kind of love, since I was clearly unable to. "He's been very diligent about taking his medication and seeing his doctor. And he's been dividing his time between working part-time at the grocery store and painting the most beautiful paintings of Saint Jude you've ever seen."

"Did he tell you he stopped by our old apartment looking for us last week?" I asked point blank.

There was a long, fraught pause. "No, he didn't mention that," she finally admitted. I was sure there were probably several other things that Patrick was hiding from her. "How do you know? If you're living out of town, I mean."

"My old neighbor told me. She said he seemed very agitated."

"That's puzzling," Abigail said. "He's very clear on the restraining order and how it will affect his chances of seeing David if he breaks it again. I'll make sure to sit down and talk with him about it. You didn't call the police, did you, since technically Patrick didn't actually make contact—"

"No," I interrupted her, because her quavering voice was pinching at my heart. "But I'm thinking about it. And if he tries it again or he sets foot on my grandparents' property, I definitely will."

"I can promise you he won't, Anna. He's really doing so much better. He's been talking about David a lot lately and how he's furious with himself for missing his early years. He seems willing to do just about anything to get to be a part of David's life again, and it is Quentin's and my sincerest hope that we could all sit down with a mediator to discuss trying supervised visits for Patrick again in October. Of course, we'll only do it with the permission of Patrick's doctor and regular updates from him. I know it's been a hard road for you, dear, but things can get better. They *will*. And we all love David, but he's Patrick's son too, and he deserves a chance to know his dad. So just think about it, okay?"

I closed my eyes and shook my head back and forth. Half of me wanted to believe in Abigail and her assessment of her son, her dream of what could be. That Patrick could pull himself out of the abyss for good and be the kind of father that David deserved. Or if not that, then at least a father who was just *there* sometimes and didn't do impulsive, dangerous things. But the other half of me knew that Abigail's impressions were clouded by motherly love. Patrick's contempt for the restraining order proved he hadn't changed as much as she thought. And I couldn't help admitting to myself that deep down I was frightened by the idea of letting Patrick back into our lives. He had hurt me deeply, irreparably, and I didn't want him to hurt David as well. I wanted David to have the kind of childhood that I hadn't had—security, consistency, and an abundance of love—and Patrick with his uncontrolled bipolar disorder didn't exactly fit into that picture.

"That's months away," I said, sidestepping her question, not wanting to bring up the more realistic likelihood of another injunction. "David's going to be starting kindergarten soon, and it's all kind of a whirlwind right now." I stepped down from the patio onto the grass. It felt dry and spiky under my bare feet.

"Our little guy, all grown up!" Abigail said with a wistful sigh and then asked about the logistics of setting up a visit with him soon. She and Quentin hadn't seen David since Easter, and I knew I wouldn't be able to put them off for much longer, but with all the other pressures in my life right now, it was one I hoped to postpone.

CHAPTER TWELVE

"Mommy, what's that?" David was pointing at the grassy field across the street from us and the packed dirt lot beyond where a few white tents had been erected and a row of port-o-potties set up. We were walking to Salsburg's tiny post office to mail a package for Duffy.

"It looks like they're setting up for the Firemen's Picnic," I said, grabbing his hand to cross the street. And sure enough, as we got closer, I could read the blue lettering on the banner hung on the side of a semi, from which brightly colored, collapsed carnival rides were being unloaded. SALSBURG FIREMEN'S PICNIC, AUGUST 9-11. The annual festivities always heralded the impending end of summer and the start of the school year.

I couldn't believe that David would be starting kindergarten in only a week and a half at Port Ambrose Elementary. I'd finally enrolled him, deciding to limit my still as of yet fruitless job search to the Salsburg area. It would allow me to live with my grandparents a while longer until I could save up enough for an apartment in Lawrenceville. Moving back to Milwaukee—where the cost of living was twice as high, and where there was now no Stacy or other supportive friends and ready babysitters, and where Patrick was apparently waiting for me to try to insinuate himself back into our lives— no longer felt like a viable option. I was trying to feel good about my decision to stay, instead of just plain trapped.

"Will they have fire trucks and tractors?" David asked, bouncing on his tiptoes to get a better view, and I could tell he was remembering the tantalizing description of the opening day parade Winston had given him. We were standing on the side of the road, watching the carnival crew's progress, with King Rex and Weeple only a few paces away. They had joined us on our walk to the post office, and I could only imagine what a strange spectacle our foursome would have made if the dinosaurs hadn't been invisible to everyone else.

"Yep, I'm sure of it," I said. From my memory, the parade was about 90% slow-moving farm equipment and local fire trucks. It certainly wasn't the glamorous Macy's Thanksgiving Day parade.

A bright red, many-legged ride, which had been compressed like an accordion was being cranked up to its full height, where it crouched like a giant spider. Two men unceremoniously unloaded the cars of a kiddie rollercoaster; the first car had a head like a Chinese lion. A truck hauled in what appeared to be a HOT WISCONSIN CHEESE stand. I didn't see the Ferris wheel or Winston's favorite, the funnel cake booth, yet.

I had always been amazed by the transitory nature of carnivals. The setting up of rides that looked too rickety to fling people into the sky and reliably return them to earth. How a camp of shabby tents and dull, creaky metal during the day could become something so sparkling and otherworldly at night. And then the next day be gone— the only signs of its existence litter and deep ruts in the ground. Carnivals were pure magic. Looking down at David's enthralled face, I caught a glimmer of his excitement. I felt almost like the little girl who'd spent nights at the carnival with Jamie and Leah Nola riding the Ferris wheel.

"You know, the parade and the carnival are this weekend," I said, as we walked past St. Monica's on our way home. "Would you like to go?"

David's eyes lit up like I'd just handed him a bag of Halloween candy and told him to have at it. "Yes," he whispered, gripping my arm and tugging it so hard it felt like it might come out of its socket. "Yes yes yes yes yes."

So the morning of the parade, which arrived with the worst possible combination of parade weather—darkly overcast, threatening rain, the atmosphere as hot and thick as a bowl of clam chowder—all four of us humans walked to Main Street to watch. Winston had driven down early with three adult-sized chairs, one kid-sized chair, and an old blanket to stake out a prime parade-watching spot, and Duffy had packed a cooler filled with bottles of water, cans of lemonade, and wedges of fresh cut watermelon in baggies. King Rex and Weeple didn't accompany us to the parade. Maybe, for the moment, tractors and fire trucks trumped dinosaurs. Whatever the reason, I was grateful for the reprieve, even though I was so accustomed to David's sidekicks that I kept doing a double take whenever I noticed they weren't with us.

The parade trickled by: fire trucks from nine different townships and villages; the William Payne High School marching band, miserable in their polyester-blend uniforms; a local chapter of Vietnam veterans; clowns on bikes and stilts; and then tractors, tractors, and more tractors. Though it had always held a place in my heart as the most pathetic parade I'd ever seen, the parade had the opposite effect on my son, who was beside himself with joy. And it wasn't just the Tootsie rolls and suckers that every group who passed by tossed at him, it was his unbridled enthusiasm over all the big machines crawling down the street. The fire trucks that flashed their lights and turned on their sirens and the tractors with wheels that looked better suited to monster trucks. He was Winston's great-grandson, after all. When he wasn't wiggling with glee on the curb, he was sitting on Duffy's lap, dripping watermelon all over (which he had refused to eat at first, until she'd convinced him it was nature's candy—just as sugary and sweet), or badgering Winston with questions about the farm machinery.

Maybe I was making a good decision by settling down in the Salsburg area after all. David could grow up with his great-grandparents in his life. He could live somewhere governed by tradition, routine, and small town values—befriending kids in kindergarten he would also learn alongside in high school, attending the Firemen's Picnic and parade every summer, ice skating and playing hockey on the frozen river every winter. It would be the opposite of the nomadic existence I'd led as a girl—four different elementary schools, two different middle schools, three different high schools, six apartments, twenty-plus of my mom's loser boyfriends, and except for our occasional *Gone with the Wind* marathons, not a single family tradition to look forward to every year.

A blue convertible drove by with a swan-necked teenager in a white dress riding atop the back. The sign attached to the driver's side door read: Fairest of the Fair, Tricia Lee Haynes, and I recognized something in her haughty expression. Her expression said *I'm better than all of you, and one day I'm going to get out of this sad little town and never look back.* And I remembered harboring that sentiment myself, once upon a time, and suddenly it depressed me that I was only a few years older than she was and had already returned, defeated.

Was I just resigning myself, then? I knew I was idealizing Salsburg and its "small town values" a tad and conveniently forgetting about my teenage boredom and disdain for the area, but I'd been so painfully naïve then, sneering at anything that seemed familiar or ordinary. Taking for granted how good predictability could feel. Just because something felt like home didn't mean that I needed to run from it. That was a lesson I was learning from my grandparents.

David wrapped his boiling little body around my already hot, sweaty legs, and I looked up to see the horse-poop scoopers and street sweepers trailing past us. At least the rain had held off for the parade.

Winston folded his chair. "If you all don't mind, I'm going to go say hello to Joe Larson. He was the one driving the Massey-Harris tractor. I'd be happy to take David along with me. Maybe Joe will let him climb up on the seat."

I didn't think David heard much of this exchange except for the word "tractor," and that alone would have prompted him to follow Winston to the ends of the earth. It was hard to know who was more smitten with my constantly thoughtful, constantly patient grandfather right then—me or David.

"You can leave the cooler and chairs here, and I'll come get them once the traffic's died down and the street opens up again," Winston said.

"Nonsense," Duffy replied. "Anna and I can carry them home. We're not delicate flowers, you know. Besides, it looks like rain." She dumped the remaining ice out of the cooler and slung a canvas chair over each shoulder.

I packed up the other two and folded the blanket into the smallest square I could. "David, you need to stay by Grandpa Winston's side at all times, okay?" He nodded impatiently, but I gratefully noticed Winston scoop him up onto his shoulders as they disappeared into the exodus of onlookers. Duffy and I headed in the other direction where slow-moving families with strollers and wheelchairs and high school band members crowded the street.

"So you and Edna are speaking again?" I asked, as we shuffled along, Duffy saying hi to practically every second person we bumped into. I felt a little guilty that "The Play Date Assault," as Edna had come to sensationalize it, had become a point of contention between the two longtime friends.

"We are, but, oh, that woman can be so ridiculous! When her precious Joy bit Kimberly when they were little, I didn't raise such a stink, and she even broke the skin! If I remember correctly, your poor mother had to get a tetanus shot."

I hadn't realized my mother was close in age to Edna's daughter; it was hard to believe that Joy had only a four-year-old while my mom had a twenty-two-year-old and was already a grandma. Yikes.

"Why, look over there!" Duffy, whose eagle eyes could spot a familiar face a mile away, said. "It's our neighbor, Wendy. Should we say hello?" Before I could respond, she was already elbowing her way through the crowd to the curb where Wendy sat alone in a manual wheelchair.

I wouldn't have recognized Jamie's mother had Duffy not pointed her out; her illness had aged her so much. Wendy's thick black hair had streaks of steel gray running through it, and her usually pleasant expression was replaced with a bad-tempered look only half hidden behind a pair of oversized sunglasses. Her legs, once tan and shapely, were now pale and skinny, lifelessly propped up on the wheelchair foot rests.

"Wendy," Duffy exclaimed. "How funny to bump into our next-door neighbor across town!"

Wendy beamed up at her, and ten years melted off her face. "Not so funny when you consider that 'across town' is only five minutes away. Where's Winston?" She smoothed the pleats of her navy shorts, and I could see that her hands were shaking. "And who's this? This can't possibly be Anna, all grown up, can it?" She lifted up her trembling arms to me, and I stepped into them, awkwardly accepting her hug.

"How are you doing?" I murmured into her hair, which improbably smelled like the butter cookies she'd always plied me with as a kid. "You look great."

She frowned as I drew away. "You're lucky I love flattery more than I despise lies. But look at you. You always were a pretty girl, and you've really grown into your beauty. I can see why my son has always carried a torch for you. Poor men. They're helpless against the pretty girls, aren't they?"

I smiled to hide my embarrassment. Duffy laughed loudly, shifted the canvas chairs, and patted her heavily hair-sprayed head, which resembled a prom updo from the eighties. "You got that right. Listen, Wendy, do you need a lift? It's so muggy out here, you're likely to melt if you sit too long. Winston's around here somewhere with the car, or Anna and I would be happy to push you home."

"That's very kind of you," Wendy said, "but Jamie's here with me. He just ran to the car with some things, but he should be back any minute now."

As soon as she said it, I unconsciously glanced up, looking for him. And there he was. Cutting through the alley between the Drop In, one of Salsburg's five bars, and an abandoned storefront that used to be a hobby shop. He spotted me the same instant I spotted him and stopped in his tracks. Our eyes locked, and a tingly feeling coursed through me as I remembered what he'd said on our drive to Milwaukee when I'd told him my fear of never amounting to anything. *You already are something, Anna. You always have been.* But we hadn't spoken since our rushed goodbye as I'd left to pick up David, and it didn't take a rocket scientist to figure out why. Probably he figured as a single, unemployed mother with a bipolar ex, I had enough on my plate as it was, which was undeniably true. But being around

Jamie felt like curling up with a good cup of coffee, and I wished we could find a way to at least be friends.

"Speak of the devil," Wendy said as he approached our little group in the shade. She reached backward to pat Jamie, but her arm jerked, so she returned it to her lap. "Look who's here," she pointed out needlessly to him, since he had already spotted us long ago.

"Hello, Duffy. Anna." He was wearing a bluish-gray concert T-shirt, and a week's worth of stubble covered his cheeks and chin. He gripped the handles of his mom's wheelchair.

"Glad you're here to take your mom home," Duffy said. "There's so much water in the air, it feels like it's going to rain any minute."

"I hope so," Jamie said mildly. "Our plants certainly need it. I just hope it stops before the carnival tonight." He met my eyes for the first time since coming up to us. His gaze felt private and heavy with meaning. "Do you ladies want a ride home?"

Burdened down by the chairs, cooler, and blanket my grandma had coerced me into carrying, sweat stinging my eyes, and still at least a ten-minute walk ahead of me, I had never wanted to say yes more. But Duffy answered for me.

"That's awfully nice of you, but we could use the exercise." She hefted the chairs and hung them over her shoulders again.

"Bah! It's too humid for exercise," Wendy said. "You just said yourself you were worried about me melting. You're coming with us, and that's final."

A sideways glance at my grandmother told me that this interaction had backfired on her, but in true Duffy form, she was going to hold her chin high and model polite, neighborly behavior for me. With Jamie pushing his mom's wheelchair in the lead, we walked a block to where he had parked, Duffy and Wendy remarking on the marching band's rendition of "God Bless the USA" and the bank's generous giveaway of both pens *and* checkbook covers this year. I was expecting to see Jamie's Demeter Landscaping Services pickup and was therefore surprised to see an unassuming white station wagon with handicapped license plates.

Duffy and I slid into the backseat, as Jamie went about the business of transferring his mom from her wheelchair to the car. He was both efficient and gentle in his movements—plainly he'd done this many times before—and the love on his face was overwhelming. I wiped the sweat out of my eyes, fiercely wishing that I could dredge up that kind of selfless devotion for my own mother. I wondered if I looked that way when I was taking care of David. I shot Duffy a significant look, but she didn't notice because she was just as intent on watching Jamie with Wendy as I was. He buckled her in, folded the wheelchair, and stowed it in the back before getting in the car himself.

The drive to the Presswoods' house took only five minutes, but it felt much longer in the presence of Jamie, his mother, and my grandmother. Wendy asked after David's whereabouts, so I had to make my overheated brain function enough to tell her about his newfound obsession with tractors, but the whole time, I felt excruciatingly aware of Jamie's long fingers expertly handling the steering wheel, his broad shoulders peeking out over the driver seat, his brown eyes darting up every so often to meet mine in the rearview mirror. Despite the air conditioning, I was sweltering. When he pulled into their garage and started unloading our chairs and cooler, I knew it was now or never.

"Jamie," I called out, sounding louder and more breathless than I had in my head. "I'm taking David to the carnival tonight." I tried to ignore the way my grandmother whipped her head around to watch us. "Do you want to come along? For old time's sake."

He straightened up and scratched his scruffy beard. Wendy, craning her neck from her vantage in the passenger seat, looked like she was holding her breath. "Sure," he finally said.

"Great! Pick us up at six, okay?" I hurried away, following Duffy across the lawn to our house before I could spontaneously combust into a cloud of girlish energy and glee.

We had hung up the lawn chairs on their garage wall pegs before Duffy couldn't hold her curiosity in any longer. "So is this, like, a date?" she asked.

"No," I insisted, more for my own benefit than hers. "Just two old friends taking a trip down memory lane and supporting a good

cause." The money raised by the three-day event almost fully sup-
ported the volunteer fire department throughout the entire year.
"Besides, David's coming."

She climbed up the front steps and held the door open for me.
"Hmm. Well, that's too bad."

"Really?" I raised my eyebrows at her. "What happened to your
'keep your distance from Jamie Presswood' tune?"

Duffy pretended to pout. "I don't know. I guess you could say
he's growing on me. I think it's nice he brought Wendy to the parade. She doesn't get out much anymore; her MS has progressed so
considerably this past year. Winston and I used to have her over for
dinner, but with all the stairs in our house, it just got to be too hard.
Joanne Gehring told me she offered to take her to the gardening club
meetings, but Wendy turned her down flat. It's good of him that he's
persuading her to leave the house."

"It *is* good of him," I said. "He loves his mom, Duffy, and he's
doing the best he can to take care of her and keep that house."

"I can see that," she said. "Not to mention, he's pretty cute when
he's not dressed like he's headed to a funeral." She winked at me
and flapped the bottom of her yellow blouse upward to cool herself,
briefly revealing her soft, fleshy abdomen.

I laughed and did my best Duffy impersonation, fluttering my eyelashes and raising my voice an octave. "But what about his troubled
past? What about what Edna told Vickie who then told Joanne who
then called *The National Enquirer*..."

"Okay, smarty-pants. Don't push your luck. I can see I've already
said too much."

I scavenged through my dresser drawers once more, hoping something different had miraculously appeared there since the last time
I'd looked two minutes ago. Jamie had already seen my "go-to" top,
the beaded turquoise one I'd worn to Carly's party, and I needed

something that was cute, sexy, and still appropriate to wear to a carnival with my son. I finally settled on my shortest jean shorts and a ruffled, sleeveless top in a soft pinky-peach that Duffy had once declared "my color." I added a pair of cowboy boots and didn't bother trying to style my hair beyond a ponytail since I knew the humidity would frizz it up anyway.

In the living room, David was dangling upside down off the sofa, flying a miniature tractor model over his head. Vivien Leigh stood on her haunches, ineffectively trying to swat the toy from his hand. "Is it time for the carnival?" he asked, bolting upright.

I peeked out the living room windows to look for Jamie's red truck in the driveway and was surprised to see him getting out. Before he could ring the doorbell and make things more "high school" than they already were, I called out, "Jamie's here! David and I are leaving now."

My grandparents were in the kitchen, eating a healthy dinner of salad, baked chicken, and steamed asparagus, so that Winston wouldn't be tempted to eat deep-fried foods at the fair later. Or at least that was Duffy's hope; I suspected it might have the reverse effect on him. She poked her head through the doorway. "We'll be leaving in about half an hour, so maybe we'll see you there."

"Okay," I said, backing up so my son could hurtle past me down the stairs.

"Anna," Duffy called, and I expected some variation of "be careful," but instead she said with a meaningful smile, "Have fun tonight."

"Thanks. You too." I took the steps slowly, feeling as jittery as if I'd just drunk ten cups of coffee. The sun had finally wrestled free of the clouds the afternoon rain showers had brought, and it was so bright, I was having a hard time focusing on Jamie and his shiny truck. He asked me a question about David's booster seat, and I was grateful to have such a mundane task to figure out. He helped me remove it from the minivan and install it in his backseat with such ease I questioned if he'd done it before, but he insisted he hadn't.

We were looking for a place to park by the time I got the courage to glance over and really look at him. He hadn't shaved, but his beard looked like it had been shaped or trimmed somewhat, and I had to admit, it made him look older, not so baby-faced, and very masculine. He was wearing sandals and faded jeans, and the only trace of black was a polo shirt that I guessed was from high school, judging by the way it fit him—tight in all the right places.

"So what do you think we should do first?" Jamie asked David, crouching down to his level.

David, never having been to a fair before, treated this like a trick question. He squinted at Jamie and turned the question around on him, a habit he'd recently acquired from Duffy, who did this to him all the time and insisted it helped develop his critical thinking skills. "What do *you* think we should do first?"

Jamie grinned at me. "Well, let's see. We could get something to eat, we could go on some rides, we could play some games, or we could talk to the firemen and check out their trucks."

Ding, ding, ding, we had a winner.

"I want to see the fire trucks," David decreed solemnly. He gripped my hand like he was going to start dragging me even though he had no idea which way to go.

Jamie guided us to the perimeter of the grounds, where a long red and white fire engine was parked and a couple of volunteer firefighters in baggy tan overalls with reflective strips were teaching kids about fire safety. They demonstrated raising the ladder and spraying the hose and even allowed kids to sit in the driver's seat of the truck and wear an oversized black hat for a photo opportunity. I hadn't thought to bring my camera, but Jamie took a picture of David with his phone and promised he'd send it to me.

"Looks like you've got yourself a future firefighter there," Jamie said to me, as my son reluctantly turned over the fireman's hat to the next kid in line.

"Yeah. Either that or a paleontologist. Or a farmer. Or a pirate."

"Hmmm. All worthy professions." Jamie lowered his phone to show David the picture he'd taken, and in his zeal, David kissed the screen. Jamie didn't even wipe off the smudge; he just laughed and put the phone back in his pocket.

We started walking to the row of food stands, for which I was grateful, because my stomach was growling and the intoxicating scent of buttery corn on the cob, roasted nuts, and cream puffs was heavily perfuming the air. How would poor Winston resist? Jamie and I each got giant slices of pizza, and David got a cloud of pink cotton candy bigger than his head. (I figured that a carnival was the one place you could get away with feeding a child spun sugar for dinner.) I was so entertained watching his deliberate progress, which reminded me of an ant nibbling on a doughnut, that I didn't notice Duffy and Winston coming toward us until they were right behind Jamie's shoulder.

"Hello, hello," Duffy said, dropping her magenta suede leather purse on the seat beside Jamie with a thump. "Thank goodness we ate before we came. It's unconscionable, the things they're coming up with to deep fry these days. Deep-fried Oreos? Deep-fried Twinkies? What's next? A vat where you can deep fry your own hand and gnaw on that?"

"Ingenious," Jamie said and winked at Winston.

"Grandpa! Grandma! Look at my cotton candy!" David cried, waving the sticky pink fluff dangerously close to my hair.

"It's lovely," Duffy said. "Just my favorite shade of pink." She leaned against the picnic table. "So, what have you all seen so far? And what were you planning on doing next?"

Oh no! She was trying to horn in on our date. Correction: not a date. Just an outing between friends who both had full and busy lives with no time for romance. I'd told her as much only a few hours earlier. But still, the thought of my grandparents chaperoning us like a couple of seven-year-olds was really unappealing. David told them all about the fire truck we'd seen, and I folded my paper plate into halves until I couldn't fold it anymore. When Jamie saw what I'd done, he reached out his hand for the plate and got up to throw our trash away.

"Do you know what we saw on our way over here?" Duffy asked David. "A game where you get to squirt a water gun at targets to win prizes! Doesn't that sound like fun?" She hefted her purse over her shoulder and gave me a questioning look. "We'd love to take him around if you guys want to…"

It was even worse than them horning in on our not-date—they were deliberately trying to force us into date territory! Could Duffy be any more obvious? I smiled apologetically at Jamie, but apparently he wasn't about to make this easy on me either. *It's up to you*, his impassive expression seemed to say. *No one else can make this decision for you, Anna.*

"Sure," I said. "That would be great. Just let me know when and where you'd like to meet up later and how much I owe you for any games or rides."

Winston shook his head. "We'll take care of everything. We'll take him home, tuck him in. Just enjoy yourselves." It was so similar to how he'd set us loose as kids, that I almost expected him to hand us each a ten dollar bill.

I asked David for a hug, and he obliged me, but I could tell his heart was already set on the water gun game. I had almost hoped for a tantrum, even just a little one, to prolong the inevitable, but David chose that moment to be an obedient little soldier. And so they left, and Jamie and I were alone.

CHAPTER THIRTEEN

"So," I said, and I found that I didn't know what to say next. I wasn't fooling anyone, least of all myself. This was officially a date now and probably had been one all along. I liked Jamie. I liked him in the cozy, comfortable way that long-time friends have with each other, but I also liked him in a kind of way that I kept wondering what he looked like with his clothes off.

But I hadn't done this—dating—in such a long time that I didn't remember how. I wasn't sure I'd ever really known how. There were the high school boys whose idea of a "date" was videogames followed by other activities I'd rather not remember in their parents' basement. And then there were the guys I'd met recently at parties or bars, whom I refused to take home to my place for fear that David would wake up. In between, there was Patrick.

"So," I repeated.

Jamie stood up and stretched, revealing an inch of taut abdomen and a black treasure trail, which I had to drag my eyes away from.

"Should we go get a couple of beers?" he suggested.

The beer tent, packed tightly with rowdy, twenty-something groups of friends and couples, restored a little normalcy to my world. Since it was where the fire department made the most money, several of the firefighters were hanging out, swapping stories, and taking pictures with flirtatious girls. Jamie bought us each a beer and then led me over to a familiar-looking group of guys who turned out to be Sam, Marshall, and another guy I didn't know (not Colin, thank

God). But just around the time I was starting to get bored with their good-natured but profanity-laced razzing of each other, Jamie said our goodbyes and led us to a small table.

"Are you sure you're old enough to drink that?" I teased as we sat down.

"I'm only six months younger than you." To prove his point, he took a swig of beer. I watched as his Adam's apple rose and fell as he gulped it down.

"Sometimes I feel older," I said, spreading my hands out, palms down on the table.

"Older than me?" Jamie's forehead creased in concern.

"No. Just older in general." We were sitting at the edge of the tent, and I could see a sliver of dusky rose sunset.

Jamie's forehead wrinkles deepened. "Well, you had to grow up fast."

"We both did," I said, not sure if I was referring to his caretaking of his mom or his battle to overcome his drug addiction.

"Do you want another beer?" Jamie asked. He had finished his.

"No, thanks."

"Me neither." His casual demeanor was wearing off, and he was starting to look as nervous as I felt. "So, how is your rocking chair?"

I looked up, caught off guard. "Oh. It's good." I laughed. "I'm a bit worried David's and my combined weight is going to break the thing, but otherwise it's good. Thank you for helping me get it. It means a lot to me, and I'm sorry if I wasn't able to properly thank you."

"No problem." He gave me a half-smile, one that reminded me of the insecure adolescent he'd been, and then turned his attention to his empty plastic cup.

"But you know what?" I asked, reaching across the table to lightly tap the inside crease of his arm. His skin felt electric and hot to the touch; I removed my hand quickly. "It was bittersweet for me to reminisce about rocking him as a baby because my 'baby' is going to be starting kindergarten at Port Ambrose Elementary in only a week."

Jamie's smile spread across his face. He leaned forward on his elbows, ever so casually flexing his chest and arm muscles. "Oh, yeah?

That's where I went to elementary school. It's a nice place. I'm sure David will like it." His dark-chocolate-brown eyes were studying me the way David's had as a newborn, with warmth, curiosity, and a hint of distrust. "Does that mean you're staying in the Salsburg area?"

"For now," I said and pulled my ponytail over my bare shoulder, teasing apart the waves with my fingers. "I don't know if it will be permanent, but it feels like the right place to be." At that moment, it had never felt truer.

Without talking about it, we both stood up and made our way outside the tent. Night was descending like a dark, silky parachute, and the carnival was finally coming alive. The round bulbs on the rides burst with electric light and energy, and everything that had looked so tacky and pedestrian before suddenly looked romantic and full of possibilities. Like Paris in the middle of small town Wisconsin. All my worries were melting away, and I felt sprightly, effervescent, and downright girly.

"Let's go on the Ferris wheel," I said.

Jamie rolled his eyes, but he was suppressing a grin. "You didn't get enough of it when you were eight?"

"Apparently not."

We bought tickets and stood in a very short line. Most of the passenger cars were unoccupied, and only a dad and a son and two adolescent girls were ahead of us. I could see why. The Ferris wheel looked even more rickety and unsafe than I'd remembered. But before I could back out, the ride operator was locking us into a car that was much smaller than I recalled. My bare thigh was snug against Jamie's jeans-clad one. How had Jamie, Leah Nola, and I all fit in the same car as kids? Granted, Leah Nola probably didn't take up much space, but still.

"Did you ever know that I used to be afraid of heights?" Jamie said, as the Ferris wheel lurched upward so another passenger car could be filled.

"No! Seriously?" I glanced at his white-knuckled death grip on the safety bar and wondered if he wasn't still somewhat afraid of heights.

"Yeah. This persistent little neighbor kid used to beg me to go on the Ferris wheel with her even though I was terrified. We'd go ten times in a row without getting off and use up all our tickets at once."

"Gosh, I'm so sorry. I had no idea. Why didn't you say something?"

"It's okay. I'm glad you didn't notice." Jamie shifted his weight slightly, and I could feel his hip pressed against mine. The Ferris wheel creaked, and we climbed higher into the night sky.

The view wasn't as spectacular as I remembered: the white tents, the port-o-potties, the other psychedelic-flashing and whirling, seizure-inducing rides. But beyond the bright lights, nestled under the cover of darkness, were modest homes, ancient trees, and farm fields that stretched for miles. And somewhere down there were my son and grandparents, the three people I loved most in this world.

I turned to focus my attention on Jamie, whose arm was carelessly touching my knee, and whose bearded face looked irresistibly handsome, and I suddenly had the urge to kiss him. Making out on a Ferris wheel was so cliché, I admonished myself, but the impulse lingered, getting hotter and more urgent with each awkward jerk of the wheel. We were on the downward swing now. Hopefully I could control myself for just ten more minutes. And then? And then all bets were off.

Jamie's warm gaze met mine, and I blushed, as if he could read my mind.

"Did you ever know that I've loved you since I was six years old?" he asked softly.

The jittery over-caffeinated feeling returned. The skin cells on my bare thigh touching his leg sparked with excitement. I gripped the safety bar too, and my palms felt slippery with sweat.

"I don't believe you," I said lightly.

"When you left, I missed you so much that I prayed you'd get in trouble again and your mom would send you back."

"And I did."

"And you did. But then we didn't see each other for all those years, and I had this idea of you in my head, this perfect, beautiful, creative girl, that I just knew wasn't realistic and that no girl could possibly live up to. But then you came back in high school, and you exceeded it. Then you broke my heart."

"I'm sorry," I whispered.

"You're not," he murmured accusingly. "You're still breaking it." His warm, calloused fingers lightly turned my chin toward his. Our lips collided, and I was suddenly no longer concerned with how cliché and adolescent it seemed to make out on a Ferris wheel. His beard felt soft against my face, not how I'd expected it to feel at all, and we were drinking each other in as though we each had been unquenchably thirsty.

We hardly noticed when the ride jerked to a stop at the bottom, the safety bar released us, and the ride operator shot us a sulky frown.

"Can we go somewhere?" I asked in between kisses, and Jamie grabbed my hand and desperately pulled me through the maze of the carnival.

Jamie's bedroom was nothing like I'd envisioned. I'd never seen it as a child, and I guess I wasn't sure what kind of room an all-black-wearing, country-music-listening, landscaping guru in his early twenties would have, but this certainly wasn't it. The room was tasteful and immaculate like a five-star hotel room. His queen-size bed was neatly made with a duvet-covered comforter that smelled like laundry detergent and sheets that felt like Egyptian cotton of a high thread count. I couldn't tell you much else about the room beyond the bed, because that was my main area of concentration. Frankly, it was very perceptive of me to notice the bed at all given the things Jamie was doing to me.

Skimming my bare legs with his rough but surprisingly gentle palms, he helped me kick off my cowboy boots and then set about unzipping and sliding off my tiny jean shorts. All through his methodical efforts to undress me, he continued to kiss me like he was a man in a desert and I was a tall glass of icy lemonade. We rolled toward the center of the bed, and I straddled him, unbuttoning the collar of his polo shirt and wrestling it over his head. I pressed my cheek against his warm, smooth chest, savoring his chiseled muscles, the clean smell of his skin, the wild pounding of his heart.

"Do you have something?" I murmured.

"Yes." Jamie twined his fingers through my messy ponytail, drawing me closer to his face, as though he couldn't bear one second when our lips weren't touching. With his other hand, he fumbled blindly through the nightstand drawer, finally producing a condom. It had always been my least favorite part of sex—the awkwardness, the bringing back to reality, the slowing down and stopping to consider: what are we doing? *Should* we be doing this? But there were none of these hesitations with Jamie. His eyes never left mine as he rolled the condom on, and then his muscular arms were back around me, guiding me, enveloping me. I felt insanely sexy and desirable, but I had felt that way before; there was more to it than that. I felt cherished. *Did you ever know that I've loved you since I was six years old?*

Afterward, we lay side by side in a blissful stupor, hypnotized by the slowly rotating ceiling fan above us. My black thong was still caught around my heel, and I lazily tried to fling it to the floor.

"Did that really just happen, or is this all a dream?" Jamie asked, gently stroking my side with the back of his hand, from my breast all the way down my rib cage.

I didn't move the sheet to cover up the pale, yet shiny stretch marks on my lower abdomen. Instead, I propped myself up on my elbow and turned to face him, noting his own scar. Three inches in length, red and raised, outlining his armpit. From the car accident, I suspected. He propped himself up too, and I reached behind him to pinch his impossibly firm butt.

"Ow. What was that for?" Jamie asked, laughing. He playfully tried to reach around me to return the favor.

I grinned and swatted his hand away. "Not a dream."

"Excellent." A black forelock fell over his eye, and he didn't bother to brush it aside. Instead, he smoldered at me with his one visible eye.

"You're excellent," I said. "I mean, wow. Just wow." I ran my palm lightly over his bearded jawline.

"That's the second best news I've heard all day," he said and kissed my fingertips.

I sat upright, hugging my knees to my breasts, and gave him a gentle push so that he lost his balance. "What was the first?"

Jamie flopped flat on his back and then stretched his arms overhead. "When you said you were sticking around Salsburg."

Another wave of contentment crashed over me. Room-darkening blinds blocked the windows, and I now considered my rushed glimpse of the house as Jamie had hurried me toward his bedroom. My blurry memory of the layout suggested that this was the bedroom on the side of the house facing Duffy and Winston's house. I was trying not to think of my grandparents or my son, sleeping only thirty yards away. Or maybe not sleeping. Maybe Duffy or Winston was waiting up for me. If they'd seen Jamie's truck drive up, it wouldn't take a brain surgeon to figure out where I was. Or what we were doing. The neon blue numbers of the clock next to Jamie's bed read 11:25, and I knew I would have to head home soon. But I didn't want to leave just yet.

"Are you ever going to go back out west?" I asked. "See the national parks you never got to see?"

"Yeah, one day. Probably not anytime soon, though, because my mom needs me too much." His hand crawled up my spine and massaged my shoulder. He tugged me gently back down onto the bed, so that I was lying with my head against his heart and my body curled around his. "After my dad left, I always had this ideal of the perfect family, what we could've been if he'd stayed, and one of the things I imagined was a family road trip out west with an obnoxiously big RV. So maybe I'll get to see Yellowstone and the Grand Canyon with my own family one day."

"That would be nice," I whispered, and it did sound nice. Teenager Anna would have turned up her nose at this stereotypical, middle-class American fantasy, but grown-up Anna couldn't help wondering if he meant me and David, or if he was imagining a different wife—maybe a brunette with sparkling green eyes and a trendy nose ring—and two or three of his own biological kids.

"What about you?" Jamie asked. He entwined his large fingers through my smaller ones and squeezed.

"What about me, what?"

"I don't know. What do you want out of life?" He tilted my chin upward to look at him.

I lowered my eyes self-consciously. "I have an idea. Kind of. I've always wanted to go to college. Take some art classes. Improve my technique and learn about working with different media." As soon as I said it, I realized it was true. That it was a desire that had been lying dormant inside me. It wasn't realistic. How would I ever get the money for tuition? And how would I both work and raise David while I was also trying to attend school? And what would a degree in art really be worth anyway? It wasn't like I would be able to find a job as an "artist" right out of school and immediately better my life and David's. No, single moms who decided to pursue college went to tech schools to get practical degrees that helped them find higher-paying jobs because that was the smart thing to do.

"I could see that," Jamie said thoughtfully. He squinted as though he were imagining it in his mind's eye. "Your drawings always were so beautiful."

I laughed. "You haven't seen me draw since I was a kid!"

"So what?" With my ear so close to his chest, his voice rumbled and vibrated. "Even at eight, you probably had more talent in your baby toe than some of these so-called artists today have in their entire bodies. I'd love to see your current work sometime."

What current work? Unless the dinosaur series I'd been secretly drawing with my oil pastels counted. I could name them similarly to Monet's haystack series. *T-rex in Sunshine. T-rex (Sunset). Brontosaurus at the End of Summer.* By capturing David's imaginary friends' likeness in painstaking detail, I'd been trying to demystify them. A kind of art autopsy. And although drawing again had made me feel more like my old creative self, it still hadn't gotten me any closer to understanding why I could see my son's imagination and what I was supposed to do with the ability. I still felt like David had handed me a secret message but neglected to include the code with which to crack it.

I wondered what Jamie would think if I showed the portraits of King Rex and Weeple to him. Maybe he'd think I just *really* liked dinosaurs. But maybe I should start taking my art more seriously again and branch out to drawing other things besides David's imagination—if I could ever find the time. The thought of showing Jamie one of my drawings was kind of nerve-wracking but in a good way. It would require me to be totally vulnerable, even more vulnerable than I was lying nude beside him. It would require me to completely trust him in a way I hadn't trusted any man in a long time, maybe ever. But with Jamie's ardent heart thumping near my ear, it didn't seem like such an unimaginable feat anymore.

"Thanks," I said. "That means a lot to me." I rolled onto my back, creating a small space between us. "Jamie? I don't know exactly how this is going to work."

He looked down at me with a slight frown. "What do you mean?"

"I mean this." I gestured to our naked bodies and took a deep breath. "Us. How's it going to work? Living next door to each other, you with your mom, me with my grandparents. Like I said, David starts kindergarten next week, and he's been going through a lot this summer, and I need to be there for him. I need to focus, really focus, on being the best mom I can be right now. I also really need to find a job. And, of course, you have your mom to take care of, and your landscaping business—"

He bent down to kiss my lips mid-sentence. "Shhh. All I needed to hear you say was *us*." He pulled the sheet up and pressed himself against me, and I gave into him with my whole being. "Anna, I've been waiting for you for a long time. I think I can be patient a bit longer."

CHAPTER FOURTEEN

"And then he said, 'Did you know I've loved you since I was six years old?'" I told my grandmother, tucking a flyaway strand of hair behind my ear, before signaling to change lanes. Though I had already given her a cursory summary of my date with Jamie, I was now fishing for additional PG-13 details to share with her to distract her from the fact that we were leaving her circumscribed safe area and she seemed on the verge of a full-blown, all-out, completely-losing-her-shit meltdown.

In the passenger seat of the minivan, Duffy looked like a nervous flyer. One fist clutched the seatbelt across her breast, the other palmed the door handle as though she might leap out of the moving vehicle at any moment. She'd been like this since we'd left the village limits. "That doesn't surprise me," she said in a small voice, unlike her own. "You were inseparable as kids, and even though you bossed him around and brought your imaginary friend with you everywhere, Jamie adored you. Winston and Wendy even used to joke about you two getting married when you grew up."

"Whoa, whoa, whoa," I said. "Let's try to avoid the M word until we've at least reached our one-week anniversary, shall we?" But this comment didn't even earn me a chuckle or a retort because Duffy's eyes were closed and she was doing Lamaze-style breathing. I had never seen her so anxious before. It reminded me of the night I'd called her in tears and she'd been my salvation, reining in her fear enough to drive all the way to Milwaukee to collect me.

We were headed to a strip mall in Glacial Hills because David needed school supplies and Duffy was out of several products for her salon. Normally, Penny Michaels, one of the women who'd rented a chair from her at *Savon Vivement*, picked them up for her, but she was on a month-long vacation celebrating her silver wedding anniversary. Duffy had started writing me a very detailed yet puzzling list (e.g., Sheen Professional Premium Creme 30 Volume Dedicated Developer, neck strip refills, and something called "cleansing pudding") until I convinced her that her order would be much more accurate if she simply came along with me. The trip would be short, we could kill two birds with one stone since the strip mall housed both a beauty supply emporium and office supplies store, and I would drive her. Finally, she gave in.

"Are you okay?" I asked, patting her tense wrist and slowing down for the world's most inconvenient stop light. The entrance to the strip mall was only a few yards beyond it. "We're almost there."

"Everything's alright," Duffy said in a flat monotone. Beads of sweat were rolling down the sides of her face from her hairline, but I couldn't tell if this was from my unbearably hot minivan or her panic attack. I could now understand why Winston's bushy eyebrows had twitched like two startled caterpillars when I'd told him my intention to take Duffy shopping in Glacial Hills. The flaw in my original plan of dropping Duffy off at one end of the strip mall to do her shopping, while David and I found the items on the list Port Ambrose Elementary had mailed at the other end and then meeting up in the middle was becoming more and more apparent. There was no way I could leave my grandma alone in this state. Clearly, I would need to help her with her shopping, and if she calmed down enough, we'd all go the office supplies store together afterwards. And if not, I'd have to make a separate trip back, which would be my own stupid fault, I knew.

"Have you seen a doctor about this?" I asked her gently. "Maybe it would be helpful to talk to someone. Maybe they could prescribe you something for the anxiety." Like a metric ton of Xanax.

Duffy snatched her purse from the floor as I parked the minivan. "Everything's alright," she repeated, but this time her voice seemed to have reclaimed its bossy-take-charge edge. "Liking to stay in one place isn't a crime, I'll have you know, Anna, and it certainly doesn't make me crazy." She was out the door and already heading toward the emporium before I had even gotten out and rolled back the door for David.

After his short, insufficient nap, David was as crabby as—well, as a four-year-old boy who's hot and tired and dreading spending an hour shopping with his mom and grandma. Who could really blame him?

Tight-lipped and pale, my grandmother was already tossing bottles into a cart when we entered. I approached her, suggesting we divide up the list to make this go twice as fast, and she ripped off the bottom third of the list for me. I was supposed to find a specific kind of perm solution, Luscious Locks shampoo and conditioner, a bottle of barbicide, and a few other items I had no idea where to find in the maze of the emporium. I grabbed a cart of my own and asked David if he wanted to ride in the front seat, which he usually enjoyed, but today, nothing was pleasing the little grump. He insisted on walking.

"Then stay close to me," I cautioned him as we tackled the first item on our list. There seemed to be an entire aisle devoted to perm solutions, and each box looked about the same to me. "Can you be a big boy and help Grandma Duffy with me? We need to find different things that she uses to cut and style hair."

David wrinkled up his forehead, eyes, nose, and mouth into a whole-face frown. It was quite a feat. "I don't want to." He fingered an artificial clump of hair hanging off one of the shelves. I scolded him when he tried to rip it off, and he let out a high-pitched whine that I was worried would lead to a full-fledged tantrum.

"You can touch the hair gently," I said. "Just don't pull it, okay?"

At last, I found the box of perm solution, which was totally gray and nondescript, on the very bottom shelf, so I was on to the next item on my list: Luscious Locks. We hurried into the shampoo and conditioner aisle, where a middle-aged lady was meticulously uncapping and sniffing each bottle of shampoo before putting it back.

"Do you know where Luscious Locks is?" I asked her hopefully.

She gave me a disdainful look. "I don't work here."

I forced myself to smile. "I didn't think you did. I just thought maybe you'd spotted it."

The lady unscrewed another shampoo cap and inhaled. "Well, I haven't. So maybe you should ask someone who actually works here."

What a class act. Discouraged, I stood back to take in the entire wall of shampoo and conditioner bottles. It would have been kind of awe-inspiring had I not been so stressed out to get Duffy's items as quickly as possible. Even knowing what color bottle Luscious Locks came in might not have helped much—every color of the rainbow and even some nature hadn't dreamt up seemed to be represented.

Duffy wheeled past the aisle, her cart nearly filled to the brim. Her color had improved slightly; maybe being in the presence of so many hair products was somehow fortifying her. "Almost done, Anna? I'm ready to check out."

"I just have a few more things to find. Do you know where the Luscious Locks is?" But she had already disappeared. I stared at the shelves, willing the brand name to pop out at me, and finally, it did. I chucked the bottles into my cart and set off in search of the barbicide.

Thankfully, the store's selection of disinfectant was limited, so I chose the cheapest refill bottle. "We're almost done, buckaroo," I said, spinning around. But David wasn't standing by the cart, where I thought he'd be. In fact, he wasn't anywhere in the aisle.

"David?" I called, expecting him to peek out from behind the display at the end of the aisle, but he didn't. "David?" I called more loudly. "You need to stay close to Mommy. Come right back, okay?"

I shoved my rattling cart into the next aisle over. No David. I backtracked to the shampoo aisle and the perm solution aisle, where he'd been so enraptured with the swaths of fake hair. No David. I ditched my cart and started a methodical search of each aisle in the store, glancing desperately up at the mirrored border near the ceiling to see if I could catch a glimpse of David, certain he was hiding.

Probably crouching behind the boxes of hair dryers and curling irons or leaning next to the wall of colorful, rippling hair extensions. But the mirrors reflected only a billion different salon products and a frantic, tiny version of me.

The mean, shampoo-sniffing lady had now moved to the hairspray section, where she was testing out each with a furtive squirt.

"Have you seen my son?" I asked her. I drew an invisible line extending from my ribs. "A little blond boy?"

She spared me a narrow-eyed glance that said *I knew you were the kind of woman to lose your son in a beauty supply emporium.* Then she shook her head dismissively and returned her attention to the hairspray. Her short hair was reddish-brown and thinning, and there was a balding patch radiating from her whorl. For a long moment, it was all I could see. The crown of her head filled my vision as hysteria bubbled up inside me.

I ran to the front of the store to ask the cashier to make an announcement over the loudspeakers.

Duffy wheeled her cart up to the front at that exact moment. "Anna, is everything okay? I thought I heard you shouting. Where's Davey?"

My panicked response was swallowed up by the loudspeaker crackling to life and the teenage clerk's whiny voice amplified throughout the store. "David Jennings, please come to the front registers. Your mom is worried about you. And if anyone sees a four-year-old boy alone in the store—blond hair, brown eyes, in a white T-shirt and green shorts please bring him up to the front registers immediately. Thank you."

I looked helplessly at Duffy, expecting the cool-under-fire, fierce mama bear to emerge and allow me to break down into the quivering pile of irrational goo I so urgently wanted to abandon myself to. But her face had turned eggshell white, and the Lamaze-style breathing had returned but more rapidly this time. "Oh no," she murmured breathlessly. "Just like I knew. Just like I always knew. He's gone. We shouldn't have come here."

I gripped her shoulders and spoke directly into her face. I think I maybe shouted in her face. I couldn't be sure. "CALM...DOWN."

The teenage cashier was watching us like we were an entertaining soap opera, the most interesting part of her otherwise boring day. I wasn't sure how much time had passed—ten seconds or ten minutes—but no shoppers had come up to the front to report David, and his white-blond head was still nowhere in sight.

"We're going to find him," I told Duffy firmly. "You stay here. Ask the cashier if there's a storage room or bathroom that David maybe wanted to investigate. See if any of the other shoppers noticed anything unusual." My throat caught around the word "unusual." I didn't even want to think about what unusual things they might have seen. "Just wait for him here in case he shows up. I'm going to go outside and see what stores are next door, see if he wandered over there, or maybe even all the way to the office supplies store."

Duffy was visibly trembling and I didn't know how much help she'd be, but another cashier was hurrying over to the registers—a heavy, capable-looking woman in a black vest, a manager, maybe, and I hoped she'd somehow magically undo the situation while I was gone.

Out on the sidewalk, facing the expansive parking lot, my stomach convulsed in fear, and I thought I might lose my breakfast. How big the world was! Inside the contained emporium, David could have been concealed somewhere in Aisle 2B. Out here, out here...Oh my god, there were so many cars, trucks, vans, so much pavement, so many streets. So many dangers to a little boy. Traffic, strangers. What if a stranger had approached him? Promised David candy and led him off to...No, I wouldn't think the worst. He was nearby. I could feel it.

A clothing boutique for plus-size women and a dollar store flanked the emporium. Hot pink and lime green pool noodles and rainbow wind socks cluttered the plate glass window of the dollar store, definitely an attractive display for a child. I stormed toward its door. A little chime tinkled as I opened it, but the check-out area was unattended.

"Hello?" I called as I skirted a table stacked with dashboard hula girls. "David?"

A guy about my age with greasy hair and a wisp of a mustache appeared from behind a bunch of helium balloons. "Hi. Can I help you?"

"Have you seen a little boy? Unaccompanied?" The young man continued to stare at me dully, so I rushed on. "I'm looking for my son, David. He's four. We were in the beauty store next door, and he wandered off. I thought he might have come in here. He's about three and a half feet tall, blond hair—"

The clerk shook his head. "Sorry. I haven't seen him, and I think I would have noticed a little kid all by himself come through here."

My heart fell through a trapdoor into my abdomen. "Okay," I said. "I'm going to take a look around anyway." I think the clerk said something else, but I couldn't hear him. My blood whooshed in my ears. David wasn't here. He was gone. Maybe Patrick had taken him. Maybe he'd come to Salsburg and then followed us to Glacial Hills and seen his chance to grab his son. He'd walked off with David, and maybe he'd take him back to his parents' house, and they'd call me, but maybe he'd take him somewhere else, somewhere far away. And maybe after his initial interest wore off, he'd forget about David and leave him there, all alone and scared. Because that was how Patrick was off his meds, how he operated. He loved you, he loved you, he loved you, until he simply disappeared and forgot all about you. I fought back a wave of emotion that was struggling to escape—tears, screams, I wasn't sure which. Maybe both.

I tried to focus on the blur of paper products in front of me—plates, napkins, gift bags, wrapping paper. Where the hell was the toy aisle? I sped around the corner and caught a glimpse of army green fabric. David's shorts?

"David?" I called, flat-out running now. I nearly tripped over a display of brooms standing against the wall, and catching my balance, I was sent flying into the toy aisle where my son crouched, looking intently at the assortment of cheap plastic toys. I was both astounded and mildly comforted to see King Rex and Weeple there too, crowding the aisle with their bulk, like bouncers at a nightclub.

"David!" I grabbed him roughly and lifted him into my arms, even though he was getting much too heavy for me. "Are you okay? Is everything okay? I was so worried about you." I pressed him to my chest, ignoring the way he struggled and squirmed against me. My wildly beating heart was trying to settle back into its proper place, but it was still too expansive with emotion.

"I'm okay, Mommy," he said.

I released him, and he sauntered back over to the wall of toys as if I'd merely disturbed him. He held up a robot action-figure. "Can you buy this for me?"

"No," I said. "Definitely no. Especially not now." I bent down to clasp his wrist, and he ducked out of reach. "David Patrick, we are leaving this store right now."

A low rumble started, like a stomach growling.

"You did a very naughty thing, running away like that," I continued, "and you scared Mommy and Grandma Duffy to death. Don't you ever do that again."

The rumbling was getting louder. It seemed to be coming from his dinosaurs. I surveyed the aisle for the black shadow, but it was nowhere to be seen. Were they growling at *me*? I tried to grab David's wrist again, but he retreated a step and King Rex slipped between us. Under the store's fluorescent lights, the T-rex looked like a ghoul from a haunted house. I knew I should have been afraid of his vampire-sharp teeth, but I was adrenaline-buzzed with a mixture of maternal relief and outrage.

"Come here this instant, David!" I ordered. "We're leaving." I reached purposefully around King Rex, and I thought I felt the side of my hand brush something cool and scaly. I flinched and fought the urge to draw back and instead caught David's forearm and started to tow him out of the store. I was panting and my muscles were twitching like I'd just run a marathon.

David was wailing with the shrill frequency and intensity of an ambulance siren as I dragged him toward the door. I glanced back to make sure his dinosaurs weren't following us, but mercifully, they had vanished. The greasy clerk watched us in half-excitement, half-horror as we left his store.

You scared me to death. Don't you ever do that again. The furious, yet loving words resounded in my head and brushed a memory loose. A time when I had run away from my own mother and scared her to death. *Don't you dare ever pull a stunt like that again, Anna Grace. You hear me?*

When I was seven years old, my mom dragged me to the East Ridge Mall almost weekly, and every trip lasted at least four hours. We didn't go there to shop for school clothes or books or toys for me; we went to shop for The Perfect Dress for her. For a while there, it felt like I spent more of my life in department store dressing rooms than I did at home or school. I became accustomed to the familiar detritus of dressing rooms—pins from dress shirts, broken hangers, crumpled up wads of tissue paper— and the sadness and secret life behind the velvet curtains. The women who cried quietly, the mothers and daughters who argued savagely over the cut of tops and jeans, the bosom buddies who boisterously discussed their personal lives from separate dressing rooms, the boyfriends who slipped in with their girlfriends and made them moan, which was almost as disturbing as the crying. To this day, I still couldn't stand dressing rooms and rarely tried anything on.

The Perfect Dress was akin to the Holy Grail for my mom. As far as I could tell, she didn't have a specific shape, style, or color in mind because she tried on nearly everything on the racks. It seemed to have to do more with how it looked on her and how it made her feel. In all our shopping trips that year, for all the thousands of dresses she tried on, she only ever purchased five dresses. Three of them she ended up returning, and the other two hung in her closet awaiting some special moment that never came. My mom never bothered to explain her relentless hunt to me, but looking back now, it seemed that the magical power of the *true* Perfect Dress would be meeting the Perfect Man, who would sweep her off her feet and away from her miserable life. And me.

One particular afternoon in December, my mom dragged me to the mall as per usual, but this time, I didn't mind as much because she'd promised we'd make a trip to visit Santa. I waited patiently in a hard plastic chair, not unlike the ones we had at school, outside the dressing rooms, while my mom glided out in a never-ending stream of festive holiday dresses to scrutinize herself in the mirror.

"What do you think of this one, Anna?" she asked of an off-the-shoulder, green velour, tight-bodiced, full-skirted number. It was her standard question, so I gave my standard response. The few times I'd tried to share my honest like or dislike of a dress, she hadn't listened to me anyway.

"It's pretty."

My mom sighed tragically and spun a few times in front of the mirror to get the full effect of the skirt. She looked over her shoulder to see if any of the other store patrons were admiring her. She fluffed up her honey-blond hair and then patted it down. "I think they had this in red too. Anna, would you mind getting me one in red? Size five. I think it was on one of the racks at the front of the store."

Some of the nicer department stores had salesladies with strong perfume who fluttered around my mom, bringing her different sizes and colors of dresses, and even recommending and picking out different ones for her. They were always bitterly disappointed when she didn't buy anything. When salesladies were in short supply, my mom sent me on her dress errands.

The front of the store opened up to the mall, and as I flipped through the rack of dresses, searching for a size five, a loud family passing by caught my attention.

"I'm going to ask Santa for a remote-controlled helicopter!" a boy cried. He was about my age, wearing a dopey-looking sweater with a turtleneck under it like it was school picture day.

"I'm going to ask Santa for a helicopter too!" a smaller boy piped up. His outfit matched his brother's.

"Copycat!" The older boy complained.

Their parents were walking behind them, holding shopping bags and smiling.

"Don't forget to say please," their dad said. "And make sure to thank Santa for all the nice presents he got you last year."

"Okay," the older boy agreed sullenly. "And I won't say anything about the Legos he forgot last time either."

I watched them walk away, presumably to Santa's Village, and burned a jealous look into the boys' backs. How lucky they were. No doubt they didn't have to endure hours of dress-shopping before they got to visit Santa.

"Can I help you, sweetie?" A saleslady's voice brought me back to my task at hand.

"I'm getting a dress for my mom," I said. "She's in the dressing room."

"Well, let me help you." After I told her the color and size, the saleslady gave the rack a few efficient flips and handed me the correct dress. She was wearing a white, fuzzy sweater with a gingerbread house pin attached to her shoulder. It looked like it had real gumdrops glued to it. My mom would've called it ugly.

"I like your pin," I said.

"Why, thank you, sweetie," she said. "I just love Christmas, don't you? I bet you're going to see Santa today."

I nodded uncertainly at her.

The saleslady glanced down at her watch and then frowned. "As soon as your mom is all finished up in here, you'll have to go there next. I think Santa and his elves are only here until four o'clock."

I rushed back to the dressing room, the red dress dragging on the floor a little.

"What took you so long?" my mom asked as she snatched the dress away, but she didn't wait for a reply. She flounced back into her dressing room and shut the saloon door with a slap. I returned to my position as sentinel on the plastic chair.

The red dress wasn't quite right either, and neither were the next four. When my mom came out with an armful of dresses to hang up on the discard rack, I grew hopeful. I stood up, but she told me to hold my horses, that she still had a few more to try on before we could go. I relayed the saleslady's information about Santa's Village closing at four, but she waved my concern away, saying we'd still have plenty of time to see Santa.

I sat back down, kicking the bottom of my chair with my too-tight snow boots.

"This is boring," a girl's voice said. Leah Nola. She materialized in front of me in her gray jumper, the kind of dress I'd always wanted my mom to buy me, but which she insisted looked too "parochial."

"Tell me about it," I whispered.

Leah Nola blew her bangs upward in sympathy. She often showed up on these dress-shopping excursions to keep me company. "Do you want me to stay with you?"

I nodded, and she sat down cross-legged on the floor in front of me. She pulled her skirt taut over her knees.

My mom appeared in a sequined black dress with a plunging neckline and a slit all the way up her leg to her thigh. She seemed to stiffen when her eyes landed on me and swept over Leah Nola.

"It's pretty," I said, before she could ask.

Leah Nola coldly assessed her. "She looks like a vampire."

My mom scowled and propped her hand on her hip. "It's terrible, isn't it? It makes me look pale and my hips look really wide. Something about these sequins." She grimaced at her reflection in the mirror before turning on her heel.

"Ask that lady what time it is," Leah Nola directed.

"Excuse me," I said to the elderly woman leaving the dressing room carrying a pair of slacks. "Do you know what time it is?"

"Three forty-five," the lady read off her watch and kept walking. A sneaking suspicion that I was going to be let down—yet again—crept over me, and I felt a little like crying.

Leah Nola gripped her knees and rocked forward. "This is boring."

"Stop saying that," I hissed. "I know it's boring. And you're not the one who's been sitting here all day."

Leah Nola's lavender eyes flashed. It was a look I knew well, her mischievous look. "Do you want to go see Santa?"

"You know I do," I said. "But my mom's not done trying all her dresses on yet. We'll go once she's done."

Leah Nola stood up and tiptoed toward the individual dressing rooms, as though listening for my mom. "You heard the lady. It's three forty-five. Santa's here until four. Your mom won't be done by then."

"She said there'd be enough time," I murmured.

"Do you want to see Santa?" Leah Nola repeated.

"Yes," I whispered.

"Then let's go." She held out her small, pale hand.

I'd like to say that I hesitated, but I didn't. We scurried from the dressing room area and hid behind a rack of dresses. The kind saleslady with the gingerbread house pin was milling around, so we waited for her to ring up the elderly lady's purchase before making a break from the store. The mall was bigger than I had thought. Louder. More crowded. I would've frozen and turned right back around had Leah Nola not been by my side.

"Do you remember where Santa's Village is?" she asked, hovering close to my shoulder.

"By the food court and the cookie bakery," I said.

"That's good." Leah Nola smiled reassuringly. "Then let's just follow our noses."

No one noticed the little blond girl and her imaginary friend as we darted between the crowds of shoppers. When we finally arrived at Santa's Village—a bustling beacon in the middle of the mall, cordoned off by a faux gold gate draped in greenery—we spotted the long, winding line of kids with their parents and realized that our adventure had probably been in vain.

"There's no way Santa's going to have time to see all these kids before four," I said.

"Why not?" Leah Nola said. "He's Santa." She guided me to the end of the line.

A man, a pregnant lady, and a toddler were in line in front of us. I didn't like the looks of the man. His hairy arms were impatiently folded across his chest, and the only times he unfolded them were to swat the toddler's hand away from the greenery and cottony snow. This mean impatience, combined with his gingery hair, reminded me of Ronnie, one of my mom's ex-boyfriends. When the man noticed me in line behind them, he smiled at me, showing all his teeth. Goosebumps pricked the skin of my arms and legs.

The line inched forward, and Leah Nola and I hung on. Not having a watch and being too afraid of the man in front of me to ask the time, I had no idea if it was four o'clock yet. It seemed like enough time had passed for my mom to have discovered I was gone, changed back into her clothes, and made a dash to Santa's Village. Surely that was the first place she'd look, right? If she knew me even a little? But maybe she'd noticed and decided to finish trying on her dresses anyway, which were clearly more important to her than me. Or maybe when she'd realized I was gone, she'd decided this was the perfect opportunity to be rid of me. Maybe she had left the mall without me.

Under my wool winter jacket, I started to sweat. Part of me had assumed I could slip out of the dressing room, see Santa, and return— my absence totally undetected. The other part of me had wished to create a ruckus, to get a reaction out of my mom. I had hoped she would come searching for me, with tears rolling down her cheeks. But what would happen if she didn't come and find me at Santa's Village? What would happen if I went back to the department store dressing room, and she was simply gone? I unzipped my jacket, hardly noticing that a sign had been placed behind me, indicating I was the last child to see Santa that day, and that only four other children were ahead of me now. Sweat poured down my chest and back, and I suddenly felt lightheaded.

Leah Nola poked me in the side. "I think I see your mom."

I followed her gaze, and sure enough, there she was. Composed and beautiful, like a mermaid on the prow of a ship, she parted the crowds effortlessly. She had changed back into her lacy blouse, jeans, and boots, and the mall's skylights made her honey-colored hair shine. My first thought was, *She doesn't need the Perfect Dress. She's beautiful without it.* My second thought was, *She doesn't look the least bit sad or worried.* For onlookers who didn't know my mom, they would've thought she looked calm and unruffled, but I could tell she was pretty pissed off.

I ducked behind the pregnant lady.

"We should hide," Leah Nola suggested. "Teach her a lesson."

I shook my head. As disappointed as I was to learn that my mom didn't love me, that my brief disappearance hadn't shaken her up at all, I knew that prolonging her discovery of me would only make her angrier in the long run. The pregnant lady stepped out of my way, exposing me, and I suddenly realized that I was next in line to see Santa. A vista had been opened up before me. I could see his big golden chair and the fake Christmas trees flanking him. The creepy man set the toddler on Santa's big, red-velvet covered lap. The toddler immediately began wailing and reaching for her mother. Santa clung to the child as if she were a slippery fish and smiled tiredly for the camera.

"I hope you're happy," my mom said, towering over me in her boots. "You just had to get your way, didn't you? You scared me to death." She bent down to my height and gripped my shoulders. Her hands felt like claws digging into my winter jacket, all the way to my bones. Her hazel eyes were abnormally bright. I thought for a moment that she might hug me, but instead, she flung me away from her, as if in disgust. "Don't you ever scare me like that again."

A young woman dressed in a green felt smock and gold tights approached us. "Welcome to Santa's Village. It's your turn to see Santa, and you're pretty lucky, because you're the last kid of the day!"

My mom sneered at the elf. "That won't be necessary." She whipped around to face Santa. "Anna Grace Jennings!" she shouted at him. "Write that name down on your naughty list. She doesn't deserve any presents this year."

The pregnant lady and the toddler were still lingering on the other side of the gold gate. She looked from my mom to me with a look of pity before her mean husband hurried her away. A few other shoppers had stopped to watch the spectacle, and I felt like burying myself in the fake puffs of snow and never coming out again.

Santa's mouth opened in a retort, but we never got to hear what it was because my mom was already dragging me away. I could feel her anger vibrating through her arms as she jerked me down a side hallway that led to where we had parked several hours before.

"Don't. You. Dare. Ever. Pull. A stunt. Like that. Again. Anna Grace." The angry click of her boot heels punctuated each of her words. "You hear me?"

I stared defiantly ahead, not responding.

"Do you hear me?" my mom demanded, the claw digging into my shoulder again.

I gave in. "Yes," I said softly.

Back in the car, she hardly paused for breath as she berated me. "How could you have been so stupid? Do you know what could have happened to you? Have I taught you nothing about public places and strangers? You don't look at them, you don't talk to them, and you certainly don't just walk away from me, when I trusted you to wait. This is a scary world, and little girls like you need to wise up fast."

My ears were plugged from crying so hard, and I caught only about half of her tirade.

"You couldn't wait five minutes until I was finished to go see Santa. You had to run off by yourself even though I promised I'd take you."

"Santa's Village closed at four," I muttered. "Leah Nola said there wouldn't be enough time."

An icy silence followed. I could see my mom's profile, and her jaw was clenched like it was spring-loaded.

"Oh, I see," she said, her volume steadily increasing. "So this whole thing was all Leah Nola's fault, huh? You were just an innocent bystander? Well, I am sick and tired of all this Leah Nola said this, Leah Nola said that crap. You did it, Anna. *You* did. Leah Nola *does not* exist." She paused to gulp in a ragged breath. "It's all in your head, and the sooner you learn that, the better. Now I don't want to hear her name ever again. Do you understand me?"

I leaned forward in my seat, eager to set the record straight. "But—"

My mom turned around quickly to fix me with her serious stare. "Do you understand me?"

I looked down at my lap. "Yes."

She shook her head. "I don't know what I'm going to do with you. You're such a stubborn little thing."

I met her eyes in the rearview mirror. "I am not stubborn. You're selfish." It had been an idea I'd been mulling over for a long time now, but something Leah Nola had only recently verbalized for me. "You don't care about me. You only care about yourself."

My words hit their target, as my mom recoiled. She adjusted her grip on the steering wheel and stared straight ahead. But then her eyes flicked back up to the rearview mirror. "If I don't care about you, why do I work two shitty jobs just to put food on the table and keep a roof over your head? Why do I put up with your constant nonsense? Talking to imaginary people and running away in malls? I'm getting pretty fed up with it, I'll have you know."

At that age, I didn't understand the difference between begrudgingly meeting someone's basic physical needs and lovingly taking care of them, so I didn't have a rebuttal. Instead I seethed in the backseat, replaying the horrific scene in the mall when my own mother had told Santa I belonged on the naughty list. Of course, she didn't end up going through with the whole no-present thing. I did get a few presents for Christmas that year, but all of the labels read "FROM: MOM." Not a single one of them was addressed from Santa, and she made a big deal out of this, acting like she'd been my hero even though I didn't deserve gifts. It was the last year I believed in Santa.

CHAPTER FIFTEEN

We arrived back in Salsburg, all three of us more or less intact, but traumatized. David had succumbed reluctantly to sleep, but his cheeks were still an angry red, and his brow was wrinkled even as he slept. Duffy was a fidgety mess, huffing-and-puffing beside me, and I was so deep in my thoughts I doubt I would've noticed if a high-speed police chase had flown past us on the highway. I had never been more relieved to pull onto Steepleview, lined with its Douglas firs.

As Duffy went about putting her beauty supplies away in the basement (the trip to the office supply store had been abandoned), I improvised a timeout chair in the dining room. I situated David in the chair and explained that he would have to sit there for fifteen minutes and think about what he had done wrong on our shopping trip. He broke out into his full-face frown again, but I stood my ground and turned him so he was facing the sun-faded mauve wall. That way I wouldn't see his pouty lips and puppy dog eyes and be tempted to cave in.

Head pounding and knees still a little weak, I collapsed onto the floral couch. The fear of losing David had burned through me like a wildfire. Never before had the possibility seemed so white-hot and real. Not when my mom found out I was pregnant and suggested I consider giving him up for adoption. Not when I found him as an infant, crying, cold, and alone in his baby bathtub. Not when Abigail Gill proposed shared custody. Standing in the strip mall parking lot, scared out of my wits, I had realized that there had been a point in time when I could have imagined my life without David and had even perhaps fantasized about its being somehow better. But now, picturing a life without him was impossible. I loved him and needed him with my whole being. But that didn't mean I still wasn't as mad as hell at him for wandering off on his own. Not to mention scared to death that a dangerous line with his dinosaurs had been crossed.

David let out a whimper like an injured dog, but I did my best to steel my resolve and ignore him. Burrowing deeper into the couch cushions, I reexamined my memory of the East Ridge Mall incident that had recently floated to the surface of my brain, clear and crisp, as if it had happened only yesterday. Leah Nola sitting at my feet, making jokes at my mom's expense, urging me to run off to see Santa, and accompanying me across the mall. It was like finding a long-lost sister. Or discovering an untapped source of strength I had never known I'd had.

But the incident's similarity to David's running away with his own imaginary friends was disconcerting to me. I disliked being cast in the role of mean mom, and I disliked even more being forced to empathize with my mother's perspective: the distress she'd obviously felt at my disappearance and her anger at my willful blindness to the menace she saw lurking everywhere. Although she definitely could have handled our reunion better—could have said just once, "I'm glad you're okay," and perhaps not sold me out in front of a mall full of people including Santa—there was love in her reaction; I could see that now. Fierce, bottled-up love, tinged with something else, though. *Fear.*

I remembered the way my mom had stiffened when she'd come out of the dressing room after Leah Nola had joined me. The way she'd grimaced when Leah Nola insulted her dress. The way her eyes sometimes flitted to where Leah Nola stood beside me, and how she'd insisted viciously, almost to the point of tears, on our drive home that Leah Nola didn't exist and was all in my head. Maybe I had inherited my ability to see David's imagination from my mom, after all. Maybe she had been able to see Leah Nola and had been afraid of her. Of *us.*

Was that the reason why she'd sent me away both summers to stay with my grandparents?

A month ago this possibility might have reassured me that I wasn't totally crazy and alone, but now it just depressed me. Because if she had had the ability to see my imaginary friend, it hadn't served as a special bond that had brought us closer together; instead, it had driven us apart. If Leah Nola had been the outlet into which I had vented all my frustration with my mom, and my mom had been able to see and hear her, undoubtedly this had caused even greater tension between us. And if my mom had thought something was wrong with her—or me—because she could see my imaginary friend, maybe she had tried to distance herself from me even more. The thought of that happening to my relationship with David was devastating. I tried not to remember the ominous way King Rex had stood, snarling, between my son and me at the dollar store. Were we already on the same path my mother and I had traveled?

I studied David's slumped shoulders across the room. He had stopped whimpering. A glance at the grandfather clock revealed only thirteen minutes had passed, but David wouldn't know the difference. To him, his timeout had probably felt like it had already lasted fifteen hours.

I gently gripped his shoulder and turned the chair around. He let out a world-weary sigh as if he were a convict being released on parole. That sigh made me want to forgive him instantly and cover his tear-stained face with kisses, but I knew I couldn't give in just yet.

"Do you understand why running away was wrong?" I asked him, tilting my head to force him to make eye contact.

"It was bad," he murmured.

"Yes, it was bad because something bad could have happened to you. A not very nice stranger could have hurt you, or you could have gotten lost, and Grandma and I were really worried about you because you're so special to us. You can't go off on your own like that."

"I wasn't alone. I was with my dino-suss."

I lowered myself to the floor and sat cross-legged in front of his chair. "I know that, but King Rex and Weeple aren't like me or

Grandma. They're not real, and you can't trust them to look after you. They're pretend."

David jutted out his lip. "They look after me. They're my friends."

"It's nice to have pretend friends as well as real friends," I said slowly. "But it's not your dinosaurs' job to look after you. It's my job as your mommy to know what's best for you and keep you safe."

"I'm not a baby," he spat and kicked out his leg, coming dangerously close to my knee.

I stilled his leg with a firm squeeze. "I know that, buckaroo. You're going to be starting school next week, and you're turning five next month. But I'll always be your mommy, and you'll always be my David, and it's so important to me that you're safe and healthy. I'm worried that you're not safe with the dinosaurs anymore. That they might hurt you—maybe on purpose or maybe by accident."

"They won't hurt me." David's eyes were as shiny as two new pennies. "They're *mine*."

His proud claim of having dominion over his imaginary friends was strangely unnerving. Though I wanted to believe in his guarantee that they would never go berserk and turn on him, I wondered about everyone else's safety. What about Jamie and Gunner? What about me? Had those aggressive actions been under David's control too? "But even if you say your imaginary friends won't hurt you, what about other people? You told me King Rex hurt Gunner, and that's not acceptable. We can't have that happening."

"King Rex said he's sorry."

Well, that was comforting—the Tyrannosaurus rex was apologetic for slashing a boy half his size with his claws. What if he was still gaining gravity, strength, and speed? And what if he used his teeth the next time David was in a situation with someone the dinosaur considered threatening? I could hear Duffy's footsteps climbing the creaky basement stairs, and I knew we needed to wrap this conversation up. But not before I'd extracted some very important promises.

"Listen to me, David. You need to control your imaginary friends so that they can't hurt anyone—not you, not me, not Grandma and Grandpa, not other children, okay? Because if you can't control them, if they do bad things, they need to go away and never come back, okay? Do you understand?"

He had never looked more like his father—the intense gaze, the conflicting emotions warring across his face. He nodded gravely.

"And you need to promise me that you're never going to run away like that again. My heart can't take it. I was so scared I had lost you."

David's brown eyes widened. "You were scared?"

"*Terrified.* I love you, buckaroo, and I don't know what I'd do without you. So do you promise not to run away like that again?"

He gestured with his cupped hand that he wanted to whisper something in my ear. I leaned forward. "Yes, Mommy," he hissed in approximation of a solemn, secretive whisper. His warm, sweet breath tickled my ear.

Over the next few days, I became obsessed with the idea that my mom had been able to see Leah Nola, and that this had somehow led to our undoing. Something major must have happened between the three of us for my mom to send me away and cite Leah Nola's arrival in our lives as the moment that I started to hate her. The parallel sets of mother, child, and imaginary friend felt like one of those algebra equations I had been so terrible at solving in high school. If x is a dinosaur, solve for y. I felt like understanding what Leah Nola had represented to me and what purpose she had served in my childhood might somehow provide the key to David's dinosaurs. And maybe understanding how my mom had mishandled my friendship with Leah Nola could teach me what *not* to do. With David's first day of kindergarten less than a week away, I was desperate to learn anything that might help him and reduce his attachment to the potentially dangerous dinosaurs.

I peppered Duffy with questions about those two summers, but she evaded them, blaming a poor memory. I knew her reluctance to talk about Leah Nola and my mom had more to do with her unwillingness to disparage Kimberly, especially around me. I had yet to come to terms with how the same leniency and forgiveness my generous, loving grandparents had shown me extended also to my mother.

I hunted through my childhood sketchbook for clues I might have missed the first time. There was one drawing that stood out to me as significant, but I couldn't figure out the context. In it, I was sitting in bed, wearing a yellow nightgown, and Leah Nola stood beside me with her arms spread out, as if she were vanquishing a bad dream. I asked Jamie about it one night, as we sat on orange vinyl barstools in his wood-paneled basement, swiveling, throwing darts, and drinking Cokes like we had as kids, but he didn't know what it meant either. He told me I had been pretty tight-lipped about my relationship with my mom, saying only a few times that I wished I never had to go back home.

Finally, I cornered my least likely source, my reticent grandfather, as he dug out the roots of a dead woody shrub in the front yard. I'd found with Winston, he was more likely to talk if you got him away from Duffy and occupied with some other activity, instead of trying to sit down for a face-to-face conversation.

"Do you need any help?" I asked, wondering why root and stump removal didn't fall under Jamie's landscaping jurisdiction. The sleeves of Winston's shirt were rolled up, and the material clung to his back and chest in two dark stains. It looked like Winston and his spade were fighting a losing battle against the gnarled roots.

"I wouldn't say no to a glass of lemonade," he said, mopping his forehead with a yellowed handkerchief. When I returned with two frosted mugs, he was leaning on his spade, contemplating the stubborn roots. "Thank you." He chugged the lemonade down in one continuous swallow, set his empty mug in the grass, and got back to work.

I sipped mine. "Do you happen to remember anything about my imaginary friend, Leah Nola?"

"Just what you told me." He punched the sharp edge of the spade repeatedly into the earth. "Orphaned as a baby. Independent, pretty, smart. A little mischievous at times." He grunted with exertion.

"Mischievous, how?" The mug was dripping condensation down my wrist. I shook it off.

He shrugged. "I can't say. We never experienced any problems with you here in Salsburg. You were pretty well-behaved for us."

"But with my mom in Milwaukee...?" I prompted him.

"Well, it's no secret you two have your history of butting heads," he said a little tiredly. "Kim never said anything specific, but it was clear your having an imaginary friend bothered her."

"Why do you think that?"

He considered this, pausing to pull his handkerchief from his pocket to wipe the back of his neck. "I don't know. Maybe she was worried you were spending so much time with her. Or maybe she just didn't under-stand. As a girl, Kim never had an imaginary friend. Luke was always the more creative one; Kim was the realist. She liked to play her flute, and she liked to collect things: wedding cake toppers, salt and pepper shakers, porcelain dolls. Not to play with, mind you, but to look at."

My mom, the realist? Ha. It sounded like something she'd paid Winston to say. The collecting part I vaguely remembered. In our kitchen, there had been a decorative shelf with several small boxes, and each box housed a ceramic salt and pepper shaker set—mushrooms, owls, gnomes, acorns, ducks—each piece an essential part of an or-dained pair. As an adolescent, I'd thought her knick-knack collection was incredibly tacky.

"Could you hand me that utility bar over there?" Winston asked.

I turned around and saw the long, steel pole to which he was re-ferring. The pole was rounded on one end and had a flat, sharp blade on the other. It was heavy; I had to kneel and lift it with both hands. "Do you think Leah Nola had anything to do with my mom sending me to stay with you guys?"

"I can't say." He angled the utility bar under the soil-packed mass of roots. "That first summer we planned your visit ahead of time. But that second summer, it was short notice. Very short notice."

His face reddened and then purpled with the effort of freeing the clump of roots from the earth, and he stopped talking. At last, the shriveled shrub fell away, revealing a cavity big enough to cradle an infant.

He huffed to catch his breath. "That second summer, Kimberly just showed up one afternoon with you and your suitcase. Of course, we were happy to have you. But it came as somewhat of a surprise."

"And she didn't say why?"

"Not exactly." Winston's tufted eyebrows knit together. "But her arm was in a sling, and she said she'd broken it falling off a ladder. I remember she was worried about waitressing and paying the bills because she was right-handed and it was her right arm."

Despite the August heat, I shivered, deeply disturbed. I had absolutely no memory of my mom's breaking her arm.

He stooped to position the wheelbarrow near the pit. "You're an adult now, so I can tell you that your grandma was concerned the 'fall' had really been a fight. We didn't like her boyfriend at the time, but Kimberly insisted he wasn't the problem."

My skin crawled. *He*, the boyfriend, wasn't the problem. What she'd left unspoken, or maybe Winston had left unspoken out of the desire to protect my feelings, was that *I* was the problem. *Leah Nola* was. Part and parcel of each other, *we* were the problem. Had the boyfriend injured my mother? Or had Leah Nola somehow done it? The thought, with the memory of what could have only been King Rex's cool, scaly skin brushing against my hand at the dollar store, filled me with a sick dread. If it was true, then imaginary things were capable of physical force. Of violence.

I took a gulp of lemonade, nearly choking. The algebra equation I'd been wrestling with was becoming only more complicated. What events had led to my mom sending me away so hastily? Had Leah Nola and I done something to frighten or injure her, and if so, what had prompted our acting out? It seemed crucial to David's safety and my own to fill in these missing variables, and there was only one person on this planet with the answers to my questions. Unfortunately, she was also the last person on the planet to whom I wanted to talk.

CHAPTER SIXTEEN

My mom's new place was in one of the well-off, northern lakeside communities of Milwaukee, and I wondered what sugar daddy she'd roped into buying or renting it for her. I'd sneakily copied the address out of Duffy's address book and entered it into Winston's GPS. The house itself was nothing impressive: a rundown Colonial with half beige brick and half white siding, rose bushes past their bloom, and two strips of concrete for a driveway with grass and weeds growing in between. There was a one-car garage set back at the end of the driveway, and I wondered if my mom's car was parked inside and she was home. It was one o'clock in the afternoon, and her waitressing jobs usually dictated a night schedule.

I parked Winston's car in front of her house and got out before I lost my nerve. I needed answers. Answers that my grandmother had pointed out, at the beginning of the summer, could only be given to me by one person. *If you have questions about that time in your life, you know who you should ask? Your mother.* But even if my mom did hold the answers I was looking for, would she be willing to share them with me?

I rang her doorbell, but when I didn't hear its chiming echo inside, I knocked as well. I started to count to twenty. If she didn't answer the door by the time I got to twenty—

She opened the door.

With her hair piled messily atop her head and her black spandex capris and aqua-colored tank top, she looked like I'd interrupted her doing yoga. I listened for a DVD walking viewers through a sunrise salutation, but I didn't hear anything. No macho middle-aged guy yelling from the kitchen, "Who's at the door, babe?" either. (Thank God.) No, there was just a long period of silence as my mom and I stared at each incredulously.

Finally she said, "Anna. What can I do for you?"

My heart gave a twinge of disappointment. Was it really so much to expect a smile? An acknowledgement that it was nice to see me after all these years? A greeting just a tad bit warmer than one she would've given a door-to-door salesperson? "Can I come in?" I asked in the most civil tone I could muster. I tried to remind myself that I hadn't come for hugs and a touchy-feely reconciliation. I'd come to learn more about Leah Nola. I'd come to see if I could glean anything to help David.

"I don't see why not." She took a step backward and opened the door wider to admit me.

The living room had hardwood floors and the walls were painted a soothing sage green. It was the antithesis of the dark, carpeted caves I'd grown up in. Only one framed photo sat on the mantelpiece—a picture of my mom with a balding guy in a gray suit who looked much older than she was. There were no pictures of me or David. Big surprise. The rest of the mantelpiece and all other flat surfaces in the living room were covered with porcelain dolls in stands: a bride, a Russian peasant, a Japanese geisha, a doll that looked like Scarlet O'Hara, a doll in a red velvet hooded cloak, a doll in a satin ball gown. And all their eyes seemed to be watching me as I sat down on one end of the couch. Creepy.

My mom reluctantly sat down in the chair across from me. She gestured to my pink cardigan, which I hadn't realized I was still wearing. "Are you on your lunch break?"

Did she even know I wasn't living in Milwaukee anymore? That David and I had been staying with her parents for the past two months? Probably Duffy had told her. But maybe my mom had forgotten already—we were that inconsequential to her. "No," I said. "I had an interview this morning."

After a long dry spell of sending out my resume with no responses, I'd finally gotten a phone call inviting me to interview for an administrative assistant position at a residential real estate office in Lawrenceville. The hourly wage was nothing to write home about, but they offered health insurance and paid sick days, and it was getting to the point where any stream of revenue, no matter how small, was simply better than nothing.

I'd dug out a pale pink cardigan from the depths of Duffy's closet and added it to my interview ensemble. With my blouse buttoned nearly to my throat, the cashmere-blend cardigan layered over it, and my long hair pulled back in a French twist, I'd looked like the kind of innocuous, wholesome Barbie that employers were dying to hire. Winston had even proposed I drive his car, so I wouldn't arrive to my interview windblown and damp with sweat. I hoped he wouldn't mind that I'd fibbed a little and told them I was meeting Carly for lunch after my interview and wouldn't be home until mid-afternoon but, instead, had driven to Milwaukee to see my estranged mother.

Janet Galloway, the realtor interviewing me, had smiled and nodded emphatically at each of my answers as though she couldn't have said it any better herself. After giving me a tour of their small office and introducing me to her two partners, Gisele Quenzel and Brandon Dial, she had squeezed my hand and said tellingly, "You should be hearing from us in a few days. Thanks *so much* for coming in, Anna."

Immediately I had felt twenty pounds lighter. I was close to securing one aspect of my otherwise erratic, up-in-the-air existence. Now if only I could get the imaginary friends situation—David's and my own—figured out.

But my mom didn't ask anything about my interview. She didn't ask where it had been or how it had gone. Instead, she directed her gaze to a foot or two above mine. "Well, you look nice."

Yeah, right. Probably like one of her porcelain dolls, cutesy in a tweed skirt and leather flats. Why was she always so focused on appearances? I fingered one of the pearl buttons on my cardigan, wishing I had thought to bring a change of clothes along. I didn't want my mom thinking I had dressed up on her behalf.

"Thanks," I said. Clearly neither of us was in the mood for girly chitchat, and there was really no way to ease into the topic I had in mind. "I came here to talk about Leah Nola." My words had the effect I'd expected them to. She clearly remembered my imaginary friend's name; she stood up from her chair as if she planned on leaving the room.

"God almighty, Anna! Fifteen years later, and you're still going on with this stupid nonsense? I would hope you'd have more important things to be worrying about."

"It's important to me," I persevered. "I don't remember much about that time period; I was so young. And it seems like Leah Nola contributed to the problems you and I had. That she was one of the reasons why you sent me to stay with Duffy and Winston the summers I was seven and eight."

My mom flopped back down in her chair and crossed her long, toned legs. "Why do you want to know? Are you writing a tell-all exclusive about your shitty childhood? Do you need more ammunition against me?" She released the sloppy bun on her head and set about rewrapping it. She sighed. "If we're being honest here, sending you away to Salsburg those two summers was probably the best thing I ever did for you. You should be thanking me."

In retrospect, I agreed with her, but at the time I'd felt so wronged and abandoned I hadn't seen it that way. I wanted to ask her point blank if she'd been able to see my imagination, but it was such a ludicrous question, and she was already on the defensive. I didn't want her to shut down on me altogether.

"You're right. Living with Winston and Duffy was wonderful. But you didn't send me there because you wanted me to spend quality time with my grandparents. You sent me there because of 'behavior problems.' Because of my overactive imagination. And I need to—"

"You need to leave the past in the past." She waved her hand dismissively. "You were a stubborn kid, a loner, who believed in fairies and all that other garbage, but you grew out of it. Well, not the stubborn part, but the rest of it. Why borrow trouble?"

"I'm not borrowing trouble," I said. Trouble was on my doorstep. Trouble was stalking my child and breathing down my neck. I needed to convey this to her, and there was only one way to do it. "David," I started—"my son"—in case she'd forgotten, "has imaginary friends too. Dinosaurs. And…" It had to come out, but it was harder than ripping off a Band-Aid. At least then, you knew you were going to feel sharp yet short-lived pain. But in this situation, I had no idea what her reaction would be. "I can see them," I forced myself to finish.

Her smooth face blanched and hardened as if it were a plaster death mask. Neither of us seemed to breathe for several seconds. Finally, she said, "That is the stupidest thing I've ever heard." She stopped abruptly. "You should just go."

Had I been totally off base with my speculations that she had seen my imagination? But no. Because even now while she was trying to brush me off, she looked shell-shocked, like I had struck a major nerve.

I pushed harder. "You know I'm telling the truth." I took a deep breath, looking straight into her hazel eyes. "You know it because you saw my imaginary friend too."

She jumped up from her chair again. "This is a fucking joke." She raised her wrist to glance at her rubbery, aqua-colored digital watch. It was color-coordinated with her tank top perfectly. "Well, it's been fun, but I need to get going to my Pilates class. Then I'm headed straight to work."

The kitchen was connected to the living room, and I followed her as she headed to the fridge to get a bottle of water. "I need to know what happened," I said. "I'm worried about David. I'm worried his dinosaurs might be dangerous."

I thought I saw her hesitate as she closed the fridge. She kept her face turned away from me.

"Mom?" I hadn't called her that in several years. As a teenager, I'd taken to defiantly calling her by her first name, and nowadays I avoided referring to her by any name. I hardly recognized my own voice; I sounded so plaintive. "Please?"

She didn't turn around. "You really don't remember?" Apparently forgetting her hair was in a bun, she forced her manicured fingernails through the crown of it, loosening strands and mussing it up. She blew out a heavy sigh. "Oh, God, what a mess."

"Was it the mall incident? When I ran away to see Santa? Was that the first time you saw her?"

"No, I saw her from the very beginning." My mom studied the Scarlet O'Hara doll on the end table beside her. It was one of the only things she and I had in common: our love for *Gone with the Wind*. The rare times we'd been at peace with each other in my middle school and high school years had occurred when the movie came on TV and we settled down to watch all six commercial-interrupted hours of it together. She glanced up at me, and I could tell she hadn't been reminiscing about the same thing, but a memory that deeply upset her. "For a few weeks, I thought she was just a neighbor girl you were playing with. But then one day, I saw her disappear right before my eyes."

"And you thought you were going crazy," I supplied, smoothing my skirt over my lap.

"I thought I was going crazy," she agreed.

I wanted to hear absolutely everything. How she had come to understand it was my imagination she was seeing, if she'd taken me to a doctor, if she'd gone to a doctor herself, what kinds of things Leah Nola and I had done together, if she had ever tried to talk to me about it. But she was as restless and edgy as a criminal about to stand trial. Our tentative truce might not last for very long, and I needed to hear the most pertinent, valuable details while she was still willing to open up to me.

"Could she touch things?" I asked. "Affect her environment?"

"She could." She raised her eyebrows as if about to challenge me, but her perfectly pink-lipsticked lips were trembling. "The little bitch."

The word *bitch* landed like a stinging slap on my cheek. It was the word we'd cruelly yet casually launched at each other all throughout my adolescence. The insult hurt even more now, though, because she was trying to tear down the friend I'd purposely created to build me up. It set my already electrified nerves on edge. Did I really want to hear the whole story, or rather, my mom's side of the story? I was suddenly scared to uncover the events that had caused me to repress Leah Nola's memory.

"What did she do?" I asked softly, grabbing the throw pillow next to me and squeezing it against my stomach.

"She made all kinds of trouble." My mom's face was so similar to my own; it was like looking into a mirror that showed me what I would look like too, one day, if I lived a life of bitterness like hers. There were more frown lines than laugh lines. She swiped absent-mindedly at her eyelashes as if she'd noticed me staring at her and thought her immaculate makeup was amiss. "But the worst of it was at the end of second grade." *Right before she had sent me to Salsburg the second time.* "She told you to smash my wedding cake topper collection."

"Your wedding cake toppers?" That sounded vaguely familiar, and I realized Winston had just mentioned them in the context of my mom's various collections as a child.

"You don't remember them? I had been collecting them since I was a little girl. I begged the bride of every wedding I attended to give me hers off her cake after the reception, and I got them from rummage sales and discount stores too." She shot me a look that implied I very well knew what had happened and I was just play-ing at forgetting to make her relive it. "I came home one day from running errands—we'd been fighting before I left, about God knows what—and I went into my bedroom, and there you were with Leah Nola, dropping the figurines off the shelf, one by one, sniveling and telling her you wanted to stop."

A chill crept down my spine, vertebrae by vertebrae, as I realized my mom was telling the truth and I remembered flashes of that day. The wedding cake topper collection had been divided among two old, scratched-up curio cabinets flanking my mom's queen-size bed. There had to have been at least forty of them—miniature smiling brides and grooms, ceramic, porcelain, and blown glass, all frozen in that eternal moment of the anticipation of a life of happiness. Some of them broke simply by sweeping them to the floor, but others needed to be stepped on with a satisfying crunch.

Leah Nola had pointed to the first one, a brown-haired man lifting a blond woman into the sanctuary of his arms, folds of her extravagant dress cascading downward. "This is her favorite one, isn't it? Let's show her, Anna. This is the only way she'll listen to you. This is the only way we can make it stop."

I lifted the figurine from the shelf and let it slip through my trembling fingers. It shattered into a hundred little pieces on the floor. "No more," I sobbed. "I don't want to do this. You're wrong."

"No, *you're* wrong," she argued. "She doesn't trust you. She trusts him. And this is the only way to get through to her." So more couples gazing soulfully into each other's eyes were split apart and decimated. Marital bliss annihilated. My mom's hopes and dreams, whatever those sentimental cake toppers represented to her, all smashed to smithereens. Only the figurines on the two highest shelves remained when she walked into the room, a look of fury emblazoned on her face.

"You know what you need to do," Leah Nola said, before vanishing to leave me with the aftermath: my mom's rage and all those sharp little pieces like tiny seashells littering a beach. At the time, I thought she'd been talking to me. But now that I knew my mom could see and hear her, I wondered if Leah Nola's comment had been directed at her. What had our argument been about? What had prompted such a mean-spirited act of revenge? I still couldn't remember everything—only bright, crystalline flickers in an otherwise murky backdrop—and it was unbelievably frustrating.

"That wasn't even the worst part," my mom said, brushing an invisible piece of lint off her stretchy black capris. "She woke me up that night, standing at the foot of my bed like a goddamn ghost. I about had a stroke. And the next day, after I boxed up the few remaining cake toppers so you couldn't break those too, I climbed the ladder to put them in the attic space, and she *pushed* me, the little shit. I didn't fall far, but far enough to break my arm in two places." She held up her flawlessly lean and tan arm as if it still bore the proof of her injury.

My mind was racing. Leah Nola was supposed to be my friend, my protector, the brave self I wished I could be. It made no sense for her to attack my mom unprovoked. Though I had been furious with my mom on countless occasions, I had never seriously wanted to do her bodily harm. Had Leah Nola slipped out of my control and taken on a malicious life of her own? If so, I could be in serious trouble with David's dinosaurs. But the memory of what Leah Nola had said, her shrouded reasoning for destroying the collection, made me skeptical of this. Also, there was my mom's tendency to never admit any wrongdoing or accept blame. Something about her short account of the events seemed fishy.

"But *why?*" I crossed my legs at the knee and pulled them toward me.

"I don't know," she shot back. "She was *your* imaginary friend, Anna. It stands to reason that you'd understand her crazy motives better than I do." The pallor that had fallen over her face when I'd first brought up our strange shared ability was being replaced by a pink flush.

"All I remember is her saying that you wouldn't listen to me," I said. "That you didn't believe me. But wouldn't believe me about what? What did she say to you? Why would she wake you up in the middle of the night?"

Red sunburn-like blotches were coloring my mom's chest and neck and creeping higher. Her lips hardly moved. "She wanted me to go to your room."

My eyes were transfixed by her blossoming red rash. I held my breath. "Why?"

"She wanted me to check on you," she said, refusing to look at me. "She wouldn't leave until I did. So I got out of bed. And I bumped into Dennis in the hall. Outside your door."

"Why was he outside my door?" I didn't blink. I squeezed my hands into tight fists.

And suddenly it was there. All of it. The drawing in my sketch-book abruptly made sense. The murky backdrop came to the fore-front, as a vision of my mom's old boyfriend, Dennis, jolted me. His sandy blond hair and mustache, his full, almost womanly lips. The presents he gave me for no reason: the ballerina Barbie doll, the silver bracelet with pink, heart-shaped beads. The way he hugged me, pet-ted my hair, offered to help me with my homework and then sat too close on the couch. Leah Nola hated him. "He's so nice it's scary. It makes me uncomfortable. You should tell your mom," she insisted. But I had never liked any of my mom's boyfriends, so my complaints fell on deaf ears. Dennis was the first of her boyfriends to show an in-terest in me—all the others had acted like I didn't even exist—so my mom couldn't understand what my problem was. And I couldn't fully explain it to her either. As an eight-year-old, it was hard to articulate a fear I had no words for or true conception of. But Leah Nola, my more intuitive self, had sensed it.

When Dennis offered to babysit me, Leah Nola and I both recoiled at the thought and persuaded my mom that I was old enough to look after myself for a few hours and that I could call our elderly neighbor, Vern, if I needed anything. But some nights, Dennis slept over, in my mom's bed, like all the other boyfriends before him; those nights, Leah Nola stood like a sentry at my door.

The night my bedroom door groaned open, I could see his sandy head silhouetted by the glow of the hallway nightlight and hear his heavy breathing. Huddled beneath my comforter, I pretended to be sleeping. Leah Nola whispered, "Hold on, Anna. I'll be right back!" and slipped out of the room like a shadow, leaving me behind, all alone and afraid. His shuffling footsteps and heavy breathing got closer but then suddenly retreated. The door had closed, and I'd heard Dennis and my mom's low voices in the hallway. Leah Nola had woken my mom up and saved me from whatever unthinkable thing would have happened next.

"He said he thought he'd heard you having a bad dream," my mom said dully, still avoiding my eyes. "He was coming to wake me up."

"And you believed him?" I kneaded the couch cushion with my fists. I felt like I might vomit. Because my mom had gone back to bed with Dennis that night, like nothing had happened, and the next day she had announced he'd be staying with us while his condo was renovated. That was when my mom had been shoved from the ladder. Not by Leah Nola, as we had led her to believe, but by *me*. Leah Nola hadn't been the one capable of physical violence. *I had.*

"I don't know how else to protect you," she had whispered, as we'd watched my mom set up the ladder, hidden from her view by the L-bend in the hallway. "She won't listen, and he's not going to stop until he gets what he wants. I'm not strong enough, Anna. You need to be strong enough for both of us now."

"But why do we have to hurt her?" I'd asked. "What if she *dies*?"

"She won't die," Leah Nola had reassured me. "It's not high enough. We just need to scare her so she knows we mean business, and he needs to leave. She needs to put you first for once and not be so selfish. I know you can do this, Anna, and I'll take the blame. We've tried everything else. It's our last chance."

Now my mom touched her neck, the tendons flaring. "Who was I supposed to believe? My eight-year-old daughter's imaginary friend?"

"Maybe your eight-year-old *daughter*." I gasped for breath and struggled to keep my nausea and fury down in the pit of my stomach and out of my scorched, tightening throat. My eyes stung in a way that I knew tears would soon follow if I didn't toughen myself up quickly.

My mom grimaced like she was in physical pain. "I sent you to stay with my parents. And we broke up not long after that anyway. What more could I have done? He was a nice guy. You and your friend…you just never wanted me to be happy with anyone. You were always trying to get attention. How was I to know that this was different? I mean, we still don't know for sure." She chewed on her fingernails, oblivious to the damage she was inflicting on her expensive manicure.

"You're right," I said in a scathing tone. "We still don't know *for sure*. Maybe if Leah Nola hadn't woken you up. Then we could've known for sure. Or maybe if she hadn't harassed you to the point of sending me away. Then we could rest easy knowing *for sure* that Dennis was a pedophile."

She was quiet for a long time, and I thought maybe she'd finally run out of excuses. Maybe I'd finally broken her down to a place where she might express horror and regret. Then she spit out a sliver of fingernail. "I don't expect you to understand, but I thought she was some kind of devil. That she was trying to possess you and was just whispering whatever lies she could think of to drive me crazy."

It would've been almost funny had I not been so completely hollowed out by my anger and sense of betrayal. "I do understand, at least sort of. David imagines playing with a T-rex and a Brontosaurus, and they absolutely terrify me. But they're as much a part of him as Leah Nola was a part of me. And she wasn't the devil. She was the closest thing to a guardian angel I had."

"Well, I hope they never turn on you." Slack-faced and tired, she stared at me as if she were seeing me for the first time. Her honey-colored hair was wild and disheveled. "I hope you...I hope you..." But she didn't complete her thought out loud for me, which was almost better in a way because then I could fill in the blank for her and imagine what she hoped for me, even if she would never admit it.

> *I hope you learn from my mistakes.*
> *I hope you are a better mother and a stronger woman than me.*
> *I hope you always listen to David and put him first.*
> *I hope you can forgive me one day*

CHAPTER SEVENTEEN

"So it's official. I'm gainfully employed now," I told Jamie. It was one of those perfect summer nights when it seemed almost criminal to stay inside, so we'd decided to take a leisurely walk through our tiny town of no sidewalks, no stoplight, and very few streetlights. Hundreds of fireflies' bulbs blinked on and off, our own private light show, as we walked along Steepleview. "Hopefully, the Salsburg rumor mill will downgrade me from a full-time mooch to a part-time mooch now."

"I'll start spreading the word." He laughed. "Congrats! Where will you be working?"

"Galloway Realtors in Lawrenceville." Melody Yarbrough's yappy little dog started barking its head off as we strolled past her house; I hoped the noise wouldn't wake the entire neighborhood.

"Like, selling houses?"

"More like answering the phones for the people who sell houses. But they're nice people, and it's a paycheck. And the hours are flexible, so it should work well with David at school half the day."

"Well, that's great. I'm really happy for you."

We came up to Main Street, and without a word, he reached for my hand as we crossed. His fingers felt good laced snugly through mine, and I was glad when he didn't let go even when we were safely on the other side. The river burbled hidden in the darkness, the moon shone on the white steeple of St. Monica's, and despite the sadness and worry that had been consuming me for the past twenty-four hours, I felt a temporary kind of peace.

Since my visit to my mom's house, I had been vacillating between feeling emotionally bankrupt and empowered. The times I felt
hollow, like a canyon that was defined by its gigantic emptiness, I
obsessed over the things I'd lacked growing up: a father, a mother
who wanted me, a stable home, the sacred bonds of love and trust
between a parent and child. Just when I thought I'd scraped the bottom and there was nothing more that could crumble away, my mom
had revealed another empty cavern that I didn't know how to fill. The
realization that I'd broken her arm made me feel somehow dirty, like
she'd been right all along about me and my behavior problems. But
the memory of Dennis, the reason for my acting out, made me feel
even dirtier and confused. Why hadn't she tried harder to protect me?
Why had she chosen him over me?

But a pity party wouldn't help David, I knew I needed to be strong
for him and succeed in understanding his imagination in the way that
my mother had been unwilling to do. It was liberating to realize that
it had been *me* all along—that I had saved myself, through Leah Nola,
and that somewhere deep inside me was a fierceness that couldn't
be squashed out by the likes of Dennis or my mom. I could tell by
his dinosaurs that my son had inherited that same fierceness, and I
needed to find a way to admire it, instead of fearing it. I needed to
study and scrutinize his imagination for every nuance and implication
as if it were a precious love letter. And if it gave me a flashing warning
sign, you could damn well bet I would pay attention.

"What are you thinking about?" Jamie asked. He switched places
with me, gently edging me closer to the shoulder of the road, as the
only car we'd seen that night sped past, shattering the stillness.

I had told him about visiting my mom, but I hadn't given him the
details. There was no way for me to convey what had happened with
Leah Nola without sounding like a total nutcase, and I didn't have
words for the rest of it. Jamie was fatherless like me, but his relationship with Wendy was incredibly precious to both of them. I feared
he wouldn't understand, and I didn't want him to look at me with
the same mixture of pity, horror, and disgust that I'd been feeling.

"I'm thinking about you," I said. "Your hands. Your heart. Your lips. Your tongue."

"Oh yeah? Is that right?" He drew me to his chest, lowered his head, and kissed me intensely, right there on the dark, empty side of the road. A thousand white-hot pinpricks of light exploded behind my eyelids and were still there even when I opened my eyes. The fireflies ecstatically twinkled their approval. All those saved-up childhood wishes were finally coming true.

White letters on a blue sign greeted us: WELCOME BACK TO SCHOOL, WHERE WE PLAY, LEARN, AND GROW TOGETHER! David and I stood outside the one-story, yellow-brick elementary school. His face was purple and teary, and I was so frustrated and exhausted from the morning's many battles that if some normal-looking person had come up to me right then and offered to take David inside, I would've readily said yes. King Rex stomped behind us. Not exactly the shiny, photo-worthy first day of school that I'd envisioned.

David hiccupped. I reached down to usher him forward, and his long Hawaiian shirt swayed like a dress. When I'd come into his room this morning to call him down to breakfast, I found him all decked out, not in the Brontosaurus T-shirt that Duffy had bought him at a rummage sale and we'd agreed upon the night before, but in Winston's old shirt that was supposed to be his art smock. It was turquoise with little islands and palm trees and leaping swordfish all over it. It was so big on him, it could've fit three Davids, and it came down well past his knees, making it look like he wasn't wearing any shorts under it. I told him to change immediately. He started bawling. I reasoned with him about the logistics of wearing his art smock: what would he wear when it was time to do crafts? I threatened and then bribed him. He wailed more loudly and flopped face first onto the bed. Duffy came into the room to find out "what all the hubbub was about," and when she saw David, she had to repress a fit of giggles. "Honestly, Anna," she lectured me. "It's just clothing. So what if he looks a little goofy?"

"But I don't want him to be the goofy kid in the too-big Hawaiian shirt on the first day of school," I hissed. "First impressions matter."

"Maybe you don't remember kindergarten, but I've been through it with enough kids. They're all the goofy kid in the Hawaiian shirt. That's the very definition of kindergarten. Nobody thinks to be cool until at least the second grade." So with Duffy and David against me, I'd lost that battle.

Last night, David had been positively giddy about starting kindergarten, and I'd thought maybe all the parental hype about The First Day of School's jitters was unwarranted. He had adoringly admired his school supplies, which had been purchased with a loan from Duffy and Winston since I hadn't gotten my first paycheck yet. There were two bottles of glue, two glue sticks, twelve sharpened pencils and two pink erasers in a red zip-up pencil case, a box of crayons, a box of markers, a pair of safety scissors, and a Buzz Lightyear folder for sending home notes. I had written his name on everything with a black permanent marker, and all of it had fit neatly inside David's crown jewel, the Spiderman backpack we had found on sale for half off.

Then David had rattled on about "kindy garden" until he grew sleepy. He was most excited about "driving the car." We'd gone to a kindergarten preview day last week, and of all the stations in the classroom—the kid-sized kitchen with the play food, the storytime rug, the dress-up corner, the art easels, the giant bin of blocks—David's favorite station had been "the car" that was actually just an old seat with a steering wheel attached to it.

I was seriously beginning to think that his fascination with wheeled machines might be usurping his love affair with the prehistoric. Would King Rex and Weeple disappear? Were David's imaginary friends, as Dr. Rosen's book suggested, a phase that he was swiftly outgrowing? The possibility filled me with hope and bittersweet relief. Maybe there would be no more dangerous brushes with teeth and talons. Maybe David was becoming adjusted to his new life and surroundings and had no more emotional need for the dinosaurs, as I had had for Leah Nola.

But I'd been dead wrong, of course. Because King Rex had been waiting patiently for us, crammed into the back compartment of the minivan when we'd climbed in this morning.

"What the *fudge*?" I cried out, immediately grateful for the way I'd been training myself to avoid swearing around David. I twisted around in my seat to face my son, wide-eyed and innocent in his booster seat, and his T-rex, glowering at me with his mustard-yellow eyes. "You know that King Rex can't come to school with you today, right? He's not allowed."

"But he wants to come," David said, tugging on the strap of his new backpack.

"I'm sorry, but he can't. Kindergarten is only for little girls and boys like you. Ages four and five." I was already envisioning a repeat of the Gunner incident, except this time on a larger scale. Multiple scratches and bites, sobbing children, angry parents. There was no way I could set loose an invisible T-rex on Port Ambrose Elementary.

"King Rex is five."

"But he's a dinosaur, and the school rules specifically state no dinosaurs are allowed." Which was hardly a lie because if the school board had realized there was a possibility someone might bring an extinct man-eater to school, I was sure they would have ruled against it in a heartbeat.

"I won't tell anyone," he pleaded. His voice sounded shaky, like tears were not far behind.

I counted to twenty and then turned the key in the ignition. We were already running late, and I figured I had the whole drive ahead of us to talk him out of King Rex tagging along. But the more I persuaded David he couldn't bring his friend to school, the more panicked he looked. The closer we got to school, the faster his legs swung back and forth. By the time we pulled in to the lakeside school's parking lot, tears were dripping from his eyes and nose, and King Rex had started a low-pitched growl that sounded like a distant roll of thunder.

I was trying to channel the mothers in my life I trusted—primarily Duffy and Stacy, certainly not my own mom—to determine what they would do if they were in this bizarre, between-a-rock-and-a-hard-place situation, but it wasn't proving helpful because they had never been in this situation. This situation was uniquely my own. Talking calmly and reasonably to David was getting me nowhere. Maintaining an authoritative, no-nonsense position was absolutely useless. I decided to stop thinking like a mom for one minute and put myself in David's shoes. It was fairly easy because of my recent memories of Leah Nola. Obviously King Rex was a kind of security blanket for David, who wanted the dinosaur with him on his first day of school, and I couldn't bear to deprive him of that comfort. Besides, I knew that David's imagination was the one really running the show here, and as frightening as that was, it was his decision to make, for better or for worse.

"Okay, buckaroo," I said, exhaling heavily. "Let's go inside. But remember what we talked about with King Rex? You promised me that he wouldn't touch or hurt anyone. Even if someone says something mean. What should you do if someone says or does something mean to you?"

"Walk away and tell an adult," David parroted. He must have sensed my relenting, because his eyes looked clearer and brighter. King Rex's snarling stopped.

"That's right," I said. I pulled back the minivan door and leaned in to unstrap him from his seat. "It's really important for you to try to make new friends today. No hanging out with King Rex all morning, okay?"

He nodded eagerly, jumping down into my arms, and immediately wriggled away. I looked up. Apparently his dinosaur had teleported from the minivan to the asphalt behind me.

Now inside and sticking close to the mint-green tiled wall, David, King Rex, and I walked toward the kindergarten hallway together. Older kids raced past us, confident and laughing: third graders, fourth graders, maybe even fifth graders. They looked huge, even to me, and I couldn't imagine how big and intimidating they must have looked to David. Another mom and son were only a few feet ahead of us. The mom's brown, perfectly-trimmed, split-end-free hair was pulled back into a sensible ponytail and she looked like she'd just walked off the cover of *Parenting Magazine*. The little boy matched her perfectly— brown hair parted down the middle and combed neatly and wearing an argyle sweater vest. Blech. The Mother of the Year must have caught a glimpse of us in her peripheral vision, because she stopped and stared with a slightly traumatized look on her vanilla yogurt face. I could see in her eyes that she was already deciding who to call first. *Have I got a story for you! You'll never believe what I saw when I was dropping Langdon off at school today…*Her equally perfect best friend? Her matching Ken doll husband? Or maybe even Child Protective Services?

So maybe Duffy was right. Kids didn't think to judge one another's clothing choices until second grade or so. But parents and teachers most definitely did. Good thing they couldn't see King Rex. If David's hideous shirt earned us these kinds of stares, I could only imagine the reaction we would get had they come face to face with the king of the dinosaurs.

We passed Mrs. Banaszynski's classroom and stopped outside Miss Hanna's. Miss Hanna didn't have twenty years of teaching experience under her belt, but as far as I could tell from the kindergarten preview day, she was nice enough and seemed competent, and she had the obvious advantage of not having the infamous Gunner in her class.

"We have to say goodbye now," I said, crouching down to David's eye level.

He jerked his head away, facing King Rex instead. One tear sparkled like a diamond in the corner of his left eye. He was still upset with me.

"I need to get going so I'm not late for work," I told him, ruffling up his blond hair, trying to look at him from only the neck up and avoid the repulsive Hawaiian shirt that made him look like a street urchin. A street urchin in Honolulu, maybe. "Can I have a hug?"

He turned his head, considering my request, and then launched himself at me so forcefully that I fell backwards into the wall. I returned his breathless squeeze.

"Have a good day at school," I said. "Grandpa Winston will be here to pick you up at 11:30, and he'll take you home for lunch, okay, buckaroo? I'll be home around four o'clock, and I'm going to be so excited to hear about all the things you learned today."

He gave me his brave face, the one that made him look older than his years, the mask that all boys learned to wear as the world required them to toughen up. "Okay, Mommy." And then he and King Rex walked into the classroom as though they were heading toward a firing squad.

The hallways had emptied some as I walked back out to the parking lot. I tried to discreetly rub my eyes on the sleeve of my blouse. Other moms and dads were exiting the building too, proud tears glistening in their eyes and on their cheeks, shaking their heads in bewilderment. *How had we all gotten to this point, our babies grown up and going to school?* But beyond that shared sentiment, we were worlds apart. While they were worrying if little Langdon would remember to tell the teacher if he had to go potty and share his blocks nicely, I was worried about David in his extra-large shirt, standing out like a peacock among pigeons. I was worried someone would say the wrong thing to him, and his T-rex friend would lash out. I was worried he would sit in the play car, mumbling to King Rex like a crazy person, and all the kids and even the teacher would ostracize him. I was worried I'd get a phone call from Miss Hanna: *Ms. Jennings, I'm just calling to tell you that your son spent the entire day talking to an imaginary dinosaur, and we think he's a little nuts and should probably see a psychiatrist. Just thought you should know.*

It had been only three days since I'd started working at Galloway Realtors, but so far, so good. The agents, Janet, Brandon, and Gisele, were all friendly, low-maintenance types, nothing like some of the demanding dermatologists I'd worked for in Milwaukee. I'd mastered my job duties by the end of the first day—answering the phone, setting up appointments, faxing and filing paperwork, and creating daily reports of new houses that came on the market. Was it an exciting, totally fulfilling job? Heck no. Did it require only a fraction of my brain power and abilities? Probably. But the pay was decent for the work I did, it was only a ten-minute drive from my grandparents' house and a fifteen-minute drive to David's school, and when things were slow, I could sketch or send text messages under the ledge of the desk. I already had one waiting for me from Jamie when I settled in to my work station.

Good luck to David today! Kindergarten=Very Big Deal, he had typed.

Thanks, I replied. *Only a few tears at drop-off.* Which was an understatement, to say the least. I set my cell phone down and scrolled through the new listings of houses that had popped up in our computer database. Only thirty seconds later, my phone vibrated, alerting me to a new message.

Yours or his?

I smiled. *A little of both*, I admitted. *But we'll be fine.* (I hoped.) Maybe typing it would make it true. I wished I could tell him the whole story—imaginary dinosaur and all—but I knew how delusional it would sound. I returned my attention to sorting through the house listings and printing out reports for Janet, trying to keep my mind off what David and King Rex were doing at that very moment. When my phone buzzed a few minutes later, I scooped it up eagerly, but it wasn't a reply from Jamie; it was a message from Carly.

A little bird told me you and Presswood were on a DATE! Woot-woot! Talk soon? I want to hear ALL about it! XO

The "little bird" was Sam, no doubt, since he'd seen us together at the firemen's picnic. I wondered if all of Salsburg already knew about us, but for once, the thought of what the town had to say didn't bother me. I texted Carly back that I was pretty busy at the moment with David starting kindergarten, but that we should get together for lunch next week.

Gisele bustled in then with a middle-aged couple who were putting in an offer on a house, so she kept me occupied the next hour preparing, photocopying, and faxing documents. By the time my lunch break rolled around, I thankfully still hadn't received a troubling phone call from Miss Hanna or my grandparents, and I knew David was home by now from his first day of school. I called Duffy to check in.

"So how did it go?" I punched the buttons on the microwave to warm up my frozen dinner.

"Just fine." Duffy's voice sounded singsong-y, and I wondered if she was trying to cover something up or if she was just in one of her "singsong-y" moods. "We're just eating tuna salad on toast for lunch now."

She really was a miracle worker; she'd diversified David's palate considerably since June. "Fine, how?" I pressed. I sat down at the small bistro-style table in the break room and anxiously crossed my legs. Brandon came in and grabbed a twenty-ounce soda from the fridge. I gave him a broad smile, hoping he wasn't planning to stick around. He smiled back and politely ducked out.

"Fine and dandy," Duffy chirped. "He drew a picture; he learned a new song. But oh, I'll let Davey tell you the rest when you get home." The oven's timer started to beep out a steady, high-pitched chorus in the background. "Oh my, I need to take the snickerdoodles out of the oven. Have a good rest of your day, darling. We'll see you when you get home."

I stared at the disconnected phone in my hand, wishing that I'd been the one to pick David up from school and feed him his lunch. I'd been hoping for more details, details that my grandparents, unfortunately, couldn't give me. What had David's face looked like right before he'd discerned Winston in the crowd of parents? Cowed and crestfallen, or eager and pleased? Had the other kids been talking to him and including him, or had he been standing a little apart? Had King Rex been standing beside him, and if so, had the T-rex ridden home in Winston's car? Was he still playing with David at that very moment? Though it was reassuring to know that no major mishaps had occurred, I still longed to see my son and hear his firsthand account. Four o'clock could hardly come fast enough.

When I arrived home, the house smelled deliciously like cinnamon, and David greeted me at the door with a snickerdoodle and an enthusiastic description of his activities at school that left little room for interruptions or questions. The tension I'd been carrying all day at the base of my neck started to dissolve. He sang his song for me, which required a ball as a prop and some audience participation.

"Roll the ball to you, roll it back to me," David sang at the top of his lungs. He pushed up his Hawaiian shirtsleeves, which puddled around his hands when his arms were down. *"What's your name?"* Here he stage-whispered to me, "Now you need to say your name, Mommy."

"Anna," I said, rolling the pink soccer ball back to him.

"No, *your* name. Mommy."

"Okay. Mommy." It would be a conversation for another time.

"And then we sing, *we're very glad you came.*"

We repeated this song at least ten more times, and each time, I felt a little more optimistic that David was going to be just fine in kindergarten, imaginary friends or not. He was not me, I was not my mom, and King Rex was not Leah Nola. Just because one hereditary pattern had repeated itself didn't mean that the whole story would follow the same plot. David's story would have a happy ending, I was determined, because I would never put him in the kind of situation that my mom had put me in.

During dinner, David told us all about playing outside during recess and the identical twin boys in his class, who both fascinated and perplexed him. "Am I two people?" he asked, and I couldn't help laughing.

But then at bedtime, he showed me the picture he'd drawn on a sheet of yellow construction paper: a black silhouette that looked somewhat like a cat.

"What is it?" I asked. "A kitty?" He squinted off into the distance, as if trying to remember his inspiration. He'd done drawings of Vivien Leigh before, but this looked nothing like those fluffy brown, black, and white imitations. "Should we hang it on the fridge? It's your first official piece of school art!" I held it up over our heads by my thumbs and pointer fingers.

"No!" He tried to snatch the paper down but couldn't quite reach.

"Why not? I think it's a nice drawing." I studied first his disgruntled face and then the drawing more carefully. Frankly, I was surprised it wasn't a drawing of one of his dinosaurs; they seemed like the only subject he and I both drew these days.

"No!" David repeated. "I don't want you to hang it up." He crossed his arms and leaned back against his pillow. After a while, he added, "King Rex doesn't like him."

"Doesn't like who, David?" Here it was: the other shoe dropping. This was where he told me about the bully in class picking on him or his run-in with Gunner on the playground. I set the drawing down on his nightstand, tucked the loose flap of sheet under his mattress, and waited for it.

But he pointed at the construction paper. "The bad cat."

The bad cat. He had used that term before. When? I sifted through my brain—*bad cat, bad cat, bad cat*—until I had it. It was the name he'd used to describe the black shadowy substance that his dinosaurs chased. The shadowy substance which, to my relief, we hadn't seen much of since early July. At least, *I* hadn't seen it, but maybe it had been bothering David when I wasn't around. Or maybe some fear had recently been resurrected to prompt its return.

"King Rex doesn't like the bad cat?" I asked out loud to make sure I had it right. "Why?" I felt like we were speaking in nursery rhymes. I longed for David to just spell out his worries for me, so that I could assuage them.

He blinked a few times, considering, and then rubbed his eyes hard with both fists. "I don't know."

I pulled his fists gently away and kissed his forehead. "You know that you can tell me absolutely anything, right, buckaroo? I love you, and if something is scaring you, I want to help."

David nodded soberly. He reached for the drawing next to him and in one quick motion, had it ripped in two. I accepted the paper halves from him and took it one step further. I tore the paper into quarters and then again and again, until the drawing was in a pile of yellow confetti pieces on the bed. David giggled in delight as he tossed a handful of the paper squares upward, and they fluttered back down on us, a few of them catching in my hair. "All gone!" he cried, and I wished that it were only that easy. That the symbolic destruction of the bad cat could somehow rid David of whatever was troubling him in real life as well.

CHAPTER EIGHTEEN

Since we'd moved in, Winston had been urging us to visit the pioneer village, where he volunteered as their resident handyman and participated in the annual Revolutionary War reenactment. Remembering my own dull trip there as a seven-year-old, I didn't think the old buildings and people in their funny costumes would hold much appeal for David, but I didn't want to hurt Winston's feelings. Besides, Jamie had offered to come along with us that Sunday, and David was in such a restless, fidgety mood that any excuse to get him out of the house was a good one. The pioneer village was on the farthest reach of Duffy's "safe zone," and as she had a few hair appointments lined up in the afternoon anyway, she decided to stay behind.

The four of us trooped out of Winston's car toward a smattering of fieldstone buildings and log cabins—the blacksmith's shop, the apothecary, the general store, the Indian trading post, the barn, and several model nineteenth-century homes. The sky was cobalt and cloudless, and my heart was soaring and wheeling somewhere up there like a seagull. Jamie and I were together, David had done well in his first week of kindergarten (even though King Rex had continued to escort him), I'd gotten my first paycheck, and the late summer's humidity was finally dissipating.

David kicked up a cloud of dusty gravel with each shuffling step he took. One of the sharp stones pelted the back of my foot.

"Ouch," I complained, bending down to rub my heel. "Pick up your feet, David. No kicking gravel."

He stopped in his tracks, chastened. There were crescent moons under his eyes, like he hadn't gotten much sleep the night before, but he hadn't woken me up like he usually did if he had a bad dream or a stuffy nose and couldn't sleep. A rotten night's sleep would certainly explain his antsy behavior that morning: teasing Vivien Leigh until she scratched him; moving from activity to activity, never settling on one for longer than five minutes; and crying at the slightest provocation. When we got home later that afternoon, I'd have to make him lie down for an extra-long nap.

"Are you tired, buckaroo?" I asked. David raised one shoulder and let it fall. "Come here. Come hold my hand." The fact that he consented proved my theory correct.

Jamie and Winston had gotten ahead of us, my normally reserved grandfather talking Jamie's ear off about the history of the village, the renovations and maintenance it required, and the upcoming Revolutionary War reenactment the following weekend. Jamie was nodding enthusiastically and asking well-timed questions. He had told me he hadn't been to the pioneer village since a fourth-grade class field trip and that he'd be game to go back. I wondered if in addition to a love for Greek mythology, he also harbored a genuine interest in American history. If not, he was a talented faker. He noticed we'd fallen behind and tapped Winston on the arm to slow him down.

The inside of the blacksmith's shop was dark and smelled like old, pungent cheese. On one wall, a forge gaped with a flickering lantern inside, weakly attempting to simulate the blazing fire that once would have burned within. Several elderly people were gathered around a man in an apron with a cell-phone clipped to the front pocket demonstrating how to operate a few filthy-looking tools. When they saw David, they made room for him, and the blacksmith asked if he wanted to give the crank a try. David half-heartedly agreed, stepping away from my shoulder to spin the rusty hand-turned wheel. The old people, Winston included, smiled indulgently. Jamie took a picture with his phone. I couldn't help being distracted by something over by the lantern-lit forge.

Was it another visitor, one I hadn't noticed upon entering the blacksmith's shop, obscured by the shadows? But when I glanced back, there was no one there. The dim light revealed that what I'd mistaken for a person was actually a huge pair of tongs leaning against the forge.

"That was pretty neat, huh?" Winston asked David, as we walked toward the next building. David's eyes never left his shoes, but he gave a sharp, perfunctory nod.

"I think he just needs a nap," I stage-whispered to Winston to try to soften the disappointment on his face.

A woman in a white bonnet was showing a family with three girls how to churn butter in the next building. While we waited for our turn, Winston taught us about how log cabins were built in the 1800's. He ran his hand along the wall, describing how sticks and mud were used to fill in the gaps between the logs. He was our own personal tour guide. Yippee.

Jamie moved closer to me, his hand only inches away from my hip. David's eyelids flickered, as if he were going to fall asleep on his feet. Maybe the nap couldn't wait; maybe it would be a good excuse to cut our visit short, but we would be letting Winston down, and I really didn't want to do that to him. David's eyes suddenly snapped open, and he looked around in a paranoid way.

"David," I murmured, not wanting to interrupt Winston's lecture. I draped my arm over my son's chest and pulled him toward me. I rested the back of my hand against his forehead in a way mothers everywhere seemed to do. He didn't feel feverish, but what the heck did I know? I pecked the top of his head. "Are you feeling okay?"

He pulled out of my grasp and dashed toward the butter-churning lady. Right. So I guessed that meant he was feeling okay now.

We trudged through the other ten buildings, enduring two lectures at each one: one from the dressed-up volunteer and one from Winston. For the most part, David seemed content enough to try out the interactive activities the volunteers offered, and Jamie seemed content enough to learn all about pioneer life in Wisconsin. I was the only one who was bored out of my mind with a steadily building headache. Duffy had been smart to avoid this trip; I was sure Winston had dragged her here several times before.

The last building was one of the main attractions (according to Winston): a huge barn with a lot of antique farm machinery inside. "Where are all the animals?" David asked as we entered the cathedral-like space.

Winston immediately launched into an overview of how much agriculture and its tools had changed over the centuries. His words fell on deaf ears as I watched dust motes dance through the streaming patches of sunlight. David trailed behind his great-grandfather, eagerly examining the old tractors and not quite understanding why he couldn't climb up on them like he could at the parade.

And then suddenly, my arms and legs felt like they'd been filled with lead. All I could do was watch in horror as David's body was cloaked in a black nimbus, pulsating and radiating, almost obscuring his blond hair with its darkness.

The black shadow. David's unnamed fear was effectively swallowing him whole, and King Rex or Weeple weren't here to chase it away this time. What should I do?

As I gaped, still paralyzed, the nimbus separated from David and formed its own shape, close beside him. It was as big as a German shepherd but moved with a slinky, almost cat-like grace. *The bad cat.* The paranoid look returned to David's face, and he hurried to follow Winston to the next tractor, but the large shadow animal seemed to be blocking his path.

"David?" I called, my voice cracking with uncertainty.

My son's chin and oval face whipped around, and just like that, whatever weird enchantment had fallen over the barn ended. A ray of sunlight obliterated the large, cat-like creature, and David darted to his grandfather's side. Still, my headache throbbed, and my blood whizzed excitedly through my veins. No matter how many times I witnessed David's imagination come to life, it could still be near-heart-attack-inducing.

"Are you alright?" Jamie asked, his warm, strong hand steadying my back.

I nodded. "Just a little lightheaded. I must be hungry. Maybe we could all get some lunch?"

Minutes later, David and I were seated at a picnic table, while Jamie and Winston went off to get hot dogs and hamburgers from the concession tent. The picnic table was near a large, grassy field where a few kids older than David were running alongside rolling hoops and trying to keep them in motion with sticks. He leaned forward on his elbow, watching a chubby boy galloping after a runaway hoop.

"What's wrong?" I asked him. I wanted to ask directly about the shadow animal, but I didn't want to give away what I had seen in the barn without David's first acknowledging it.

He glanced over his shoulder, almost like he was expecting the large cat to be lurking right behind him. The circles under his eyes looked like bruises, like someone had pressed their thumbs under his eyes until it had left a mark. "Nothing. Can Grandpa Winston take me for a tractor ride?"

"Maybe later," I said. "You'll have to ask him nicely." I straightened up on the picnic table bench and spotted Jamie in line at the concession stand about fifty yards away. Even from this distance, I could see his strong, sexy back and the way his black hair curled messily around his neck and ears. My heart felt like it was being clamped in a vice. Because I knew I needed to ask David about Jamie.

I needed to know if it was only a coincidence that the bad cat had appeared twice now when Jamie was present, and that King Rex and Weeple's first instincts had been to ambush him, or if Jamie was somehow contributing to David's fears. I'd made a promise to myself that I wouldn't ignore the warning signs of my son's imagination, and this seemed like a pretty conspicuous one.

Though I didn't entertain the thought of Jamie having a child perversion for one second, perhaps there was something else worrisome or threatening about him to David. Or maybe David was just concerned by the idea of my dating, period. Either way, I would never forgive myself if I didn't at least open up the conversation to my son. How might things have gone differently if my own mom had been willing to do the same and had actually listened to me?

"I want you to tell me the truth, David," I said. "What do you think of Jamie?" I tried to keep my expression neutral, but the vice grip around my heart was tightening.

He returned his attention to me from the kids rolling hoops and then smiled hugely, the kind of smile usually reserved for spaghetti night or new action figures. "I like Jamie. He's fun."

The vice started to loosen. I blew a strand of hair out of my face and relaxed my spine a little. "I'm glad. But if he ever says or does something that bothers you, please tell me right away." I felt kind of guilty for even suspecting Jamie of any potential wrongdoing because he was such a good guy, a guy I was quickly losing my heart to, but probably my mom had thought that about Dennis too. And as far as I was concerned, until I could figure out what was upsetting David, I couldn't be too cautious. "Is the bad cat bothering you?" I asked.

He nodded and let out a cavernous yawn. "Sometimes I wish he'd just go away," he whispered fervently.

David slept for the rest of the afternoon, and I pulled out *Imaginary Friends, Your Child, and You,* which I'd written off weeks ago as totally useless. But I was getting desperate, so I paged through it until I got to Chapter Nine, which was aptly titled Boogey Monsters, Bullies, and Shadow Men.

Scary Imaginary Companions. *The dark. Thunderstorms. Spiders and wasps. Big dogs. The list of childhood fears is extensive and well-known. Though not all children are afraid of the same things, inevitably between the ages of three and eight, there will be at least one significant thing that scares them. This is a perfectly normal occurrence, so much so that overcoming these fears is often seen as a rite of passage in many cultures.*

But what happens when your child seems to be afraid of his or her imaginary friend? Though it is more common for children to create imaginary friends who are submissive to them and whose sole purpose is to entertain and make the child happy, there have been several cases reported of just the opposite. Case studies have shown that some children have imaginary friends who insult them, make them cry, and even seem to "haunt" them at night, making it difficult for the child to sleep.

Many parents are disturbed and confused by this turn of events. "Isn't my child the one who invents the imaginary companion?" they wonder. "Why would my child intentionally create a boogey monster to tease and torment him or her?" Other parents jump to extreme conclusions, suspecting that their child might be haunted or possessed. But just like other more friendly imaginary friends, these "scary" companions are serving an important purpose for the child too.

Consider, for instance, the case of Sierra B., age seven, who started having sleepless nights after a Shadow Man took up residence in her bedroom closet. Her parents performed nightly "closet checks" and bought her an extra bright nightlight. But still Sierra woke up in the middle of the night from vivid nightmares about the Shadow Man standing over her, tugging off her blanket, and proceeding to count her fingers and toes, which she was sure he was going to bite off.

Poor kid, I thought. What a creepy nightmare. I glanced at the black and white photo at the end of the chapter. It depicted a girl with pigtails, smiling happily, as her strong, hardy-looking father checked under the bed, presumably for monsters. Definitely not Sierra B., I suspected.

After months of disrupted sleep, Sierra B.'s parents tried having her share a room with her younger brother, emptying out the entire closet so she could see there was no one inside, and sleeping with the light on, all to no avail. The bad dreams continued. The family went to see a child therapist. Over several sessions, it was determined that Sierra B., an aspiring ballerina, was putting too much pressure on herself to perform well in her dance classes and recitals. Her parents made her take a break from ballet, and the Shadow Man disappeared, the nightmares stopped, and everyone could have a good night's sleep again.

What is most important about the boogey monsters, bullies, and shadow men is not what form they take, but what fear they represent to the child.

It is important to talk to your child, on your own or with the guidance of a therapist, about what he or she is afraid of. Once the source of the fear has been determined, it will be easier to "exorcize" the scary imaginary friend. Just remember that conquering fears is a natural part of childhood, and an imaginary friend is just a resourceful, external way for your child to do that.

Sure, right, of course. It was very "resourceful" of David to have a shadow creature stalking and scaring the bejesus out of him. Way to go, David's imagination. The moral of the book seemed to be that every odd, freaky aspect of children's having imaginary friends was "PERFECTLY NORMAL," "HEALTHY," "VERY COMMON," and "A SIGN OF CREATIVITY." I wanted so badly to believe that the book was right and I was just reading too much into things. That maybe David was scared of something as mundane as the dark or thunderstorms, and his imagination would help him work through these problems. Perhaps my laying eyes on the ominous-looking dinosaurs and black cat was just riling me up unnecessarily—the dark underbelly of childhood to which parents simply shouldn't be privy. I wanted to think that, but my own history with imaginary friends as harbingers had me predisposed to believe the worst.

Over a dinner of hamburger noodle casserole and cornbread, David still seemed tired and grouchy, picking at his food in silence. Afterward, Duffy suggested a game of Candy Land, David's favorite, and he cheered up considerably. Duffy, David, and I played the board game at the kitchen table, while Winston washed the dishes, served us bowls of ice cream, and then joined us for a second round. Despite his long nap, David seemed ready for bed at his usual time but declined hearing one of my made-up stories, so I read him *Where the Wild Things Are* instead. When I asked him if he wanted me to check in his closet before I left, he looked at me like I was insane. He didn't seem scared, lying there in his green striped pajamas, atop his rocket ship comforter, and I felt like maybe I was starting to let *my* imagination run away with me. My son was just fine. Things were going to be just fine for us.

Since my worries about David had made me kind of cold and distant to Jamie at the pioneer village today, I was longing to see him and make up for it. The Presswoods' garage door was wide open, and light spilled out onto their driveway when I crossed the lawn. I poked my head inside and heard a country music station crackling over the radio. Dressed in only boxers and a T-shirt, Jamie was bent over a work bench, peering inside a cardboard box.

"Do you always hang out in the garage late at night in your underwear?" I teased, wrapping my arms around him from behind.

"Only when I'm hoping my hot neighbor will show up," he said. He nodded toward the cardboard box. "I thought you might like to see this. It's the box I found your sketchbook in."

"Oh." I moved around him to inspect it. "One of your mom's memory boxes?"

"Yeah." The way he bit his lip made me wonder if he'd been lying about that. If he had been the sentimental one all along, not Wendy, boxing up and collecting my happy memories for me to return to at a later date. Perhaps in the hopes that I would return to *him* at a later date.

"It's mostly garbage. I don't know why I kept a lot of it," he said. "And I haven't the faintest clue what some of it means. Like this, for example." He held up a long, brown-and-black-striped feather.

I shrugged. "Beats me."

We sifted through the box's contents together. There were empty, flattened boxes that had once held sparklers; loose bills of Monopoly money; smooth, gray river stones; mason jars with holes punched in their lids; cryptic lists compiled of random words: *pickle, kangaroo, fart.* It was the debris of a short-lived, yet happy time in my childhood, and even though it was mostly junk, it had once been prized by Jamie and me. At the bottom were a few faded three-by-five photographs. Jamie flipped through the pictures and then handed them to me.

The first were fuzzy, off-center snapshots of the backyard and what appeared to be a turtle. The next was a shot of Wendy, looking younger and stronger and more beautiful than I'd remembered, clipping a checkered tablecloth to a picnic table. The last two were pictures of me and Jamie, glowing with suntans, grinning wide smiles dotted with missing baby teeth. I was nearly a head taller than him, and the way our arms were looped around each other with an intentional gap in between, suggested that maybe Leah Nola had been there with us.

"Can I have one of these?" I asked.

"Of course." Jamie carefully returned one of the mason jars to the box, as though it were a Ming vase, not something he should probably toss in the recycling bin. I saw it then. Even more so than the night of the firemen's picnic or any of our time together since. He loved me. Really, really loved me. And it wasn't a fleeting whim; it was something he'd been growing and nurturing, like one of his rose bushes, since he was a little boy. I felt ashamed that I'd even speculated he had anything to do with David's shadowy fears. I felt undeserving of a heart as precious and kind as his.

I leaned forward to kiss his collarbone and then stood on my tiptoes to kiss his lips. He hoisted me up and I wrapped my legs around his waist as the kiss grew more passionate. He fumbled for the garage door remote, not breaking our kiss, and set me down on the work bench as the door began to creak closed.

"Not here!" I laughed as he started to pull my shirt over my head. "There are spiders...and engine grease...and someone could see!"

"Spoilsport," Jamie teased. "Maybe the spiders want to watch." But he led me noiselessly through the house, so as not to wake Wendy, and up to his bedroom, where we not as noiselessly tumbled into bed together, and he proceeded to make our first mind-blowing, earth-shattering night together look like amateur hour.

I felt too dazed for words, too dazed for thoughts, even, and it was such a solace, just lying there in his arms, utterly satisfied and exhausted. The ceiling fan wobbled as it spun. Jamie rubbed small circles on my back as he talked about another lawn makeover job he had scheduled for this week in Lawrenceville. His first clients had been so pleased with his work that they'd recommended him to their neighbors, and as a result, his September was quickly booking up with landscaping jobs. His business was finally taking off, and he was starting to feel cautiously optimistic that he could actually make a go of it. That he wouldn't have to sell the house to pay his mom's medical bills or go to work at the printing factory with Marshall.

"I am so proud of you," I said. "Can you hold that thought for just one minute? I need to use the bathroom." I slithered down the bed and walked naked to the en suite bathroom, pleased that I was able to conceal my usual post-sex insecurity and that I was giving Jamie an eyeful.

I flicked on the light switch and shut the door. The bathroom was in keeping with the rest of the bedroom's chic, hotel-seeming décor. So clean, it almost seemed like it was never used. White tile floors, white porcelain pedestal sink, spacious bathtub enclosed by a charcoal gray shower curtain. When I went to wash my hands, I noticed the only thing out of place, the only thing betraying that somebody did in fact use this bathroom. A little orange pill bottle with a white cap. I dried my hands and told myself not to look, that it wasn't any of my business. But I couldn't help myself. I snatched up the bottle and glanced at its script. *Oxycodone*, the bottle read. *Wendy Presswood. Take two pills daily, or as needed, for pain.*

I tried to replace the pill bottle where it had been balanced precariously on the edge of the pedestal sink, but it tipped over and fell to the tile floor. I didn't bother picking it up. I opened the mirrored medicine cabinet as quietly as I could, and there it was. The evidence of what I'd been refusing to believe all this time. Each shelf was occupied by a neat row of orange prescription vials. Some full, some empty. All made out to Wendy Presswood. All with recent dates ranging from six months ago to one week ago. Duffy had been right all along. He was abusing his mom's prescription medications. He wasn't a recovered or recovering drug addict; he was just a drug addict, period.

I clicked the cabinet shut. Standing naked in his bathroom, I felt foolish and vulnerable. The fluorescent bulb and white walls washed me out, and my face in the mirror looked pale. Pale and angry. More angry at myself than at Jamie. Why hadn't I learned my lesson? If something seemed too good to be true, it was! Why hadn't I listened to my grandmother and the entire town? Why had I been so blind, choosing to see only what I wanted to see, when the facts were so pitifully obvious? I scanned my memory for times when he'd seemed overly mellow and detached or giddy and euphoric. Had he been high the night he told me he'd loved me since we were kids?

Even if he did really love me, it still wasn't enough. Patrick had loved me too, and look where that had gotten us. Even if Jamie was the best friend I'd ever had and probably would ever have. I couldn't put myself through what I'd gone through with Patrick again. It wasn't fair to David either; he was enamored with Jamie right now, but if Jamie was still hooked on painkillers, there was no way I was letting him near my son again. Maybe David's subconscious mind had somehow sensed Jamie's duplicitousness, and the shadowy animal was a manifestation of that. The thought further infuriated me.

I opened the bathroom door and stalked into the room. "I need to go," I said, stooping down to grab my bra and underwear. I hated that I was still naked in front of him when he'd betrayed me so badly. I found my shirt halfway under his bed and held it against me as a partial covering while I slipped back into my underwear.

"Anna, what's wrong?" He'd been lying provocatively against the pillows with a big smile on his face when I'd come out, but the smile had quickly been erased. He bent forward, tugging the sheet self-consciously across his lap.

"I think you know what's wrong," I said and pulled my top over my head. Now where the heck were my shorts?

"No, I don't know." Jamie huffed out an aggrieved sigh. "That's why I'm asking. Can you please tell me so I can try to fix it? I don't want you to go."

I thought about going back into the bathroom and dramatically tossing the vial of oxycodone at him. But that would take too long, and frankly, all I wanted was to get out of there, back to my grandparents' house, so that I could slip into my son's bedroom and kiss his forehead while he slept.

"The painkillers," I said.

His eyes widened. "You went through the medicine cabinet?"

"No," I snapped. That had come after. "There was a bottle out on the sink."

He climbed out of bed, slipping into a pair of cargo shorts, not even bothering with boxers. "Prescribed to my mom, I hope you noticed. They're not mine."

"How convenient," I said. I spotted my shorts on the other side of the room, bunched up against one of the legs of Jamie's desk. One of my sandals was near it, too. I hurried to retrieve the shorts and sandal, all the while keeping my eyes peeled for its mate.

"I know it looks bad, but it's not what you think." Jamie dropped his heavy, calloused hand onto my shoulder. "Stop. Just stop. Let me explain."

I ducked out from under his grasp. "Why? So you can tell me more lies about how you're rehabilitated and all you're doing now is dutifully taking care of your poor mom? And so what if you refill her scripts for your own personal, illegal use occasionally? No biggie."

"No. That's not what I'm doing. Anna, would you please just stop moving and sit down for just one minute so we can talk?"

I spied my other sandal under the draped comforter on the floor and jammed it on my foot. "No, I can't, because you forget that I've been through this same kind of shit before. This is the part where you try to explain everything away and make me a whole bunch of promises you never intend to keep. Or aren't capable of keeping—whichever—but the point is, it never ends happily. And I really can't do this because I have a son who's counting on me, and I refuse to put him through this again. He deserves better. We both do."

Jamie sat down on the foot of the bed, hunched forward. "I'm not your ex, Anna," he said softly. "And if you knew me even a little, you would know that I wouldn't do something like this, and you'd give me the benefit of the doubt and let me explain, instead of jumping to conclusions."

I forced myself to walk away from him and put my hand on the doorknob. I would not cry. I would not give in. I needed to be the type of mother who made sacrifices for her child, who put her child before herself and her own stupid desires, no matter what.

"Well, maybe that's part of the problem, then," I said, avoiding his eyes. My heart ached like a bruised apple. "We don't really know each other so well after all."

CHAPTER NINETEEN

I crept up the stairs, feeling like a caricature of myself as a teenager sneaking in after a wild night. Except this time, I almost hoped Duffy would catch me. I wanted her bossiness and overbearing love, so I could hurl my anger and sense of betrayal at her. *How could you let me fall for him?* I wanted to shout at her. *You knew, you knew, you knew, and you didn't stop me!* I wanted her to hold me and rock me until all my miserable tears were spent and I was exhausted enough to finally close my eyes and sleep. But it was after two o'clock when I got home, and she and Winston were sleeping soundly and didn't stir. I was utterly alone with my wretchedness.

I stripped down to my underwear, threw on an old oversized T-shirt, and climbed into bed without even turning the lights on. As I flopped down, my shoulder and hand brushed against something. Something solid and warm and taking up half my bed. I bit back a scream. My eyes adjusted to the light, and I quickly realized that it was David, curled up and sleeping in the middle of my bed.

How long had he been asleep in here, and why had he wandered to my bedroom? David had never been a sleepwalker. Had he come to my room seeking comfort from a bad dream, only to find my bed empty? I stared down at his now peacefully sleeping face and noticed pillow creases on his flushed cheeks and what looked like dried tears crusted on his eyelashes. Had he cried himself to sleep? I brushed a damp lock of hair off his forehead. He didn't stir.

In my guilt, I thought about letting him sleep in my bed all night, but it was a twin size bed and much too small for a grown woman and a growing boy. His warm, long-limbed body seemed to be everywhere at once; I couldn't get comfortable, and I was downright exhausted. I scooped him up as gingerly as I could, trying not to wake him, and carried him back to his room.

When I laid him back in his bed, his eyes shot open. "Mommy?" he cried, reaching out for me.

"Yes, David. It's me," I whispered. "I'm here. Go back to sleep."

He sat upright, rubbing the sleep from his eyes. "Where were you?"

Guilt, as sour as curdled milk, flooded my mouth and stomach. I was just like my mom, leaving a child in the middle of the night to deal with whatever trauma might arise on his or her own. No, a part of me argued, Duffy and Winston were here. My mom had left me totally alone. But that logic couldn't bear much scrutiny. David had wanted his mom, and I hadn't been there for him. He was only four, and I had known he had been having trouble sleeping. And I had left him to go across the yard to the next door neighbor's house, a drug addict's house, to have sex. But it would never happen again, I resolved fiercely.

"I was outside," I said. "Did you have a bad dream?"

"No." David buried his head in my armpit. "I can't sleep in here."

I flipped on the small lamp on his nightstand. A pool of light spread across the bed, dispelling the shadows a little. I hugged David tighter, inhaling his little-boy scent.

"Why not?" I asked. "What's wrong?" My question made him start to cry. "It's okay, it's okay." I rubbed his back.

"I don't know what he wants," David choked out between sobs.

The hair follicles on my arms stood up, as a chill passed through me. "Who?" I asked, trying to keep my voice calm.

"Under the bed," David whispered.

I tried not to think of Sierra B. and her dream of the Shadow Man biting off all her fingers and toes. I tried not to think of every scary movie I'd ever seen where a gray-skinned ghoul dragged the protagonist under the bed to kill him or her. Instead, I tried to imagine the black-and-white photo in chapter nine, that had showed the fearless daddy checking under his photogenic daughter's bed for monsters.

"There's nothing under the bed except for some forgotten toys and dust bunnies," I teased. "Would it make you feel better if I looked?"

"No." David clung to me, his fingers digging into the ribs in my back. "Don't look, Mommy."

I certainly didn't want to. My heart was battering against my chest, like it was trying to run away, and every inch of my skin was covered in goosebumps. But I was being ridiculous. There was nothing to be afraid of. No boogey monsters, no shadow men. They were all just imaginary. The problem was I could see imaginary things.

I pried myself free of David's death-grip and knelt down on the floor. I seized the navy blue dust ruffle with sweaty fingers in preparation to fling it upright.

"Mommy," David whined, huddled against the headboard.

"It's okay, David," I said. I took a deep breath and counted to three and—

A pair of large, green reflective eyes with black pupils stared back at me. I couldn't help it. I screamed. David screamed with me. I scrabbled backwards on my hands and knees, but the dust ruffle stayed flipped up, and the green eyes continued to watch me hungrily. They seemed to belong to an enormous, muscular cat of some sort with black, shiny fur. The bad cat was…a panther? It was hard to believe it was able to hide under something as small as a twin size bed. It opened its mouth, revealing a rough pink tongue, and the sharpest incisors I'd ever seen, and it let out a bone-chilling growl.

"Anna? David?" Winston, wild-haired and breathless, ran into the room, wielding what looked like a hammer. "I heard screams. What's wrong?"

Neither of us was capable of speaking. The bad cat still had me fixed in its hostile gaze.

Winston followed my eyes and bent down to look under the bed. I almost cried out for him to stop, to save him from getting his head chewed off, but he popped back up with a confused look. Of course. The panther was invisible to him.

"For the love of God, can you please put the dust ruffle back down?" I asked him. David hiccupped and nodded wildly in agreement.

Winston dropped the dust ruffle back into place, and the panther mercifully disappeared from view. But this time, I knew what was lurking under the bed.

"What is going on here?" Winston asked. Duffy appeared in the doorway behind him, a pink satin eye mask pushed up onto her forehead.

"Nothing," I said. "Bad dream, that's all. Everything is fine now, but I think David might sleep with me tonight." There was no way I was making my son sleep in a bed with a panther under it. Especially one that might have physical properties and the power to hurt us. Especially one that David cowered from, suggesting it wasn't under his control.

Winston scratched his head. Duffy pursed her lips. David leaped off the bed toward me, and we carefully edged our way past my grandparents and out of the bedroom.

"Seriously. Everything's fine. Go back to bed. Sorry for waking you."

It took David a long time to fall asleep, and it took me even longer. Our bodies were still trembling with shock as we curled together. What did *Imaginary Friends, Your Child, and You* have to say about a freaking panther under the bed? What fear did *that* represent? Fear of being mauled to death by a large carnivorous cat? Because if that was the case, I was afraid of that too. I lay awake until the sky turned a milky white, wondering how the hell we were going to survive David's imagination.

The next day Carly and I had planned to meet at La Frontera in Lawrenceville—according to her, the only halfway authentic Mexican food you could find within a thirty-mile radius—for a quick lunch. I considered canceling because of my grainy eyes and lack-of-sleep-induced headache, and most of all, because I knew she was going to give me the third degree about Jamie, and I'd have to admit what had happened between us. But it had been weeks since I'd seen Carly, and I figured her brand of humor and some margaritas (okay, well, maybe only one margarita, since it was the middle of the work day) would help take my mind off David's panther and my otherwise crumbling life.

When I arrived at the restaurant, Carly was already seated at a table near a reproduction of a Diego Rivera painting. She stood up to get my attention and waved me over. After squeezing me in a tight hug, she handed me the laminated drink menu. "Here. You look like you could use this."

I nodded and studied the menu with unseeing eyes. "Let's just get a pitcher of margaritas." So much for responsibility.

She grinned. "My thoughts exactly." Our waiter appeared then with two types of salsa and a basket of warm tortilla chips glistening with oil. She gave him our drink order, and he hurried off. "So what's up? No offense, but you look kind of exhausted."

"None taken. I *am* exhausted. I was up really late last night with David. He had a nightmare."

"Oh, poor thing," she cooed, scooping up some salsa with a chip. "I sometimes have this recurring nightmare that I'm late for a precalculus test in Mr. Crunkle's class—do you remember that old dillweed?—and when I finally get there, I realize I'm totally naked." She laughed and pretended to shiver. "Probably not the same kind of nightmare David's having though, huh?"

"A little different." I attempted a smile and ran my fingers over the blue tiled tabletop. The panther's twin incisors, at least two inches long, flashed in my mind. His green eyes like two glassy marbles floating in the darkness. The kind of nightmare that didn't vanish even when you were awake with your eyes wide open. "I don't think I was in Mr. Crunkle's class with you," I added quickly, to change the subject. "You were one semester ahead of me in math, remember? I would've been in geometry with Mrs. Yetz."

"That's right. I had her too. She was so sweet. One of the only teachers who ever believed in me." Carly tapped her short, somewhat square fingers against her water glass. "But we're not here to reminisce about high school math teachers, are we? I want to hear all about Jamie, and don't even think about leaving out a single detail. Start from the beginning, please. So how did you guys finally get together?"

I could see our waiter over her shoulder heading our way with the tray of margaritas. "Look what's here!" I exclaimed, buying myself some time. The next few minutes were taken up by the waiter sliding our salt-rimmed and lime-wedged glasses toward us as expertly as a poker dealer, positioning the pitcher in the middle of the table, and jotting down our food orders.

Carly carefully sipped her margarita. "I have to say that in high school, I never would have imagined you two together. But when you started talking about him the day we took the boat out, I could totally picture it. When Sam told me about seeing you guys at the fair, it all clicked; you two being a couple just made sense. I'm really so happy for you."

She wasn't going to make this easy for me. I took a swig of my margarita and remembered the medicine cabinet chock full of pill bottles, all prescribed to Wendy. I tried to focus on that—his addiction, the blatant lies he had told me—instead of the earlier part of the evening when he had sweetly shown me his box of childhood memories and we had made love. The way I saw stars when he kissed me. How in his arms I felt safer than I'd ever felt in my life—before I had known the truth.

"Well, it didn't last very long," I said, raising my shoulder to my ear. I exhaled and let it drop. "We broke up last night."

"Really?" She cocked her head and leaned in. "What happened?"

I gripped the base of my margarita glass and then pinched the stem. I didn't want to be a cog in the Salsburg gossip machine, but I also knew Carly would be skeptical of any other excuses I could give her. She would know I was lying if I told her there was no chemistry between us (we were practically a combustible explosion in bed) or that Jamie was put off by my being a single mother with baggage, when he actually accepted me like no one before him ever had and was really great with David to boot: a bottomless source of patience and kindness, a little boy at heart himself. So vague lies definitely wouldn't cut it, and in a way, I felt like Carly deserved to know the truth about Jamie. Her fiancé was his close friend, after all, and maybe there was something they could do to help him. Maybe they could talk him into going back to rehab.

"The rumors about him are true," I said. "He's addicted to oxycodone, and I told him I can't be with someone with problems like that. For David's sake." I fingered my paper napkin bundle of silverware and glanced up at Carly.

"Really?" she repeated, but she didn't sound as surprised as she had the first time. "Sam told me about the car accident and how Jamie got hooked on narcs the first time, but I thought that was in the past. That he went through the program and hardly even drinks beer now."

I shook my head. "That's what he told me too. But he lied." The Rivera painting on the wall next to us made me sad. The massive bunch of calla lilies, the young woman's black braids, her strong back and arms open wide; all of it would have filled me with hope yesterday. It would have made me think of Jamie and the way he took an interest in my art, making it seem like not such an unattainable goal, but something alive and shimmering. But today the dream of pursuing an art degree seemed impossibly out of reach again.

"If you don't mind my asking, how did you find out?" Carly removed the lime wedge from her glass and tossed it aside.

"I found the pills," I said simply and rested my throbbing forehead in my palm.

"But how did you know they weren't his mom's?" she asked, draining the rest of her margarita. "I mean, with her MS, she's got to be on a whole regimen of different drugs, right?"

"They *were* his mom's. Prescribed to her at least. But he's clearly the one taking them. They were in his bathroom, out on his sink, plain as day."

She lifted the pitcher to refill her glass. She topped off mine too, but there wasn't much space for her to refill it since I'd taken only a few sips. Her tone was light and thoughtful as she asked, "So what did he have to say for himself?"

"I didn't care to hear it. I left." I sat up, scanning the restaurant for our waiter, hoping our food would be arriving soon to save me from this line of questioning, but no luck. "Can we—"

She interrupted me. "But maybe there's a reasonable explanation. I know the evidence seems pretty damning, but something's not quite adding up. Why would Jamie lie to his friends when he told them the truth about everything else? When Marshall has acted almost as a kind of sponsor for him? And why now when Sam says Jamie is the happiest that he's ever seen him? There's something else bugging me too. A few months ago, before you moved back, Jamie asked Sam for help moving some furniture around. He and his mom were switching bedrooms because she could no longer climb the stairs. So maybe—"

"Carly, please. I know you're just trying to help, but I really don't want to talk about it anymore. Jamie and I are through, which is probably a good thing anyway, because I have my hands full enough without someone else's drama. So please. Tell me about your wedding dress hunt. Or what's new at Ruby's. Or absolutely anything you want, unrelated to Jamie."

"Fine. Just one more thing, and then not another word." She pushed a curl out of her eyes and leaned forward. "I just think you should hear him out. At least listen to his side of the story. You owe him that much." Then she made an elaborate show of zipping her lips and wiping her hands clean of the topic.

Our waiter mercifully showed up at our table then with our enchiladas, rice, and beans, and I dug into the food, somewhat because I was hungry and would need to return to Galloway Realty soon, but mostly because I was glad to have a reason to underscore the end of our conversation about Jamie. Carly chatted away about the prohibitively expensive mermaid sheath wedding gown she'd fallen in love with online but couldn't find in any of the local boutiques for cheaper. I recommended a discount designer bridal store in Milwaukee that she should check out, and she eagerly jotted the name down on her napkin. She told me about Sam's intramural baseball league and a tournament his team had recently placed second in. She offered up his services to play catch and do some batting practice with David.

I listened with half of my brain, the other half mulling over the objections she had raised on Jamie's behalf. Most of them were easy to dismiss as the talk of a friend who didn't want to believe the worst of Jamie. I understood that all too well. But the bedroom switch with Wendy was interesting. It would certainly explain why both his bedroom and bathroom had looked so clean and unlived in, with no real personal touches.

But if Wendy could no longer climb the stairs anymore, why would all her medications be upstairs where only Jamie had access to them? And why was it specifically oxycodone, his drug of choice, out on the sink? All the holes in the story still weren't satisfactorily explained, and I felt naïve for even hoping that maybe Carly was right and I might have jumped to conclusions. What was that old saying? *The simplest explanation was usually the right one.* It was painful to grasp onto a fraying thread of hope, but it was even more painful to just let it go.

Duffy had sent me to bring the clothes in off the line because a squall was approaching and she was trying to get dinner on the table. David darted outside with me, zigzagging across the yard for a five-minute game of tag with King Rex and Weeple. Thunder rumbled in the distance as I squatted to drape one of Duffy's blouses across the laundry basket, so I didn't see or hear Jamie approaching until he was only a few feet away.

"Holy *cats!*" I said, taking a step back. "You scared me!"

He was wearing his work uniform of khaki shorts, tan boots, and a black T-shirt with Demeter Landscaping Services, LLC screenprinted on the breast pocket and carrying a handful of tiny tomatoes. His bronzed face and arms had that flushed glow of someone who's just been doing hard manual labor in the sun. It physically hurt to look at him.

"I'm sorry," he said stiffly. "I saw you from our garden. I called your name, but you must not have heard me."

I unpinned David's pirate ship T-shirt and tossed it into the basket. I didn't trust myself to speak. In my tornado of thoughts, who knew which words would tumble out? *"I love you, regardless of what problems you have"* seemed just as likely to pop out as *"How could you have lied to my face? I can never trust you again."*

"I don't think I can talk to you right now," I said. Another clap of thunder reverberated, closer this time. I sought out David, half-hidden by the clothes still on the line. His dinosaurs weren't on the offensive, as I'd expected, and Jamie's presence hadn't inspired the panther, in its shadowy or more solid form, either. Instead, David waved excitedly at Jamie before flitting away to tag Weeple.

Jamie gave him a hesitant wave back, as if he wasn't sure if he was still allowed to wave at my son. "Fine. Don't talk then." A vein at his temple bulged as he gritted his teeth. "Just listen."

"Time to go inside, buckaroo, before you get soaked!" I shouted. "Can you please help Grandma Duffy set the table and tell her I'll be right inside?" When the screen door slapped shut behind him, I turned to Jamie. "Okay. You probably have about five minutes until the sky breaks open. I'm listening." As if to prove my point, lightning crackled in a faraway part of the sky, covering up the staccato hammering of my heart.

He started talking rapidly as though he thought I might interrupt him or walk away any second. "I know you'll believe what you want to, but the pills are my mom's. For her muscle spasms, which are really painful. Most of them are anticonvulsants that seem to help when things get really bad, but she occasionally takes oxycodone for the pain too. Sunday was one of those days. Her meds are in my bathroom because it's not really my bathroom. I moved her downstairs to my old room and my stuff upstairs in May, because the stairs were just getting to be too hard for her. But we kept the bathrooms as is because the upstairs one has the bigger tub. With a lower lip too, so it's easier to get into and out of. Her nurse comes twice a week and carries her up the stairs to bathe her. If you don't believe me, you can look in the tub sometime. Her bath seat is in there, along with all her favorite shampoos and body washes. I get ready downstairs in the guest bathroom, and my shaving stuff and all the mildew can prove it."

He squinted at the slate gray storm clouds, as if considering what other questions I might be wondering, and rubbed the back of his deeply tanned neck. "Her doctor asked me to keep the drugs out of her reach, which is why they're in the upstairs bathroom because she...so she doesn't take too many. We tried the top kitchen cabinets, but that didn't work. If she really put her mind to it, she could still get to them. So I brought them upstairs, where only the nurse or I could access them. I know you probably won't believe me, but I've never taken any of my mom's pills. Not a single one, and no oxycodone since I've been back. I'm clean. I can see how you'd think I'd be tempted, and to be honest with you, sometimes I am still tempted. That's why I rarely set foot in that bathroom. It's my mom's. It's her stuff, and when she needs something, I get it, but otherwise, the door stays closed."

He held out his splayed hands in front of him, the small tomatoes cradled in his fingers, as if I could read the truth in the deep lines of his palms. He looked so earnest right then, like the little boy I'd grown up with, big-eyed with his heart safety-pinned to his sleeve. I felt stunned and sheepish, incredulous yet hopeful as hell, and I wanted nothing more than to press my nose against his chest, breathe in his cedar smell, and let him wrap his arms around me and hold me up.

But something black and cancerous was growing in my abdomen, preventing me from making a move toward him. The panther under the bed, David's pitiful question of why hadn't I been there for him, my mom's appalling taste in men, Dennis lurking in my doorway, Patrick pleading with me to never leave him, that he'd kill himself, that he'd kill us all if it was the only way we could be together. It was all getting jumbled together, roiling in a sea of black, and Jamie was there too, with his former drug addiction and everything I didn't know about him and all the ways he might let David and me down if I gave him the chance.

"Thanks for telling me," I said softly. "I'm sorry I didn't listen to you right away." I removed the last few pieces of clothing from the line and folded them on top of the mounded pile in the basket. Despite the fact that it was only six o'clock, it was nearly pitch black now. The atmosphere was thick and almost magnetic with the impending storm.

"That's really all you want to say, Anna?" Jamie asked, narrowing his eyes and rocking backward on his heels.

"I'm sorry," I repeated. "I believe you're telling the truth. But I told you this isn't a good time to talk." The first drop of rain, warm and dime-sized, plopped on my shoulder.

"You're probably right," he said, blinking, as a raindrop pelted his cheek. "So when can we?"

I hugged the laundry basket to my hip, as if this could somehow protect the clothes from the rain. A tempestuous range of desires swirled within me. I wanted to forgive him and invite him inside for dinner. I wanted to drop the laundry basket and passionately kiss him, rain and clean clothes be damned. But I also wanted to flee inside and pretend this whole thing had never happened. I wanted to punish him for failing to somehow convince me sooner and sparing us the humiliation and heartache. I wanted to blame him for David's fears and the way he distracted me from being the kind of mother my son needed.

"I don't think we should," I whispered, as raindrops fell more steadily, wetting my bare arms and the crown of my head. "I don't think I can be in a relationship right now. David needs me too much. I've only got one chance to get this right, and I really think I need to focus more on him."

Nestled in Jamie's black hair, raindrops refracted the light like tiny diamonds. "I really don't understand you, Anna. You're a great mom, and David is a great kid. I'm not asking you to demote him as your number one priority, so why are you acting like this is about him? Are you just trying to spare my feelings?"

A bolt of lightning lit up the sky, like a bright white scar, and a thunderclap followed not thirty seconds later. I jumped. "It *is* about David!"

His jaw muscle twitched. "Come on. You can't tell me you don't see the pattern here. You can only afford to like me when it's convenient for you. Because I'm here and I'm what's available, and as soon as there's the slightest problem or someone better comes along, you move on without a glance back. Like you've always done."

"That is really unfair," I said, even as his words plucked a chord of ugly truth, which resonated in my chest. I wanted to defend myself against his accusations that I'd treated him as the boy next door, my plaything who would always be right there where I'd left him, while I could come and go as I pleased. In childhood, in high school, even this summer. But I knew there was a kernel of truth in what he'd said. I had used him in some ways, and I was still doing it, toying with his heart when I was too busy being a single mother to engage in a romantic relationship. Too busy and too broken after what Patrick had put me through. Would a normal person without trust issues and the constant expectation of being let down have reacted the same way to the prescription medicine as I had? I honestly didn't know.

It started to rain in earnest then, as if God had turned his showerhead from a misty rainforest setting to a high pressure deluge. Our clothes were instantly soaked and clinging to our bodies, but it didn't seem sexy like it did in the movies. It just seemed like a very sad, very final ending.

CHAPTER TWENTY

"Anna bean!" Duffy hissed. She was shaking me harder than seemed strictly necessary. "David's going to be late for school, and you're going to be late for work if you don't get a move on." Her face appeared upside-down and frog-like as she leaned over me on the couch. "What are you doing out here?"

I struggled to kick free of the chenille throw blanket and sit up, but Vivien Leigh was curled on my stomach, and she let out an indignant meow. She'd been skittish and clingy the last two days, avoiding the upstairs at all costs, which made me wonder if somehow she could also see the panther. That my house cat could intuitively sense the much bigger imaginary feline seemed no weirder than anything else in my life these days. But how could I explain to Duffy that the panther hiding under David's bed had taken up residence under my bed last night, exiling us to the living room?

"What time is it?" I moaned. There were no digital clocks in the living room; only the grandfather clock that had woken me up every hour on the hour as it boisterously rang out the time. There was a crick in my neck that made the muscle feel like a crimped piece of pie crust. An unexplained feeling of emptiness washed over me, and I gradually remembered my break with Jamie.

"Seven-thirty." She turned to the loveseat where David was still sprawled out as limp as a rag doll and started gently stroking his face and exposed arms. "Time to rise and shine, grasshopper."

So I had overslept by half an hour. Normally by seven-thirty, we were sitting down to eat breakfast and argue over David's questionable wardrobe choices. Drop-off time for kindergarten was between eight and eight-twenty, and normally I took David closer to eight, so I could still get to the real estate office by eight-thirty to open it up. Our mornings were carefully orchestrated chaos in a very narrow window of time, and now I'd gone and screwed that up because I hadn't remembered to drag my alarm clock out into the living room, plug it in, and re-set it when the panther had resolved to terrorize us the second night in a row.

"Time to get dressed," Duffy sang to David. "You've got to hurry, though, or Grandpa Winston will eat all the pancakes, and there won't be any left for you."

"Pancakes?" David's sleepy face lit up. The purplish circles under his eyes were gone, and I was relieved to know that at least one of us had slept soundly last night.

"You bet," Duffy said. "But you need to be quick and pick out a nice outfit you know your mommy will like, okay?" She spun around and pointed at me like I was vermin she wanted to shoo from her house. "You! Go hop in the shower. Winston can drive David to school this morning if need be. We don't want you getting fired for lateness in only your first month."

With Duffy the drill sergeant's instructions, Winston was able to leave by 7:55 with David who had been washed, dressed, and fed, more or less. He gave me a syrup-sticky kiss on the cheek before he left, and I squeezed his shoulder, wanting to fortify him somehow against the panther who I was worried might follow him to school next.

Since I wasn't driving David all the way to Port Ambrose, I still had a few minutes before I needed to leave for Lawrenceville. I dropped into one of the kitchen chairs, zipping up the side of my skirt with one hand and reaching for a mug of coffee Duffy had just poured me with the other. The effect of my sleepless nights left me feeling like a leaky inner-tube being tossed about by the ocean. My eyes hurt. My back and neck hurt. My brain hurt. But most of all, my heart hurt.

Duffy handed me a plate stacked with two golden, fluffy pancakes, drenched in maple syrup. She put her hands on her hips. "Sunday night, we hear screams and then you let David sleep in your bed, and now last night, you're both sleeping out here. What in the name of Pete is going on?"

I chewed slowly, letting the heavenly pancake melt on my tongue. The pancakes looked soft and pillowy, like a great place to rest my head for just a moment. "I told you, he's having nightmares."

She sat down across from me. "I understand that, and I'm sorry to hear it. But I don't understand why he needs to sleep in your bed or you both need to camp out in the living room. It seems like that might send the wrong message to him. You want to take his nightmares seriously, of course, but not so seriously that you're encouraging him to continue being afraid. You need to teach him to face his fears and see they're not so scary after all. Giving him this kind of special treatment and attention seems like it might enable him." She was starting to sound like Dr. Rosen's book. "Do you remember what we used to do when you had a nightmare?"

I shook my head, which felt like it weighed twice its usual amount. I remembered having a bad dream once at my mom's house. I had probably been only five or six. I couldn't remember the dream, but I remembered my mom in a pink negligee slipping into my room like an apparition to push my head back against my pillow and whisper, *Hush. It was just a bad dream. You're going to have a good dream now. Close your eyes, and you'll be a beautiful princess living in a castle in the clouds far, far away from here.*

Duffy toyed with the white bandana covering her hair. "It was Winston's duty mostly, soothing kids after bad dreams. I figured it was the least he could do after the baby years of nightly feedings. But then he got so gosh darn good at it that even if I wanted to try to console Kimberly or Luke after a nightmare, they didn't want me. They wanted their dad." She shrugged. "I tried not to take it personally."

"What did he do?" I took a sip of my coffee and leaned forward. Did my grandfather have some handy-dandy nighttime blessing or bedroom enchantment up his sleeve that he could teach me?

"He would sit on the bed, pull you onto his lap, have you tell him about the dream, and then kiss you good night."

Disappointed, I sat back. "That's it?"

"That's it," she said defensively. "Anyway, it seemed to work."

It was worth a try, but I suspected that Winston's trick wouldn't work with a two hundred-pound panther. Duffy was right in her own way; we couldn't keep letting the panther bully us and drive us from our beds, but there was no way I was leaving my son alone in the dark with a lethal animal that belonged in a cage at the zoo. Imaginary or not. I had experienced the terror first-hand last night as we lay together in my bed, and suddenly a deep growling had started up from beneath the mattress. We had only stayed long enough for me to strip the pillows and blanket from the bed.

"I've tried something similar," I said. "David keeps dreaming that there's a black panther under his bed, and it wants something from him, but he doesn't know what. That's as far as we can get, and he's terrified of it."

Duffy puckered her lips, deep in thought. "A panther? Where could he have come up with that? Has he been to the zoo recently?"

"No. His preschool took him to the petting zoo last year, but the meanest thing they had there was a llama. He's got a very active imagination." I pushed off from the kitchen table, wishing I could eat more of my pancakes, wishing I could go upstairs and back to sleep in my hopefully no longer panther-occupied bedroom. "I think I'm going to call his pediatrician and see if she can refer me to a good—" I couldn't bring myself to say 'child psychiatrist,' so I stopped. "This book she loaned me was talking about how I need to figure out what his imaginary friends and his bad dreams symbolize. What he's really afraid of."

Last night, as I'd listened to the grandfather clock chime and tossed and turned restlessly on the couch, I'd brainstormed a list of possibilities. An aversion to Jamie or any man in my life was probably out, since David continued to see the panther even when Jamie wasn't around, and he'd professed to like our neighbor. (I wasn't looking forward to explaining that we probably wouldn't be spending any more time with Jamie in the future.) Anxiety about school seemed off the table too, since David enjoyed his mornings in kindergarten and talked enthusiastically about them.

So was it a more generalized fear? Perhaps watching Gunner's Titanic video had made him more aware of death, and now he was subconsciously worried about losing his grandparents or me. Or maybe since the panther seemed to be haunting *me* equally, it represented *my* fears for David, my insecurities as a mother, my constant worries about his happiness and safety, his lack of a stable father in his life, the possibility of mental illness lurking in his future. Maybe David had created the shadow animal, but I had inadvertently fed his fears and made it more solid and ever present. I didn't know if that was even possible, but since the situation was already so outrageously surreal, I wasn't going to discount it until I had answers. That's why I needed to get David in to see a child psychiatrist to discuss his imagination, so we could uncover the truth about the panther before it got even more out of hand.

Duffy raised her eyebrow and cleared my plate away. "A panther isn't scary enough to warrant its own fear?"

"I know. It's really freaky." I grabbed my purse from the counter. "Well, I better get going. Thanks for whipping our butts into shape this morning. You're a lifesaver."

"You're welcome, snickerdoodle. That's what I'm here for." She started to run hot water over the breakfast dishes in the sink. "I know you're headed out now, but I need to talk to you later, so remind me, okay? I want to talk to you about David's birthday and what you want to do for it. Do you want to have a party, and if so, should we do it that Saturday or Sunday? What kind of cake should we get? Does David have any little friends he wants to invite, or should we keep it to family? Your mom called the other day and—"

I cut her off. "You flatter yourself and us if you think my mom gives a damn about David or his birthday."

Duffy turned off the tap and faced me. "Listen to me, Anna. She disguises her feelings just as well as you do. She told me you stopped by a few weeks ago and said how pretty and professional you looked.

She's proud of you, honey. She just doesn't know how to show it. And I bet if we invited her to David's birthday, she would love to—"

"I can't think about this right now. I need to go." I swung my purse over my arm and left the kitchen. *Pretty and professional?* That was her takeaway from my visit? Never mind the accusations we'd let fly about Leah Nola and my mom's child molester of a boyfriend.

"That's fine. We'll talk about it later. I just wanted to make sure it was on your radar."

Ha. Sure, it was on my radar. I imagined a neon green circle and several blinking missiles converging on me all at once. Dealing with the large black cat menacing my son seemed just a tad more important than planning a birthday party right now. David would be turning five in what—two weeks, now? Oh my god. Only two weeks. And even if I blacklisted my mom, I knew the Gills would still want to see David and bring over gifts. Maybe I could arrange something separate with them at a restaurant the following week?

Last year we'd met them at Chuck E. Cheese for a couple of hours, and they'd given him an overabundance of expensive outfits and toys, including his remote-controlled dinosaur, but it didn't seem like Abigail would be satisfied with that same kind of arrangement this year. She wanted quality time with her grandson, and in another month, when my injunction against Patrick expired, she'd want me to let them try supervised visits again. The thought made the rhythm of my heart stutter. The timing couldn't have been worse. David certainly wasn't ready to "meet" his father right now, when he was already in such a fragile state, dreaming up dinosaurs to protect him, cowering from a panther under his bed, and I doubted Patrick, with his flagrant indifference to the restraining order last month and his agitated behavior, was truly ready either.

The real estate office was blissfully slow. Brandon was out showing houses, and Janet and Gisele were tucked away in the back room on a four-hour conference call. Every so often, a phone call would trickle in, and I would e-mail the message to the respective agent. That left me ample time to deal with my own personal crises.

I called Dr. Rosen's office to get a referral for a child therapist. Even the psychiatrist's name, Oscar Da Costa, sounded impressive and expensive, and I could already imagine the jokes he probably made to his fellow doctors at medical conferences: "Of course, I can help you, but it's going Da Cost-ya." Har-har. The soonest he could squeeze David in was next Friday, but I jumped at the appointment, even though my new health insurance wouldn't be kicking in until next month, because a) I didn't think David and I could wait any longer to be rid of the panther and b) I doubted my meager health insurance would cover a luxury like child psychiatry anyway.

I had no sooner ended my call with the clinic when my cell phone started ringing. By this point of the day, Winston normally had David home from school, and I'd trained Duffy to relay a brief report to me. But it was a phone number I didn't recognize. I glanced over my shoulder at the conference room, but the door was still shut.

"Hello?"

"Is this Anna Jennings?"

The high-pitched, chirpy voice was familiar, but I couldn't quite place it. "Yes."

"This is Lindsey Hanna, your son's kindergarten teacher."

I sank back heavily in my wheeled receptionist chair, and it rolled at least a foot backwards. I smushed my ear against the cell phone. "Is everything okay?" I hoped against hope that she wouldn't say "your son has been mauled by a panther" or "your son attacked another child and is blaming it on a dinosaur." I pictured David, bruised hollows under his eyes, arms around his knees, rocking himself in the corner next to the play car while the black panther paced circles around him. Had the panther finally followed him to school then?

"Ye-es," she said, stretching the word out into two syllables, as if unsure of it herself. "I was just hoping you could come in for a chat sometime this week to talk about David."

I twitched the computer mouse to dispel my screensaver and read the time on the monitor. "How about now? I could come in on my lunch break."

David's teacher laughed. I could hear her shuffling papers in the background. Perhaps she had a whole list of students to call, and she'd forgotten which one was David. What else could explain her levity? "That's nice of you to offer, Ms. Jennings, but afternoon kindergarten starts in a few minutes. If today's a good day for you, we could meet at 3:30 or 4:00. Otherwise any afternoon this week would be—"

"I can come at four today," I said.

"Wonderful. I'll be looking forward to it." How could she be so nonchalant about David's very serious problems? Maybe it was a technique they taught all education majors: when contacting parents about bad news, make sure you sound your perkiest so you can lure them in, and then BAM—hit them with the announcement when they're least expecting it.

I hurriedly called Duffy to let her know I'd be home a little later because of a meeting with David's teacher. Duffy didn't seem to think there was any cause for alarm and suggested the meeting was a routine introduction, a kind of get-to-know-you for all parents. She put David on the phone, who informed me they'd gotten to play The Farmer in the Dell at kindy-garden that day, and he'd been chosen as the dog. He demonstrated his very convincing bark for me and didn't seem distressed in the slightest.

Despite this, I still couldn't stop myself from pondering a slew of terrible scenarios of what Miss Hanna wanted to communicate to me. Between his uncombed hair today, his sleepy eyes Monday, and the Hawaiian shirt on his very first day, maybe she suspected I was a negligent, unfit mother. Or maybe David or King Rex had scratched another child? Or maybe the other kids were picking on him because he didn't know how to interact with anyone other than imaginary beings? When Janet and Gisele finally finished their phone conference, they had a whirl of requests for me, and I was grateful to keep my mind off my 4:00 meeting at Port Ambrose Elementary.

When I arrived at the school, the parking lot was practically empty except for a few teachers' cars. A handful of students carrying what looked like violins and trumpets in black plastic cases were being picked up by their parents. After-school music lessons. I wondered if I should be signing David up for something like that or if it was still too early. My mom had never signed me up for any extracurricular lessons—no ballet, no gymnastics, no soccer—no matter how much I'd pleaded, and I'd always been so jealous of my friends who tossed their hair and complained about how boring their piano lessons were. It was a good thing Jamie and I had broken up, so I could dwell on these kinds of important questions.

Miss Hanna looked up from sorting through a plastic tub of hand puppets as I entered the room. "Well, hello. Thanks again for coming to see me on such short notice." Blunt bangs were cut in her strawberry-blond hair, and she was wearing a bright yellow cardigan with a red belt around her narrow waist. "Why don't we have a seat over here?"

She shepherded me over to her desk, where two adult-sized chairs and two child-sized chairs were arranged. I selected one of the adult-sized chairs and nervously sat down. I had so many questions to ask that I felt like I would burst, but I knew I should let her do the talking first since she was the one who had asked me here.

"How does David like kindergarten so far?" she asked.

Was this a trick question? I crossed my legs and wiggled one of my feet. "He seems to like it very much," I finally said. "Every day he comes home with a new song or fact to teach us."

"Excellent." She grinned, and I could see that despite her otherwise classically pretty looks, her upper teeth were crowded and trying to hide behind each other. "I'm very glad to hear that." She rifled through one of her desk drawers and slid a manila folder over to me. "These are some of David's drawings that I thought you might like to see."

Oh no. I gripped the folder, reluctant to open it and see what was inside. A gruesome drawing of the panther dismembering someone? A pack of dinosaurs with teeth and claws as sharp as steak knives? Or maybe a sad, confused family portrait? *Your son seems very disturbed,* Miss Hanna would say.

I folded the file's cover back and breezed quickly through my son's illustrations, relieved to see there was nothing too out of the ordinary. They were the same type of crayon drawings he did every day: red tractors and fire trucks, a self-portrait of David kicking a pink soccer ball, a green dinosaur (Weeple), and then several pictures of the black panther. More than I would have hoped for. I stared down at the last drawing in the bunch, another of the panther, feeling a weird sense of déjà vu sweep over me. Clearly, it was the panther I had seen the night before and the night before that. So why the bizarre feeling of a deeper recognition? David's sketched version looked almost cartoonish, and that seemed more right to me somehow than the furry, muscular cat that was currently living in the upstairs of our house.

I was reluctant to look back up. I felt like a witness being asked to okay the sketch artist's composite drawing of the perpetrator. *Yes, ma'am, this is the panther that's been terrorizing my son.* But when I looked back up, Miss Hanna wasn't casting me a practiced, teacherly look of concern; she was practically pulsating with eagerness. She reached out for the folder, and I returned it to her.

"Ms. Jennings, to be quite frank, these are some of the best drawings I've ever seen a four- or five-year-old do." She paused dramatically, as if allowing the news to sink in, before continuing on. "I don't know how familiar you are with the artistic ability of children David's age, but let's just say it's nowhere near as advanced or creative as this."

I crossed my legs in the other direction and waited. Was this some strange way of easing me into a conversation about how poorly he was doing in another aspect of kindergarten? Buttering me up with his strengths before dropping his weaknesses on me? His teacher was staring at me expectantly, so I said, "Thank you. David's always been very imaginative and good at drawing. I'm very proud of him."

"You should be." Miss Hanna nodded emphatically and pulled out another file from her desk drawer. "He's a very bright student in other ways as well. We always do an initial assessment of the incoming kindergarteners, and he scored very highly. I'd like to talk to you about getting David set up in our gifted and talented program. It meets twice a week, on Tuesdays and Thursdays, during recess."

She continued to describe the "enrichment curriculum" that my son would be exposed to, and I continued to stare at her crooked teeth in a daze. It was like getting called into your boss's office, sure you're going to get canned, only to discover you're being given a promotion and a fat raise. David, a gifted and talented student? I'd always known that he was a very creative and sensitive little boy, but, of course, I was a little biased. And then there was the fact that when he was interested in something like dinosaurs or tractors, he could soak up every detail like a sponge. Maybe that wasn't so typical for a four, going on five-year-old.

"So can we sign him up?" she asked hopefully.

"Sure." I read over and signed all the paperwork she passed to me. Even though I knew I should have been feeling a mix of relief and pride, I still couldn't help feeling a bit anxious in that classroom. The cheerful colors and smiley posters didn't match the foreboding vibe I was getting on the other side of Miss Hanna's desk. "So besides his drawing ability and high test scores, how is David doing?" I asked.

Miss Hanna scribbled something on the form in front of her, looked up at me, and blinked.

"Does he get along with the other kids?" I prodded her. "Does he seem shy or withdrawn?"

She shook her head. "David plays well with others, shares toys, takes turns. He's made marvelous friends with the identical twins in the class: Maddox and Mason. They're like the Three Musketeers."

"So no problems then? No unusual changes in behavior?" I asked, the tightness in my chest finally loosening. "That you've noticed," I added.

She considered. "Well, now that you mention it, David did seem a little spooked when he came in from recess today."

"Spooked?" That was an odd word but probably a fitting word to describe a child being haunted by a black panther. I cast a glance at the low bank of windows that overlooked the playground and woods.

"At first, he sat kind of apart from the others on the storytime rug and didn't seem to be paying much attention. But then Maddox encouraged him to join them, and he seemed fine after that. I thought maybe there had been a tussle on the playground." Before I could ask her, she supplied, "It wasn't my day for recess duty, so I can't be sure."

I peered at the color-blocked storytime rug and then out the window again, at the orange plastic slide. A scuffle with another kid certainly could have happened out there, but I suspected his spooked mood had more to do with the panther. I would definitely have to ask David about it.

Miss Hanna returned the folders to their drawer, flashing me her cluttered-tooth smile. "Nothing to worry about, I think. They seemed to resolve it fine on their own." She stood up then and offered me her hand across the desk. "It was so nice seeing you again, Ms. Jennings. I really appreciate your coming in and talking to me about David. I think he's going to have a very bright future ahead of him."

On the drive home, I listened to a voicemail message that had been left during my meeting with Miss Hanna. Not Jamie, as I'd briefly (and naïvely) allowed myself to hope, but Stacy. "Hi, Anna, just hoping to catch you. We're loving our new house and would love to have you and David visit sometime. Maybe for Thanksgiving unless you're planning to spend it with your grandparents? Oh, and Breanne said something strange the other day, and I just wanted to run it by you. I really miss having you guys close by. Call me to let me know how you're doing, okay? Ba-bye!"

I knew it would be a marathon phone call, so I added it to the bottom of my steadily growing to-do list. As I piloted the Caravan to Salsburg, I tried to hold onto Miss Hanna's words like a talisman: *He's going to have a very bright future ahead of him.* Please, please, please, I prayed silently. Let her be right. Let David have a bright future free of fear. And bad cats.

CHAPTER TWENTY-ONE

The September evening air was surprisingly brisk, so I'd nabbed one of Winston's old hooded sweatshirts from the coat closet as Duffy and I headed outside to monitor David playing. The sweatshirt smelled a little like alfalfa and my grandfather's musky cologne, and I had to roll up the sleeves three times for my hands to peek out. Duffy had politely withheld her questions about my meeting with Miss Hanna all through dinner, but I could tell she was close to exploding with curiosity. Now, as we settled side by side into the deck chairs and I relayed the news about the gifted and talented program, my grandmother's eyes shone with the unadulterated pride and excitement I knew I should have been feeling.

"Our Davey's a genius." Duffy clapped her hands. "I always knew it. Just wait until I tell Edna." She hopped up from her chair, nearly tipping it over, and hastened to the door.

"Where are you going? You're not seriously going to call Edna to gloat, are you? Duffy, please don't—"

She shook her head, held up one finger, and disappeared inside. Wonderful. Just what their already overwrought friendship needed. I wondered if Gunner would be in the program too; for David's sake, I certainly hoped not.

David was winging a frisbee from one end of the yard to the other, as if in hopes of his dinosaurs' fetching and returning it to him. I didn't know if it was because they lacked the knowhow, the desire, or the physical strength, but each time they didn't, he blew out an

exasperated sigh and chased after the frisbee himself. I doubted anyone would suspect him of being a genius now. King Rex was pacing
along the tree line in a very fierce "king of the dinosaurs" way, but
Weeple was sticking close to David. He lumbered after him like a
faithful, oversized Saint Bernard every time David set off in a different direction. I thought about joining him in his game of frisbee, but
just then Duffy reappeared with an uncorked bottle of champagne
and two glasses.

"Champagne?" I gaped. "Honestly, I think you're making a bit too
much of this."

"Don't be silly." Duffy poured a fizzy glass and handed it to me.
"I bought this for our thirty-eighth anniversary back in May, and
then we forgot to drink it. You know your grandfather and I aren't
big drinkers. And this seems like something to celebrate." She set
the bottle on the table and raised her glass. "Here's to our little boy
growing up and starting off his school days so brilliantly. And here's
to you, dumpling, for choosing a job close to us, so we can be a part
of your lives." She winked at me as we touched glasses.

My chest tightened with emotion. As extravagant as it was—drinking champagne on a Tuesday night—just having Duffy there to share
the news with, someone who had as much a vested interest in my
son as me, was incredibly meaningful. I remembered last September,
when David had gotten his first run in T-ball, and we'd come home
from the game, totally jazzed up, with no one to share our excitement.
Stacy and her kids had been out, my other friends my age didn't have
kids and weren't the slightest bit interested in T-ball, and who else
was there nearby to celebrate with? I'd ended up ordering a pizza for
the two of us, and we'd eaten it in the living room on paper plates.
I'd let David stay up until eleven, when he'd finally fallen asleep on
the couch still in his dirty uniform.

I started to speak, and Duffy hushed me. "I know it's not Harvard,
it's only kindergarten, but I'm really proud of Davey. The Jennings
don't produce dumb kids. I mean, look at you! Bright as can be, with
talent to spare. I can only imagine how well you would've done in
high school if you only would've tried. It's no wonder Davey is so

good at drawing with two artists for parents…" She trailed off as Patrick, and whatever else David might stand to inherit from him, floated between us.

"Well, thank you," I said quickly and took a swallow of champagne. "I'm really happy for him too; I just want to get all this nightmare business sorted out, and then I'll be ready to celebrate."

Duffy glugged back her glass. "I understand. You want him to be happy and healthy in all parts of his life."

I did, more than anything, and it seemed incongruous that she and Miss Hanna could be so convinced of David's success and well-being right now, while I was frantically scheduling an appointment for him to be mentally evaluated. Who was right? The experienced mother and grandmother? The kindergarten teacher who'd studied children's learning and development in college? Or me, the bumbling mother who believed she could see her child's imaginary friends? I knew who a jury would believe, but I also knew my son.

I twirled the champagne glass in my fingers by the stem and turned to watch David, who had given up on his frisbee and was now singing The Farmer in the Dell in a loud, off-key voice to King Rex and Weeple. They were standing loosely in a circle, so it was hard to determine who was the farmer, who was the wife, and who was the child. He looked so relaxed and confident playing with his dinosaurs that I wished they could effectively scare the panther away once and for all. But King Rex and Weeple didn't seem to be a match for the roaring, rumbling panther under the bed since he'd ceased to be an ethereal black mist.

The color was draining away from the backyard as the sun dipped behind the trees. It was nearing David's bedtime, and I was dreading it. I didn't think I could survive another night on the couch, worrying that either David or I would wake up with the panther's ghostly green eyes studying us, ready to pounce. The champagne was compounding my sleepiness, and I wondered if I had finally built up enough of a sleep debt, that regardless of all my apprehensions, I would somehow drop into a deep and dreamless sleep tonight.

I sipped the bubbly, sweet liquid and rubbed my arms vigorously in an effort to wake up. Jamie's backyard was empty, but I could see a light on in what I now knew was their kitchen. Were Jamie and his mom eating a late dinner? Or was Jamie alone, scrubbing pots and pans, loading the dishwasher, peering out the window? Could he see David in his bright blue, long-sleeved T-shirt? Was he thinking about me? My eyes watered, and I let out an involuntary yawn.

"That looked like a pretty heavy conversation you two were having last night," Duffy said, nodding toward the Presswoods' house. Of course, she'd peeked out the screen door at us. When I'd sent David in and hadn't followed quickly behind with her laundry, she'd probably wondered what was holding me up. "Is everything alright?"

"Not really," I said, trying to keep my tone light and easy, as if I were about to tell a really good joke, but my voice cracked. "We broke up."

She arched one of her perfectly plucked eyebrows. "You broke up? Whatever for?"

I wasn't looking forward to a repeat performance of what had happened at La Frontera. I didn't want to admit to her that I'd found painkillers in Jamie's medicine cabinet; I didn't want to re-experience with her the same feelings of betrayal and self-righteousness that I had already cycled through. I didn't want to listen to her verdict when I finally told her Jamie's version of events, and I really didn't want to try to explain my black muddle of emotions and the stoic way he had reacted, like he'd been preparing for me to break his heart all along. *You can only afford to like me when it's convenient for you.* I didn't want to, but I knew I needed to, so I took a deep cleansing breath and I let it all out.

To her credit, my grandma didn't interrupt me once. She didn't gasp dramatically or make murmuring sounds of disapproval. She sat very still, her bright eyes leaving my face only every so often to monitor David playing. By the time I was finished, the first stars were peeking through the gauzy fabric of the sky and David and his dinosaurs were three silhouettes prowling and playing in the murkiness. I stopped talking, and a profound silence fell over the backyard.

"It sounds to me like maybe you're both a little scared," Duffy said, tapping her copper-colored fingernails on the table. "Jamie feels like you're abandoning him again like you did in high school. Maybe a part of him thinks you're even right to do this and he's not good enough for you now because of his history with drug addiction."

"I'm sure he'd appreciate the psychoanalysis," I said wryly. I made a face and hugged Winston's ratty sweatshirt around me.

"I'll send him my bill tomorrow," she quipped. "Seriously though, it's not called 'falling in love' for no reason. It's scary! It's like jumping out of a plane with no parachute. Or bungee-jumping without your cord attached. Or hang-gliding with only one wing."

"I get the picture. But in case you've forgotten, I've done that once already, and it didn't work out so hot."

"Of course I remember." She set her champagne flute on the table and leaned back in her chair. "It's clear that you're scared now to trust another man with your heart. You're worried that something that seems so good will likely blow up in your face like it did with Patrick. That you can't trust your instincts anymore, and you need to be doubly skeptical of everyone because of David."

Startled by her shrewd observation, I met my grandma's eyes. They were hazel, like my mom's, but crinkled up mischievously, and they seemed capable of seeing into my heart where all my secret worries and fears were hidden.

"I know a little something about fear, honey," she said with a tired sigh. "I know what a relief it feels like to give into it at first. It's not hard to persuade yourself that you're doing the right thing—that you're making the smart, safe decision."

I pressed my spine into the back of the chair and hugged my knees to my chest. I had never heard my grandmother talk so candidly about her anxiety before.

"But fear is insidious," she said, smoothing her hair back. It looked more white than blond in the dusky light. "It takes anything you're willing to give it, the parts of your life you don't mind cutting out, but when you're not looking, it takes anything else it damn well pleases too. I started out persuading myself it was just the highway traffic

I wanted to avoid, the parallel parking on busy streets, the pushy crowds. But now, a decade later, I find myself looking up and realizing I'm virtually on an island. I've given up so much, and it may be too late for me to dramatically change course now, but it's not too late for you, Anna."

"But Duffy, if you want help, then—"

She cut me off with a resolute shake of her head. "This isn't an intervention for me, dear. Forgive me—I know I'm being a terrible hypocrite—but I don't want you to miss out on living your life and following your dreams. You're much too young to be so scared and jaded. You need to learn how to trust people again and follow your instincts."

"But how do I do that?" I asked, feeling like the world kept proving me right that it was a scary, hardhearted place. My mom had started the lesson, Patrick had continued it, and lately, even David's imagination was conspiring against me. There were so many things to be afraid of—some real, some imagined—and it seemed impossible to know the difference until it was too late.

"You need to be brave," Duffy said simply. "The only thing more powerful than your fear is having a reason worth abandoning it. In my case, one of the only times I was able to leave Salsburg was for someone I really loved—you—that night I came to pick you up in Milwaukee. And in your case, Jamie is your reason, because someone that perfect for you doesn't come along every day. You need to give him another chance because not enough young men today have his integrity and steadfastness. Winston and I have been watching him with you and David, and we like what we see. You already look like a family."

We both thoughtfully considered the shadowy shape of David flitting around the garden like some kind of woodland sprite. I remembered the way Jamie and I had chased each other in this very same expanse of deep, velvety green as children, capturing fireflies in canning jars, demanding they release their magic and grant us wishes. The way afterwards, dog-tired from our running around, we lay in the grass together like a human pinwheel with our heads together and our legs pointed out.

"I thought that once too, before this whole fallout with his mom's pills," I confided. "But I don't know if he wants to be with me anymore. I might have hurt his feelings too much. He thinks I don't believe in him and that I view him as just the boy next door, a diversion when I'm living here."

"Well, then you need to set the record straight and tell him how you really feel." Duffy leaned forward and put one hand on either side of my face. "Anna, you are so loving, so beautiful, and so resilient." She stroked my hair, as if I were still seven years old. "I know you're capable of great courage. You can do this. You *need* to do this."

"Thank you," I whispered. "I'll try." I looked once more across the lawn to his house. The kitchen had gone dim; maybe the front of the house and the living room were lit up now. I wished I could run across the grass to him right then, pour out the contents of my heart, and let him hold me until I fell asleep in his arms, but I had David to tuck into bed and a panther to contend with. Jamie, unfortunately, would have to wait for one more day.

I stood up, exhaustion seeping into every fiber of my being. "David! It's time to go inside and get ready for bed."

His dinosaurs seemed reluctant to say goodnight to him. They flanked him, showing their loyalty, like buddies sending their friend off to a schoolyard fight they knew he didn't stand a chance of winning.

Upstairs, David was somber and calm as he changed into his pajamas and brushed his teeth. He seemed resigned. I listened for the panther's growling in his bedroom and then mine but didn't hear anything. Could it be that the phantom panther had given up its terror tactics? I hardly allowed myself to dare to hope that maybe today at recess David had overcome whatever fear it represented.

"I talked to your teacher, Miss Hanna, today," I said as he climbed into bed, hoping to distract him from whatever pattern of nighttime fears we'd gotten into. "She said that she thinks you're a very gifted student and that your drawings are excellent. She wants you to take a special class on Tuesdays and Thursdays where you'll get to do all kinds of fun things: solve problems, do puzzles, and make creative projects with a few other kids."

"Will Maddox and Mason be there?" he asked, rolling onto his side.

"I don't know," I said honestly. "But even if they're not, you'll be in class with them most of the time and can still be friends with them. It's just one hour per week." I decided to pull out the big guns. "And Miss Hanna said there will be a unit on dinosaurs."

Instead of looking gleeful at this prospect, David seemed preoccupied by other thoughts. He nibbled on his thumb. "Does the zoo really have dino-suss?" he asked abruptly.

"The zoo? I don't think so. Do you mean the museum?"

"No, the *zoo*," David repeated more loudly, as if I were hard of hearing. "An atomic zibbit."

Oh, the animatronic dinosaur exhibit at the zoo! Just the other day, Winston had mentioned to me the special fall exhibit that would be opening; perhaps he had mentioned it to David too. "I guess the zoo does have dinosaurs," I amended. "But I don't think you'll be doing a field trip there with your school, if that's why you're asking."

"Does the zoo have a train too?"

"It does," I said, thinking now this was clearly a thinly-veiled attempt to get me to take him there. "And also, incidentally, a whole bunch of animals. Would you like to go there sometime?"

But David shook his head briskly as though he were trying to get water out of his ears. "No! I don't want to go to the zoo."

I bit my lip, feeling a flutter of concern in the pit of my stomach. Was his fear of the panther making him nervous about seeing other exotic animals? Why bring up the zoo if he had no interest in going? "Okay, we won't go," I said. "Some other time maybe." I pulled the sheet up to his chin and tucked it under his shoulders. "Your special class is on Tuesdays and Thursdays during recess, so you'll have to give up recess on those days, but you'll still get to play. It will just be a different kind of playing indoors."

"I won't have recess tomorrow?" David asked. He didn't sound as mutinous as I'd expected.

"Tomorrow is Wednesday, so you'll still have recess. But on Thursday, the day after tomorrow, you'll go to your special class for the first time and miss recess." He closed his eyes. I leaned on the bed and rested my cheek close to his. "I really hope you sleep well tonight, buckaroo. With no bad dreams. Should I look under the bed?"

David's pale eyelids wrinkled and creased. "He's not there. He's waiting for me at school."

I inhaled sharply. So Miss Hanna was right. Something had spooked David at recess today: the panther, just as I had feared. But I needed to confirm my assumptions. "Who's *he*, David? Who's at school waiting for you?"

He shrugged listlessly. "I don't know what he wants. He watches me at recess."

Sweat prickled my otherwise chilly skin. No wonder he didn't seem too bummed about giving up recess. "The big black cat?"

David nodded and slid down the bed a few inches. I ran my fingers through his corn silk hair.

"You don't have to be scared," I whispered. "We're going to meet with a nice doctor next week and figure this out, okay? But in the meantime, I'm not going to let it hurt you. I'm not going to let anyone ever hurt you. Okay, buckaroo?" Now if only I could find a way to fulfill that promise.

I glided to my bedroom, so tired I felt like I was already dreaming. I was doing my best to protect my son from the real dangers of the world; how could I protect him from the dangers of his own invention as well? How could I fight something that wasn't real? I lay down on my bed, still dressed in my jeans and Winston's sweatshirt. As my muscles sank into the soft mattress, I thought fleetingly about Jamie next door, but he seemed so far away.

David and I sat in the minivan in the parking lot outside Port Ambrose Elementary. His face was a mask of misery. Even fresh-baked chocolate chocolate-chip muffins hadn't been enough to cheer him up this morning. Lately, he'd been looking too big for his booster seat, but now he seemed dwarfed by it, and his new red and white sneakers dangled over the edge as if he were only a toddler. King Rex hadn't accompanied us for the first time, and his absence in his usual spot in the back of the minivan was glaring. But instead of rejoicing that David no longer felt the need to bring King Rex as a security blanket to school, I felt troubled by the T-rex's sudden time off. Why now when David seemed to need him the most? I remembered Leah Nola's comment that she wasn't strong enough to help me any longer, that I needed to help myself, and I really wished I understood what was happening in my son's psyche.

I'd been planning on personally walking him inside like I'd done on the first day and having a quick chat with Miss Hanna, but now that we were there, I honestly felt like peeling away, calling us both in sick for the day, and heading to the beach or the park. But that would be irresponsible, I rebuked myself, and I would be setting a bad example for David—that it was okay to play hooky from school and that you should run from things you were afraid of. It had been those two reasons, along with my dread of what Duffy would say, that had prevented me from keeping him home in the first place.

"Time to go in," I said, trying my best to sound cheerful. "We don't want you to be late. I need you to remember something for me, okay, David? Something very important. You are a smart, strong, creative boy. Your imagination can't hurt you if you don't let it, okay?"

David gave a slight nod as I unbuckled him from his booster seat and he slid down into my waiting arms. I felt like someone was chiseling away at my heart. Slivers of it were chipping off and crumbling. How could I just leave my baby here, alone and inconsolable, to face whatever horrible thing was waiting for him?

The kindergarten classroom was in full swing when we arrived, and about twelve other little boys and girls were settling into the tiny communal tables and chairs that were arranged in the center of the room. Two black haired boys with identical devilish grins waved at David, and he waved back and gave them the first smile I'd seen all morning, but he was still hesitant to leave my side.

"Is that Maddox and Mason?" I asked.

David nodded. "They're twins."

"Do you want to go say hi to them while I say hi to your teacher?"

Lindsey Hanna was stationed at the blackboard, drawing shapes in strong, even chalk lines. When I said hello, she jumped back, her ponytail twitching. "Oh, Ms. Jennings. You surprised me. What can I do for you?" She brushed the chalk off her hands, clearly too busy to talk to me right now, but I needed to make myself heard.

The problem was what to say. How could I appropriately express my concern for my son to her? And what did I really want to ask of her?

"David's had a rough morning," I said, forcing a laugh. "I was just wondering if you could pay him a little extra attention today, and if you notice he seems upset or anything else out of the ordinary, would you be able to call me?"

Miss Hanna looked like she was trying hard not to roll her eyes. She was probably pegging me for a helicopter mom who thought she deserved special privileges now that David was enrolled in the gifted and talented program. But to her credit, she patted my shoulder and smiled a close-lipped smile. "Sure thing. We'll try to turn his bad day around."

"And you'll call me if—"

"Definitely, Ms. Jennings." She set her chalk down on the metal tray and pointedly walked around me toward the children. Class would be starting any minute now. I needed to leave.

David and the twins were gesturing excitedly and making what sounded like rocket ship sounds at their round table. He's okay, I told myself. The panther and whatever fear it represented would blow over soon enough because David was making friends and gaining self-confidence. And next week, after meeting with Dr. Da Costa, maybe we'd have some concrete answers and coping strategies. We just needed to get through this day by day.

I caught David's eye and gave him a small wave as I backed toward the door. *I love you,* I mouthed to him. His eyes widened in panic for a second, but then that little boy look of brave resolution slid in place.

He waved back and stared down fiercely at the table, as though he was trying not to cry.

I sat at my desk like a zombie all morning, answering phone calls and taking messages on autopilot. Both Gisele and Janet asked me more than once if I was okay, and I waved them off, joking that I was still having a hard time adjusting to my little boy being in kindergarten. Janet, who had three older kids, nodded sympathetically. Normally I kept my cell phone in my purse on vibrate, but today it sat on my desk with the ringer turned on, in case Miss Hanna called me.

By almost eleven, I still hadn't received a call from the school, which I tried to take as a good omen. I wouldn't be able to fully relax, though, until I'd heard from Duffy.

Brandon came into the office in the best mood I'd ever seen him. He had just sold one of our most expensive properties, a six-bedroom house on the bluffs overlooking the lake, and he was in the mood to celebrate. He wanted to treat us all to lunch, and no matter how politely I declined, the three of them insisted I come along. Brandon swore that it was my friendly demeanor over the phone that had laid the important groundwork with the buyers, and that I deserved to reap the benefits of his sale too. Janet suggested we close up shop for the hour and turn on our away message on the phone. She offered to drive us all in her Lexus.

I was uneasy, but I forced myself to act upbeat. My coworkers were trying to be nice and bond with me, and I appreciated it. Once I got my phone call from Duffy, it would be much easier to enjoy myself.

It turned out they wanted to drive all the way to Salsburg to Ruby's Diner. Apparently, it was Gisele's favorite, and Brandon loved their meatloaf sandwiches and milkshakes. Go figure. The glass dessert case was full of baked goods, so I could tell Carly had already left for the day, which meant that thankfully I wouldn't have to give her an update about Jamie. The counter was crowded, but only half of the booths were full, so we were seated immediately. I slid in next to Janet, across from Brandon. They were all highly entertained when our waitress, Lorraine Schiff, greeted me by name.

"I keep forgetting you're a Salsburg native!" Gisele said. She had grown up in Madison, and both Janet and Brandon were transplants from other parts of Wisconsin too.

"I wouldn't say I'm a native," I said. "My grandparents live here, and I spent a couple of summers with them as a kid. I grew up mostly in Milwaukee." I wasn't sure why I was distancing myself. The last few weeks had made me really embrace small town life and view Salsburg as my home, but in the face of these well-dressed, Lexus-driving, college-educated real estate agents, I didn't relish being associated with Lorraine Schiff and the rest of Salsburg.

Our food arrived, and Duffy still hadn't called. The clock on the wall said it was 12:00, and Winston normally picked David up at 11:30 on the dot. Had Duffy decided to make David's lunch first and then call? Or had the news about the gifted and talented program somehow made her think I no longer needed these daily updates? I dug through my purse for my cell phone, just in case it had somehow switched to the silent or vibrate setting, but it wasn't there.

"Is everything okay?" Janet asked, picking at a wilty-looking salad (not Ruby's specialty).

"Yeah, fine. I just realized I forgot my cell phone at the office." I pictured it, right on my desk where I'd left it like a total space cadet. Had Duffy left a message, surprised that I didn't pick up? Maybe Miss Hanna had too. I squirmed in my seat. *You're being paranoid*, I told myself. *And obsessive.* If there was a message from Duffy, it probably said something along the lines of, "Hi, Anna banana. David learned a new song at school today that he really wants to teach you. We're having hot dogs and baked beans for lunch. See you when you get home."

"Do you need to make a call?" Gisele asked. "You can use mine." She fished around in her handbag for it and then glanced down worriedly at the screen, where there were obviously a few messages waiting for her. "Hold on a sec. I just need to return this one call, and then it's all yours. Anyway, we should probably be heading back to the office soon. I've got a 1:30 showing." She hurried outside to make her call.

Thank God, we would be leaving soon. Brandon took a long drink of his milkshake through a straw, clearly disappointed that his celebration was going to be cut short. I glanced down at my mostly untouched club sandwich and French fries.

"So tell me about this house," I said, trying to keep the conversation going and wanting to keep my mind off David. "I think it was listed before I started working here." I felt bad for Brandon that lunch wasn't working out as he'd expected.

He took the bait readily and soon was describing the house's huge master bath and the wood-burning fireplace in the family room. I tried to look suitably impressed and not distracted.

Gisele returned, clicking loudly in her five-inch heels. "God, I hate diva clients. Sorry that took so long. Do you still need my phone?"

I glanced down at the complicated-looking smart phone in her hand, and I realized that in this day of speed dial and cell phones, I didn't even have my grandparents' home phone number memorized. Was it 8821 or 2281? I couldn't remember.

"It's okay," I said. "It can wait until we get back."

On the drive back to Lawrenceville, the three agents were deep in discussion using some closing terminology I wasn't yet familiar with. I tried to follow along but found I was too anxious to focus, so I looked out the window and thought about Jamie. I remembered what he'd said to me after we'd made love for the first time: *All I needed to hear you say was us. I've been waiting for you for a long time. I think I can be patient a bit longer.* Without my realizing it, he had made my life start to make sense in a way it hadn't in years. I just hoped I wasn't too late and things between us weren't totally irreparable now.

"Whose car is that?" Brandon asked as we pulled into the office.

I'd been so deep in thought I hadn't even realized we'd arrived. I unbuckled my seat belt and stretched my neck to look at the car in question. It was my grandparents' little beige car. Or at least, it looked like it, but it couldn't possibly be, right? Why would Winston be at my office on a Wednesday afternoon? I scrambled out of Janet's Lexus, and that's when I saw my grandmother. She was knocking in vain on the locked front door. My surprise doubled at the sight of her.

Duffy, here in Lawrenceville, when she was so terrified of leaving her little cocoon of safety? Why? It set off a red flag immediately.

When she heard our car doors slam, she whirled around and saw me too. She looked like a drowning woman. More anguished than her last panic attack, more anguished than when David had disappeared at the beauty supply store…

David. Where was he, if not with her?

My legs began to shake, and I steadied myself on the side of the car.

"Anna, I've been calling your cell phone and the office for the past hour," Duffy called out to me half-accusingly, half-apologetically.

"I forgot my phone. We went out to lunch." My whole body was starting to tremble, and I couldn't make my lips speak the question I was so dreading the answer to. *What's wrong? Where is David?* Somewhere in my peripheral vision, I could see Janet, Gisele, and Brandon exchanging confused looks, but like me, they were frozen in place. No one made a motion to unlock the office door. They could sense something was terribly wrong too.

"So you don't have him?" Duffy pleaded pathetically. "He's not here with you? I thought maybe—that was my last—"

I stared back at her, shaking my head slowly, reluctant to understand her painful meaning.

She doubled over against the wrought-iron banister, and I feared she might collapse, but I couldn't bring myself to move toward her. "Winston went to pick him up … 11:30 as usual…" Stifled sobs and gasps punctuated each piece of her story. "Wasn't there … teachers couldn't find him … thought maybe someone else had picked him up…"

With great effort, she straightened herself and raised her platinum blond head. "He's gone, Anna. David's gone."

CHAPTER TWENTY-TWO

There were ten missed calls on my cell phone and five new messages. The office machine was blinking too, but I couldn't bring myself to listen to Duffy's distraught progression of voicemails, each one more frantic than the next. The one time I had accidentally left my cell phone behind—how cruelly, bitterly ironic.

Somehow Duffy was able to convey to me that Winston was at the school talking with the police. Somehow I was able to persuade Duffy that she couldn't ride with me, that she needed to stay strong and drive her own car because we'd certainly need it. Somehow we were both able to make it to Port Ambrose Elementary, where there were indeed police cars parked out front. Those official-looking cars, connected with grisly scenes of murder and other ghastly crimes, were here because David was missing.

Missing. Somehow the word seemed worse than Duffy's use of "gone." It brought to mind those mailers and grocery store bulle tins with the smiling, ghostly faces of missing children on them. Kidnapped children, runaways, victims of molestation and abuse. I pushed those images away as fast as I could. David wasn't missing. In the foggy time since Duffy had showed up at the office until now, I had convinced myself that David had only wandered off, like he'd done at the strip mall. He was probably only hiding somewhere. Maybe the panther had frightened him, and he'd concealed himself somewhere very clever. The teachers just hadn't looked hard enough. I was his mother; I would find him immediately.

"Is this the mother?" I heard one of the police officers ask as I approached. I was The Mother. The Mother of The Missing Boy. Among the blur of faces was Winston's haggard, grief-stricken one. He reached for me, and I submitted to his strong embrace.

"It's going to be okay," he said. "Everything's going to be okay. We're going to find him." He held me as if I were waking up from a nightmare, and I sincerely wished that I was.

All I wanted to do was go to David's classroom and call him out from wherever he was hiding, but the police wouldn't let me. They asked me a never-ending stream of bewildering questions. What had David been wearing that morning? What size shoe did he wear? When was the last time he'd gone to the dentist? Was there anyone else in the family who might have picked him up from school? Any close family friends that David would've trusted? Why had I asked his teacher to keep an extra close eye on him that morning? Did I have any reason to believe he would go missing?

There was that word again. It threatened to capsize me if I dwelled too long on what it meant, as well as why the cops were asking about his dental records. There was no way to explain the imaginary panther that had been tormenting my son, much less my bizarre ability to see it, so I kept my mouth shut and muttered something about David having a bad dream the previous night.

Finally, Winston and one of the police officers escorted me to David's classroom, where Miss Hanna was sitting with her head in her hands, looking even worse than I suspected I did. She started to cry harder when I came in, blubbering out apologies, but I didn't have time for her. I had to find David.

"David?" I called, methodically searching the room. Behind the play car. Under Miss Hanna's desk. "David?" In the nook of cubbies for coats, boots, and hats. I flung open the doors of the pretend fridge and stove, which were much too small for David to hide inside.

"What about the playground?" I asked. "Has anyone looked for him out there?"

Someone, the police officer, maybe, replied in the affirmative, but no one was going to deny The Mother of The Missing Boy a chance

to look around the playground. No one wanted to deny me my last
sliver of a hope.

Outside, the day was misleadingly sunny and bright. Since the
superintendent had canceled school for the rest of the afternoon,
the playground was eerily abandoned, making all the brightly colored equipment—the slides, jungle gyms, and monkey bars—seem
haunted. The playground looked securely fenced in; the only entrance or exit seemed to be through the school. One side faced the
parking lot and the other two sides were bordered by a small forest.
I remembered how David had told me the panther had watched him
at recess. Had I been misunderstanding him all along? Had he not
been talking about the imaginary panther, but some stranger who was
hanging around the parking lot, peering in at the children? I shuddered at the thought.

"The twins are here," Duffy said. I wasn't sure how long she'd been
standing next to me. Had she just walked up or had she been there
all along? "Their mother says she thinks one of them saw something
funny at recess. The police are talking to them now."

I didn't want Maddox or Mason to have seen "something funny"
at recess. I wanted it all to be just some huge misunderstanding. I
wanted David to pop out from behind the merry go-round with his
dinosaurs beside him, like they'd done at the dollar store. I wanted
to have the luxury of being angry at him for scaring us so badly.
I wanted to forgive him quickly and shower him with hugs and
kisses. I wanted to buy him a stupid robot action figure. Ten robot
action figures.

"Why don't we go inside and have a seat?" Duffy was suggesting
from somewhere very far away. "We can get you something to drink,
and then we can find out if the police officers have learned anything new." I let her shepherd me inside to what must have been the
teachers' lounge, not because I wanted to sit down and have a drink,
but because I was all out of ideas.

David's principal, Mr. Crane, whom I had met only once and
briefly at that, made a fresh pot of coffee for Duffy and me. He seemed
overly solicitous, and I wondered if he was worried I was going to

sue the school for losing my son. For letting my son disappear. For letting him get kidnapped.

I decided to listen to my cell phone messages. Anything would be better right now than the terrible refrain in my head, the guilt-inspiring chorus of "if only's." *If only I had listened to David more closely…If only I had pressed him for more details…If only I hadn't made him go to school today…If only we'd gone to the park instead…If only I'd followed my gut when I felt like something was wrong…* The first two messages were from Duffy. The next was from Mr. Crane, sounding very professional and grave. The fourth and fifth were from Duffy again, the hysteria in her voice nearing a breaking point. I deleted the messages and closed my eyes.

In my mind's eye, I replayed the morning's events, searching for clues that weren't there, and then rewound to the night before and the promise I had made to David. *You don't have to be scared*, I'd said. *I'm not going to let it hurt you. I'm not going to let anyone ever hurt you.* I had broken my promise to him; I hadn't been able to protect him at all. David had told me that the panther wasn't under his bed anymore, that it was waiting for him at school, and now he was gone.

I felt sick as I imagined the panther with its thick, bluish-black fur and green reflective eyes. I remembered the last of David's drawings that Miss Hanna had shown me, the cartoonish one of the panther, and how it had felt familiar to me. I struggled to pinpoint where I had seen it—that sinewy black silhouette; that long curving tail; that ferocious, gaping maw; those stark white claws hooked as if sinking into skin…Skin? Suddenly it all made sense.

I conjured up Patrick before me, the way he'd looked the first day I met him. His dark, doleful eyes and the black tattoos covering his chest, arms, and back. A wild mustang, a hawk, a Chinese dragon, a Celtic cross, and a *panther*. The panther was inked on his left bicep and its long tail snaked down his forearm. David's drawing had looked familiar to me because it was a fairly good reproduction of Patrick's tattoo.

Patrick was the panther. He was the one haunting David.

He was the one making it hard for David to sleep. He was the one making David scared to go to school. David had seen Patrick, whom he didn't recognize as his father, watching him from the parking lot at recess. The black panther tattoo had clearly made an impression on him, and that's how Patrick had manifested himself in David's imagination. As a scary, muscular cat who wanted something from David and was always hungrily watching him. That's what he'd been trying to tell me. That's what the panther had been a warning of. But I hadn't figured it out in time, and I had failed him. I had failed my son, and now maybe it was too late to get him back.

"Patrick has him," I said aloud. "I don't know how. I don't know where. But he has David."

I called Abigail Gill. She answered on the fifth ring and sounded short of breath. "Oh, Anna," she chirped. "I've been meaning to call you. I—"

"Where's Patrick?" I interrupted.

"He's not here right now," she said slowly. "Why? Were you hoping to talk—"

"David's missing." I was pacing around the teachers' lounge, clutching my cell phone as if it were a live grenade. "He disappeared from school today, and I think Patrick had something to do with it."

"David was taken from school?" She gasped, and then for a long time, all I could hear was her muffled weeping on the other end.

I sucked in a sharp breath. "So do you know where Patrick is? Is it possible he was in Port Ambrose today?"

"Anna, I'm so sorry. If I had only known…" Her pause lasted an eternity. "Patrick didn't come home last night after his shift; we haven't seen him all day, and he's not answering his cell phone. Quentin called his manager, and apparently Patrick didn't even show up last night, and he's been coming late and blowing off work for the past few weeks. I don't know why his manager didn't let us know, and I have no idea where Patrick has been going instead. He's been acting so even keel." And then she burst into tears again.

I handed the phone off to a police officer. They were already working on dispatching a squad car to the Gills' house to investigate. One of the twins, Maddox or Mason, I wasn't sure which, had reported seeing a man lurking near the fence by the parking lot at recess. Today, and apparently last week as well. The man had "yellow" hair and tattoos covering his arms. It was the perfect description of Patrick when he had his dark hair bleached.

The police asked me for a list of Patrick's hang-outs and other places he might have taken David. His house seemed unlikely, because his parents would alert me to David's presence, and then he'd have to give him up. Maybe he had an apartment his parents didn't know about? All of Patrick's favorite haunts—the Basilica of St. Josaphat, Gesu Church, the coffee shop on 22nd street, the university's art history library—seemed like odd choices to which to bring an abducted child. But then again, if Patrick was off his meds and snatching his son from school, he clearly wasn't making very smart choices.

I knew that suspecting Patrick was the kidnapper instead of some complete stranger should have reassured me slightly, but it didn't. Though he could be incredibly gentle and loving, he could also be demanding and harsh, moody and forgetful. I couldn't help fixating on all the reasons why I had petitioned so hard to get sole custody of David and then eventually found it necessary to get an injunction against Patrick. His fleeting attention span. The loose pills he haphazardly left all over the house—on the kitchen table, between the couch cushions, in his shoes—some of them prescription drugs to treat his bipolar disorder, while others, like the candy-colored tabs of ecstasy, decidedly were not. And of course there were the supervised visits we'd tried where Patrick had held David so tightly he'd wailed. Then he'd scolded his nine-month-old son, "Stop crying, dammit. Don't you love me? Is your bitch of a mother teaching you not to love me?"

So while I didn't think Patrick had it in him to ever *intentionally* hurt his son, I knew the possibility still lurked. If Patrick was in one of his manic moods, he might recklessly put David in a dangerous situation and then neglect to watch over him or forget him there entirely. Or he might lose his patience with David, if David frustrated him, like he'd lost his patience with me when I was pregnant. I prayed that wouldn't happen and he wouldn't harm a hair on David's head. I prayed that Patrick wouldn't leave our little area of southeastern Wisconsin. *Please, please, do not leave the state. Do not disappear on me.* I prayed that we would find them quickly, before anything could happen to permanently traumatize my poor little boy. If he hadn't already been emotionally scarred by the abduction.

Duffy appeared in the doorway of the teachers' lounge. Her blond hair was disheveled and looked like a lopsided wig. There were puffy bags under her eyes from all the crying she had done. I knew I looked ten times worse.

"The police say it's time for us to go home," she said. "There's nothing more for us to do here."

I slowly assessed the teachers' lounge, which I'd come to think of as kidnapping case central. Here my grandparents and I would sit, drinking coffee, answering the police's questions, and getting constant updates until David was returned to the very school where he had been taken from. But clearly that wasn't how things were going to work. They wanted us to go *home*?

"I'm not going home," I said. "What am I going to do there?"

Duffy rested her hands firmly on my shoulders. "I know it's hard, Anna, but now we wait. We go home and we wait for the police to call us once they've met with the Gills, and while we're waiting for that, we eat some dinner and we—"

I stood up, brushing her hands off me. "I don't want dinner. I want to find David. I'm going to go look for him."

Duffy followed me down the hallway. "I want to find David too," she called after me. "But we have to stay calm. And we have to be there to help the police. We can't all go off disappearing on our own."

I passed Winston, who gently snagged my arm. "Let me drive you," he said, walking quickly beside me.

I sat in the back, next to David's empty booster seat, deep in thoughts of my sweet child somewhere, petrified and God knows where, with his unfamiliar, frightening father. I kept picturing Patrick as the crazed, half-naked man who had ambushed me two years ago outside my old apartment. So deep in the world of his delusions that he was unrecognizable as the man I had once loved. What would have happened that night if Stacy hadn't called the cops? We needed to track them down immediately.

The thought of Stacy made me realize I should call her to let her know about David, just in case she had any helpful information for the police. Since she no longer lived in Milwaukee, I doubted it, but maybe she could give me our old landlord's phone number, and I could pass it along to the police, in case Patrick decided to stop there for some reason. It was farfetched, but I was desperate. I was hoping to just leave a message, so she could get in touch with the police department on her own, but she answered on the third ring, and I had to break the news for a second time. It wasn't getting any easier, and Stacy's horrified reaction didn't help.

"Oh, God, Anna, this is awful," she cried. "I think he's been planning this for months. That was what I wanted to tell you yesterday. When the kids started their new school, we gave them the 'stranger danger' talk again, and Breanne mentioned that someone had approached them in the front yard when she was babysitting David a few months ago. I guess Brett pulled up right then, thank the Lord, and the guy fled. I couldn't believe she waited this long to tell me! When she described the man and his tattoos, it totally matched Patrick, but his hair sounded like it was black at the time and longer than usual. This would've been in early June, right before you guys moved, and a few weeks before he rang my doorbell looking for you."

I numbly gave her the lead detective's phone number, asked her to report the information to them, and disconnected. Without my realizing it, Winston had driven me home. Before he had even fully stopped the minivan, I jumped out and ran up the front steps. Inside, the house was silent except for the relentless ticking of the grandfather clock. Normally at this time of day, the house was filled with the sounds of David singing and a clanging and beeping from the kitchen as Duffy fixed dinner. I hurried to the upper level of the house, to David's bedroom and my bedroom.

I first flipped up the dust ruffle on David's bed and then mine, but the space beneath both beds was empty, as I had expected. David was gone. His imagination was gone too.

"I hate you!" I screamed at the space where the panther had once crouched, growling. "How can you do this to him? To me? Bring him back, Patrick. Bring him back right now!"

I would've given anything to wrestle with the two-hundred pound cat right then. To channel my useless adrenaline and energy into such violence. To feel its claws sink into my soft flesh, diverting me from the agonizing emotional pain that felt like it would be the death of me. Stacy was probably right; Patrick had been planning this all along, and a part of David must have known the mysterious man posed a danger to him. When he had first laid eyes on Patrick in the front yard was around the time he had invented his protective dinosaurs, and the black smoke, which would later become the full-bodied panther, had first materialized. On the edges of his subconscious, but always there. And I, who had been given nearly clairvoyant insight into my son's imagination, still hadn't understood what he was showing me. Even with almost all the pieces of the puzzle in hand, I still hadn't figured it out in time. I still hadn't been able to save him. How stupid I was! And sorry. How very, very sorry.

Time was becoming more elastic, speeding up and slowing down in unpredictable ways, so I had no idea how much time had elapsed when Duffy finally found me in my bedroom, rocking violently in David's rocking chair, hugging his pillow to my chest.

"I made some butternut squash soup," she said. "I thought you might like to come downstairs and have some with us." Leave it to my grandma to make her famous cold and flu remedy, in the hopes that it would help alleviate the suffering of a kidnapping too.

"I'm not hungry."

"Come downstairs anyway. Winston just got an update from the police about the Gills."

"Did they find Patrick and David?" I asked, propelling myself from the chair.

She shook her head sadly. "Well, no, but they had some information the police found useful."

On the kitchen table, three bowls of orange soup were cooling. Winston sat on one end of the table with a photo album spread out in front of him. When I came in, he held up a glossy photo of David. It was a picture taken a few months ago, of David squatting on the living room floor, playing with his racetrack and his matchbox cars. In it, David was grinning broadly, and Vivien Leigh's bushy black tail made an appearance in the corner of the picture. He looked smaller and younger; his nose was a little sunburned, but his hair hadn't been lightened by the sun yet. He had grown and changed so much over just this summer alone. If Patrick kept him from me, I wouldn't get to see him continue to grow and change—I quickly banished the thought from my mind.

"Do we have anything more recent?" Winston asked, tapping the photo.

I didn't have any more recent pictures because I was a terrible mother who was constantly failing my son. More recent pictures had been taken of him—next to the fire truck at the fair, for example, or at the pioneer village—but those had been photos taken by Jamie, and they were still on his phone. And presumably Jamie had no idea that David was missing, and even if he did, he had no reason to want to approach me now. I was the girl who had made it perfectly clear I didn't have room for him in my life anymore. The girl who always let down those closest to her, those she loved.

I shook my head and sat down in front of one of the steaming bowls of soup. "So what was the police update? What did the Gills tell them?"

Winston closed the photo album and filled me in. The Gills had cooperated fully, letting the police search the guest suite above the garage where Patrick lived, giving them a description of the car they let Patrick use and its license plate number, recounting Patrick's unusual behavior the past few weeks—how they'd recently learned he'd been ditching work a few days a week, how he talked of little else except seeing his son, how they hadn't seen him in over twenty-four hours now. Quentin didn't keep any guns in the house, and they didn't seem to think Patrick could've gotten his hands on one legally because of the restraining order, so they didn't suspect he was armed. (*Armed!* I had never even thought to worry about a gun!) The police found a couple of gas station receipts in Patrick's garbage can, dated from the last two weeks. The gas station was in Port Ambrose, somewhere he had no business being. Apparently Patrick had been driving to David's school and watching him for days now. Watching and waiting for the perfect opportunity to grab him. The thought chilled me.

"The police have put out an Amber Alert," Winston concluded. "Describing David and Patrick and the car. I guess they've already gotten one sighting. Someone saw his car traveling south on Highway 45 near Menomonee Falls about half an hour ago."

"So he's headed back to Milwaukee!"

"It seems like it. The police are going to keep an eye out for him at all the places you and his parents suggested he might go."

I stood up from my chair, bumping the table in the process. My untouched bowl of soup quivered a little but didn't spill. "Good. I'm going to go look for them, too."

"Anna, no!" Duffy got in my way. "Let the police do their job. We need you here. How else can you hear the police updates? What if they need to ask you more questions?"

I stepped around her. "That's what cell phones are for. Call me if you hear *anything*."

Winston remained seated, his large hands folded calmly over the photo album. I knew if he said just one word, I would stay here. If he truly believed my staying home was what was best for David and me, I would do it. But he didn't say anything.

"David needs me, Duffy," I said. "I'm his mother."

She nodded at me, jarring loose tears that rolled down her cheeks. "Okay," she said grimly. "Be safe. But call me every hour on the hour to update me and let me know you're alright. Otherwise, I'm coming after you." She looked beseechingly at Winston, as if expecting him to offer to go along with me, but he was still staring down at David's photo.

"I need to get this to the police station," he said. "Good luck, Anna."

Outside, I was surprised to see that the sun was starting to set. How much time had passed since David's disappearance? Eight hours? It felt like a lifetime. I trotted to my minivan, digging in my purse to make sure my cell phone and its charger were there. I didn't notice Jamie striding up the driveway until he was almost at my car door.

"Anna," he said.

I whirled around, nervous energy coursing through me. Jamie's face was sadder than I'd ever seen him. Although the sight of him would have filled me with joy only twenty hours ago, now I felt only impatience for his timing and a jolt of guilt. Because maybe if I hadn't been so focused on my relationship with Jamie, I would have figured out what was going on with David sooner and stopped Patrick from taking him.

"I'm sorry. I don't have time to talk," I said, climbing into the driver's seat. "David is missing."

"I heard," Jamie said, "and I am so sorry. I can't imagine how scared you must be feeling right now." He took a hesitant step toward the minivan. "I'd like to help. Is there anything I can do? Can I come with you to look for him?"

I fumbled with my car keys and managed to turn the minivan on. Every second that passed that I was sitting here was a second that David was getting farther and farther away from me, scared and confused.

"Can you send one of the recent photos you took of David on your phone to the police department?" I asked. "I don't have any really current ones."

"Definitely. Consider it done."

"Thank you." I stepped on the brake and shifted into reverse. "I need to go."

"Anna, please let me come with you. Please let me help. As an old friend." There were deep wrinkles of concern on his forehead, and I could see that he was genuinely worried about David's safety too.

"Get in," I said.

CHAPTER TWENTY-THREE

Jamie kept me talking the entire drive to Milwaukee. The only time he paused in his stream of questioning was to call information and get the police department's phone number, so he could send them David's picture from his cell phone. I told him what little information I knew from the police about David's disappearance. I told him about Patrick and the custody battle and how we'd been estranged for the past four years. I told him about the smashed piggy bank and his suicide threats and the way I'd found David alone in his bathtub as an infant. I told him about Patrick's run-ins with the law, his hospitalization, and later unwillingness to take his medication and see his doctor on a regular basis. Then I bit my lip and tried not to cry when we passed an electronic sign over the highway proclaiming my son's Amber Alert.

Once we got to Milwaukee, we were running low on gas, so Jamie suggested we take the opportunity to fill up and switch drivers. It was pitch black by this point, and it was becoming apparent how naïve my hopes of simply driving around and spotting Patrick and David on the streets were. But there was no way I could just give up and sit still while my poor little boy was still out there somewhere. Even driving around the streets of Milwaukee aimlessly was better than doing nothing. Jamie cruised past my old apartment and then asked me to direct him to Patrick's favorite cathedrals (which were both closed at this time of night) as well as the coffee shop (no luck) and art history library (also closed). Duffy called twice to check in and tell me that no other tips had come in about Patrick's whereabouts and she thought I should come home and try to sleep. When I told her that Jamie was with me, she seemed relieved but then wanted to talk to him. "I'm supposed to tell you to take a break and go home and get some rest," he conveyed, shaking his head sympathetically. We kept driving.

Jamie proposed we look for Patrick's silver car in some of the local motel and hotel parking lots in the area, in case Patrick and David were holed up for the night. I went along with his idea, even though there were about a million places to stay in Milwaukee and its suburbs, and we'd probably have a better chance of finding them if we looked in the phone book and randomly started calling people to ask them if they knew where David was. We weren't in Salsburg, with its total lack of hotels, motels, and bed and breakfasts, anymore. To top it off, I wondered if Patrick had already abandoned his car. Maybe they were on foot or taking the bus or train. Maybe they had been swallowed up in Chicago or an even bigger city by now.

"What's that noise?" Jamie asked, a little after three in the morning.

It took me a minute to realize it was my stomach growling, and when I admitted that I hadn't eaten much of anything since breakfast, he recommended that we stop at an all-night diner to keep up our energy for our search. He was just like my grandma, always believing that a good meal was the solution to everything. Drinking a cup of coffee and eating a huge strawberry and whipped cream-covered waffle did make me feel momentarily better.

The diner was close to campus, where Patrick's old apartment had been, and I tried to remember if we had ever gone there together. We hadn't left the house much in those early days of staying in bed, making love. Despite the fact that it was the middle of the night, there were several bleary-eyed college students packed into the booths. I couldn't tell if they'd been up all night partying or cramming for a test.

"So we've already checked out Patrick's favorite spots," Jamie started, "but did he ever mention places he wanted to take David when he grew up?"

I leaned on my elbow, trying to make my sluggish brain dredge up something new. "Nothing in particular that I can remember." I let my eyelids drift shut and thought back to when I was pregnant and Patrick was so excited he would keep me up late, whispering to my stomach. *Baby Panna*, he would say, *We're going to have so much fun once you're born.* I squeezed my eyelids tighter. What had he promised he'd do with David? Where had he promised he'd take him? *We'll go to the pumpkin farm and go on a hayride...* It was much too early in the season for him to do that. *And I'll draw your portrait every month, and I won't make you cut your hair ever if you don't want to.* None of that was particularly helpful.

But maybe David and his panther had dropped hints I hadn't realized were clues. In frustration, I mentally reviewed all the recent conversations I'd had with David, but everything he'd said about his panther had always been so cryptic. Then, out of nowhere, I remembered his spontaneous questions about the zoo last night, right in the midst of our conversation about recess and the panther.

Was it possible that Patrick had talked to him during recess while he'd spied on him? Had he tried to find out David's interests and then lured him away with promises of a trip to the zoo to see the animatronic dinosaurs? Perhaps David had found Patrick's offer both attractive and frightening, and that was why he had talked about it in such a roundabout way and then insisted he didn't want to go. Had he been afraid of running straight into the panther's den?

"I think we should check out the Milwaukee County Zoo," I told Jamie, "because of something David said last night. It's a long shot, but it's something."

"What time do they open?" he asked.

"I don't know. Nine o'clock?"

And that's how we found ourselves parked on Blue Mound Road, along the tree-lined fence of the dark, closed zoo, at four-thirty in the morning. I called Duffy to alert her to this newest turn of events, and she sounded just as wide awake as I was, despite the time. She wanted to forward this suggestion on to the police, but I begged her to hold off on doing that. How Patrick might react to armed officers closing in on him in a public place unsettled me. There had to be a way for me to first pacify him and remove my son from harm's way. At that point, I realized how much faith I was investing in the belief that Patrick would be bringing David to the zoo tomorrow. Of all the places he could be, of all the places he could convey him, what were the odds that he would show up here, I wondered. Probably not very good. But it was the only lead we had at the present, so I clung desperately to it.

I leaned my head against the headrest of the passenger seat and let out a deep breath.

"Maybe you should try to get some sleep," Jamie said. In the shadows, I could barely make out his stubble-covered face and weary yet alert eyes. "I can watch over you."

"I can't sleep," I argued. "I can't sleep while David is somewhere out there —" My voice cracked and I fought back the coming tears with what little energy I had left. I remembered how much the panther had scared him. How he had been unable to sleep. The dark-blue crescent moons under his eyes. How he had adamantly called him "the bad cat" and wished it would just go away. How it had been his dinosaurs' jobs to chase him away, but in the end, they hadn't been up to the task. All signs pointed to David being terrified in Patrick's presence right now, wherever they were. To sleep, to forget his plight for even one second, would be to betray him.

"Come here," Jamie said, stretching his arms across the front seat to embrace me. He held me tightly to his chest, not making any promises he couldn't keep, not whispering meaningless platitudes of consolation. He just held me, and for whatever reason, just being in his arms comforted me. If someone that strong and steady was helping me, finding David seemed not so far out of reach.

"I don't know what I'd do without you right now," I whispered into his T-shirt.

Jamie didn't say anything; he just continued to hold me against his chest, and, there, I somehow fell asleep, because when I opened my eyes, the clock on the dashboard read 7:58, and bright sunlight was pouring through the windows. I squirmed free of Jamie's grasp, and he started to stir too. Thankfully, no cops had driven by and busted us for sleeping in the minivan. I grabbed for my cell phone and immediately called Duffy. Patrick and David still hadn't been found, she reported unhappily, but another tip had come in last night that Patrick's car had been seen on the east side, which meant that he was still probably in the area. Thank God.

Since we had time to kill before the zoo opened, we walked to the gas station across the street to use their restrooms and buy cups of coffee. By the time we came back, more cars were parked on the street behind the minivan, and families were pushing strollers toward the zoo. My heart thumped hopefully in my chest. This was it. And if they weren't here…I had no Plan B. I had no idea what to do next. But I wouldn't think about that right now. We joined the crowd of zoo patrons who were purchasing their tickets. I hadn't been to the zoo since high school when a boy had taken me there on a date and we'd made out in the dark of the snake and reptile house.

"What do we do if we see them?" Jamie asked as we passed the penguin tank, around which a few children, but no David, were huddled.

"We call the police and let them handle it," I lied.

We made a thorough loop of the zoo, walking through each building and area, keeping our eyes peeled for Patrick's bleached blond head and David's natural blond one. In particular, we checked out the dinosaur exhibit and train station, with no luck. The zoo grounds were so vast, I was starting to think that even if they were there, there was no way we would ever bump into them at the same place at the same time. Exhausted after walking constantly for two hours, we decided to sit down on a bench by the lake where swans and ducks were swimming peacefully.

"This was a stupid idea," I said, with my head in my hands.

"I think it's a great idea," Jamie said. "It's just hard because there are only two of us. Why don't we call the police, see if they can send some plainclothesmen in here to look around too?"

The crick in my neck had returned with a vengeance, and I rubbed it forcefully and then swiveled my head from side to side. The third time, something caught my eye—the shine of tattoo ink.

And that's when I saw Patrick standing in front of the polar bear's enclosure. My eyes rapidly scanned the area around him, and yes, there too was David at his side. I quickly pointed them out to Jamie, who looked both as relieved and alarmed as I felt.

"I'm going to go talk to Patrick," I said, standing up from the bench.

"What about letting the police handle it?" Jamie asked.

"Call the police," I said. "Please. But I can't wait for them to get here and run the risk of losing him again. I'll be okay."

"But what if he's angry? What if he's dangerous?"

"Then it's all the more reason to get my son away from him," I replied and dashed off before he could stop me.

David was still wearing the same red T-shirt, jeans, and red and white sneakers I'd dressed him in the previous day. His hair was sticking up in about ten different directions. His shoulders were slumped in a tired, defeated way. I could tell all this just by seeing him from the back. I wondered if he'd slept at all last night. I wondered where he'd slept and if Patrick had fed him anything. I wondered if he'd cried or shown Patrick his brave, big-boy face.

When I was only about ten feet away from them, Patrick turned around and caught sight of me. He smiled and waved.

"Anna!" he called, as if we'd been planning this all along and he'd been expecting to see me. As if we were a normal family who was having a day at the zoo, not a broken family embroiled in a kidnapping situation.

David turned around at Patrick's greeting, and when he saw me, he looked like he might burst into tears of gratitude. I lurched toward him, my body drawn to my son like metal to a magnet. My fingers were only inches away from grasping his thin shoulder when Patrick stepped between us. His elbow caught me sharply in the ribcage and jostled me backwards, and David disappeared from view behind the wall of Patrick's body.

"I don't think so." Patrick's archangel eyes were shining bright. "You've had your time with him, Anna. It's my turn now. So if you can't play nice, you should just go home."

"I'm not playing," I said, trying to sound more assertive than I felt. "You're breaking the law. You could go to jail for being near either one of us right now. So why don't you give David back to me, and we'll pretend this whole thing never happened?"

He leaned forward so close that our noses were almost touching, and I could see his dilated pupils. I instinctively took a step back.

"I don't care about the legal system," he ranted. "It's stripped me of all my rights to be a father. Just because I have a mental illness! *They're* the criminals. They're the ones who should go to prison for discriminating against me and depriving me of the first five years of my boy's life. Not me, just for taking him to the goddamn zoo."

That tirade didn't sound like Patrick at all. The legal system stripping him of his rights and depriving him of fatherhood? I wondered who had been telling him he'd been wrongfully discriminated against because of his mental illness. I doubted it was his mom. David's red and white sneakers poked out from behind Patrick's scuffed oxfords. If I could only distract Patrick for just one second and get him to move away slightly, I could grab David and run into the nearest building, find a security guard, tell them to lock down the zoo, and wait until the police arrived. But what if Patrick's parents and the police were wrong? What if Patrick was armed? If he'd gone to so much effort to find David's school and stake it out day after day, certainly the thought could have crossed his mind to have bought a gun. I really didn't want to find out.

"You didn't lose your custody of David because you're bipolar," I said. "You lost your custody because you refuse to do anything about it. You don't seem to want to get better, and David can't be around you when you're like this. Just look at him. Can't you see how afraid of you he is?"

Patrick sneered at me but then turned around and crouched down to examine David. He didn't seem to notice the way David flinched when he raised his hand to flatten one of his son's cowlicks, and he didn't seem bothered by the purple shadows under David's eyes. In his mind, today was a beautiful, harmonious day and David was grinning with delight. He had his son and he was taking him on an outing, and he couldn't recognize that David wasn't having the time of his life.

"He's not afraid," Patrick snapped, satisfied with his assessment, and straightened up. "Just bored. We came to the zoo to see the animals, not stand around arguing with you all day." He reached down and seized one of David's hands. "Should we go see the big cats now? The lions and tigers and cheetahs..." The black panther tattoo gleamed on his arm in the sunlight, the ink as shiny as a puddle of oil.

David's face had turned a grayish white, but he didn't speak up. My heart was beating rapidly, and my mouth was so dry I felt like I could hardly crack open my lips to form words. "David's afraid of big cats," I said. Where the heck were the police officers when you needed them? Shouldn't they have been here by now? Why hadn't I agreed to let Duffy call them right away?

"I'm going to teach my son to be fearless," Patrick said loudly, and it wasn't clear if he was addressing me or David or maybe the crowd in general.

"There are other more important things to teach him." I was stalling for time. I was so close to them now that I could've grabbed David's hand, but Patrick still had a tight grip on his other one, and I really didn't want to get in a tug-of-war contest with my son in the middle. "Like integrity. And steadfastness."

Patrick scowled and started to pull David away from me. David was resisting, dragging his sneakers, so Patrick slung his wiry arm around David's back to shove him forward. "He's my child, Anna, like me in every way, so you better get used to it. Now, say goodbye."

"He may look like you," I shouted after him, and the people around us all turned to look. I wanted to make a spectacle, to draw attention to what was going on, so Patrick couldn't just disappear into the crowd again. "But David is my child through and through." I fought for air to fill my tired lungs and shout even louder. "He has my creativity and imagination. He has my spirit. He has my fight." I ran after them, but Patrick was picking up speed and charging up the hill toward the big cat house. Suddenly, out of nowhere, Jamie was resolutely blocking his path.

And finally! A flash of black—two police officers in black uniforms. They flew up the hill and restrained Patrick, breaking his grip on David. In an instant, Jamie had picked up my son and was carrying him over to me. I was so overcome with relief that I fell to my knees, right there on the concrete, and David ran into my arms. Holding my son had never been sweeter. I plastered his face and the top of his head with kisses. I was murmuring to him, but I hardly knew what I was saying, and I doubt what I said mattered to David at that point either. He was safe in his mother's arms. In his mother's love. We were back together, and I was never going to lose him again. And that was what mattered most.

The Milwaukee police took Patrick into custody and led David, Jamie, and me into the zoo's education center to question us about the last twenty-four hours. I held David on my lap, not wanting to miss out on a single second of physical contact with him. He leaned limply against me and every so often reached up to touch a strand of my hair, so I could tell he felt the same way. In this position, he recounted the whole frightening ordeal. Patrick had been watching him at recess but not every day; by David's estimate, he had visited the school a total of four times. Most days, he leaned against a car in the shadowy parking lot and watched the children play, and David gave him a wide berth, but sometimes when the teachers congregated on the other side of the playground, he asked David questions about himself, like what he liked and where he lived, and sometimes David answered, and sometimes he didn't. On the day Patrick had taken him, he had called David over to the fence by name, and this had both startled and impressed David. "David Patrick Jennings Gill," Patrick had called him with a friendly, non-threatening smile. "Do you know how I know your name? Because I'm your dad."

David hadn't believed him, but the man persisted and told him he would explain after school and they could go out for ice cream together. David turned him down, knowing that Grandpa Winston would be there to pick him up like always and that I wouldn't like it if he talked to strangers. But when the final bell rang and David went outside with his other classmates to look for Winston's car, he spotted Patrick first. And Patrick spotted him too. Patrick picked him up, shoved him in the car, and drove off—in the front seat of the car with no booster seat, David specified, clearly shocked by this—before David could make a peep or anyone had even noticed in all the bustle. It was disturbing how easy it had been for Patrick when there were so many potential witnesses.

Then they drove for what seemed like a very long time to David and stopped at an ice cream stand. Patrick made him eat his ice cream cone in the car, which also surprised him. At this point, David assumed the man would be taking him home, but Patrick insisted he still wanted to spend time with him and there was someone he wanted him to meet. And so they drove for a very long time again to a house, and David was tired and scared and didn't want to get out of the car, but Patrick carried him inside. There were several barking dogs and a lady with blue hair, and Patrick asked her to go out and bring them some dinner. When she came back with Chinese food, David refused to eat it, and Patrick was very upset with him at first, but then he poured him a bowl of cereal with marshmallows instead. Afterwards, the blue-haired lady made up a bed for David on the couch, but it smelled yucky like dog hair and he had a hard time sleeping anyway because he was so sad and afraid. And then this morning, Patrick had given him more marshmallow cereal for breakfast before shepherding him to the zoo and promising a fun road trip to a place called Montana.

He wasn't ever planning on bringing him back, I realized in horror, squeezing David against me. And who was this blue-haired woman? A friend of Patrick's? A girlfriend, maybe? Most likely, the person who'd been whispering in his ear about his rights. The police wanted to track her down for questioning, and because of the tip that had placed Patrick on the east side last night, they thought she might live there.

Now that we had David back, all I wanted to do was bring him home to Salsburg. Winston and Duffy would be as overjoyed as I was to see him and hug him and smother him with kisses. Finally, after what seemed like hours, the police had everything they needed from us and allowed us to leave. Jamie offered to drive so I could have my hands free to make phone calls to my grandparents, the Gills, the school, Stacy, and my coworkers at the real estate office, updating everyone. I strapped David into his booster seat in the backseat of the minivan, and he fell asleep before we had even merged onto the highway. When my voice was starting to get hoarse and scratchy from telling the story so many times, I tucked my cell phone back in my purse, slipped my shoes off, and sat barefoot and cross-legged in the passenger seat. I kept turning around in my seat to steal glances at my sleeping son to make sure he was really there and that I hadn't dreamt our reunion. I prayed the whole ordeal wouldn't scar David emotionally. I prayed that we wouldn't spend the rest of our lives looking over our shoulders, watching for Patrick. But for right now, Jamie, David, and I were all safe together in the minivan, and I allowed myself a deep sigh of relief.

"Did you ever know that you've been the best friend I've ever had since I was seven years old?" I asked Jamie.

He turned to me and gave me a half-hearted smile and then fixed his attention on the road ahead.

"You're dependable and trustworthy. You're absolutely essential to me. And I'm really sorry if I made you feel disposable." I pressed one of my knees to my chest and studied his unreadable profile. "Duffy helped me realize that I've been harboring a deep-seated fear for a while—it sounds kind of pathetic when I say it aloud, but here it is anyway—that I'm not really worthy of love. And I didn't want to turn out like my mom, looking for love in all the wrong places when she had this child, this perfect vessel of love for her, *me*, right there in front of her. I wanted David to be enough, all the love that I needed, because I didn't trust my instincts with men anymore, and I didn't want to make a mistake that would eventually hurt him."

Jamie adjusted his grip on the steering wheel. "I understand, Anna. You forget that I was raised by a single mother, too. My dad abandoned us, and my mom never dated again, even before she was diagnosed with MS. And after this nightmare with your ex, I can kind of see why you were quick to jump to conclusions when you found my mom's pills. It looked really bad, and you were just trying to protect David."

"I was," I agreed. "But even after you told me the truth, I still couldn't admit to myself that you were different." I thought of the 3 x 5 photo buried in my purse. The photo of us as rowdy, sun-bronzed dreamers with no idea what the future held in store for us. The photo that he had held onto for all these years. While I had been clinging fiercely to Leah Nola and, in effect, myself, he had been there all along. Jamie my protector, Jamie my champion. Jamie my best friend, Jamie my lover. How was it possible that someone who had known me for so long could love me so profoundly? I still didn't feel worthy of that kind of love or devotion, but for once, I wasn't going to question my good fortune. "You said you knew right away when we were kids that you loved me. But it took me a lot longer. Maybe I'm stupid, or maybe I'm just really slow to recognize good things."

I leaned toward him, against the gentle tug of my seatbelt. "Because you are a very good thing. In fact, one of the best that's ever happened to me. I couldn't have survived the last twelve hours without you, but I want you to be more than just the person I turn to for help. You are so much more to me than that." I took a deep breath. "I want you to be the person who teaches me the names of flowers. I want you to be the person I show my sketches to. The person who memorizes every inch of my body—from my ticklish zones to the pleasure spots. The person who compliments my grandma's cooking and humors my grandpa when he's on a history ramble. The person who goes to David's games with me to cheer him on. The person who helps me teach David how to catch fireflies and make wishes on them." I lifted my arms, sweeping them open to encompass the front seat, the back seat, the road ahead of us, everything. "The person I rent an RV with one day to go out West and wherever else our hearts desire. I love you, Jamie Presswood, and I really want to be your girlfriend, if you'll have me."

Jamie let out a deep belly laugh, the kind that made me want to laugh right along with him and never stop; it felt so good to finally have a reason to laugh. He reached across the front seat and cupped my knee. "You have no idea how long I've been waiting to hear you say that."

EPILOGUE

A full year had passed, and we were celebrating David's sixth
birthday. My grandparents' backyard and the Presswoods' backyard
had been transformed into one huge soccer-themed extravaganza.
Two goal posts were set up on either end, and Winston had even
spray-painted the grass in an approximation of a soccer field. A lumpy
soccer ball piñata hung from one of the trees; black, white, and green
balloons bobbed from the patio railing where they were tied; and the
picnic table was covered in a spread of hot dogs, fruit salad, potato
chips, soccer-ball cookies, and green-frosted cupcakes topped with
miniature plastic soccer balls. David was zooming around the backyard, kicking a soccer ball with his best friends Maddox and Mason;
Izzy, whom he'd met a few months ago on his co-ed soccer team; and
even Gunner, who turned out to be an acquired taste.

On the patio, the adults milled around, chatting and snitching
soccer-ball cookies: Duffy and Winston, Wendy, Carly and Sam,
Abigail and Quentin, Edna and Chuck, the parents of David's friends,
and even Stacy and Brett and their kids, all the way from Rhinelander.
Duffy had convinced me to invite my mom as well, and though she
RSVP'd yes, she'd called Duffy a few days ago to say she wouldn't be
able to make it after all because something had come up at the last
minute. She'd sent a birthday card with a fifty dollar bill inside it
instead, and I had to admit to myself that I wasn't too crushed.

Jamie strode across the lawn from his house—*our* house, I cor-
rected myself. David and I had gradually been moving in for the past

few months, and our transition was almost totally complete. Duffy and Winston didn't say as much, but I knew they were happy to have some of their old privacy and lazy days back, although they were still over the moon that David and I were only a stone's throw away, and David still spent many of his afternoons with them. As Jamie walked past the wild and disorganized soccer game in progress, he gave the ball a light kick to help it back into bounds, and David and his friends cheered. Jamie was carrying a huge present, the one that we had picked out together. It was a plastic artist's easel and a huge kit of art supplies—pencils, wax crayons, oil based crayons, charcoal, watercolor, and tempera paint. We wanted to nurture David's creative, artistic side.

Jamie had been encouraging me to nurture my inner artist as well. Last spring, I had enrolled as a part-time student at the University of Wisconsin-Glacial Hills, and since then, I'd accrued twelve credits in various art classes and one creative writing class. My major goal was to write and illustrate a children's book called *David and the Dinosaurs*. In addition to other children's reading and enjoying it, I wanted it to be a kind of memory book for David, a record of the amazing things his imagination had created one summer in Salsburg. I thought that one day when he was older, it would be the perfect centerpiece to start a conversation about how I'd been able to see his imagination once upon a time and how it helped me to understand him and appreciate all the beautiful things about him. He'd met with Dr. Da Costa for a few months following his abduction, and we hadn't seen the panther since.

Jamie reached the patio, and I leaned my head over the railing to kiss him. "Is it time for presents yet?" he asked eagerly.

"I don't know," I said. "What do you think? Piñata, cake, and then presents? Or presents, piñata, and then cake?"

"Let's start with the presents," Jamie said. "I don't think I can wait much longer to see David's face when he opens his gift."

We gathered the lawn chairs in a loose circle on the grass in the shade. Jamie helped his mom maneuver her wheelchair. Abigail and Quentin sat a little outside of the circle, a present that rivaled our own in size balanced on their laps. They both looked older and more care-worn than they had one year ago. David's kidnapping and Patrick's subsequent sentencing of eighteen months in prison had really taken a toll on them. He would be getting out in April, maybe even sooner for good behavior, and it was something I tried not to think about, but something I suspected they thought about all the time.

With his friends clustered around him, David joyfully unwrapped a steady stream of presents. When he opened ours last, he grinned and said, "Thank you. I already know what I want to draw!"

"What's that?" I asked, leaning forward in my chair, bringing Jamie's hand, which was clutched tightly in mine, with me. My diamond engagement ring sparkled in the sun.

"Our family," David replied with a big smile.

The rest of the birthday party was a huge success, judging by the squeals of glee from the kids. Around four o'clock, our guests started to leave, and Winston, Duffy, Jamie, and I all started to clean up the party's aftermath. David was still sitting in the backyard, his pile of presents surrounding him, as he carefully examined and touched each one. Duffy and Winston disappeared inside to put the leftover food away, and Jamie set off to our house, lugging behind him a garbage bag full of dirty paper plates, wadded-up napkins, and crumpled-up wrapping paper.

"I'll be right back to help carry the presents over," he said.

"Okay, thanks." I glanced back at the picnic table and patio, but really there wasn't much left to be done, so I watched David, trying to freeze this moment in my mind, trying to keep him from growing any older.

King Rex and Weeple had joined him. I hadn't seen much of the dinosaurs since he'd started first grade, and even now, they didn't look as colorful, crisp, and life-like as they once had. They were fading, and I didn't know if this meant I was losing my ability to see them or if David was gradually letting his imaginary friends go.

They both lowered their heads, bowing before David, as though they wanted him to pet them. He reached up to each of them, laying his palm flat against their leathery, prehistoric snouts. His lips moved as he talked to them, but I couldn't hear what he said. Weeple was the first to turn away and amble toward the trees. King Rex continued to study David for much longer, and David had to give the Tyrannosaurus rex a second urging. King Rex gave him one last look, and then he followed Weeple to the tree line, where they both slowly started to dissolve until they were gone.

ACKNOWLEDGEMENTS

In preparation for writing this novel, I read psychology professor Marjorie Taylor's *Imaginary Companions and the Children who Create Them*, which helped me to understand this childhood phenomenon. It also assisted me in writing my fictitious version of the book Anna reads, *Imaginary Friends, Your Child, and You*, although of course, I took great liberties and stretched the truth for my own purposes.

I am deeply indebted to my early readers, especially Becky Vinter, Kate Blakinger, Rebecca Adams Wright, and Kodi Scheer, whose invaluable feedback helped me navigate the sometimes murky waters of Anna's journey and David's imagination.

Thanks to my wonderful agent, Stephany Evans, for finding the perfect home for *Imaginary Things*. Thanks also to the terrific people at Astor + Blue for their enthusiasm and the great care they showed my novel, especially my brilliant editorial team, Robert Astle and Jillian Ports, and my publicity and marketing gurus, Tony Viardo and Shelby Howick. I sincerely appreciate the talented Julie Metz for designing my gorgeous cover, which I fell in love with immediately.

My heartfelt thanks go out to my family, both nuclear and extended, as well as my in-laws, the Lochens, for all their support and encouragement. I feel so blessed to belong to such a warm, loving bunch of people who would do absolutely anything for each other.

And last, but certainly not least, thanks to the love of my life, Matt, who has been a great champion for this book from the very beginning. Without his thoughtful insight and unwavering belief in me, I'm not sure this story of Anna and David would have ever made its way out into the world.

BOOK CLUB DISCUSSION QUESTIONS FOR IMAGINARY THINGS

1) At the start of the novel, Anna feels defeated to be returning to Salsburg, which she connects with boredom, failure, and provincial attitudes. What changes her perception of life in the small town, and how does it change?

2) Duffy and Winston each have their own personalities and styles of being a grandparent. How does Duffy demonstrate her affection, and in what ways does Winston show his? How do their different approaches help Anna in different ways? Do you see examples of either in the way Anna parents David?

3) After the end of her relationship with Patrick, Anna speculates that "mania *was* true love. And it could consume you like it had consumed Patrick, or it could leave you feeling tired and used up, like it had left [her.] Nothing seemed to exist in between." How and why does her attitude about love change over the course of the novel?

4) Why does it take so long for Anna to see Jamie as someone other than her childhood friend and the "boy next door?" What qualities does he possess that make him a good fit for Anna?

5) Why do you think David creates his dinosaurs? What do King Rex and Weeple individually represent and what roles do they serve for him? In contrast, why does he create the panther and what function does it perform?

6) What do you think *really* happened between David, Gunner, and King Rex during the disastrous play date? In the world of the novel, do you think that imaginary friends could be capable of physically affecting their environments? What other clues might suggest this?

7) As a child, why does Anna dream up Leah Nola as her imaginary friend? What role does Leah Nola play in her life, and what light does this shed on Anna's own personality and past?

8) What do you think of Kimberly's character and the choices she made as a parent? Do you agree with Anna's assessment of her? Why or why not? Do you think the mother and daughter could ever restore their relationship?

9) Do you think seeing imaginary friends is a hereditary trait, or do you think there is some other reason both Anna and her mom, Kimberly, were given the opportunity to see their child's imagination? Compare and contrast the ways the two women handle the surreal situations.

10) Did you or your child ever have an imaginary friend? How do you think this and other games of make-believe affect children's development? In what ways do adults use their imagination? Is there anything we can consider as imaginary friends for adults?